Her Last
Promise

BOOKS BY CATHERINE HOKIN

Her Last Promise

CATHERINE HOKIN

bookouture

Published by Bookouture in 2023

An imprint of Storyfire Ltd.
Carmelite House
50 Victoria Embankment
London EC4Y 0DZ

www.bookouture.com

ISBN: 978-1-80019-627-8
eBook ISBN: 978-1-80019-626-1

For Tina for keeping this ship sailing steady!
Many thanks for it all

CHAPTER 1

The scream came from nowhere, a jagged swoop of pain which tore through the house, swallowing the air, silencing the chatter swirling up from the foyer. The force of it caught Hannelore in mid-pirouette and froze her instantly to the spot, the swish of her new party dress completely forgotten.

What's that? and *What's happened?* collided immediately into *What do I do now?*

Hannelore had no more of an answer for the last question than she did for the first two. And she didn't have any guidelines to follow, which was another disorienting shock. Feeling untethered, having no clue which way to turn wasn't a normal state of affairs for her or for anyone else in the Foss household. Her home was a highly regulated place in which all forms of behaviour were governed by rules that its inhabitants knew better than to break. It wasn't a place where people screamed. It wasn't a place which tolerated raised voices of any description. The house ran on whispers and murmurs and the careful anticipation of its master's wishes. And now somebody had stepped out of line and the house was holding its breath.

Maybe I should stay in here. Maybe I should wait until whatever it was has passed over, until someone comes and tells me what I'm meant to do.

That would have been the safe and sensible choice. Unfortunately, Hannelore had a curious streak that her father hadn't yet managed to break, so she pushed safe and sensible to the back of her head. She edged towards her bedroom door instead and eased it gently open. The upstairs hallway had returned to its usual silence. There wasn't a sound from downstairs beyond an awkward cough or two. Her father's guests – who a few moments earlier had been clinking glasses and braying about the evening's long-anticipated party – had all apparently been struck dumb. Hannelore's skin started to crawl. A private disturbance in the house's smooth fabric was bad enough, but a public one?

He'll be all smiles on the surface and seething inside. Please God he doesn't think it's my fault.

The thought of Reiner's anger unleashed her way was almost enough to send Hannelore scuttling for the safety of the space under her bed. It was a struggle not to bolt straight there, but her curious side was still winning, even if she had to grip on to the door frame to steady her nerves. Hiding from their fathers was something that frightened children, not thirteen-year-old girls did.

I wonder if Luise does it. I wonder if I should have taught her to.

The image of her four-year-old little sister cowering in fear was a horrible one. And trying to explain to such an innocent little mite why having a hiding place might be a good idea was unimaginable. Hannelore couldn't think about that any more than she could think about her father looking for someone to blame.

Maybe I misheard. Maybe it was an owl screeching in the

trees outside, or a mouse that's got into Mama's bedroom and made her shriek.

Those were calming thoughts, better than picturing Luise at the mercy of her father's bad temper. And owls and mice were hardly dangerous things – they might cause upset but they wouldn't hurt anybody and they wouldn't ruin the night's plans.

Hannelore didn't want to be selfish – that was as childish as hiding – but she really didn't want anything to wreck those. Tonight's party was full of milestones she was desperate to scale. Tonight, for the first time, she wasn't going to be left with the other guests her own age and their chaperones; she was going to cross the bridge to the wonderfully named Peacock Island side by side with her mother. And she was going to be wearing a new peach gown that was the most beautiful dress she had ever owned. It had a dipped neck, not a little girl's prim collar, and a thin diamante belt rather than a child's satin sash. Tonight was special. Tonight marked her entry to a new grown-up world. Nothing – not strange noises nor her father's moods nor worrying whether she was a good enough big sister – was supposed to spoil that.

Hannelore managed to hold on to the hope that the evening would settle again for another moment or two, crossing her fingers to make it come true. She pretended that the sound tearing down the corridor hadn't shivered with pain. She pretended that the guests hadn't heard it and that her father would still be smiling. Until a second scream shattered the air and there could be no more pretending about anything at all.

This one was louder, more piercing and filled unmistakeably with fear. It was also cut through with an anguished 'Somebody help me!' which landed on Hannelore's skin like a burn. The voice in distress was her mother's.

All thoughts of the party and pretty dresses melted away. Talie was the gentlest creature on earth – nothing was meant to hurt her.

Hannelore raced into the corridor, the threat of her father's anger as forgotten as her clothes. And she wasn't the only one now on full alert: the foyer below her was crackling. Heels clicked against marble as the guests jostled at the foot of the stairs, craning up, straining for a glimpse of the normally unflappable Talie Foss in a state of panic. Listening for another cry which would feed the gossip they were already brimming with. Hannelore ignored them and she ignored the footsteps which began mounting the stairs with the slow heavy tread that marked them instantly as her father's. She was too focused on the sobs coming from the nursery where Luise slept to worry about him. Sobs that were as frightening and out of place as the screaming.

'What's the matter? What's going on? Has something happened to my mother or Luise?'

She reached the nursery's partially open door but got no further.

'Go back to your room, pet – this isn't the right place for you now.'

Her mother's maid Emmi, who was more of a friend to Talie than a servant, had slipped through the gap, blocking Hannelore's path. The woman was small and delicate-looking, but when it came to Talie, she was fierce. Hannelore tried to stretch round her but all she could see was an empty strip of Luise's crumpled bed.

'You have been told what to do, Hannelore, so do it. Go and wait in your room.'

Reiner Foss had arrived, his squared shoulders and lowered voice pulsating with fury. He pushed past her, and pushed past the maid whose name he had never bothered to learn, and stormed into the nursery, shutting the door firmly behind him. The frightened look on Emmi's white face left no room for argument. Hannelore knew all too well that, if she stood her ground and demanded answers when her father had told her to go, the maid would be the one to suffer. Reiner liked his daughter to understand that bad choices always had wider consequences than her when it came to doling out punishments.

Hannelore returned far more slowly to her room and sat on the bed, holding her body tight so that it wouldn't dissolve into shivers. If the commotion was because Luise had been taken unwell, that in itself wasn't unusual. The little girl was delicate and tired easily, but Talie had assured Hannelore that she would grow out of that. And being delicate didn't mean she was sick, at least not in any serious way, or there would be regular doctor's visits and Mama would surely be far more anxious than she usually seemed.

But Mama screamed and Mama never screams.

Didn't that turn delicate into something more sinister? Hannelore shut that thought down. The idea of her sister in the kind of distress which would make Talie lose control was unbearable. She scrabbled around again for a less frightening explanation.

Maybe Luise fell and hurt herself. Maybe she had a terrible dream or was sleepwalking and that frightened my mother.

None of that sounded convincing but when Reiner finally appeared in her doorway and blamed the disturbance on a particularly bad nightmare, Hannelore was relieved enough to believe him. Until he followed his terse explanation with a brusque 'Now get yourself downstairs; your mother's not coming', which didn't make sense. And until he repeated the same excuse to his guests, although he explained both the noise and Talie's withdrawal from the party in a gentler tone and with the addition of 'What can I say, she's such a devoted mother.' That was when Hannelore knew for certain that he was lying.

Talie Foss was the perfect hostess, whatever the circumstances. Hannelore had seen her mother smile and attend parties when she was suffering from a migraine or the flu because that was what her role as SS Obergruppenführer Reiner Foss's wife demanded. And tonight wasn't the kind of party anyone with an invitation dared miss. It was a ball to celebrate the end of the Berlin Olympics, hosted by the Propaganda Minister Joseph Goebbels. He was the reason Hannelore had been invited in the first place – he had seen her taking photographs at the Games' closing ceremony and had pronounced himself enchanted. He had asked Hannelore to send him some of her photographs and insisted that she should attend the closing reception as a special guest and capture all its delights. He was also the kind of man who expected all his whims to be met, and he was very easily offended. Which was why her father's 'You'd better click away with that camera and be your most charming tonight – I don't need him choosing to turn your mother's absence into an insult' as he hurried her into the car was unnerving, but it wasn't a surprise.

The night hadn't started the way that it should have done and Hannelore didn't see how it could improve. She spent the drive worrying about her mother and her sister, who she hadn't been allowed to see. She didn't want to be in the car; she wanted to be at home, with them. Refusing, however, had not been an option. But enjoying herself? That was a different matter entirely.

All I have to be is polite. I don't have to be impressed by anything.

And then they pulled into the parking lot opposite Peacock Island and all her plans to be unimpressed flew out of her head.

The scale of the party was breathtaking. From the second Hannelore stepped onto the pontoon bridge which led across the narrow channel from the mainland, her head was in a whirl.

Lanterns lit up the trees, throwing dancing reflections into the dark waters of the River Havel and turning the leaves and branches to gold. Clouds of white flowers covered a miniature fairy-tale castle at the top of the path. Peacocks wandered the lawns, their tails spread out behind them like dowagers' trains. Ballerinas disguised as satin-clad nymphs ushered the guests between the dining tables and the dance floors and the velvet-draped stage where the orchestra sat. The female guests shimmered in diamonds and silk; the men steering them were splendid in tailcoats as immaculately fitted as the uniforms they normally wore. Hannelore was so spellbound she could barely drink it all in. Until its host turned her into the star of his show and the lights instantly dimmed.

'Here she is, our charming little photographer, the Reich's next Leni Riefenstahl. Do you know what she told me when I saw her taking pictures at the Games? That she chooses the image she photographs with her heart and with her feelings as much as with her eyes. Isn't that delightful? And her pictures are as pretty as her words. You must all have your portrait taken by Fräulein Foss tonight – I insist on it. She is a great talent in the making.'

Goebbels' welcome was loud and effusive and gathered a crowd round Hannelore which delighted her father. Hannelore did what was required of her. She smiled at the Minister, she said *thank you* and she took all the pictures he demanded. She acted the part of the perfect little pet, precisely as was expected. And she did the exact opposite of what Ezra Stein had taught her three years earlier as she stood on the balcony of the Adlon Hotel watching the procession to celebrate Hitler's appointment as Germany's Chancellor. She didn't look at her subjects through wide-open eyes so that she could capture every hidden detail. She forced herself not to look at anyone clearly at all.

The Führer's master of ceremonies and perhaps one day his rival.

That was how Ezra – the man who had introduced

Hannelore to the art of photography as well as the personalities of the men who had swept into power – had described Goebbels. Clever and ruthless and a man to be wary of. Hannelore had listened to that warning as carefully as she had listened to his tips on how to best use a camera. There had been an honesty about Ezra which made her take him seriously even though he was a stranger. *I don't know whether to be thrilled by the events he can pull off or be terrified.* That was the other thing Ezra had said about Goebbels that night, as the two of them had watched the torches and the streams of carefully orchestrated National Socialist supporters pass by. Hannelore hadn't spoken to Ezra since then but she imagined he would have plumped by now for terrified.

The Propaganda Minister still specialised in dramatic parades, but it was his speeches he was better known for. They were delivered in a roar far bigger than his small body and were filled with phrases about pride and courage and the will of the people which his audiences were expected to memorise and cling to. Hannelore had sat through plenty of those and nothing she had heard suggested that Ezra's advice about the minister had been wrong. She had followed that advice ever since and carried on watching the world very carefully. Now she was wary not just of Goebbels but of all the loud-voiced men who flocked round her father once he also became one of the Führer's favourites. How could she be anything else when the views they subscribed to were so utterly wrong?

Ezra was one of the kindest people Hannelore had ever met. Reiner hadn't cared about that – he had been furious with Hannelore for saying it. Reiner had hated Ezra on sight and so would all his cronies, for the simple fact that Ezra was Jewish. According to the new rules on what it was to be German, that made Ezra possessed of *bad blood*. It also made him *other,* a word that was forever on Reiner's lips and was shorthand for *not us and not German.* According to Reiner and the National Socialist Party he was pledged to, Jews were the enemies of the world, the incarnation of evil. Goebbels had described them as a contagious infection. After five minutes with Ezra, Hannelore knew that couldn't possibly be true. And her grandmother, who hated what her son had become, had told her that there was no such thing as bad blood – that the people who insisted there was were the true monsters. So Hannelore was wary, but she wasn't a fool.

When Goebbels asked why she had developed such an interest in photography and Reiner's hand sank claw-like into her shoulder, Hannelore didn't mention Ezra. She told the Minister instead that taking lessons had been her father's idea. That it had been a passion of his as a boy and an honour for her to continue. Everyone clapped at that; no one guessed it was a lie. Or that it wouldn't be the last one Hannelore would have to tell about the evening's entertainment. She would have to thank Goebbels for his hospitality and sound sincere enough to fool his sharp ears. She would have to tell her father what a delight the evening had been and be sure to sound enthusiastic. And she would have to keep smiling at these men at every event she was trotted out at. Even though the more she grew to understand them, the more their plans for the way the world should be run dismayed her and the lies turned sour on her tongue.

But what else can I do? I have to find a way to live among them whether I want to or not, because this is where my father has put me.

That was a confusing, unsettling thought. Once it jumped into her head, the party's gloss quickly tarnished even if her performance didn't falter. Her father's loosened grip on her shoulder proved that. So did the compliment he tossed her way when she finally climbed back into the car – sleepy from too much roast goose and too many sour cherry pastries, her eyes and ears dancing from a firework finale loud enough to clear a battlefield.

'I wasn't disappointed with you.'

He rarely praised her, so that should have meant something. If only his thin smile hadn't immediately disappeared behind an image of Ezra sadly shaking his head.

'We're home, Miss. Your father said you were to go straight to bed.'

Reiner had left the car and left her lying in it asleep. Hannelore thanked the chauffeur and scrambled out, shivering as the cool air fluttered through her thin dress. The house was dark; there was nobody waiting.

She went inside, wondering if Reiner might have told her mother that they were back. She didn't want to go to bed without knowing Luise was well again or without Talie's kiss and, if everything was calm again in the nursery, a cup of hot chocolate and a chance to tell her mother about the better parts of the evening. The house, however, was as silent as it was dark, all its doors firmly closed.

Hannelore made her way slowly up the stairs, dwarfed by the wide corridors and the acres of family portraits. Upstairs was as quiet as down but there was, to her relief, some sign of life there: a thin sliver of light spilling under the door of the nursery. And there were no more sobs, which had to be a good sign.

Her spirits lifting a little, Hannelore removed her shoes in case Emmi was lurking ready to leap out and shoo her away and tiptoed towards the door. This time she reached it and slipped inside without interruption, and her luck held: her mother was curled up on a chair in the corner.

'Oh, I'm so glad you're here!'

Hannelore stopped, her excitement quickly fading. Nothing

about the scene in front of her felt right. Talie was wrapped in a blanket instead of her usual chiffon layers. Her body was hunched and her eyes, which were firmly fixed on Luise's bed, were feverish. She looked like an older, harder version of her mother, one Hannelore was suddenly afraid to approach. And Luise did not look well. The child was asleep but her skin was waxy and her hair clung round her face in damp tendrils. Hannelore remembered the screams and she shivered.

'Is she all right? Is she sick? Is that what the fuss before was about?'

She moved closer to the bed but Talie shook her head as Hannelore reached out to touch her little sister.

'Leave her be. She needs the sleep. She can't take another one.'

There was a sourness to the room, a scent of sickness, or fear. Hannelore's skin began to prickle. She dropped her hand and stared at her mother, who barely glanced her way.

'I don't understand. What's wrong with her?'

But Talie carried on talking as if she hadn't heard.

'Don't let him fool you. He'll throw you little crumbs. He'll praise you when he has to, to keep you in line. But he hasn't got a heart, Hannelore. Don't ever make the mistake of thinking that he has.'

There was no bitterness in Talie's voice; there was nothing but a bone-deep exhaustion. And there was nothing else to come. She turned away from Hannelore the minute the warning was done and switched whatever energy remained in her crumpled frame back onto Luise.

Hannelore couldn't stay. There was a darkness in the room that she couldn't make sense of. The nursery felt as if it would suck her down if she swallowed another mouthful of its stale air. She backed away, retreated to her bedroom and crawled under the covers, still wearing her party dress. *She can't take another one* ran on and on through her head. Something was wrong with her beloved little sister. That was bad, that was unthinkable; Hannelore ached to protect her. But that wasn't what kept her awake until the sun came pressing in at the curtains. What kept Hannelore awake and kept her afraid was *he hasn't got a heart.*

Because she knew in hers it was true.

CHAPTER 2

4 MARCH 1963, WEST BERLIN

Hanni sat at the gingham-covered kitchen table, her camera and spare lenses spread out in front of her, methodically packing her bag ready for the day. It was a calming exercise, a ritual. A moment of peace before the street below their Rüdesheimer Straße apartment filled up with shoppers on their way to the market, and the apartment filled up with Leo.

She sipped her coffee and glanced at the clock. Another ten minutes before she had to wake him and unleash the day's round of door slamming. Even if she had another sixty she wouldn't be ready.

Where did my little boy go?

It was a treacherous thought she clamped down on the moment it surfaced. It was hard to stop it bobbing back up. Her Leo was still in there somewhere, Hanni knew that. The laughing child who had run rings round her heart from the moment he was born. Who still held her heart captive. But now that boy came wrapped in the body of a furious twelve-year-old who went to bed cross and woke up still spoiling for a fight.

The coffee had grown cold. Hanni pushed it away and began picking, as she had been picking since dawn, at the row which had soured the previous night and, unless she could somehow divert it, would no doubt colour the start of today.

'I'm sorry Leo, but it's work and, besides, you've got school. You can't come with me.'

Her refusal to give in to his pushing the previous night had acted on him like a match. And when frustration finally defeated her determination to stay calm, her 'If I'd said no to my father at your age, the heavens would have opened' had turned that spark into a fire. Another evening had been spent in separate rooms, with Leo sulking and Hanni hovering by the phone, longing to call Freddy and ask for his help with their son. She hadn't done it; she never did. What could Freddy do? He hadn't caused this mess they were all forced to navigate their lives around. Her mistakes and her lies had done that.

Hanni glanced at the clock again and started to pack her bag quicker. Today's assignment – an interview and photoshoot commissioned by *Der Spiegel* magazine – one of her best clients – would be fraught enough without Leo tagging along. Her subject, Valentin Gessner, had become the darling of the political world following his recent election to the Berlin House of Representatives, and the darling of the media who filled dozens of columns with his wit and his film-star looks. He was also, for reasons Hanni was struggling to fathom, Leo's new hero. Unlike her son, Gessner's charm left Hanni cold. And what she had uncovered about his background troubled her: he was a man with secrets Hanni was determined to expose. So she needed a clear head to prepare for him and a morning which began calmly, with smiles and apologies and hugs. She was as ready as ever to try, but Leo was in no mood to oblige her.

'I don't see why I can't come with you. Gessner's got way more interesting things to say about politics and history than any of my teachers. He's not scared stiff of the past for a start, and he doesn't apologise like they do for being born a German.'

Leo had suddenly barrelled into the kitchen in a whirlwind

of spidery legs and gangly arms and, as Hanni had wearily expected, still stuck in the middle of last night's row. She bit her lip to stop herself flaring back at him. She didn't have the energy or the will for another fight, but she also didn't quite have the heart to tell him to stop. His passion was misplaced but his determination to craft a winning argument turned him perfectly into Freddy.

He should be here; we should be sharing this. Being cross and proud together. Sneaking a look between us that says, yes he's exasperating but isn't he clever?

Her and Freddy playing happy families with their boy. It sounded wonderful, until Hanni tried to properly picture the scene. The reality of doing something as intimate as eating breakfast together in her kitchen would be horribly stilted. Leo would worm into the cracks that ran through the base of his parents' relationship and push them against each other in an attempt to push away his own pain and confusion. Nothing about the meeting would go well. The three of them didn't have a rulebook for anything other than the public faces imposed by restaurant meals, and the days when she and Freddy had giggled their way around a stove together were long gone. Those were part of a past the two of them pretended nowadays had never happened.

Part of a past that's never been bettered.

That was a traitorous thought too and not one Hanni could afford to indulge. She had no time to waste on daydreams – the situation she and her broken family were now in worked because Hanni worked to stay thankful. Life as parents, if not as anything else, had finally become a manageable thing. She and Freddy had found a way of living politely around each other that Hanni hadn't believed would be possible before Leo's birth, in the terrible months when their lives had exploded. They had maintained that politeness for over twelve years. And no, being able to function around each other as carefully and unemotionally as they now did wasn't soul-crushing. She wouldn't let it be. It was an accommodation to be grateful for. It was a positive thing, like so much of her life. She had Leo, who was the centre of it. She had work that she loved and was very good at; she had interesting friends. There had been men who had cared about her, who could have been a more permanent fixture if she'd let them. She had a full life, a steady life. There was nothing to be gained by wishing for the moon.

Except we're still married. We've never managed to take that last step, so maybe the moon is still waiting.

'Are you even listening?'

Hanni pulled herself back from the father to the son who was all clenched up in front of her and tried to ignore the similarities.

'I told you: I like Gessner and I respect him. Aren't you always telling me I'm supposed to find people to respect? He's different – all my friends think so. He's not like other adults. He doesn't go around talking about guilt and blame and the burden Germans are meant to carry for something that happened nearly twenty years ago. I might actually learn something of value from him. What's wrong with that?'

What's wrong with that?

Hanni didn't know how to start explaining all the things that were wrong with that to a boy who could dismiss the war and its horrors as *something that happened.* And as for who Leo had chosen to respect... That was a minefield she couldn't bear to step into. His new friends, who were too old and too rough for him and also thought Gessner was a saint, were another one.

'It's late, Leo. I don't have time for this now.'

There were no smiles and no apologies. Instead she said no again and he slammed the door again, accompanying that with curses she thought he was too young to know.

Where did my little boy go?

Hanni sat alone in the kitchen, her camera bag and Valentin

Gessner forgotten. She knew exactly where the answer to that question lay. With the day three years earlier which had fractured her family. With Freddy slumped across the table from her and the chaos that was Renny. A day that was still all too vivid...

'It was her fault. She told him everything we've tried to avoid and that's what upset him.'

Freddy's hair was a bird's nest; his collar was unbuttoned. He had clearly raced to her apartment the moment he had finished grilling his sister without a thought for his appearance.

Hanni stared at him, her hands hidden under the kitchen table where he wouldn't see that they were balled into fists. She had managed to control her temper when she phoned him; she wasn't confident that control would continue.

'He's not just upset. He's confused and angry and convinced we're all liars. What happened? When I left Renny in charge they seemed happy enough, but when I came home he was hysterical and she stormed out. What does *told him everything* mean?'

It took Freddy a few moments to answer. Hanni didn't push him although she wanted to: she was too uncertain of where the conversation might lead to do that. The two of them managed the present because they never revisited the past. Which meant that a lot of shaky ground still stood between them, and the subject of Renny occupied a very fragile share of that. Freddy had been trying to mend the damage wreaked by the first years of Renny's life for almost a decade, ever since he had discovered that his little sister hadn't been murdered by the Nazis along with the rest of his family but had survived imprisonment in Theresienstadt and was living in Prague. He had brought her back to Berlin full of plans for their happy future, but he hadn't succeeded in repairing the harm that had been done to her.

That ran far too deep. Neither he nor Hanni blamed Renny for that and neither of them ever discussed Prague, or the part Hanni's father Reiner had played in the chaos that had enveloped them there. Hanni had wished Freddy nothing but joy in finding his sister; she still hoped that joy could be found. That the reality had proved to be very different was another not-to-be-mentioned subject on a far-too-long list.

Renny might not have been the target of Reiner's revenge when he and Hanni had locked swords so brutally in 1950, but she had become its casualty. The holes Reiner had torn still gaped. Renny couldn't forgive Hanni for being a Nazi's daughter and hiding that fact. She couldn't forgive Freddy for coming back into her life without bringing her mother. None of it was logical; all of it was real. Renny was lost and Renny lashed out. Hanni could forgive her for that. She could forgive Renny's fury for keeping her and Freddy apart long after she suspected Freddy was ready to step closer. Hanni had betrayed them both so badly, she felt her punishment was deserved. But now Renny had hurt Leo and Hanni's capacity for forgiveness was wearing dangerously thin. She didn't tell Freddy that either.

'She told Leo about the Holocaust and what the Nazis did to the Jews, in quite graphic detail from what I can gather. And that your father, his grandfather, was one of the worst. That Reiner helped set up concentration camps and sent whole families to the gas chambers, including our mother and father and that she was supposed to have been murdered there too. And that you knew but you lied and pretended to be someone else entirely. Someone, as she put it to me and presumably to Leo, who I would love.'

His words came out with a struggle but they still came out, and they hit Hanni like a punch. Not that she had a defence. Everything Renny had said was the truth.

'Why did she do it, Freddy? He's only nine years old. The

same age as she was when we found her. Can't she remember what that was like, how frightening discovering the truth about her own past was? I know she hates me, but couldn't she let Leo have his childhood? Did she really have to blow that apart?'

Freddy's face had slipped its moorings. Her bones had aged.

Why can't we be who we were? Why can't we fall into each other's arms and pull through this together?

He was looking at her so intently, Hanni thought she must have said that aloud. She also thought, for one beautiful moment, that he was thinking the same thing. Until he spoke and the gulf that still sat between them, the one neither of them acknowledged or knew what to do with, cracked even further open.

'I don't want to stick up for her, Hanni. When she confessed what she'd done, I wanted to throttle her. But it wasn't done from malice or because she hates you. I don't even know if that's true now, or not like it was. She did it because she's obsessed with the truth; she's blinded by it. She thinks that we shelter Leo – like everyone born after the war gets sheltered – because no one wants to look back at those years with honesty. And she's on a crusade to change that. In her words she wants to get justice for the dead who don't have a voice. Surely if anyone can understand the need to do that, it's you.'

It was a gentle rebuke but it was a rebuke all the same. It made Hanni want to curl up.

I was going to reveal Reiner's crimes to the world. I was going to bring my father to justice. I was going to bring that to you as proof that I wasn't him.

She had sworn that to Freddy when their world fell apart. She had sworn the same promise to herself for years. But her words and her actions had come too late. She had failed and others had paid the price; she could hardly blame Renny for wanting to do better. So she said nothing because there was nothing to say and she let Freddy carry on.

'What happened to her has left deep scars and she's afraid, although she hides it very well. She doesn't think Germany will ever be safe. She doesn't understand how anyone with Jewish blood – including me – could have stayed after the war, or still stays here now. And she's sorry, she's really sorry. She knows what she did was wrong. That we hadn't told Leo about Reiner or any of the rest of it not because we wanted to lie to him or pretend, but because it's a mess he's far too young to understand. She'll apologise to him; she'll apologise to you. Can't that be enough?'

A mess.

It was too small a word to describe the limbo they were living in. Not together, not properly apart. Both in and out of other relationships that never stuck. Unable to deal the final death blow to their marriage by signing divorce papers, despite all the years that had passed. Unable to discuss why. And that hadn't been the time to tackle it. So Renny's promise of an apology had had to be enough...

Even though I lost a part of my son that night which I might never get back. Even though he thinks I'm a liar who ruined his father's life.

Hanni pulled herself back from the past and cut that thought off: if it took hold, she wouldn't be able to function. Leo was angry with the world and so was Renny. Freddy wasn't hers to love or be loved by anymore. And her father was still out in the world, still flooding it with his acolytes and his poison. Hanni got up and swung her camera bag over her shoulder. She didn't seem to be able to solve Leo, or her situation with Freddy. There was so much she couldn't change but, for today at least, she could do something to slow down Reiner Foss.

. . .

Valentin Gessner's press schedule was overcrowded and falling behind, but Hanni's *Der Spiegel* accreditation moved her quickly up the waiting list.

The hotel reception room which the politician had commandeered for the day was all velvet drapes and gleaming chandeliers, its gloss creating an effect that was positively presidential. Hanni made a mental note not to comment on it.

Gessner was waiting wreathed with smiles, his hand out to greet her and usher her into a carved tub of a chair. It was obvious that he was expecting another easy walk through his life and another raft of congratulations. It was also obvious that he assumed he was the one in control. Hanni didn't say anything beyond the usual round of *thank you* and *hello* and, instead of sitting, she began to set up her camera. Rather than talking she let him take the conversational lead. Since she had extended her skills to writing the interviews that went alongside her pictures, she had quickly learned that starting with a series of flattering photographs was the quickest way to catch her subject off guard.

'I saw your last exhibition, Frau Schlüssel. Your shots of the Wall going up were quite brilliant – they really captured the suddenness of its arrival.'

He continued his charm offensive as she checked the lighting and asked him to pose, something he was perfectly delighted to do. He complimented a piece she had done on the Beatles, a British pop group who were causing something of a stir in Hamburg, for *Stern* magazine. He showered her most recent book – a compilation of photographs contrasting street kids from 1945 with the Americanised teenagers who had filled Berlin's streets ten years later – with praise. And he waited for her to reciprocate the flattery. Hanni smiled and thanked him but she had no intention of inflating his already buoyant ego. She finished her last frame, sat down, clicked on the tape recorder and opened one of the notebooks that was filled with background information. And then she stopped him the moment he began his prepared speech.

'Forgive me but I do have a copy of the talk you gave earlier this morning, Herr Gessner, and I will refer to it. But I'd rather find out about you the man. It's been quite a trajectory so far. Glory with the medal-winning Olympic shooting team in Rome. A successful law career. Elected to the Berlin House at thirty and now tipped as a candidate for the Bundestag in the federal elections. Has it been as dizzying as it sounds?'

She gave him a few moments to expand and to preen. To talk about the opportunities that came with the sense of self-worth he hoped all Germans would one day recapture. Then she moved in.

'And where did you find that confidence, Herr Gessner? Who taught you to, as you put it, "hold your head up and be proud of the country which raised you"?'

Hanni recorded his bland answer about loving parents who wanted nothing but the best for their only son. She had no intention of using it, not when the truth was already captured in her notes. Valentin Gessner's parents' love or otherwise had very little to do with the man sitting in front of her now. The real Gessner, as opposed to the one he shared with the world, had detached himself from them as soon as he could find a more comfortable home inside one of the Third Reich's educational incubators. And he had continued to follow that path even when the Third Reich was done. Valentin Gessner was one of her father's boys. The twelve-year-old killer the Nazis had created had been forged into a man by Reiner. A product of the school system he had built to fill young men with his twisted ideals before he sent them out into the world as fully-fledged, if well-camouflaged, fascists.

My boys will be natural leaders. They will be so perfectly suited to running the show, who would want to stop them?

Reiner had announced his vision to her on a bench in

Prague thirteen years earlier and he hadn't missed a step since then in turning that dream to reality. He had raised the money he needed for the first school so quickly, Hanni assumed that the pledges had already been in his pocket when he described his plans. As to where those pledges had come from? She didn't want to know – she assumed that his benefactors were as good at reinventing themselves as he was, and as rotten at the core. The three schools he now ran from his main centre close to Goslar, a small town nestled on the slopes of the Harz Mountains, were flourishing. Their first successes were safely launched out into the world, Valentin Gessner among them.

Hanni flicked through her notes as Reiner's star pupil sat back, satisfied that he had fooled her. And then she took control.

'That's an answer you've given before. But I wonder if there isn't a different story? I wonder if your sense of pride and your sense of self weren't perhaps learned in the elite Third Reich school you attended for two years, or in the Hitler Youth? Some of the boys who were members of that at the same time as you have painted me quite an interesting picture of the young Valentin. Do you mind if I run through their testimonies?'

She had chosen that word, with its connotations of courtrooms and witnesses, deliberately. Gessner's face flickered but he indicated that she could carry on.

'I think it's fair to say that you had quite a reputation for outstanding devotion to the cause in those days. One incident I've been told about particularly stands out, or it does to me. I wonder if you remember it? It happened at a concert on April the twelfth 1945, the last one held by the Berlin Philharmonic before the city fell. The Hitler Youth played a prominent part at that, didn't they? It must have been quite a sight, all of you in your uniforms, stationed round the hall holding baskets of cyanide ampoules, offering a way out to the 'loyal servants of the Reich' who feared being seized by the advancing Russians. That can't have been an easy thing to do: you were, after all, only eleven or twelve; you were still children. But, according to my source, you embraced it.'

She glanced at her notes, giving him a chance to challenge her. He didn't.

'Here we are, here are his exact words: "Valentin told anyone who took a pill that they had to kill at least one Russian before they swallowed it or they would go to their deaths as worthless cowards. His fervour was frightening – it went way beyond the rest of us. It was bred into his bones." That's quite a statement, don't you think?'

Hanni had to give Gessner his due – he barely reacted, beyond dismissing the allegation as 'the kind of malicious slur those of us in the public eye too often encounter'. Followed by the defence that she expected, that: 'Those were very different times and all of us were caught up in events which ran past our control.'

She let him have that. Then she turned the page.

'I wonder if this is a malicious slur too? You see I also have a report that, in the last days of the street fighting in Berlin, when your youth division was called up to fight, you put a bullet in the heads of two of your comrades – boys who were twelve years old, just like you – because they were terrified of the advancing Russian army and wanted, quite understandably, to run. The word used to describe your actions was "execution".'

He reacted now. His 'Who the hell told you that?' burst out in a snarl which Hanni ignored.

'And I also have it on record that you did the same to a fellow "Werwolf", as you liked to call your band of resistance fighters, when you were hiding out in the Harz Mountains and refusing to surrender even though the war was done. And that you met Hitler in the days before his suicide and he awarded you a medal to mark your bravery. A medal you still wear at private functions. Are they all slurs too? Or are you going to tell me that you were just a boy caught up in events?'

His bland surface cracked. He leapt to his feet, towering over her. That was also an entirely expected response, and it didn't work. Hanni had been threatened by far more intimidating men than Valentin Gessner, and she had left her fear of what they might do to her in a cellar in Prague. So she let him stand there, fists clenched, face bunched, telling her that she had no right to talk to him like that, then she suggested that it might be better if he sat down. And waited quietly until he did.

'Thank you. So, cards on the table. I intend to write an honest piece about you, Herr Gessner, not a fluff one. About the man behind the charming façade. About the boy whose reputation for cruelty was honed when he won a place at a Napola school where the future leaders of the Thousand-Year Reich were trained, and whose brutality was unleashed on the streets of Berlin in 1945. Who continued to fight for his beliefs, with an unparalleled level of savagery, long after the war was done, until he found his way from the mountains to a school run by another man just like him. I want to show the real Valentin Gessner to the world. Not a politician working for the good of the common people and trying to lift Germany's head back up, but the Valentin Gessner whose National Socialist beliefs were bred bone-deep, ready to be refined in one of Emil Foss's elite academies. The fascist who still holds the swastika close to his heart. And before you ask me why, it's simple. It's because I don't want you and your kind ever getting comfortable in the world again. I want you stopped.'

It was a long speech. It was followed by a long silence. Hanni gathered her notebooks back up, unclipped the tape from the machine and packed her camera away. She doubted that he would be foolish enough to hurt her, but she didn't trust him with her equipment. She was on her feet ready to walk out when he finally spoke.

'Reiner warned me that you would be like this. Vengeful. Irrational. With a tendency to be brave when you really ought to be quiet. It was quite entertaining to see how hard it was to give you a fright.'

Reiner. He doesn't use the false name, Emil. He's letting me know how close the two of them are.

Hanni turned back to face him, forcing herself not to react.

Gessner smiled. 'Really, you thought all the squaring up and looming over you was serious? You thought I didn't know who you are? Oh dear, Frau Schlüssel, that is unfortunate.'

His mocking tone could have been Reiner's. Hanni didn't sit down again, although Gessner clearly expected her to, and she didn't reply. She waited for whatever threat was coming.

'You've kept your little secret from the rest of the world rather nicely, haven't you? Another change of name from Winter to Schlüssel, another inch or two of distance from your father. But you can't hide from us, from his boys. We're his eyes now – we're watching you for him. You've done your share of interviews too, haven't you? And you do go on about the importance you place on telling the truth through your pictures, don't you? You're a stuck record. Have you never considered what a risk that is, given that the truth is your Achilles' heel? Germany is a very moral place nowadays, Frau Schlüssel, or haven't you noticed? The churches are full and, while nobody cares about Nazis anymore, liars are a very different matter. Oh, how the vultures will come feeding – I can't wait to see it – when the real story of how you took your most heartbreaking photographs in the Theresienstadt ghetto is unmasked.'

He smiled wider and stretched out his legs, a perfect clone of the man who had crafted him.

'So a positive piece would be best, don't you think? Not a load of nonsense about old hatreds and new conspiracies nobody will want to read. Or write what you want and see how your editor reacts when you're the one who's exposed. Watch your life get destroyed, not mine.'

The cruelty she had accused Gessner of was all there. And

the control. And the certainty that his will would be the one which prevailed. Fear, brute force, blackmail: whatever it took. Once upon a time, one or all of those things would have worked on Hanni, but those days were done.

Reiner's got eyes on me but he's still blind. He doesn't know that I've changed, that my life is no longer his to play with. That, by ripping my world open, he set me free.

She smiled too and was pleased to see how much that discomforted Gessner.

'That was quite a speech, but you're rather behind the times. You're certainly wrong that nobody cares about Nazis; the Eichmann trial has changed that and there's no going back. There will be more criminals hunted down, more punishments, more jail sentences to come.' She let him have his snort before she went on. 'And you're wrong about me too. I don't care if you stand on a rooftop and shout to the world who my father is, who I was. Which you won't by the way – or not before I do – because that would reveal him too. My son knows. My husband knows. Reiner, or Emil, whichever you call him, has done all the damage to me he can do. So have your fun, blow my world up. I really don't care. It is, after all, the fate I'm planning for you.'

She walked away while he was still shouting that she would be sorry, that she didn't have the first clue, leaving the door open so that the press pack milling around the foyer could hear their golden boy in all of his colours. For almost thirteen years, ever since she had become a mother, she had left Reiner to his world while she focused on hers. She had stopped the quest she had been on since the war's end to make Reiner pay for his crimes entirely because of Leo.

Good luck with my grandchild.

Those were the last words Reiner had said to her in Prague. Hannelore had heard the warning in them: that any arrow she threw at him would fling itself back at her son. So she had kept away from her father and kept her boy safe. And then Leo had found a new hero in Valentin Gessner and Reiner's poison had touched him anyway.

Hanni hurried into the street, the article already taking shape in her head. Reiner's influence was spreading, exactly as he had promised it would. Reiner's influence had reached Leo.

So this was where it stopped.

The apartment was empty, which it shouldn't have been. Leo was supposed to be at home, grounded again for mixing with a group of boys who spelled trouble. That was another fight she would have to have. Hanni pulled out the tape recording and her notes, determined to make a start on the article while her blood was still racing. She couldn't settle. Her head was too full of her son and the bad crowd he was sliding so easily into.

I don't know him.

A handful of years ago, when she'd known every thought in Leo's head, that disconnect would have been impossible. Now it was frightening.

Hanni got up, picked up a pile of laundry and went into Leo's room. She didn't try to fool herself that putting the folded clothes away was anything other than a pretence, an excuse to do something she never did: open the drawers and start digging. She set about the task quickly so that she didn't have to weigh up its morals. There was nothing in the chest by the window, or the one by the bed; she was certain that didn't mean there was nothing to find.

Hanni stood in the centre of the room, trying to remember what she had been like at Leo's age, when she had also had secrets that were best kept from her parents. Her letter from Ezra and the first photograph she had taken of the Hitler Youth boy screaming in hate. The other images she had slipped away from her mother over the years to capture. The signs forbidding Jews to enter Berlin's theatres and parks; the smashed shop windows and hate-filled graffiti; the old man curled at a police-man's feet, trying to protect his head from the swinging boot. Her catalogue of a world spinning out of control. *Where did I put them?* The answer sent her straight to the right hiding place.

The box she pulled out from under a jumper at the back of Leo's wardrobe looked innocent enough. Until she took out the old copies of the *Fix und Foxi* comic he hadn't read in years and dug deeper. What she found turned her blood cold. Under-neath the childhood mementos was a stack of magazines produced by the unashamedly right-wing DRP, the Deutsche Reichspartei. Hanni flicked through the articles, her stomach churning at each opening sentence.

The war crimes attributed to the Third Reich were a slander, spread by the Jews.

The Poles massacred fifty thousand Germans in 1939 and started the war.

She sped past the photographs of SS officers labelled *Our Heroes*. And the eulogies to Goebbels and Hitler. She tried not to think about Leo reading them. She tried to quieten the voice in her head which was an echo of Renny's. That was filled with, *This is your fault. You've hidden the past. Because Freddy won't engage with his Jewish heritage, you've never given Leo any sense that he could have a share in it.*

She put the magazines to one side and pulled out a copy of *Mein Kampf*, whose ramblings she could only hope he hadn't been able to penetrate. And then she picked up and opened the first of a bunch of carefully folded newspaper cuttings and it was hard not to retch. Reiner stared back at her. He stared out of all of them. Every article Leo had saved and stored at the bottom of his box full of Nazi memorabilia was about his grandfather and his award-winning schools. And every one of them was soaked in the flattery Gessner had expected to hear.

'What are you doing?'

She hadn't heard him come in. Now Leo was standing in the bedroom doorway, his body rigid with anger.

'Leave those alone. They're private – they're none of your business.'

'Of course they're my business! The magazines, this hateful book? They're filth that you've no business to be messing with!'

Her fury galvanised him. He rushed forward, snatched the papers out of Hanni's hands and began stuffing them back into the box. Hanni forced herself to take a deep breath. She wanted to keep yelling; she wanted to tip the whole box into the bin. She wanted to shake Leo until she forced some sense into him. She couldn't do any of it. She had to keep calm despite her revulsion, or she really could lose him. She swallowed hard and forced herself to soften her voice.

'Okay, okay. I'm sorry that I went through your things. You should be allowed privacy and I was prying. But I'm not sorry for how I feel, and I was prying because I'm worried about you. And now I've seen this lot, I think I've got good reason to be. Never mind your grandfather – we'll come back to him – the things you've collected and have presumably been reading are dreadful. You do know that, don't you? That they've been written to keep a dreadful way of thinking alive? And I don't understand why you'd want to read them. Can you at least explain that?'

His face snapped into the sullen expression that normally heralded an explosion. Hanni tried again.

'I'm trying my best not to judge or be angry here. Do you need more answers about the world or the past than your father and I have given you? Is that it? I can understand if that's the reason, although I can't condone what you've been doing. Come on, Leo. You're a clever boy. You must know that reading these lies is absolutely not the way to find the right answers. You know what happened to your father's family and why. You know he's Jewish, and okay fine, that doesn't mean that you are but it surely gives you some sense of connection? And you know how Renny spent the first years of her life.' She swallowed again, conscious that her voice was rising. 'The point I'm trying to make is that the people who committed those terrible crimes in the war, the people who these magazines have cast as heroes, were evil. So why do you want to know more about them?'

'Because you say all those things but I don't know if they're true.' The answer burst out of him with a force that stunned her. 'I don't know what they did, or not really. Everyone repeats the same number all the time: six million Jews were murdered in the war. But then they say that nobody in Germany knew it was happening. How can that be right? It doesn't make sense. But if it is and if my grandfather was involved like Renny said, why didn't somebody stop him? Why didn't you? And why didn't he go to jail at the end of the war? If that many people were murdered, why aren't the jails bursting with their killers?'

Hanni stared at him, groping for an answer that was better than 'I tried' or 'There were too many to prosecute'. For something that didn't come with a raft of excuses she didn't believe any more than Leo would. She hesitated too long and that hesitation simply fed into the impossible stance he had chosen.

'You can't give me an answer, can you? So why should I believe any of it happened? The Holocaust, I mean. I don't believe in it. I think it's made up.'

She had expected confusion and questions that were too hard for the easy answers he wanted, and his anger at being discovered, but not that. She shook her head as his words bit at her.

'Wait a minute, what did you say? You don't believe that the Holocaust happened?'

The instant she said the impossibility of that out loud, her tightly held anger flared.

'Are you serious? What exactly are you saying here? That your father and Renny are liars? That everything that was said at the Nuremberg Trials was false? That all the testimony at the Eichmann trial, which you watched on television sitting next to me, was fake? Honestly, Leo? Could we take a pause here and really consider the possibility of that? You think that the witnesses in Israel, who wept on the stand as they described gas being pumped into buses and hearing the screams coming out, who were forced to dig pits and load bodies into them with their bare hands or were shot themselves and only climbed out by scrambling across the corpses of their husbands and wives, were spinning stories? Is that truly what you are saying?'

Her pulse was racing; her skin felt too tight. Surely this time she'd got through to him? To her horror, Leo shrugged.

'Not all of it. I think that some bad things happened and some people died as a result – it was a war after all. And maybe the Jews were targeted, but how am I meant to know if that's true? I've never heard it at school. I don't know any Jewish people except Dad, who says he isn't Jewish anymore, and Renny, who shouts slogans at me or treats me like a kid. And where's the proof? Lots of people have said that the photos were altered, that the witnesses were bribed. Are all of those people lying? And you've always said that the Nazis were monsters but Eichmann was so scrawny he looked like my history teacher. Am I honestly supposed to be scared of him?'

Some bad things happened; some people died.

Hanni couldn't feel the ground. Where was Leo's empathy? How could he so easily reject the evidence? She couldn't make sense of it, until she remembered the phrases which had been trotted out so often since the war they had rung round Germany like a refrain. *I didn't know. I didn't see. I never met the sort of people who were taken – they weren't our kind.* The step from turned-away heads and shrugged shoulders to *it didn't happen* suddenly seemed frighteningly close. And it wasn't a place where she could allow Leo to stand. She made one last attempt to rein herself in.

'I'm trying here, I really am. I'm trying to believe that you don't mean what you just said. Tell me that's right, Leo. Tell me that you've made a mistake. That you've read some things that confused you but you don't really think like this. Take a moment and remember how upset you were when Renny told you about the war, and what happened to her afterwards. Remember how upset you were then and how upset you've been since, and tell me it's because you believed her. Don't be this boy – be the one that I know with the kind heart.'

Her words fell unheard. He flicked his hands as if he was pushing away who he had once been.

'I was nine when she told me that stuff. I'd only just stopped believing in Father Christmas. I would have believed anything at nine. And Renny was angry when she said it; she always is – she'd say anything to kick up a scene.'

He was all squared up, his body switching from a child's to a man's the way his voice had started to do. Hanni stared at her son and couldn't see anything but a stranger.

Is this what too much silence has done? Does he honestly believe that Germany was some kind of innocent victim of the Third Reich, or that all the hatred wasn't true?

It was as if Leo could read her thoughts.

'And why are we still the only bad guys? Germans don't even get to mourn our own dead. That's not right. You go on about all the millions who were murdered, but what about German soldiers, all the millions of them who died too? When do we get to be proud of them? In Britain and France they build monuments and they say thank you. Why don't we get to do that here?'

He was parroting his magazines which refused to believe

that German soldiers had been anything but honourable. The complaint about nobody mourning the Wehrmacht was also at the core of Gessner's latest speech, although Leo had stripped that of its clever language and twisted facts and simplified it down to an adolescent boy's confusion. And that was something Hanni could tackle.

'You got that idea from Valentin Gessner, didn't you? Or the bones of it. Maybe he has a point about us not paying enough attention to our dead, I don't know. But I do know that he's not who you think he is and he's not someone you should be listening to. He's a killer, Leo. At the end of the war, when he was twelve years old like you and fighting in the last street battles, he executed two boys who didn't want to fight anymore because the war was done, who just wanted to go home. He did the same a year later to another man who was supposed to be his comrade.'

But Leo's answering, 'You mean that he was brave, that he had a cause to believe in,' dismissed Gessner's crimes, and her, so casually, Hanni's temper finally blew.

'You don't have a clue.'

She grabbed one of the magazines and ripped through it until she found the picture she had spotted earlier: a group of SS officers standing on the rim of a crater and laughing into the camera.

'That's an execution pit, down there, below them. If the shot had gone wider it would have picked up the carnage. They're laughing at dead bodies, Leo. They're having fun. Like they did when they tricked women and children into the gas chambers at Auschwitz or worked hundreds of men to death in a day at Buchenwald. Or sent boys like you to be slaughtered in some pointless last stand the officers weren't stupid enough to take part in. And swap their uniforms for a jacket and tie and yes, they look like history teachers or accountants. Or your grandfather. That doesn't mean they weren't monsters. Because that's what they were, Leo, whatever they might look like now. Evil monsters who committed murder on an industrial scale. Can't you get that into your head?'

She had lost him. The photograph was evidence to her but not to him – he couldn't see past its borders. And she had picked the wrong example in Reiner. Leo reached back into the box himself and pulled out a press cutting.

'Oh here we go. My wicked grandad again. Okay, if he really is as awful as you make out, how come he's so popular with the newspapers? Why do rich people send their sons to his schools? How could a war criminal be as successful as he is?'

'Easily. Germany was so desperate to move on, anyone could reinvent themselves, even a man as vile as Reiner. He changed his name to Emil to hide his identity – I've told you that. He pretended to be a brother he never had. Doesn't that at least throw up a red flag?'

But Leo didn't listen – he talked over her. It was a moment or two before Hanni realised what he had said.

'What was that? Where do you want to go?'

'To one of his schools. He'd take me like a shot. And he might tell me the truth about the war, not make up stories about it.'

There was a shadow in the room, one Hanni knew all too well. She could barely get the next words out.

'How do you know he'd have you? Have you been in touch with him?'

For the first time since he had burst in on her, Leo had the grace to look a little shame-faced.

'Yes, I wrote to him. I knew there was no point in asking you, and I told him I wanted to get to know him, that I thought his schools sounded really great. He said there was a place for me whenever I wanted one.'

Hanni thought she was going to be sick. She told Leo that and she told him no, that he would go to one of those dreadful places over her dead body. The row that erupted then was bitter and painful. In the end, Leo screamed at Hanni to get out of his room and Hanni gladly went.

Her first impulse was to phone Freddy and beg for his help. She couldn't do it. She couldn't tell him that Reiner was so horribly back in their lives again. She went to bed instead and lay awake most of the night, desperate to go to her son and erase all the fury between them. Repeating over and over to herself that Leo hadn't meant what he said, that he was under the sway of bad influences. Determined that, as soon as morning came, she would make him see the truth and make everything right.

But when morning came it was too late.

Leo's bed was empty and Leo was gone.

CHAPTER 3

Freddy groaned awake as the alarm clock burst into life.

It was only Tuesday and already the week had lasted too long. He groped for his watch on the bedside table, hoping that he had set the alarm wrong and there might be another half hour that was totally his. He hadn't and all the wishing in the world wouldn't change the fact that, once he was up and moving, nothing of the day would be his at all.

When Brack, his old and unlamented boss, had finally been eased out of the chief inspector role at Friesenstraβe police station and the title had passed to Freddy, he had beamed for days. And he had done very well at the job. The station now had a reputation not for the dubious wartime past of its boss but for being the place where Berlin's brightest young detectives wanted to train. Freddy had built bridges with the American military authorities he had regularly upset when he was head of the murder squad. He had forged ties with the burgeoning intelligence community in the west of the city and maintained enough old ones in the east. Friesenstraβe was held up as the perfect example of a modern police station and Freddy was held up as the architect of that. Which was all wonderful, except Freddy was bored.

Being in charge meant being stuck at a desk. It meant too many forms and too many decisions and not enough of the hands-on detective work that he loved. And far too many hours lost to meetings whose nit-picking attention to every detail of the job drove him to distraction. He was starting to feel old and he wasn't ready to feel old. He was also starting to look it – whatever his last date had murmured about the grey hairs dotting his temples being distinguished.

Which is all fine in theory but she'd have run a mile if she'd met the cause of them.

He fought off the impulse to pull the covers over his head and pretend another day wasn't coming.

Please at least let this one start without every door in the flat slamming.

Freddy made the same wish every morning but it rarely came true, not with Renny in the house. He loved his younger sister more than he had words to say, but the gap between the girl he had gone searching for in Prague a dozen years ago and the one who whirled through his life like a hurricane now was a wide one. Freddy was aware, although she had only admitted it once, that Hanni woke up most mornings wondering how she had lost Leo. He woke up wondering why he had never properly found Renny. It hadn't been for want of trying.

Something is broken but I'll fix it, I swear. If she'll let me.

It was all he had wanted to do when he finally found her. He hadn't managed it. When he brought the damaged child back to Berlin, his only aim had been to give her a secure and happy life. He was fairly certain he failed at that too, or at least at the happiness part. Renny wanted a life he didn't know how to give her.

And lying here feeling sorry for her, or for myself, because we're permanently at odds won't remedy anything.

He forced himself out of bed. Fretting over Renny and feeling useless was not how he wanted to start his days. Any more than he wanted to get sucked into the other problem which permanently circled him – Hanni. Freddy had to think about Renny even when thinking about her exhausted him because she was his sister and he was determined to do what he could to make her life better. He wished that he didn't have to think about Hanni, other than as the other parent of his child; there was no solving her at all. And no getting rid of her either. The number of mornings when Hanni leapt into his head, even, to his shame, when there was another face on the pillow, had gone past counting long ago. Which was why the remedy of another face on the pillow never worked. *Why can't I let her go?* was as common a tune in his head as *Why can't I help my sister?* And neither of them were doing anything for the advancing grey in his hairline.

He was rubbing at that when Renny's door crashed open.

She was incapable of starting a day quietly, or she was now. In those first awful weeks when he had brought the confused and frightened nine-year-old home, she wouldn't leave her room and she had been so silent it had terrified him. Now she hit every morning at full blast and top speed. She raced everywhere and lapped up everything, as if, at twenty-two, she was already in danger of missing her chances. She took more courses than she was required to at the University of West Berlin and she was rarely at home in the evenings. She spent most of those with a youth group she had cast her lot in with at a synagogue near their home in Bergmannkiez, when she was thirteen and bursting with questions about her family's faith that Freddy had no idea how to tackle. Following the Jewish faith wasn't a possibility for him anymore; it hadn't been for years. He couldn't explain that to Renny. He could barely put into words the pain his family's fate could still stir in him if he let it. Or the irrational anger that stemmed from wishing his parents had been born into a religion and a culture that would have allowed them to live. He wasn't proud of that feeling – it put blame where blame had absolutely no right to be – but he couldn't shake it off either. Which meant that there was no place for him among the kindly men and women at the synagogue.

Despite that, he had been happy that Renny had found herself a clan she was comfortable with. Now, however, he was increasingly worried. The shy boys and girls she had met at thirteen had turned into angry young people. Ardent Zionists who believed, as Renny did, that Germany was no place for Jews. Who didn't want to live 'sitting on packed suitcases' as she put it, waiting for the next Holocaust to consume them. Who could only see a future in Israel.

They weren't a bad crowd – not like the right-wing little thugs Leo seemed to have latched on to – but the intensity of their desire to leave Germany, which Renny very vocally shared, troubled him. That and their increasing determination to make a name for themselves. There was hardly a weekend which went by without Renny disappearing on a protest or a demonstration in support of somebody or against somebody; he could barely keep up. Not that she would be doing any more of those, not if he had any say in it. After the group's last outing, he'd found himself standing on the wrong side of a desk in the police station at Tempelhof, where Renny had been taken to cool her heels after shouting abuse at a member of the government. That was an uncomfortable experience which had quickly worsened when the officer in charge realised who he was dealing with.

So what did I do? Did I say yes, Renny, you're right, that politician's no good and his past is questionable. Did I listen to her fears and suggest that she look for a better way to express her anger than a street brawl? No, I yelled at her instead and dropped us straight into another bitter fight.

He groaned at the memory. Fighting was all he and Renny

seemed to do. The one the previous night was a copy of one that played out on an endless loop. It began with Renny delivering a lecture on the opportunities offered by emigration. It continued with Freddy trying to explain that he was German before he was anything else, and that he couldn't leave the place where his son lived. It boiled over somewhere in the middle of, 'How can you stay here when you know what these people have done and what they're still capable of?' Their disconnection was exhausting, their disagreement was never-ending.

But better that than to face up to the thought of her leaving. Which she doesn't know is something I worry about because I never tell her.

That was a sharper wake-up call than any alarm clock.

Freddy began pulling on his shirt and running through topics they could talk about which might make for a more digestible breakfast. He was working on a method of saying 'Please stay, stop scaring me by talking about going' that she might listen to when the telephone rang. He didn't hurry to answer it – an early morning call was a common occurrence – the station apparently couldn't go more than a few hours without him. Renny's phone manner was far politer than his so he left the pleasantries to her and concentrated on the calm demeanour and the warm smile he intended to present her with. Which disappeared the instant that he walked into the kitchen. Contrary to his expectations, Renny wasn't spoiling for a fight. She was staring at the phone as if the words coming out of it didn't make sense, and her face was a frightened little girl's again.

'It's what I was afraid of – he's with Reiner. A telegram arrived from the Goslar school twenty minutes ago.'

Hanni's hand was trembling as she handed it over. The message was short and horribly to the point.

Leo is here asking to be enrolled stop it will be
my pleasure to accommodate him stop

The fear Freddy had been swallowing since Hanni's phone
call turned into a sour ball of rage.

Reiner Foss had his son.

Freddy wanted to smash walls. He wanted to kick and yell
and break heads. He wanted to scream at Hanni, *Reiner is your
father so this is your doing*. He handed the telegram back. He
managed to grab hold of himself. He tried to focus on *she is not
her father*.

Freddy hadn't seen Reiner Foss since the man had
destroyed his and Hanni's future, but Foss still loomed too close
to his life. That was partly because Freddy could not let him go.
He had devoured every morsel he could find about the Nazi
who, in a cruel twist of fate, was his father-in-law, in an impossible attempt to understand what motivated Reiner to keep
following the fascist path he had set out on in the 1930s. Very
little of what he could find tallied with what Hanni had been
forced to tell him when Reiner had unmasked her in Prague.
The Emil who Foss now presented to the world, the educator
who graced society parties and was interviewed surrounded by
beaming students and their wealth-dripping parents, was very
different to the sneering, heartless SS Obergruppenführer
Reiner Foss who Freddy had met. To the man Hanni had
described cracking his whip as the inmates of Theresienstadt
were pushed onto the trains which would carry them to their
deaths. That man ran with hate where his blood should have
been.

And his daughter is a very different creature.

Freddy finally understood that, although he had spent years
getting to that point. He had never found the right words or the
right time to tell Hanni that he had reached it.

And I can't do it today, no matter how much she might need to hear it. Not with my boy under threat.

He also couldn't add to her pain by heaping on blame, so he stayed silent as Hanni poured out her shock and he forced himself to listen the way a detective not a terrified father would.

'I thought Reiner would be the one to make a move. I've had nightmares for years about him snatching Leo, but I had it all the wrong way round. Leo chose to go to him. He thinks Reiner's some kind of a hero, that he's not guilty of anything. I can't make sense of it. I didn't even know he'd gone, so what kind of a mother does that make me? He must have sneaked out in the night and caught an early train. And I need to go to him, I need to bring him home...'

Hanni's voice finally cracked on *home* and it broke him.

Freddy was halfway across the hall, his arms outstretched, when she waved him away. Part of him was glad that she did: touching her, even purely for comfort's sake, would have plunged them back into intimacies they no longer knew how to navigate. And part of him was simply sad that comforting her was no longer his to do. He took a deep breath and stepped back again.

'What happened? I assume you didn't have any idea what he was planning?'

Facts were steadier ground. Approaching the reasons for Leo's actions from the point of view of a policeman rather than a parent might stop him from cracking.

Hanni shook her head. 'No, I hadn't a clue. I only found out last night that he'd been in contact with Reiner, and I only found that out because we'd had a blazing row. We've had too many of them lately. This one started because I wouldn't let him go with me when I interviewed Valentin Gessner, and then I made it worse by snooping in his room.' She suddenly shook her head. 'No, I'm sorry for the row but I'm not sorry I did that. I had no idea how deeply he was getting sucked in to the wrong kind of thinking so thank God that I did. And I found some things that you need to see.'

Freddy followed her into the sitting room where a box was waiting on the coffee table. He sat down and flipped through its contents as quickly as his stomach would let him. By the time he reached the press cuttings, he'd had more than enough. When he glanced up at Hanni she looked equally sickened. She couldn't keep her voice steady.

'I've had this wrong too. I thought he was just pushing boundaries, that these older boys he's got in with at school were rough and leading him astray but they'd all grow out of it. I didn't realise they were trainee Nazis.'

Freddy pulled himself back together. It was too easy to let Hanni carry all the guilt; he'd made his share of mistakes too.

'Keeping tabs on who Leo's mixing with and what he's reading isn't just your responsibility. I should have come down on that gang harder. They're piling up enough petty crimes to pull them all in and that would have given Leo enough of a fright to get him out from under their influence. And never mind that, I should have dealt with the subject of Reiner when Renny exploded that bomb over us, not shied away.'

Hanni shrugged.

'And I should have handed my father over to the Russians in 1945 and told the truth from the beginning. We could both pave our lives with *should* and it won't change where we are standing. Which is why I'm going to catch the next available train and bring him back.'

'Wait a moment – slow down.'

He knew instinctively it was the wrong course of action but Hanni was up and moving so fast, he was forced to chase after her and grab the suitcase he had suddenly noticed was set ready in the hallway.

'You can't. I know you want to, and so do I, but that's not the right way to do this.'

Hanni stared at him as if he had gone mad.

'What? Why on earth not? Don't you want to come too and bring a squad if needs be? He's underage and not capable of making these decisions so surely it's a police matter and not just a personal one? Well I'm going – I'm not going to stand by and let Reiner twist up my son.'

She tried to snatch the case back and push past him but Freddy shoved himself in between her and the front door.

'Hanni, I know this is a nightmare but will you take a second and listen to me? Will you stop?'

She slumped without warning, her shoulders hitting the wall, the energy that had propelled her through finding Leo's empty bed and the telegram's arrival draining away. This time Freddy caught her. He kept a tentative hand on her arm and steered her back into the sitting room. He led her to the sofa and sat her down, repeating, 'It'll be all right,' over and over and wondering which one of them needed to hear it the most. And he didn't let go of her jacket, because he wasn't convinced she would stay.

'I know you're afraid; I know you want to fly after Leo. So do I. If I could get my hands on Reiner, I'd kill him for encouraging this. But that's the problem, Hanni. It's encouragement, what he's done, not kidnapping. I could turn up there with half Berlin's police force but there's nothing I could actually charge Reiner with. And what if we make things worse, which I think that we might. What if us turning up mob-handed and angry, demanding that Leo comes home, goes the wrong way? What if it pushes him closer to Reiner? God, Hanni, I know this is hard – it's killing me to have to say it – but I think we have to wait. Maybe Leo has to learn the truth for himself. Maybe that's the only way he'll accept who his grandfather is. I'm as scared about what Reiner could do to warp Leo's thinking as you are, I swear it. But I'm more scared that, if we don't get this right, we could lose him for a very long time.'

Freddy didn't know if it was *we* or *lose* or the way his voice finally faltered on both words which broke the dam but Hanni's tears wouldn't stop once they started. This time he broke all his rules and he properly held her.

It wasn't much of a movement, a hand on an arm becoming a hand round a shoulder. Her head lowering an inch or two onto his chest. And, despite the years of distance, it wasn't new. Their bodies had learned this rhythm long ago – it was printed inside them. How to mould to each other, how to fit. Her hands pressed into his shirt. Her cheek tucked under his chin. The position they slipped into was safety and home. It was everything his tired heart needed. Or it would have been if Freddy hadn't glanced up from her hair and caught sight of Reiner's face in one of the articles his rummaging had tipped onto the floor and his body pulled back before he could stop it.

'I'm sorry.'

They both said it. Neither of them was certain what they were apologising for. Hanni got up and moved to the safer haven of another chair.

'I don't like it at all. But I trust you and I'll do it if that's what you think is best. I won't go, or at least not today. But he can't stay there, Freddy – we have to make a plan. He might be safe with my father for now but what if that changes? And he can't breathe the same air as Reiner's boys. He can't become one of them.' A shiver suddenly ran through her. 'Valentin Gessner went to the Goslar school – did you know that?'

Freddy didn't but he wasn't surprised. On their one meeting he had found the man cold and his famous charm reptilian.

'He did and he's so like Reiner it's frightening. It's as if Reiner's built a mould and he'll be desperate to force Leo into that. That can't happen. There has to be something we can do that's more than just sitting around waiting for Leo to come to his senses.'

And then she jumped up so fast, Freddy was ready to go

chasing after her again. Instead she ran over to the desk in the corner of the room and snatched up a notebook.

'He has to learn the truth for himself – okay, I understand that, but we could speed up the process. Or I can.'

She sat down again, clutching the little book to her chest as if it was a talisman.

'I interviewed Gessner yesterday. He was vile and so full of himself. He has to be brought down the same as Reiner before he gets even more power. Which is why I'm going to write an exposé on him that will ruin him. And that's how we get Leo back.'

Freddy was lost. Hanni was running ahead of him. That didn't worry him; it wasn't new. It usually meant that she had seen an angle a moment before he had.

'I'm not with you. Explain.'

Her pace picked up, the way it always did when an idea hit her.

'The piece I'm planning to write will discredit Gessner, but it will discredit Reiner more. And once his real story is out in print, all the rich parents and the support he's built up will fade away. Leo will have to accept the truth about him then, won't he? It's supposed to be published the week after next. And when it comes out, it will bring our boy back – it has to.'

If anyone could write Reiner's story and make it believable, Freddy had no doubt that it was Hanni. But whether anyone would actually publish what she was planning to write was an entirely different story. He doubted that many people had any interest in pursuing individual Nazis, never mind an appetite for conspiracies that involved a whole posse of them.

'It will work, Freddy – it's got to. Not just because we need it to, but because the tide is turning against Reiner and his kind.'

She had read the doubt in his eyes – she had always had a knack for spotting that.

'Think about it. The television broadcasts from the Eichmann trial put war crimes into ordinary people's homes. Questions are being asked about Nazi atrocities that haven't been asked since Nuremberg. If I'd tried to write this at any point in the last ten years, nobody would have listened, but Germany's ready to examine itself now – or it's going to be forced to. So the time to go after him is finally right.'

It was a plan and they needed a plan to keep them both sane. Freddy had no idea if it would work but it was surely better than dragging a furious Leo away only to have him run off again.

The time is finally right.

Something apart from whether the idea would succeed or fail was niggling. Freddy closed his eyes and let his brain scroll through the latest stack of briefings that had clogged up his desk. It took him a minute but he finally remembered the article. It wasn't one that he currently wanted to face.

'It might be right, but it's running out. The statute of limitations on war crimes is due to expire in less than two years. There's pressure to extend it, but no guarantees. Which means it could be harder not easier to bring a case – these things take forever and no one will want to start an investigation that won't make it through to an end. And that's the problem: your piece could damage Reiner's reputation, and Gessner's, but it might not lead anywhere except to you being hit with a libel suit.'

The thought that thousands of war criminals would never answer for their actions whatever way public opinion ran was a bitter enough one to momentarily push his fears for Leo to one side. And there was worse.

'And, Hanni, I'm sorry to ask it, but even if your article is as damning as you intend, does it hold enough proof to stand up to scrutiny? At the moment, isn't it your word against Reiner's and a handful of photographs you took in Theresienstadt, which he'll say were faked? It might be enough to sow a few seeds with Leo, or...'

She filled in the pause.

'Or Leo will say it's more lies and ignore it, and I'll have wasted my best shot.'

He nodded. 'You've got testimony to back up your allegations, haven't you?'

He relaxed a little when she said yes, and then his heart sank at 'Against Gessner anyway.'

'That won't be enough to catch Reiner as well. I'm sorry, Hanni, but look at how the Israelis finally caught out Eichmann. All those months of testimony, all those charges against him that he shrugged his way through as hearsay and other people's doing, and it all boiled down in the end to one order that he couldn't deny. If we want to catch Reiner, we have to do the same: we have to find one indisputable act to tie him to. One thing that has his fingers all over it.'

It wasn't a blow Freddy wanted to deliver but he couldn't let Hanni move on with false hope. She was quiet for a moment, and then she drew herself up.

'I do have witness names I can cite, so writing the piece isn't a problem. And maybe the thrust of it will be Gessner, but it will discredit Reiner – he'll be forced to defend himself. And that's when we go to the school and build on the doubt and persuade Leo to come home. Or better still, we use the time between now and publication to get more evidence together so that Reiner is fully implicated as well.'

And then she suddenly slumped.

'Except how do we do that? I've tried that route time and again but he was too clever to leave traces of himself anywhere – he prided himself on it. And there's no files on him that we can access, or none that I know of. We're back where we've always been, and no closer to rescuing Leo.'

He could see she was on the verge of running for the door again. Now Freddy was the one who had to be a step ahead. He concentrated as hard as he could on everything she had ever told him about Reiner.

'Luca, the Stasi agent from East Berlin.'

The name came to him from nowhere but he could feel something stir in it.

'Remind me, why was he hunting for your father in Prague? Why were the East German secret police interested in him?'

Hanni frowned, but she didn't waste time on questions. 'Because of the sabotage that was happening to factories and farm equipment in the East back then. The GDR didn't want to admit that the trouble was caused by their own people, so they were looking for ex-Nazis to blame, to be scapegoats. The plan was to arrest Reiner and stage a show-trial. It would have solved some of their internal problems, and catching war criminals who the West wouldn't convict was also a propaganda win for them.'

Freddy nodded. 'That makes sense and it also means that the GDR must have compiled a file on him. I bet they still have it. They're always announcing lists of ex-Nazis they think the West should have prosecuted and haven't. That desire for a propaganda win has never changed. I've not seen Reiner's name in any of the ones that have come over my desk, but that doesn't mean they're not aware of him.'

She was in step with him now – her face had lost some of its fear.

'They might have information that we've never seen. That could place him somewhere I don't know about.'

Freddy nodded again. 'It won't be straightforward. There's no guarantee they'll hand anything over even if they've got it, and the Stasi are not my favourite people to deal with – if anything their grip on the East and their levels of control are getting more hardline. But I've retained a few contacts who might talk to me if I try. And if your exposé does get traction, perhaps they'll be happy to pile the pressure on. The GDR love to shout about how our side never cleaned up our act the way that they did. How many times have you heard an East German official say that if you scratch a West German politician or banker or judge, you'll find a Nazi underneath? And we both know that Reiner has done his research into the kind of education well-off and ambitious parents want and it's the kind provided by Eton and those sorts of private schools, not what German ones that still haven't properly recovered from the war can offer. If the publicity is right, he's already attracting British and American pupils from the diplomatic and military families here who don't want to send their kids abroad. I bet the East could make a lot of capital out of that.'

Hanni was on the edge of her seat, ready to send him straight out on the case.

'And if they do, then Leo would see Reiner for who he really is.' She stopped and the adrenaline that had been powering her suddenly fell away. 'But how long would it take to do things this way? The thought of him in Reiner's clutches for one night is bad enough. Now we're talking about two weeks until the article's out. What if the rest takes three, or a month, or more? I don't think I could stand it, I really don't.'

She was doing her best to stay calm but her knuckles were white. Freddy desperately wanted to make her feel better. He wanted to promise her that two weeks was the absolute limit, that it could all be done much faster – he wanted to hear that himself. It wasn't a lie that would help.

'I know. I can't bear the thought of him spending even an hour in Reiner's hands any more than you can. So I'll do my best – I'll push as hard as I can on my side.' He couldn't quite manage a smile but he did his best to sound hopeful. 'And even if it does take a bit longer, it will be all right. Reiner can't ruin a boy as good as ours in the space of a few weeks.'

He had struck the right note. The tight lines around Hanni's jaw finally eased.

'He can't, can he? Leo will come through this unharmed. Because we did make him good, our boy, didn't we, despite everything else that went wrong?'

Freddy had to leave when she said that. He needed the solitude of his car to give in to the tears that had been burning his throat since he had heard Renny say, in a voice that was far too small to be hers, 'Leo's gone missing.'

The worst had happened – Reiner had appeared and struck directly at them, and they had managed not to tear each other apart. They had managed instead to come together, as a team. And he had held her, and the body in his arms had never felt more right. Freddy sat in the car replaying the feel of her.

His heart was bursting with fear for his boy and fury with Hanni's father but – for the first time in years and despite the terrible timing – there was also a space opening up in it for Hanni.

CHAPTER 4

6 MARCH 1963, UNIVERSITY OF WEST BERLIN

Freddy blamed her for Leo's disappearance – Renny had seen it in his eyes when he came back from meeting with Hanni, although he had quickly tried to hide it.

When she had asked, 'Is there anything I can do? Is there anything Hanni needs?' Renny had genuinely wanted to help. Freddy's response – 'Leo's gone to his grandfather and, given that his obsession with Reiner began with your outburst, you're probably the last person Hanni wants to see' – had crushed her.

Renny bitterly regretted telling Leo the truth about his messed-up family. She had regretted opening her mouth the moment the shocked little boy had burst into tears. She doubted anybody believed that.

Because your apology was rubbish and you've never tried to explain why you did it, or not honestly anyway.

Renny stopped folding the leaflets promoting her Zionist discussion group's next meeting before she tore through and ruined another one. Deciding it was time to open Leo's eyes – and then the way she had dealt with the fallout – had not been one of her finest moments.

'Maybe I said it badly but he needs to understand who his

mother is and what his grandfather did. Or we leave him in ignorance and he turns into yet another bystander incapable of taking a stand against evil. Is that what you want? Isn't the truth more important than a few tears?'

She knew now that her speech had been pompous and self-righteous and barely merited the title apology. It was no wonder that Freddy had blown his top and called her fixation with making everyone face the truth just as dangerous as running from it.

'You need to get off this crusade, Renny, before you do any more damage. To yourself as well as your family.'

She in turn had blown up at that and any chance for an honest conversation about the whole sorry episode had vanished. The irony of that hadn't been lost on her. The truth was that Renny hadn't been on her crusade when she told Leo that his grandfather was a Nazi who had murdered her family. She had told him that because she was jealous. She had been forced to watch Hanni wrap the boy up in her arms and cover him with kisses and she couldn't stand it.

Jealousy caused by the never-filled hole left by the loss of her mother, not a fixation on honesty, had made Renny forget that Leo was a child. And anger. Anger was her permanent state. She burned with it. For Hanni, for making her believe, for a moment when the two had first met in Prague, that new love could help heal the scars left by the love which was lost. For Freddy, for finding her and being family but for not being enough to heal the empty space where her dead mother should be. And with the world which had snatched her from her safe life when she was little more than a baby, for being dangerous and unpredictable and her enemy. Renny had been angry for so long, most other emotions were drowned by it.

Except jealousy and loneliness and fear – they seem to survive well enough.

She pulled herself up off the floor. If she sat there any

longer, she would give in to the weight of all her bad feelings and curl up in a ball, and she didn't want anyone to find her like that. It wasn't as if the bad feelings were new. They had been with her since long before she left Prague and came to Berlin. That move, to a city full of people who looked respectable but could have been responsible for organising deportation trains or designing gas chambers, had simply cemented them under her skin.

Those first months in Germany were still so profoundly with her, they had shaped all the rest. The smothering panic she had felt at entering a schoolroom where the German language she was suddenly expected to speak was an alien, forbidden thing that the citizens of Czechoslovakia had closed their ears to. The impossibility of making friends with children whose parents could have murdered her own. The shame of constantly saying the wrong thing, because *ovens* and *concentration camps* and *ghetto* apparently weren't nice words for little girls to use.

Renny had retreated; she had lost her voice. She had turned silent and invisible to be safe.

And Freddy refused to understand, because he was too busy being German to be Jewish.

When Renny realised that being Jewish was something that mattered to her, the loneliness in Freddy's refusal to engage had been dreadful. He wouldn't talk about the faith he said he had left behind him in Buchenwald; he wouldn't talk about what that faith had meant to their family or what it might mean to Renny. He had constructed the little sister he wanted, a girl who walked with a far lighter tread through the world than she did. A girl she could never be. The loneliness in that was the worst.

'If you want to go there that's fine but don't keep asking me to come. I came, I tried like you wanted me to, but it's just not for me.'

There was the Fraenkelufer Synagogue, a short walk from

their Bergmannkiez home and *not for me* was where the gaps in her and Freddy's relationship had split into a chasm neither of them could find a way across. The synagogue had welcomed her; it had tried to welcome Freddy. Its stories of loss and resistance as well as the happier lives which had flourished despite the tragedies had given Renny roots. And the boys and girls she had met in its youth group had been searchers like her. She had grown up with them. She had found friends and a community with them, and now they were older and had moved out into the world, she had found a cause. She wished Freddy could be happier about that.

'Germany isn't safe; Germany hasn't changed. No one with Jewish blood in them will ever be safe here.'

She said it constantly but her brother wouldn't listen and wouldn't take her fears seriously. Not even when she showed him proof in the newspaper: photographs of swastikas painted across a synagogue in Cologne next to the words 'Germany demands Jews out'. That had happened four years ago and it still terrified her. She had nightmares which roared through her head in an unstoppable tide of barking dogs and marching men and ended with her being dragged onto a train. The threat of a repeat of what had happened to her in 1943 had been all too real, but Freddy had dismissed the graffiti as the work of right-wing idiots who would disappear back into their lairs. Which they hadn't done and which they wouldn't do because the vandals had turned out to be members of the Deutsche Reichspartei, an actual legitimate political party and a Nazi one by any other name, which so many people supported, it had won seats in the Bundestag. Renny had cried when she found that out. But then, as the swastikas and the same vicious words had started to appear on walls in Berlin, she had stopped crying and grown furious.

'I want to leave. I want to go and live in Israel – it's the only place Jews will ever be safe.'

Freddy refused to discuss even the possibility of that. He left the room every time she as much as mentioned emigration. Renny refused to give the idea up.

Israel was the goal of everything she did. All her friends were determined to get there, one day, one way or another. The country was their holy grail and the Israelis were their heroes. Germany had let ex-Nazi after ex-Nazi creep back into the high-ranking positions in politics and finance and business and the law that they had held during the war, because their experience apparently outweighed their crimes The Israelis had gone Nazi-hunting instead.

In 1960, Israeli secret agents had tracked down Adolf Eichmann, the architect of the Holocaust, to Argentina, to the little city of San Fernando north of Buenos Aires and they had swooped in and kidnapped him. Renny had memorised every glorious detail of the raid. From the daring way the Mossad agents had kidnapped Eichmann and dragged him to a safe house – where they had established his identity from a scar on his chest and his oddly small feet – to the description of them throwing their hooded captive into the boot of a car and then smuggling him, drugged and disguised as a crew member, by plane to Jerusalem. She had watched every televised moment of the trial with equal glee and cheered when the judge ordered the death penalty. Now there were rumours that those same agents were on the trail of Josef Mengele, the doctor who had butchered children in Auschwitz, and Renny and her friends were beside themselves with excitement. To be one of those agents was their dream. And the only way to achieve that dream was to be worthy of it.

Renny gathered up the leaflets and sorted them into bundles, ready to be posted through letter boxes and into pigeonholes. The discussion group was an excellent forum for exchanging ideas, but she and her group no longer believed that the world could be saved by talking – nothing of use was ever achieved by that. The Mossad agents were their idols but there were other heroes closer to home they wanted to copy. Jews who had stood up to Hitler in the war. Resistance fighters from the Warsaw ghetto and from Vilna who had escaped to form partisan groups in the forests. There hadn't been many of them perhaps but their exploits were the stuff of legend. And their spirit lived on in the group.

Renny and her friends weren't fighting the same war as the partisans had waged, they were well aware of that. The Nazis they were determined to silence didn't stride around in uniforms; they didn't do their dirty work in public. They daubed their swastikas at night and hid their identities behind the pseudonyms they used in their filthy publications. Like Leo's grandfather, they were well protected and harder to drag into the light. But they were out there. They could be traced and tracked down.

And if Renny was going to be forced to stay in Germany, she wasn't going to step back and stay silent. She was going to stand up for all the people who could no longer raise their voices or their fists. She was going to do her bit for justice.

CHAPTER 5

13–14 MARCH 1963, WEST BERLIN

'We can't use it, Hanni, I'm sorry. It's a fascinating if disturbing read, I'm not denying that, but it won't stand up in court.'

Noah normally jumped up and beamed when Hanni entered his office, and the start of their meetings was usually lost to industry gossip. Today her editor had stayed seated and formal and he could barely meet her eyes. And his refusal had completely wrong-footed her. Hanni had worked on a freelance basis for *Der Spiegel* and for Noah for years and he had never rejected her work before. She'd thought, or at least until today, that the kind of meetings where an editor would smile politely and praise her work and still pass on it belonged to the earlier and more hand-to-mouth days of her career. She couldn't remember how she was supposed to respond.

'Are you saying that you don't believe it?'

Noah shrugged, a gesture which sat awkwardly on his elegant frame. 'Whether I believe it or not isn't the point – it's what we can get past the lawyers.'

He glanced down at the closely typed pages spread across his desk. Every one of them was slashed through with red ink.

'The rumours about Gessner are legion; they have been

since he popped up in the Olympic shooting team and became a media darling. Some of what you've got here is new – I've not come across the cyanide capsule story before and it's a horror – but as for the rest? The allegations that he turned his gun on his comrades in the battle for Berlin and his exploits as a Werwolf? They've been doing the rounds between journalists for years, but nothing will make them stick.'

Hanni breathed a sigh of relief: perhaps there was still something to salvage.

'But I provided sworn affidavits for everything I wrote – all you had to do was check them.'

Noah was starting to look tired. 'Which we did, Hanni. This is hardly our first controversial story. We contacted every name that you gave us, but we couldn't get corroboration – Gessner either saw the list of your sources during the interview or he already knew how to get to them. No one will go publicly on record. Every single one of them backtracked. Which means that this isn't an article we can go with; it's a lawsuit we don't have the coffers for. And as for Reiner Foss, or Emil, or whatever he chooses to call himself...' He shook his head. 'That will be another dead end. There's as many stories about him as there are about Gessner, but Foss is the slipperiest of the lot.'

He flicked over a page which was as covered in scribbles as the rest. 'I don't doubt that this education programme he's set up is suspect, not given his credentials. Everything you've said about the schools being a continuation of the Nazi Napola system rings true, from the castles and mansions he's sited them in to the whole concept of deliberately educating an elite. But there's no point in pursuing it. Foss – and whoever the men are who back him – is untouchable. There's not one provable link between him and the war crimes you accuse him of. And the Brits and the Yanks with enough money to afford what he's peddling love all the 'gateway to the world' promises he makes them, never mind all the Germans who flock there. How can our homegrown schools, which are still short of textbooks and overwhelmed by too many kids in each classroom, compete?'

He was right, but that didn't make it bearable.

'By being decent? By teaching democracy, not hatred? By not having killers in charge?'

Noah didn't reply. He gathered up the pages Hanni had spent hours labouring over and passed them back across his desk.

'I know you're passionate about bringing him to justice and I understand why, especially now I know the personal angle. But that's the other thing, Hanni, what you've admitted in this about your relationship to him. I get it – it's a piece about honesty – but it's potentially also professional suicide.'

'I don't care about that.'

That wasn't a conversation Noah wanted to have; he stood up and made it clear that she should do the same.

'We can use one of your pictures for a cover shot but not the words, I'm sorry. Why don't you use the research you've done for a book instead? If you could get some more ex-members of the Hitler Youth to talk, there could be something interesting in that. Send me a proposal if you like and I'll put out some feelers.'

His secretary knocked with the details of Noah's next meeting before Hanni could regroup or reply. She emerged out of the magazine's offices onto the busy Kurfürstendamm with no idea what she was supposed to do next. The article had been her lifeline, the only thing stopping her from ignoring Freddy's advice and physically dragging Leo back to Berlin. Writing it, and imagining the trail her words would blaze from Gessner to Reiner and on to the prison sentence that would ruin him, had consumed her. And now, in every sense, it was done and there was nothing left to hide her fears behind.

What's he doing to Leo? How long am I meant to be able to stand this without going after him?

Hanni walked past the shop windows decked out in bright yellows and greens without noticing their springtime displays. Every open door was playing the same tune – 'Junge, Komm Bald Wieder', a song which had topped the charts for so many weeks its first note normally set Hanni's teeth on edge, never mind its message appealing for a boy's return which suddenly resonated far more than a silly song should. Today she was deaf to it. Reiner was the only refrain in her head.

He's untouchable. There's not one proven link.

Noah's verdict on Reiner had been an echo of Freddy's insistence that they needed a crime with her father's fingers all over it. They were both right. Hanni slowed down and began looking around her, at the ordinary people with their ordinary faces whose lives might be anything but.

You said that the Nazis were monsters but Eichmann looked like my history teacher.

Which was how he had managed to live out in the world undetected for almost twenty years, and why Leo hadn't been even vaguely frightened by him when he watched the televised trial. And Freddy was right: tying Eichmann to one specific act that had his fingerprints indelibly on it had been the only way to convict the man, when, despite the wealth of evidence produced by the courts, a conviction hadn't felt certain. At one point, Hanni had been convinced that the trial would fall apart and Eichmann would walk free. Nothing had touched him. Not the documents that were laden with details but couldn't provide a record of his name where it could do real damage. Not the equally detailed witness testimonies which Eichmann was deaf to. Not even his own confession.

Maybe I had been drinking when I made it, maybe that was added afterwards... I had nothing to do with the killing, I never killed a Jew, I never killed another human being... I don't know... I wasn't there... I was a law-abiding citizen, a small cog in the machine, I was only dealing with train timetables.

Eichmann's denials and his rambling and his lack of any kind of a reaction had carried a force of their own. Until the moment came. The one that none of them glued to the television had expected, when Hausner the prosecutor found the one crime his Nazi prisoner could be directly associated with.

'You initiated the foot march. You proposed it.'

It was a simply put statement, made in the same measured tone Hausner had used throughout his questioning. A barely there description of a death march from Budapest that had taken the lives of tens of thousands of Hungarian Jews. But this time Eichmann didn't bat it away. Hanni thought at first she had misheard his response – so, or it seemed, did the lawyers – but she hadn't. She didn't understand why he had finally told the truth and she didn't care. With Eichmann's equally unemotional 'I will admit that much, yes', the prosecution team had the confession it needed and Eichmann's conviction was secured.

Hanni came to a standstill as the memory of that seemingly impossible moment flooded back and reignited her courage. Her strand of the plan she had agreed with Freddy had failed with Noah's rejection but that didn't mean the whole plan was done. They still had the second route, the possibility of tracking Reiner down in the East. She latched on to that to stop herself running to the train station and heading straight for Goslar and Leo. The moment she did so, a voice she hadn't thought about in years leapt into her head.

You were a monster from the start. You volunteered for every obscene job that was available.

Luca – the Stasi agent whose hatred of Reiner couldn't be stopped by broken bones or by the fear of death – had hurled that accusation and more at her father. Luca had known the details of Reiner's war far better than Hanni had, which had to mean that Freddy had been right about that too: there was a file, somewhere in the GDR, which told Reiner's complete story.

And if anyone can find that, he can. Or we can, together.

In the middle of the worst shock she and Freddy had encountered as parents, they had said *we,* they had said *us.* Small words perhaps but their impact was a blanket around her. Leo's running away could have driven the two of them further apart but instead it had pushed them together.

And he held me.

The memory of his arms was so warm all it took was a moment's pause to still feel them.

Freddy held me and there was love when he did it.

She had lost track of the street again. She was forced to move aside as an irritated pedestrian jostled past her. She barely noticed: she wasn't on the Kurfürstendamm; she was on the sofa in her flat with her head pressed against Freddy's chest. They had managed the shock and the guilt surrounding Leo's disappearance together. They had calmed each other down and come up with a plan to bring him home, together. Their bodies had fallen back into their old conversation as if that link had never snapped. Surely there was a flicker of hope in that.

'I know we agreed not to chase after him, but I couldn't not phone. Not that it made a difference. He wouldn't speak to me, or he wasn't allowed to. And now this has arrived.'

Please don't contact me again. I am happy here – that's all you need to know.

Hanni handed Freddy the note which had reduced her to tears the moment she read it. Its lack of even the most basic affection had torn another wound in her heart. *It's not Leo's work* had been her first desperate thought; *Reiner dictated it* had been her second. The comfort that brought lasted barely a handful of seconds: the terse dismissal in Leo's note was too clearly an echo of the furious mood he had left her in. And, as if to underscore that, Reiner had added a message of his own which was thick with his brand of cruel amusement. Freddy was still chewing his lip when Hanni passed him the second piece of paper which had been folded inside the envelope.

> *To be granted custody of the next generation – is there a more wonderful honour than that? I promise I will do everything in my power to make our boy into the most perfect young man.*

Our boy.

It was the way she and Freddy had spoken about Leo and now Reiner had turned the words obscene. Freddy's face darkened as he read the message. The hope Hanni had been nurturing since their last meeting instantly withered and all she was left with was guilt.

'Maybe Renny was right. Maybe we did over-protect him. Maybe I should have been showing Leo pictures of the camps every day to make him understand who his grandfather was, or reading survivor testimonies not nursery rhymes to him at night.'

There were no outstretched arms waiting to hold her this time, no reassuring words – not that she expected them. Freddy was still staring at Reiner's letter as if he could drill through the words and get a hold of the man. Hanni was caught fast in his silence, reading too much into it, struggling to manage the weight of blame she was carrying. When he still didn't speak, her misery overflowed.

'This is all my doing. I've blamed Reiner for everything. I've acted like I was a victim, a passenger in his life but it's not true. I wasn't a child in the war; I was sixteen when it started. And I was Leo's age when I really entered Reiner's world. Well Leo's certainly proved he can steer his own life, even if he's doing it badly, so why couldn't I? My father didn't lock me in a room and force me to stay – I could have run away like Leo did. I could have argued and asked questions and said no. So why didn't I make braver choices?'

It was an over-simplification of her past perhaps, but it was heartfelt. Freddy finally looked up but whatever he was thinking was carefully hidden.

I have to face my own past, not just Reiner's was a realisation that had come newly to her. She was bitterly ashamed by that. She hadn't intended to share that new awareness with Freddy; she didn't know yet what to do with it herself. Watching her boy weighing up the world, sifting out what he needed to take from it to create himself had been a fraught and frightening process. It had also forced Hanni to reflect on the twelve-year-old she had once been, the girl who had so perfectly played the part of an SS officer's daughter.

And not just on that girl. She had also been forced to reconsider the fourteen-year-old who had sat through Goebbels' speeches vilifying the Jews – and the school lessons incorporating his evil message which had followed – and never dared ask why they were so hated. And the fifteen-year-old who had closed her bedroom window against the smoke and her hopeless fears for Ezra and his family when the fires raged in the synagogues on Kristallnacht. There was very little in any of those images that Hanni liked, but all of those girls had been, and still were, her. They weren't strangers she could cast off and pretend had never existed. And Reiner had stood those girls in front of Freddy when he revealed the truth about her past. The question burst out of her before she realised what she was saying.

'With all that I was, how could you ever forgive me?'

There was no taking it back. There was only one answer she wanted: *because I know it wasn't really you.* For a moment Hanni convinced herself the answer she craved was coming: Freddy's eyes were focused so intently on her it felt as if her soul was being stripped bare. But then he shook his head and turned away, and Hanni hadn't the heart to ask him if the question was impossible or if they were.

'I'm sorry. That was unfair. This is about Leo and what we do next to get him home, not me. So where are we with that? Have you managed to make any progress with Reiner's trail in the East?'

She managed the switch from personal to professional because she had to, and she did it smoothly enough to allow Freddy a way back into the conversation.

'I think so. I've found an official over there who has agreed to a meeting. My rank means I will be able to get both of us permits to cross into East Berlin hopefully by early next week. I can't promise it will lead anywhere, but it's a first step.'

Organising the details of what was needed for that was quickly done and was much safer ground – making impersonal, transactional arrangements had been the bread and butter of their relationship since Leo was born. Neither of them strayed back towards personal matters. They didn't discuss the fears for their son's safety they were both trying not to drown under. They didn't remind each other that they had set out on this kind of quest before, when they had made the crossing over the border into Czechoslovakia and gone searching for Renny. They had been newly married then, deeply in love and full of beginnings. Neither of them needed to be reminded of that.

Or of how damaged the child at the end of the journey had been.

CHAPTER 6

Hanni still couldn't get used to the Wall – it was too fresh a scar on the city.

She stared out of the window as Freddy circled round the Tiergarten towards the Chauseestraße crossing point, her fingers playing with the scarf at her neck. The slightly faded length of blue and green checks was Leo's and too short to sit comfortably inside her coat, but it was at least some kind of a connection to her son. The Wedding route they had chosen as their point of entry into the GDR was a far less visible option than Checkpoint Charlie, the passage to East Berlin which was the main military and diplomatic channel between the two halves of the city. That was why it was perfect. The last thing either of them wanted to do – particularly after Gessner's warning about watching eyes – was to draw attention to their journey.

It had been a long time since Hanni had visited East Berlin. She had stopped going there in the late 1950s when wandering around its streets with a camera had started to become problematic. The new rules governing movement, which the Wall had brought with it, meant she couldn't have made the crossing at all now without Freddy. Like the majority of West Berlin's citizens who lacked the required official credentials, Hanni was forbidden from travelling to the missing part of her city. The once fluid division between East and West – whose human traffic had flowed, in Moscow's opinion, far too heavily in the wrong direction – had literally been set in stone overnight. And, also like her fellow West Berliners, Hanni could vividly remember where she had been when that happened.

'I was at a cinema in Flensburger Straße on the night it went up, watching Marilyn Monroe in *The Misfits*. Which could also—'

Hanni managed to stop herself before she finished the sentence. She had been about to say 'have described the date I was on' before she remembered who she was talking to. Instead of making a fool of herself, she relapsed into the silence which had deadened the whole journey. Telling Freddy about a bad date was hardly the right way to switch them out of the professional mode they had retreated into when Hanni had brought up the subject of forgiveness. And if there was ever a day which did not need to be clouded by personal matters, this was it. Although Freddy had downplayed what they were doing, the stakes were high, especially for a West German police chief. They were not only about to enter the East; they were heading for Stasi headquarters, a place from where – if even half of the rumours were correct – people disappeared. They needed their wits about them; they needed to remember the kind of people they were dealing with. Not that the looming Wall would let them forget.

'I saw the photographs you took of it being built. Of the soldiers pointing their weapons at the crowd on the western side and their stunned faces. I thought they were some of your best. You really captured the shock, and the fear.'

Freddy's compliment took Hanni by surprise. When she

turned away from the view and back to him, he wasn't smiling
but his jaw had softened.

'It's interesting that you say that. I can see it now but I
didn't feel the fear at the time – I was too focused on getting the
shots. The second I saw the weird blue light over the Gate –
those massive arc-lights they used to turn night into day – and
heard the tanks coming, I grabbed my camera and went running
towards it. It wasn't until later, when I developed the pictures,
that the real force of what had been done hit me.'

The whole night still felt blurred to her, even when she
tried to describe it. She had barely noticed the crowd she had
run with through the Tiergarten towards the Brandenburg
Gate. Or the eerie silence everyone fell into when they saw the
ring of GDR soldiers waiting to meet them with raised guns.
The crowd had frozen but Hanni had flown into action, her
fingers dancing across the camera, taking picture after picture.
Of the troops guarding the workmen whose hydraulic drills
sliced through the slates and the cobbles with an almost balletic
ferocity. Of the tanks and the armoured personnel carriers
ringing those troops. Of the broken cobblestones and the newly
laid bricks which rose with a dizzying speed and the barbed
wire whose twists and spikes carried the shadows of camps and
older confinements. Despite the photographs which had been
exhibited and widely praised, she had never quite managed to
shake the sense of unreality which had gripped her as the first
negative slipped into the chemical bath and turned into an
image.

'It made no sense to me – I do remember thinking that. I
mean, I know we'd lived with the idea of division since forty-
nine, but to see that turned into stone and mortar and reality?
To have buildings suddenly knocked down or boarded up and
the line of bricks getting higher and higher. To see people who
were used to paying Sunday visits to their families in Mitte and
Friedrichshain physically disappearing or throwing themselves

out of the last remaining windows to freedom was surreal. And as for the things I couldn't capture – the level of control the Wall represented, the broken families whose relatives were caught unawares and got stuck on the wrong side.'

She shuddered and fell silent, momentarily overwhelmed by the pain of the enforced separation which was now her own daily reality. From the way Freddy's face tightened again, it was clear he was tumbling into the same hole. She was about to stretch her hand towards his but his shoulders tightened and his chin lifted before she could.

It's not the time, it's not the place. We can't go under here.

They were almost at the crossing point. Hanni straightened herself up too and blinked away the tears for Leo which were threatening to blind her as they approached. Chauseestraβe was no Checkpoint Charlie. That bristled with signboards and official notices about which sector travellers were leaving and entering and sported a huge Stars and Stripes in case anyone was in doubt. The guard hut at Chauseestraβe was a ramshackle affair which needed a coat of paint, and the lone policeman waiting to inspect them seemed more interested in huddling inside his grey overcoat and staying warm than scanning the road for traffic. Freddy began to slow the car down anyway.

'There'll be more security and more scrutiny of our papers on the other side, and we'll have to leave the car there. That and an escort driver has all been arranged but I imagine they'll draw the operation out and pile on the drama. Don't let it throw you.'

He turned towards her and finally managed a smile. This time Hanni didn't hesitate. She put her hand on his arm as they pulled up at the first barrier.

'Are you worried about this? Asking the Stasi for a favour could put you in debt to them.'

Freddy didn't reply until the western guard had glanced at their papers and waved them through towards a set of staggered concrete blocks on the eastern side that kept his speed to a crawl.

'It's not an ideal situation, no. But it's for Leo, so if there's debts to be paid, then there's debts. And we've got Reiner and Luca, so we've got bargaining chips too.'

He turned to her as the first of a much bigger group of GDR soldiers began to approach them.

'Are you good?'

Hanni nodded. It was for Leo, so she was good.

The city they crossed into was Berlin and it wasn't.

There were no garish advertising hoardings looming over the pavements. There were far more soldiers and far fewer cars, and the ones that were on the road were all the same make – the boxy GDR-produced Trabants which West Berliners mockingly referred to as 'sparkplugs with roofs'. And the concrete had spread out from the Wall to create new buildings which were square and regular and totally lacking in features.

Hanni assumed that their driver was more than a driver so she kept her observation – that the streets looked drab and drained of energy – to herself. He hadn't spoken to either her or Freddy beyond checking their names since he had collected them from Chauseestraβe. Now his main concern seemed to be looping the car through so many twists and turns that both of them, despite having once known the whole city well, quickly lost their bearings. By the time they reached the huge compound which housed the Ministry for State Security, Hanni was starting to feel nauseous.

The building itself was vast, with long wings stretching out from a rectangular centre and far more windows than Hanni had expected. She hadn't admitted it to Freddy – because he would have rolled his eyes and told her to stop watching spy movies – but part of her had expected them to be swept into it via a darkened back entrance, possibly wearing black hoods. Instead they were whisked into a highly polished foyer and greeted by a reception committee with handshakes and smiles. It was all rather disappointingly bland, which Freddy's contact momentarily threw her by acknowledging as he led them into his spartan wood-panelled office.

'I think you were expecting something a little more secret agent novel, Frau Schlüssel, and rather less dull corporate workplace.'

He laughed when she blushed. Then, when the introductions were done and tea had been ordered, he tried to wrong-foot her again with: 'And there are far fewer people listening to us than you might think.'

Hanni returned his smile but she had seen her father try the same kind of disarming technique too often to be fooled by it. Major Rühl had emphasised his rank as he shook her hand, and his uniform jacket was sporting a raft of medal ribbons. And she assumed that his reputation for loyalty was as spotless as his manners if he was permitted such close, and unsupervised, contact with Westerners. Freddy's 'Don't give him anything you don't have to' hadn't been needed. When she didn't take the bait, the major continued.

'So you want our help to catch a Nazi? It's an unusual request.' This time he turned his smile onto Freddy. 'As I am sure you will appreciate, Chief Inspector, any request from your side is unusual, but Nazis? That did come as a surprise. We were under the impression they weren't an issue for the West nowadays, that they had all been welcomed back into the professions they'd previously disgraced.'

Rühl's opening gambit wasn't unexpected. Both Hanni and Freddy had been prepared for a lecture on how the West had failed in its duty to purge Third Reich loyalists from its institutions after the war, and another on how the Communist Party had been the cradle of resistance during it. And however many lectures they were forced to sit through, Freddy had made it clear that he would be in serious trouble if either of them did more than listen.

'Accepting the grandstanding is the price we have to pay to get their co-operation. Whatever's said about Western negligence towards war criminals, I can't comment and you mustn't either. I don't want to find myself quoted all over the GDR as the chief inspector with Nazi sympathies, or across the West as a communist.'

With that warning in mind, Hanni waited for Freddy to steer the conversation to safer waters. He didn't get a chance to. Rühl concluded his point with an expansive shrug and steered it in his own direction.

'And that is an argument for the politicians and not for us, don't you think? I would rather stick to what's really of interest here.'

His focus was suddenly so intently on Hanni, she had to force herself not to shift away from him.

'Can I assume that the Reiner Foss you've come searching after is your father, Frau Schlüssel?'

His smile had gone, and that was easier. Hanni had been close enough to a Stasi agent before to know that nothing good came from trying to be friends with them – it was always preferable to get straight to the point. And given that one agent had known her identity, she was hardly surprised that Rühl did too.

'Yes, it is. And he is most definitely a war criminal but, as I assume you know, he has never faced justice. If anything his life after the war has been an even bigger success than his years spent serving the Reich. Which is not a state of affairs that can continue.'

Rühl's grimace confirmed that he was fully in agreement with her assessment.

'I can't argue with that. But even if we are on the same page in our attitudes, why do you think we can help?'

And this was it, her moment to make the pitch she and Freddy had agreed had the best chance of winning Rühl's help. Hanni met his gaze and jumped in.

'Because you have a stake in this too. Reiner would be a big catch for the East, an excellent example for you to expose the way the wrong people have prospered.' She shook her head as he shrugged her idea away. 'Don't tell me the propaganda win wouldn't matter, Major, because I won't believe you. The Stasi has been on Reiner's trail before, in 1950, for exactly that reason and the competition between our two sides to be the best Germany has hardly faded since then.'

She paused, hoping that the next reason she had to offer meant as much to him as she needed it to.

'And the agent the Stasi sent to try and catch Reiner then – who went by the name of Luca – paid a heavy price. I thought that you might also want justice for that.'

'What do you mean?'

Rühl's face had changed completely at *heavy price*. He suddenly looked much younger than his display of medals suggested, and more vulnerable than Hanni thought a Stasi major could be. When she quickly ran through the events in Prague and what her father had done there, it took him a moment to gather himself.

'We trained together, Luca and I. He was a good friend and his disappearance was... difficult. You have solved a puzzle for me. But that still doesn't explain why you have come here. Never mind what the GDR says in public, we know attitudes in the West towards war criminals are changing, that the spotlight's been turned up since Eichmann. You've a new Central War Crimes Commission, haven't you? Which our intelligence estimates has collated eighty thousand names in the last five years. Why didn't you go to Ludwigsburg, to them? It's a far less complicated journey.'

'Because they've got too many names and not enough people to look into them.'

Freddy was right but it wasn't the whole story.

Hanni leaned forward. 'We could, but we think you have files on Reiner which are far more detailed than anything they have. And also because nothing has changed since Luca was sent to lure him to Prague rather than trying to catch him in Berlin – he's too well-connected in West Germany; he's got even more layers of protection now than he did then. No one on our side will go after him, believe me, even though his power is growing.'

Hanni told him about the schools and about their graduates like Gessner. Then she let Freddy explain why they needed to pin Reiner to one specific crime before the time to stop him ran out. When that was done, he passed the baton back and Hanni told the major about Leo and how afraid they were of Reiner gaining any more influence over their son. Neither of them knew which part of the plea worked but something did. When they were both done, Rühl sat in silence for a moment and then he left. When he came back, he was carrying a folder.

'You can study it and copy from it but you cannot remove anything. And if Foss is ever brought to account, you must acknowledge our part in it.'

He left again the instant they both blurted, 'Of course.'

Freddy made no move to open Reiner's file; they both knew that job was Hanni's. She was all fingers and thumbs with its knots when she did. Whatever was inside was Reiner's story, but it was also hers. The places it catalogued, or at least a portion of them, would be places she knew, places that carried memories she desperately didn't want Freddy to stand witness to. Hanni the SS officer's daughter was suddenly far too vividly in the room and Hanni couldn't look at Freddy for the shame that brought with it. When she spread the twenty or so pages the folder contained onto the desk and divided them into two equal piles, her hands were shaking.

Some of the reports were typed, some were handwritten, some were far more detailed than others. Freddy took his share without comment; Hanni took hers feeling sick. They sat in a silence that was worlds away from comfortable, reading and scribbling notes as the clock ticked the afternoon away. Neither of them looking up, both of them pretending that they had never sat together hunting through Nazi files for evidence before, or remembered where that last time had led.

The papers in Hanni's pile told Reiner's Third Reich story from its start, beginning with an SS training school at Dachau she had never heard of. The sparse descriptions of the belief system that was instilled there perfectly encapsulated her father. When Hanni read it, particularly its last line, and thought of Leo she couldn't remember how to breathe.

> SS *obedience is a matter of the heart... officers must show iron toughness... the whip is an iconic weapon... camps are a stage for humiliation and violence, terror is a public performance... the leader is a role model whose approval recruits ardently seek...*

Everything else she read after that was familiar. Theresienstadt featured heavily but Hanni already knew that the answer wasn't there. Or in Sachsenhausen, another place Reiner was noted as regularly visiting. The sparse notes which accompanied the dated entries showed Reiner following his SS training and wielding his whip without mercy in both those places, and at the Petschek Palace in Prague. Nothing in them was new or surprised her. Hanni had heard Reiner's boasts about how quickly he could ruin a prisoner; she had seen him use that same whip to herd the residents of Theresienstadt onto Auschwitz-bound trains. Nothing was a shock and nothing linked him to specific people who had died at his hands. For all the traces he had left at his torture sites, Reiner might as well have been a ghost.

In the end she pushed her share of the folder away, defeated by digging at names that were already well known to her and already hopeless.

'I can't see anything in these that will help. I can't find anything or anywhere new.'

Freddy didn't answer her at first. Then he pushed a sheaf of his own pages towards her.

'I can. Look at these entries – there's dozens of them and they're all for the same place.'

He pointed to the name he had underlined in his notebook so hard the pen had torn through the paper. His face was set in the unforgiving lines Hanni hadn't seen since the days after Prague and had hoped she would never see again.

'Why did you never tell me that your father was such a regular visitor to Buchenwald?'

CHAPTER 7

20–23 MARCH 1963, BUCHENWALD, EAST GERMANY

Freddy hadn't exaggerated. There were over a dozen visits to the camp listed, starting in 1937 when it was first built and ending in 1943, not long before Reiner had been posted to Theresienstadt and taken Hanni and her mother with him. Unfortunately the details recorded against each date were vague, giving little information beyond 'inspections and expansions'. Until Freddy enlightened her – in a terse voice which suggested that she should already know – Hanni hadn't realised that the network of sub-camps and armament factories which had spread out from Buchenwald's main site by 1943 was such a vast one, or how many prisoners, including him, had passed through it.

'There were over a quarter of a million of us. Over fifty thousand were killed there and God knows how many were tortured. It must have been a hell of a playground for him.'

Freddy's disgust was well placed. Hanni didn't know how to respond to it except for a heartfelt, 'Please God you never came into contact with him yourself?'

It was a relief for her when he shook his head, but not for Freddy.

'I didn't but I knew men who were whipped, who couldn't stand for days afterwards because of the pain. Who died of the wounds the lash left. If I'd even suspected that your father was the one who'd wrecked them...'

He didn't finish the sentence. He didn't look at her. When Hanni offered him a shaky 'I'm sorry', he shrugged her inadequate apology away. Freddy had never got a chance to strike back at Reiner in Prague – his whole focus then had been on trying to stem the damage inflicted on Renny. He had never pretended to be happy about that. And Hanni didn't want him lost in that day now.

'It could be a good thing, couldn't it, that he was there so often? Someone might remember him, especially if he used his whip as often at Buchenwald as he did at Theresienstadt.'

She hurried on, formulating the start of a plan to keep Freddy in the present and breathed a little easier when he blinked himself back.

'He wasn't mentioned at the Buchenwald trial or we'd know, but – given that was sixteen years ago – maybe some of the officers and guards who were imprisoned then might be free again now. Maybe some of them would talk to us, if we could track them down.'

'They've probably all started more respectable lives and won't want to know' was Freddy's first response, but the seed had been sown and Hanni knew he would pursue it. And that he was right: chasing contacts who would be lukewarm at best about reliving their most shameful days wouldn't be enough.

We have to go there ourselves.

She didn't need to say it out loud, not that she could have suggested it. Freddy's pinched face told her that he was ahead of her and dreading even the thought.

So I'll go there alone. I won't put him through it. If there's anything to be found which leads us to Reiner, I'll uncover it myself and bring back the evidence.

The search for Renny had taken her back to Theresienstadt and that had been a soul-crushing experience. A return to Buchenwald would be far worse for Freddy: Buchenwald was where he had been turned, in his own words, into something less than human, and the scars of that experience still ran deep. Hanni was about to lay out her plan to spare him the ordeal, but Freddy was already shaking his head.

'No, Hanni. I know what you're thinking but no. Buchenwald is the last place I want to return to but, if that's where this journey is heading, then I'm going there too. This isn't just about me – this is about finding a way to get Leo home, body and soul. And I know you mean well, but Leo belongs to us both so bringing him back also belongs to us both. So we do this, we go there, together.'

His use of *we* made Buchenwald seem smaller; it made the challenge seem simple. It was a fiction they both silently agreed to stick to, even though neither of those things were true. Whether Freddy could navigate the return or not was a moot point: there was no guarantee they could even get there. Buchenwald was three hundred kilometres away, far further into East Germany than a car ride across Berlin. Without Rühl's agreement and co-operation, the camp was no more than a tenuous lead pointing to another dead end.

Rühl's 'What on earth do you want to go there for? You won't find anything now' was dispiriting but at least it wasn't the immediate no they had both been expecting.

Hanni passed him the file pages and Freddy's notebook.

'Because it has to be worth a try: look how often Reiner visited it. And maybe Buchenwald will lead to nothing, the same as Theresienstadt and Sachsenhausen did, but it's the only other camp he appears to have spent a significant amount of time at so it makes sense to check.'

Rühl flicked through the entries but he didn't look any more convinced. 'Isn't it just one more camp in a list of camps where Foss seems to have been very good at staying invisible? What do you expect to find there that you haven't found anywhere else? A letter with his signature arranging a transport? A photo of him flaying open someone's back?'

He sighed as Hanni's expression suggested that yes that was exactly what she was hoping for.

'If you believe that then you've far more faith in the universe than I have. Besides, Buchenwald is not the place it was in 1945 – it's been turned into a memorial site. If those things ever existed, they're long gone.'

'Which doesn't matter.' Freddy gathered his notes back up again. 'He was there. Perhaps there are people still living beside the camp in Weimar who remember him; perhaps there are workers at the site. People are drawn back to these places for all kinds of reasons – we learned that at Theresienstadt. And a lot of those people are still looking for endings.'

Rühl put the papers back in the folder and closed it. Everything about his stance suggested that their time with him was up.

'Even if you are right about that, Chief Inspector, none of them will talk to you. Have you forgotten where you are? This is the GDR: the thing that we are best at is managing our people.'

He paused for a moment and then came to a decision. 'If you're determined to do this, I may as well warn you what you are getting into. Our people watch each other; they tell tales. They believe that anyone they meet could be an informer and that the best mark of loyalty is denouncing a neighbour, and they do that because that is what we have trained them to do. Our citizens walk a tightrope every day because the system we have built is based on their fear of what will happen if they don't and their total belief that we know every inch of their lives. Even if we only had fifty informants in our network, which I promise you we do not, in their minds we have fifty thousand. It's a perfect system. It's delivered us a country with far more walls than the one we've built to contain it. There's not a question you can ask that will get past those.'

They believed him but he still hadn't said no and, as far as Hanni was concerned, that meant he still could say yes. She glanced over at Freddy, aware of how deeply he hated using his personal tragedy as a bargaining tool and ready to jump in and spare him that effort too. But she wasn't the only one who parenthood had changed.

'Perhaps it won't. But you see, I was in Buchenwald. I was held prisoner there from 1943 to its liberation. I lost part of myself in there but I was lucky, if that is the correct word to use, because I walked away.'

Freddy's voice was perfectly even, as if he was offering the facts of somebody else's life.

'Tens of thousands, however, did not, and if Reiner Foss left his mark on anyone who suffered there, I want to be the one who finds it.'

He paused. He looked at Hanni and his voice was no longer steady at all. The pain in his eyes ripped through her.

'You have no idea, Major, what that man stole from me or the misery he inflicted. So yes, this is about stopping Foss spreading his disgusting beliefs and it's about rescuing my son from his clutches, because the thought of that man with his claws in my boy is killing me. But it's also about revenge, and surely you, who lost a friend to him, have to let me take that, however misplaced my methods sound.'

Rühl stared at him and at Hanni and then, to Freddy's evident relief, he nodded.

'Fine. If you want to go to Buchenwald, go to Buchenwald. There will be forms to sign and documents to process, and it will take a day to organise accommodation and a suitable driver but, if it matters that much to you, why not? Perhaps, Frau Schlüssel, you could take some photographs there which would show us in a better light than the ones you took of the Wall going up – if nothing else that might make my agreeing to this look a little less unconventional.'

That was an easy request to agree to. Rühl left them to begin the form-heavy process and to find them a hotel room in East Berlin for the night. Freddy left to place a call to Renny to explain why their trip had been extended. And Hanni waited until they were both out of earshot before requesting that Rühl's secretary – who immediately made a separate note of the request in her boss's private diary although Hanni asked her not to – allocate them not one bedroom but two.

They left East Berlin in the early morning under street lights which bathed the grey buildings they were driven past in a softening sepia glow. Breakfast had been a snatched and largely silent affair and – with all the nuances carried by *a suitable driver* – the silence continued as they settled into the back of a Tatra limousine which was bulky enough to roll over the Trabants it lumbered past.

On paper the drive should have taken little more than three hours but nothing in the GDR worked as simply as paper would have it. It took closer to five to progress along a road whose broken asphalt was a challenge even for the official car's solidly built chassis. There was very little to see apart from the tractors dotting the vast farms which dominated the landscape, although Hanni stared out of the window as intently as if was covered in castles. It was the only way to stop herself sneaking glances at Freddy's pale face and initiating a conversation about his feelings that he wouldn't welcome, whether the driver was listening or not. He seemed determined not to give them even one private moment.

Their bags were collected from the boot at the hotel in Weimar without the need for anyone to leave the car. There was no time to catch more than a glimpse of the city whose inhabitants Freddy had once described as 'the cowards who left us to rot' before they were driven out of it again. So when their silent chauffeur suddenly stopped at the bottom of a hill a short drive from the city and announced that they had two hours at the site on their own, Hanni wasn't immediately sure what to say. It was hard not to assume that being left without supervision meant that there was nothing of value to find. And Freddy's face was now so white, she wasn't convinced that he should get out of the car.

'We can leave if you prefer and drive back to Berlin.'

It was the first time that the driver had turned round and directly addressed her, and it was a ridiculous idea. Hanni had no choice but to shake Freddy's arm.

'We're here. We're at Buchenwald.'

It didn't need saying; Freddy knew exactly where he was, but the words jolted him out of his fog which was what Hanni had intended. Until he got out of the car and froze again within seconds.

'You need to lead the way, Freddy. I can't.'

His first reaction was to take a step backwards but then he shook himself and set off up the steep slope through a ring of birch trees he muttered should have been thicker and at a pace which felt like a run. Hanni followed, glad that he had taken charge. Whatever else happened, he had to reach the top first and he had to go through the gates first. Then, once he was standing back inside the camp, he could scream or cry or freeze again, whatever his body dictated, and without her standing over him.

Hanni could still all too clearly remember their return to Theresienstadt when they had been hunting for Renny, even though it was thirteen years ago now. The first steps she had taken through the archway there had plucked her instantly out of the present and toppled her into a past that was so real she could smell it. She didn't want Freddy to suffer that same level of shock, but there was nothing she could do to stop it. His return to Buchenwald wasn't hers to shape. Her only job was to wait, and then to hold him or to step away while he settled himself, whichever was needed.

She slowed a little as they neared the ridge, her eyes fixed on his back, her arms ready to reach for him. But when she did catch him up, he wasn't empty-eyed and seeing ghosts the way that she had done. He was shaking his head and staring around the bare landscape as if he had somehow landed on the moon.

'It's not here. None of it is here.'

He began to pace, first to the left, then to the right, then back in a looping circle towards Hanni again, his hands flung out as if he was trying to trace out a view.

'The gates have gone, and the barracks. I can't get a sense of it. And I don't know what that is.'

He was pointing at a construction which resembled a vast bell tower and his voice was starting to break.

'Where is it, Hanni, where's Buchenwald? I could have drawn every inch of this place but it's all disappeared. Rühl said it was a memorial site but how can it be when everything that it was is gone? How will anyone remember the dead, or the living who suffered here, if there's no trace of them left?'

He turned again and again, scanning the skyline as if they might be on the wrong hill and the camp whose memories were so deeply scored through him was hiding behind the next ring of trees. Not knowing what to do or to say – because she had also expected to be confronted by gates and barbed wire and barracks – Hanni moved beside him and put a hand on his arm. Her touch didn't stop him shaking.

'There is an order of some kind here.' She pointed to the paths and the circular constructions fanning out from the tower.

'Maybe we just don't know how to read it. Why don't I go and see if there is someone who can help?'

She didn't want to leave him but she didn't have any answers, and Freddy was more in need of those than meaningless words of comfort he would hate.

There was a guide, or a caretaker – Hanni wasn't sure which title the old man wore and he didn't offer to enlighten her – huddled in a hut at the far side of the hilltop. He was buried in a newspaper and in no hurry to help her until she pressed more money than she guessed he would be worth into his waiting hand. When she led him over to where Freddy was still rooted, Freddy immediately launched into a series of questions, all of which were completely ignored.

The old man led them round the site but stuck to a prepared script which placed the glory of the communist resistance firmly at its centre and held no room for anything else. He took them to the crematorium which Hanni had mistaken for a small house and waited while they read the plaque dedicating the building to the communist fighters whose bodies had been consumed there. Then he led them along the path to the circular pits which contained their ashes and shrugged when Freddy asked, 'But where are the graves for the Jewish prisoners and all the others who died here?'

He pointed out the stone slabs marking the places where the barracks and the infirmary had once been and took them to the tower which had been built as a monument to the freedom the GDR's brave citizens had fought for.

Eventually he told them where the stone which commemorated the camp's murdered Jewish population could be found but he didn't take them to it. And he met every question about survivors living close by and where records for the SS personnel who had served there and the testimonies of those who had been imprisoned might be stored with a shake of his head. Then he left, and Freddy exploded.

'Is that it? A begrudged stone slab for us and not a mention of anyone who was held here unless they were a communist? And no care for what any of the spaces he dragged us through once meant?'

He waved a hand at a patch of wasteland which stretched out from the main path. 'He walked past that as if it was nothing but that's where the roll-call square was. That's where they took us every day to decide if we had a chance of living through another one. Once the whole camp was made to stand there for over seventy-two hours for no other reason except to see how many of us would collapse and die, and he ignored it.'

His breath was coming thick and fast; his voice was cracking. A moment later Freddy was on his knees, sucking at the air, his face haggard and wet.

'How can there be nothing left? Not just of Reiner but of me and all the other men and women who were left to rot here? Why can't I feel what happened? The ground should be soaked with the suffering but there's nothing. And how can this be a monument to freedom when nobody who came through this place will ever be free?'

His hands clawed at the dry soil as if he was trying to trace the prints of the wooden clogs and the bare feet which once had pressed into it. He tipped his head back as if he was listening for cries still caught on the wind. Hanni was instantly on her knees at his side, her arms around him, whispering 'Hush' and 'Breathe' until his shuddering body gradually calmed and he came slowly back.

'It hasn't gone, Freddy; it's inside you. You don't talk about it, you bury it, but you carry Buchenwald's walls and its cruelties with you wherever you go.'

She took a deep breath of her own, aware of the thin line she was walking. Not wanting to bring her Theresienstadt burden into his misery by trying to share his pain with an inappropriate 'so do I'.

'There are parts of the past you need to hold on to – your memories of your mother and father and your brother. But maybe there are also parts you need to start letting go.'

He didn't argue, which felt like a way forward. Hanni dropped her arms from his shoulders but she stayed close. If she was going to push him, she also had to be there if he fell.

'Could this be where you start?'

He blinked at her. 'What do you mean?'

Hanni had thought about this moment of Freddy unburdening himself many times, and about what she could say to encourage him when she had seen him either struggle with a memory or retreat from the past. Her guilt had always held her back. Now she waited until he was properly focused on her and hoped that some of the trust that had once run so strong between them was still there.

'Tell me something, Freddy: let me in. I know how your time here started and how it ended, and I know how Elias's friendship helped you survive, but tell me something that happened in this place. Let me take that from you and maybe the burden will start to ease.'

It was a gamble mentioning Elias Baar, the man Freddy had regarded for years as his brother and the man who – because of Reiner's manipulations – had been forced into a betrayal which had ended their friendship. The blame for that had hung over Hanni since Prague, but she needed to bring Elias back, if only to make the camp real.

Freddy rubbed his eyes. He was staring at a tableau that Hanni couldn't see.

'You know how I came to be captured – I've told you about that, and about the later days. But the bit in between? What happened when I arrived? That's where I always get stuck.'

Hanni slipped her hand inside his as his voice shook. He didn't appear to notice.

'So tell me about that now, if you can. Share that with me. Whatever it is, if telling it helps you, I want to hear it.'

It took him a moment to focus, to find a steadier rhythm for his voice, but he gripped her hand back as he did so.

'It's not easy to describe, but I'll try. There were so many work details here then and the Nazis didn't care who survived any of them – we were all replaceable. But the cruellest of them all, the one everybody was afraid of, was the stone quarry. And that was where they sent me. I'd call it hell but the word doesn't seem big enough. Everything about it was designed to kill us. It was a six-mile walk there and back and the return journey was made lugging carts laden with limestone bricks that needed teams of horses to pull them, not the broken men they turned us into. And when we were actually there... We were beaten on the way up the steps and the terraces that led to the digging areas, and we were beaten on the way down again. The working day lasted nine or ten or eleven hours depending on the whim of the guards, and there was barely any food to sustain us. Four or five times a day there were these deafening explosive blasts which tore through the stone and left mangled bodies behind them, because so many of us were too weak to run away quick enough – or weren't given the chance. There were so many accidents, Hanni. Pickaxes slipped; hammers broke. Hands and fingers and legs were crushed. I had nightmares for years that were filled with the screaming.'

He stopped, his body shuddering. Hanni stayed silent, stayed holding him and turned her face away so that he wouldn't see her shock and stop talking.

'I don't know how I lived through the first day let alone the first week. I stopped thinking, I know that much. I stopped feeling. The guards had all these games... They forced prisoners to climb the slopes out of the pit like monkeys and then they kicked anyone who reached the top back down again. They ordered others to jump off. There were so many bodies some days it looked more like a grave pit than a quarry. In the end I turned myself blind. I made myself deaf. It was that or go mad. And then it was me who fell. My hand slipped – I don't remember how – and my leg got caught as a cart toppled. I honestly thought I was done for. If it hadn't been the end of the shift, I would have been: the guards would have shot me for falling. As it was, I managed to roll so the bone was bruised but it didn't break. And I dragged myself back to the camp, leaning against the cart whenever I could, letting it pull me along. I got back in one piece which was a miracle in itself. I certainly didn't expect to survive the next morning's roll call in the state I was in, and I wouldn't have done, except that for the next two days it snowed so heavily that nothing and no one in the camp could move.'

He drew a sudden breath and his voice slowed. 'There's a madness to that too. Something so simple as a shift in the weather and it saved me. I was able to hide my injury; I was able to recover. After that, from nowhere, like a guardian angel or so it seemed, there was Elias and you know the rest.'

He came to a shaky stop. Hanni let his hand fall as his head dropped onto his knees and took a quiet moment of her own. She didn't know the rest, she knew only its highlights, but now she knew Freddy a little more.

She waited until his trembling had eased before she spoke. 'Were you afraid?'

Freddy looked up. His eyes were clear again. 'Of dying?'

She nodded.

'I don't know. In an abstract way perhaps. I was aware of the possibility of it every waking second in the same way that I was aware of the sky and the clouds. It was there, it existed; nothing I could do would change it. Maybe that's the hardest thing for anyone who wasn't imprisoned here to understand: Buchenwald wasn't a prison in the way prisons exist in the outside world. There were no rules here, no fixed sentences; there was no hope of release. Punishments existed because they existed. There was no connection to a crime. There was no reason for punishing anyone except to make the rest of us live in fear. The only thing that we were certain of was that death could come at any second. So the only thing to do was to try and stay alive until it came.'

He suddenly looked like himself for the first time since they had reached the top of the hill; as if he was in control of where he was, not the other way round.

'I've not really thought about this before today, but I think I was more afraid when I got out, when I realised how few of us had made it. The nightmares went on for months. Sometimes they still come back. I see the quarry; I see flames burning as bright as if I had been thrown into the ovens. There were times when I didn't believe I was alive. And I grew so used to that, it became an odd kind of normal. I'm not sure I've ever considered the toll that must have taken.'

He could so easily have been killed here. I might never have had a moment of him.

And now it was Hanni who couldn't breathe, who wanted to gulp at the air and cry for all the dead who surrounded them and for all the horrors Freddy had seen. She didn't let herself give in to that. She pulled herself back: Buchenwald's suffering wasn't hers to latch on to.

But it's not for hiding from either.

'That must have been horrible to relive but thank you for sharing it. That means a lot. Your war was such an impossible thing and mine was...' She shook her head as Freddy tried to stop her. 'No, don't: saying nothing is far too easy; it's been the default for us both. I was clumsy in the flat, blurting out nonsense about you granting me forgiveness. I'm not asking you for that now. But I do want us to go forward knowing each other better, for Leo's sake. Our silences, our refusal to look at the past, haven't helped him. So I want to tell you something of me in return, if you think you could listen.'

He looked away but he nodded, so Hanni told him the story of Peacock Island. There were so many other things she could have told him but she had realised, as she decided to share something of her life with him, that Peacock Island was the start. That was the night her adult life had begun and the start mattered. So she told him about the disturbance in the house which meant she had attended the party without Talie's watchful eye and as her father's pet. How that success had led to her increasingly playing the role of his hostess when the world overwhelmed her mother and the people that role had brought her into contact with. And she told him both sides of the coin: how she had lived inside Reiner's world and taken advantage of the opportunities it offered her, despite being all too aware of how rotten those opportunities were.

'I took the photography scholarship Goebbels arranged for me because I wanted it – there was no other reason than that. I knew what he was; I could have made up an excuse and refused and no one would have cared beyond a few moments' embarrassment. My father would have been angry but that would have passed. And he used to enjoy pointing out my double standards to me. He taunted me for watching everything from inside what he called my safe world, for doing nothing publicly to challenge what I attacked him in private for being. He said he would have admired me more if I'd run away and joined the resistance. He called me a coward. I railed against that, but he was right. I could have stood up and denounced him, if not during the war then certainly after. If I had fought harder, if I had trusted you more and accepted my part in the crimes my father committed, perhaps we wouldn't be where we are now. And I'm not telling you this because I want your absolution, or because I'm going to start making excuses for who I was. I just want to do better for our son.'

Freddy said nothing for a while. Hanni would have understood if he had walked away and said nothing at all. When he finally turned to her and said, 'Thank you,' those two words were better than any of the *I forgive you* scenarios she had played out in her head.

They went down the hill far more slowly than they had come up. They returned to Weimar, where they visited its town hall and two or three of its oldest pubs before they abandoned any hope of its citizens looking kindly on them. The driver followed them everywhere. No one in the town hall's offices had any idea where information on Buchenwald might be kept. No one in the bars would even answer an opening hello. Whatever cruelties Reiner might once have inflicted on the prisoners in the camp had vanished along with the barracks and the bodies.

Rühl had been right: there weren't any answers in Buchenwald, or not to the question of how to stop Reiner. But there were other things to be found. They both spent a sleepless night in their separate rooms, their heads filled with each other. The next morning they went back to Berlin, empty-handed in terms of their quest perhaps, but closer to the Hanni and Freddy who had met in the ruins of a Third Reich palace than they could remember being for a very long time.

CHAPTER 8

24 MARCH 1963, HARZ MOUNTAINS, WEST GERMANY

The boy was an even bigger disappointment than his daughter and proof, if proof was needed, of the deadly damage the wrong blood could do to a line.

Reiner sat at his leather-topped desk facing the window, staring out at the grounds swooping down from the school to the lake. Their upkeep cost a fortune. It was a good thing his investors had such deep pockets and that the parents who competed for his attention were so free with their wallets. For all the time and money that was spent on it, it should have been a perfect view. It almost was. The lawns were neatly manicured. The bushes edging the path to the lake had been shaped into equally sized globes. The roses edging the drive had been newly replanted. And yet... He sighed. The view, like his grandson, was spoiled. Leaves dotted the grass. One of the shrubs had yellowed. Soil from the planting had spilled onto the neatly laid gravel. He made a mental note to fire the gardener, and the maid who had delivered his morning coffee a degree cooler than he chose to drink it.

Which will be a moment's diversion but it won't be enough.

Because the person he really wanted to humiliate was his daughter, and his daughter hadn't come.

Reiner dropped the second pencil he had snapped that morning into the bin. Trying to work out what Hannelore was up to was straining his patience and swallowing too much of his time. Leo's unexpected arrival should have brought her to his study, never mind the telegram and the letter that had followed implying that he now had full control of the boy. He had expected her to arrive with all guns blazing and hopefully with the Jew in tow.

Your son chose me, Hannelore. I didn't have to do a thing.

What a joy it would be to say that. To parade Leo, to parade his victory. To pretend that the boy wasn't the weakling he had turned out to be but a shining addition to his empire. Except all that pleasure remained uncollected because she hadn't come. Apart from one phone call, she hadn't made any protest at all. Which suggested that she was up to something. Reiner was going to make her regret that.

A sudden shout from outside caught his attention. It was a pack of his final-year students, the boys he had chosen as his favourites, as he did with an elite group every year. A group who would do anything to please him, who all the other boys wanted to be. They were dressed in their running kits, pounding down the drive and laughing despite the rain which had started to fall in cold steady sheets. He stood up to watch them go by. They were exactly the kind of pupils his schools excelled in: strong and fearless and loyal to a fault.

The complete opposite of Leo.

Reiner had to turn away from the window before he threw his cup through it.

'There is a young man calling from Goslar station saying that he is your grandson.'

What a phone call that had been. Reiner would have hung

flags from the battlements if he had been able to use the ones that mattered to him.

'My grandson will be the perfect pupil, a blueprint for the leaders we are here to create.'

He had boasted, something he rarely did or needed to do. He had sung the praises of a boy who was supposed to be himself in miniature. And then the real one arrived and Reiner, for the first time in his life, had felt like a fool.

Leo was a tongue-tied mess of gangly limbs and a sullen disposition which had already marked him as an outcast. Reiner knew exactly where the problem lay – the boy was too much his father's son. The Foss genes had been tainted by bad blood. That sickened him. It was also a secret that could never be revealed, a stain that would have to be bred or beaten out of him. Until then the boy was an embarrassment, and as for Hannelore...

Reiner sat back down and rang for the useless gardener, determined to get some value out of his morning. Despite everything he had done to prove who was in charge, Hannelore apparently hadn't learned her lesson. She still thought she could outwit or beat him. She hadn't come running to rescue her son. What she had done instead was to try and outflank and discredit him. To get her nasty little exposé of Valentin Gessner – her exposé of him – published.

Every time he thought about the lies she had written, which he did far too often, Reiner's hand curled around an imaginary whip. The damage she could have done to his reputation with that piece would have been hard to recover from. Luckily the magazine's editor hadn't been as big a fool as Hannelore – and his lifestyle regularly outstripped his wallet, which helped – so the piece, which Reiner had read and been maddened by, had sunk without trace. But not her.

According to Reiner's sources, she and the Jew had requested permits to visit East Berlin, where they had been picked up at the border crossing by a Stasi driver before disappearing below his radar for days. Reiner didn't believe in coincidences. Whatever Hannelore was up to, her trip suggested a level of digging into the past he was not at all comfortable with. It also suggested that she had grown complacent over the last thirteen years. That she had forgotten that his eyes were always on her and that his web of contacts was wider than any network she could call on. That he would break her completely if she ever tried to ruin him again.

Or she hasn't forgotten anything – she doesn't care.

Reiner wouldn't have thought such a level of stupidity was possible, if Gessner hadn't planted the seed in his head.

'She's a lot stronger than you said she was, or a lot less afraid of consequences. Perhaps you took the brakes off her when you told the husband who she really was. And now the son knows the truth about her too, she doesn't care about the rest of the world finding out. And there's something else.'

There was always something else and it was never good.

'One of our police contacts says the Jew is sniffing round the statute of limitations and asking about the likelihood of extensions to it. He took a copy of the memo on it to the GDR. Could there be something specific they're looking for?'

Something specific – that had rattled Reiner more than he let Gessner see. A specific crime had been the bedrock to the Eichmann prosecution and now it looked as if Hannelore and her Jew had decided to follow that precedent once the print attack failed. He had sent Gessner away then, shrugging off the suggestion that there was anything to pin directly to him as impossible, to stop the man harping on about threats to his reputation. But it wasn't impossible at all.

There was a knock on the door, tentative enough to suggest that the gardener knew what was coming. Reiner settled himself more comfortably in his chair. Perhaps when he had done with the gardener and the maid and his temper had eased a little, he should summon Leo. The boy was easy to confuse and as eager to be liked as a puppy. Perhaps it was time to pour on the charm again instead of the vinegar. Hannelore would come, Reiner was certain of that if not of the timing, and the boy was too obviously afraid of him. For Hannelore to see that wouldn't do. It would lessen her punishment, and Hannelore deserved only the worst kind of punishment.

Even though she doesn't know what she's looking for, so the winning hand will stay mine.

His daughter searching through his past for some way to destroy him was a concern but it wasn't necessarily fatal. Not if he got to the evidence first.

If there is even any evidence left to find.

Reiner called the gardener in and left him standing ignored in front of the desk long enough for the man's knees to start shaking.

He had had years of practice at this: shutting problems down, silencing loose tongues; setting watchers and setting traps that could never be traced back to him. And that was also another point in his favour. Years had gone by – who could possibly be left to tell the tale?

The gardener was white-faced and ready now. Reiner looked up at him and smiled. Even if by some misfortune she did uncover what he'd done, what did it matter?

He had Leo.

He had Hannelore's heart in his hand.

CHAPTER 9

3 APRIL 1963, WEST BERLIN

The world kept turning but Hanni was stuck.

Going to Stasi Headquarters. Going to Buchenwald. Telling herself that they had found meaningful leads in Reiner's file. Growing closer to Freddy. Doing those things had kept her moving. They had given her back the belief that the plan to bring Leo home would work. They had offset the panic which flooded through her every time she imagined Leo standing beside Reiner and drinking him in. But now that sense of purpose and hope was gone. Now it had been replaced by nightmares in which Leo and Reiner kept merging into one person and the man they became was laughing at her.

Freddy was stuck too, although he had tried his best to keep the search for Reiner going when they returned to West Berlin. He had used far more police resources than he should have done to track down the defendants from the Buchenwald trials. The main target of those had been the camp commandant and the doctors who had ignored their medical oaths and performed agonising and deadly medical experiments on their prisoners instead. Of the dozens who had been imprisoned in 1947 – which was a fraction of those who should have been charged –

all but one had been released in the late 1950s. None of them
would speak to Freddy. They replied to his request as if they
were no longer responsible for their earlier selves. And as for
the one who was still held in custody and available to him...
Freddy filed a request for a meeting but Hanni refused to let
him anywhere near her. Ilse Koch, the wife of the first commandant and known since her trial as the Witch of Buchenwald,
was a sadist even by Nazi standards. She was said to have
removed tattooed skin from the camp's dead and saved the
pieces in a macabre souvenir collection. Hanni couldn't bear to
think about Freddy breathing the same air as her so she had dug
in her heels and argued until he gave in. The trip to Buchenwald hadn't unlocked every vault in him, but he had been
moving with a lighter step since they had returned. She wasn't
going to let him be brutalised again.

Buchenwald had opened personal doors for Freddy, but it
was a dead end in the search for a crime to snare Reiner. Theresienstadt and Sachsenhausen led nowhere. Dachau had also
been mentioned a number of times in the file but Hanni knew
they would meet the same blank wall there. Aside from those
places and their associated sub-camps and factories, there was
nothing else that triggered possibilities in her notes. In the end,
she was so desperate she took over Freddy's notes too, even
though he promised he had scoured them through and through.
Hanni didn't doubt that but his memories weren't hers, and his
eye was drawn, consciously or not, to the places that made his
skin burn. So Hanni took the pages and crawled through every
inch of them until finally, late one night when she was ready to
rip the sheets to shreds, she found the name almost obscured by
his notes.

Hadamar.

It wasn't a place Hanni recognised. She couldn't find it on
the list which detailed the regime's forced labour and killing
camps. There was also no information recorded against the

entry beyond the visit's date, and when she telephoned
Freddy, he couldn't remember it and was mortified that he had
overlooked anything. Hanni didn't blame him for that; she
understood: Buchenwald had loomed larger than the other
words on the page and the date for him was just a date. It
hadn't caught at his throat the way it clawed at hers – it
couldn't have done.

The tenth of December 1938. That was the only day
Reiner was shown as having visited Hadamar. To Freddy it was
just a date in a long list; it was anything but to Hanni.

The tenth of December 1938.

The day Luise had died.

'It wasn't on our camp lists because Hadamar was a medical
facility. It still is – it's still operating. All I know about it so far is
that it specialises in the treatment of psychiatric patients, but
Luise was physically ill, wasn't she? So Reiner's visit can't have
anything to do with her condition, despite the date. It must be a
coincidence.'

Freddy had gone immediately into investigative mode the
moment Hanni had flagged the entry up to him, but he was
struggling to make any kind of connection. Hanni was struggling not to. Coincidence and Reiner had never been a concept
that worked together before.

'What was wrong with Luise anyway? You've never really
said.'

Hanni was suddenly ashamed of the answer. 'That's
because I don't exactly know. I've been going over and over it
since I found the entry, but I don't remember anyone ever
listing her symptoms or labelling her with a specific illness. I
don't remember her getting any medical treatment at all.'

What she could remember was a nursery door that was too
often closed and the sound of stifled weeping and a sense of

something hidden which had become part of the muted rhythm of the house.

'And it's odd but what stands out more than her being sick are her absences. She stopped going anywhere with us as a family for at least two years before she died. And that became normal too.'

Hanni frowned as she tried to pull together a disjointed patchwork of her life in Charlottenburg that she hadn't thought about enough at the time and hadn't thought at all about in years.

'Everything seems so much more significant when I look back than it did at the time. I don't think I questioned anything then. She was there at the Adlon Hotel in 1933 when we went to watch the procession on the night Hitler became chancellor, I'm certain of that. She was a baby then and her nanny came with us so that my mother wasn't distracted from her guests. And she was with us at Nuremberg in 1935 for the rallies and at the Olympics' opening ceremony the following year.'

She winced as Freddy flinched from the images she had thrown at him.

'I'm sorry. I know that's not a life you want to hear about, but that is who we were: my father's perfect family trotted out to make him look like the perfect Nazi. And Luise was part of that – she was everyone's little darling. Or she was until Peacock Island.'

Hanni paused as the swirling memories started to settle. 'I told you at Buchenwald that my life shifted that night but I'd completely forgotten the other thing that changed. We were never a complete family again after that, or not in public, because that was when Luise stopped being allowed to come anywhere we were invited to and it was a fight to get my mother to do her job, as Reiner put it, and appear at his side.'

She stopped again, as another side of the story edged forward. 'And I never asked why. I accepted that Luise was sickly. I believed that she would grow out of whatever the problem was because my mother said that she would. But I didn't ask what was wrong, or about her treatment, or why, if she was poorly, the doctor never came. I loved her, I did, and I saw her whenever I was allowed to, but *what's the matter with Luise?* became one more thing that was never discussed. How did I let that happen? How did I take so little notice?'

It was another question, like *how can you forgive me?*, that Hanni didn't expect Freddy to answer, but this time he did.

'Because you were a child yourself, Hanni, even though you were made to act like an adult. You were a child for a lot longer than the guilt you feel now is letting you remember. And you're looking at her illness now through a mother's eyes, the way you worry over Leo when he's sick. The responsibility of Luise's illness or her care wasn't on you, and the date of her death aligning with Reiner's visit to Hadamar most likely means nothing. You weren't there when she died; you've told me that, and, yes, she was a poorly little girl when she was alive, but there doesn't appear to have been some long-term reason for that or surely your house would have been filled with doctors? I don't think this is what we're looking for, Hanni, and I certainly don't think Luise's illness or death is something to blame yourself for.'

The words were kind; his voice was warm. Hanni knew that he meant it, that he was offering her, unasked, some of the forgiveness she craved. But something else was nagging at her far louder than his kindness and it was telling her that Freddy was wrong.

'She told me Reiner didn't have a heart.'

Freddy frowned. 'Who did?'

'My mother, on the night of the party when she screamed the house down.' Hanni closed her eyes briefly as her mother's haunted face swam back up through the years. 'It was a warning but perhaps it wasn't about me being careful around him, the way I thought at the time. Perhaps it was about him and Luise.'

She picked up Freddy's notebook and ran her finger over a name that only hours ago had meant nothing to her.

'And maybe this isn't a coincidence. Hadamar is part of Reiner's story. And so, somehow, is Luise's death. There's a connection, Freddy, I can sense it. I just don't know how to join up the dots.'

But she knew how to start.

'All of this began at the house so I'm going back there to see if I can fill in any of the blanks. And although I really appreciate the offer, I have to do this bit alone.'

Now that Hanni was standing outside the family home in Lietzenseeufer, which she hadn't ventured close to in almost twenty years, she wished she had let Freddy drive her there and wait in the car. The house was still lovely. Its yellow stucco-work front had been repaired and was gleaming, and the front lawn was flower-edged and immaculate. In a different life it would have been where she brought her husband and her child to visit her loving parents. Instead, the house was full of ghosts and the last fear-filled days of the war. And the terror of Reiner's unexpected return.

Hanni hovered halfway down the neatly swept drive, convincing herself that she didn't need to knock, that there would be nothing left inside to find. That the British army officers who had taken over the house in the immediate aftermath of the war, and any families who had lived in it since, would have wiped the Fosses away. And that she wasn't pursuing a lead by being here but delaying the trip to Hadamar she knew she had to make but wasn't yet ready to tackle.

'Can I help you? Do you want something?'

The door opened while Hanni was turning to leave. The woman standing with her arm blocking the hallway behind her didn't offer a smile, and her tone was as cool as the day. It wasn't the most auspicious start but it was a start. Hanni retraced her steps, stuck on a smile and stuck out her hand. The woman watched her come but she didn't take it.

'I was hoping that you might be able to help me, yes. My name now is Hanni Schlüssel and I'm a photographer, but a long time ago when I was a girl, I used to live here.'

She'd hoped that introduction might make her sound respectable and win her a warmer welcome. The woman stepped further back into the shelter of the doorway instead.

'Don't tell me, you want to come in and have a root through the attics and see if there's anything left of your long-lost family?'

Her voice wasn't merely cool now, it was hostile. Something was clearly wrong. The moment Hanni recognised that, her immediate thought was *Reiner*.

'Has someone else been here?'

The woman frowned. 'Of course. I assumed that's why you've turned up: to see if your approach would work any better than his. Or are you going to tell me that two of you turning up in the same week with a sudden urge to investigate your dead relations after twenty years of ignoring them is a coincidence?'

It had to be him, or more likely one of his boys. He was watching her, guessing where she might go.

Which is frightening, but it has to mean that I did the right thing in coming, that there is something here to find.

Hanni didn't move any closer – she didn't want a door slammed in her face – and she didn't waste time on denials.

'No, I don't think it is. Was it a young man who came? Probably attractive, certainly charming and perhaps too forceful when you hesitated about letting him in?'

The woman's manner didn't immediately soften, but her shoulders loosened a little.

'Yes to all of that. And to the fact that I didn't let him in: there was an air about him that I didn't like, as if I was supposed to immediately jump and do his bidding. I sent him on his way instead. I'm assuming from your expression that was the right thing to do.'

Hanni nodded, glad that she had chosen honesty. This was clearly a woman who wouldn't settle for anything less.

'Yes, it was, although I hope you won't do the same with me. And yes, I have come about my family. Something happened here, or started here, a long time ago before the war that I think may have played a part in the death of my younger sister. I don't know any more than that, although I do think that your previous visitor might have been trying to get in my way. And I understand if you don't want to get involved given how strange and complicated that sounds. If you ask me to go, then I'll go.'

Hanni waited, her fingers mentally crossed, while the woman considered what she had said. And didn't hide her sigh of relief when the house's new owner stepped back and waved her in with a 'Call me Greta' and at least the edge of a smile.

'We bought the house in 1955 when the army was finished with it. We never met the original owner – he didn't want any more to do with it apparently and the sale was all done through lawyers and banks. I could see why someone might not want to return. The place wasn't in the best state inside or out. The garden was a swamp and most of the rooms had been turned into offices – the paint looked like someone had taken a plough to it. And the attic is a mess which I've never tackled, although we were told we could get rid of anything that was still here – one look at the chaos the army had left up there was more than enough; we haven't touched it since. You're welcome to go and try to make sense of it. It's always upset me a little, to be honest, that a whole set of lives could be so easily forgotten. But then, if there's the sort of secrets that you're hinting at waiting up there, maybe that was for the best.'

Hanni didn't attempt to answer that. She was too busy trying not to disappear under the tide of memories pushing around her. She followed Greta along the hallway and up the stairs refusing to look anywhere but ahead, ignoring the doors which had once led to bedrooms and nurseries and secrets. Focusing not on Luise or strange screams in the night but on Leo, who was alive and needed the protection her little sister had moved far beyond.

'It's up here. I suppose I don't need to tell you to take care on the ladder.'

Greta didn't. The slightly rickety pull-down construction was the same one Hanni could remember climbing up as a child, despite all the warnings she had been given not to. Not that the trouble she had got into then had been worth it. In Hanni's ten-year-old head, the attic had been a magical treasure-filled kingdom, a gateway to new worlds. In reality, it had been a dark and dusty labyrinth dotted with broken bits of furniture and rusted old trunks that scratched her hands and wouldn't open. Now it was as crammed as a scrap yard. She squeezed into it, overwhelmed by all the pieces of her family which had been tumbled together without any care for how much they had once mattered. *How can I start if I don't know what I'm looking for?* thudded through her head. The strands she was clutching were too fragile to be clues. An upturned night and a warning. A sick child who nobody had called a doctor for. Holes in family outings where her mother and her sister should have been.

She began to push her way forward, stopping whenever a chair or a table or the corner of a cobwebbed mirror looked familiar. Resting her hands on them, closing her eyes; trying to see the objects where they had stood when the house was hers to walk around. She had buried the memories so deeply, it wasn't easy to call them up now that she needed them, but then her knee banged against a low surface and one came surging back.

She can't take another one.

Talie's voice was as clear as if she was also standing in the attic. Hanni sank down onto the bed her knee had found, the white one which had belonged to Luise. It was covered in dust and the covers were gone but the carved teddy bears her sister had talked to every night were still intact on the frame.

My sister lying like a wax doll, my mother's eyes on fire.

The image was so strong, Hanni could almost feel Luise's tiny body curled up behind her in the bed. It was Luise's sickness which had caused her mother to scream. The connection was so obvious, Hanni couldn't understand why she hadn't put the two together before. Talie had been hunched beside the bed like a sorceress that night, staring at her daughter as if she wanted to wrap her up in a spell. The dots suddenly started joining up round her.

She wasn't trying to keep Luise safe from the illness. She was trying to protect her from my father.

Hanni closed her eyes even though the attic was gloomy, the past surging back so fast it was all she could do to stay upright. Her father's anger and his lies had spilled over from that night into every other public occasion the family had attended. Luise hadn't joined them at any event outside the house – or any in it which involved outside guests – after Peacock Island, but it hadn't been Talie keeping her daughter away from the parties and celebrations. Talie had dressed Luise up in her pretty little frocks and her pink buckled shoes and brought her downstairs chattering with excitement and ready to join in whatever excursion was planned.

And Reiner sent her back upstairs again. Every time. So what was he afraid of?

It wasn't of over-tiring his fragile daughter, Hanni was certain of that. Reiner never put anyone's needs above his own – he had rarely let Talie stay behind with her child; he had insisted her place was at his side, even when she begged him not to. He had only let her step away from her duties if her mother had... Hanni opened her eyes and stared at the little bed. If her mother had what?

Said that we might not be able to hide this one if I'm not here.

She had no idea where that echo came from. She couldn't pin it to a particular night or a particular event but she knew as surely as she knew her own hand that she was right. *We might not be able to hide it* had stopped Reiner shouting at Talie to get her coat and be a proper wife. It had propelled Hanni out of the door behind her father with instructions to act as his hostess and behave like a lady.

And the look in her eyes frightened me into not asking what she meant, although I'd forgotten that too.

Hanni forced herself to get up. Her mind had suddenly turned blank, closing itself off from the strain of any more recollections. She carried on moving anyway, weaving her way around the clusters of furniture, wondering if more echoes would stir, but all the pieces she touched remained silent.

Who else was in the house on the night of the screaming? Who, besides my father and my mother, knew its secrets?

She pushed and pushed at the fog filling her head, but the names wouldn't come and the faces were hazy.

Photographs, I need photographs. Or my mother's writing desk and her letters.

Having something to focus on finally made the attic seem smaller. Hanni had grown up in a home that was cluttered with silver picture frames, where every Christmas and birthday was captured by an official photographer and Hanni had been encouraged to catalogue the rest. Whatever else had been dumped up here, there had to be photographs.

She couldn't find the desk. It took her a while to find the boxes into which the family's personal items had been tipped, and her clothes and hands were filthy by the time she located them. It didn't matter. There were letters, torn and tattered maybe but still legible, and the frames were there. Their silver was tarnished, their edges were chipped and most of the glass that had covered them lay in shattered fragments. But the pictures were intact and so were the ones in the albums piled in on top of them, and the faces staring back at her hadn't faded at all.

CHAPTER 10

4 APRIL 1963, HARZ MOUNTAINS, WEST GERMANY

He had made a really bad mistake and he didn't have a clue how to undo it. And he missed his mother dreadfully and he didn't have any way to tell her.

Leo peered out of the grime-laden window onto the lawns spread out far below him, feeling impossibly small and alone. It was all supposed to have been such an amazing adventure. So why had it all gone so wrong?

Because you were an idiot and you didn't have a clue what you were doing; you just wanted to win.

The voice in his head sounded exactly like his father. He missed his father badly too. The voice was also right. His mother had been wrong to go through his things but the fight that followed had got so out of control, Leo had lost himself in it. All he had wanted was for his mother to listen to him and answer his questions, but she kept saying the same things over and over again – *you don't understand, your grandfather is terrible, you're stupid, this is how you should feel.* He shuffled on the window seat. Perhaps, if he was being fair, she hadn't exactly said those things. But that was what he had heard, so he'd fired back the worst thing he could think of to upset her and then got completely carried away.

He hadn't been serious when he'd threatened to go and live with his grandfather, although it was too late to tell his mother that now. He had liked the look of the schools, that was true, but all his friends were in Berlin and he was far more at home in the city than he was in the countryside. But she had reacted as if he had stabbed her and he'd been blinded by the scent of victory and then...

She yelled and I got angry and I couldn't calm down.

It was anger that had propelled him out of the house and onto the train. Then, once he was actually on board, excitement had kicked in. He had never travelled further than the distance across Berlin from his mother's flat to his father's on his own before and even doing that was a recent thing. To sit on a train for hours by himself, and to have enough money left over from his pocket-money stash to buy breakfast in the restaurant car, had felt impossibly grown-up. And when he had telephoned the school at Schloss Braunsberg and explained who and where he was, his grandfather had sent a car and a driver to Goslar station to collect him. Leo had loved every moment of that – the car had smelled incredible and the chauffeur had bowed – and then he arrived at the school itself and his jaw had almost cracked against the back of the seat.

Leo had sat in the leather-lined Daimler twisting around until he made himself dizzy. He had never been anywhere so fantastic – it was like something out of a storybook. The lions on top of the gold-patterned entrance gates looked real enough to leap off and chase him. The trees circling the lake were so bright and full their reflections had turned the water emerald green. There was a honey-coloured set of cloisters on one side of the central building and an ornately carved round structure he couldn't identify but thought might be a church and more turrets and towers than Leo could count. It was as if someone had mixed up a monastery with a palace and dropped it all into the middle of a fairy-tale park. The school was every bit as special as Leo had hoped it would be, and his grandfather, who was waiting at the top of the stone steps to greet him, was as tall and elegant as a king. It had been the most perfect beginning. Until he'd managed to mess it all up.

Leo wormed his way further into the dark recess beside the attic window where he could watch for the bullies and they couldn't find him. One handshake and he'd been made to feel like an idiot. He still couldn't understand how that had happened.

'Well, that needs work, young man. That's got *weak* stamped all over it.'

His grandfather had smiled as though he was really pleased to see him. And he had smiled around at everyone else, but that was the first thing he had said. He didn't say it loudly; he didn't make a fuss. But he also didn't say *welcome*, or *what a pleasure this is* or even *how is your mother*. He said *that needs work*. And after he said it, Herr Foss – which is what the driver had said Leo should call him at the start, the same as the rest of the boys – had stared at Leo's hand the way he had once seen his mother stare at a dead rat in the park and let it drop. That had confused Leo a lot. He couldn't marry up the way his grandfather spoke or the way that he flinched with the warmth of his smile. It had turned out to be Leo's first lesson in the difference between his grandfather's public face and his private one. A distinction Leo still hadn't worked out what to do with.

Except get things wrong all the time and mess up even more.

What had come after the welcome was a conversation with his grandfather which had felt like a series of tests and everything had gone from bad to worse. Leo hadn't been able to do anything right. He didn't speak particularly good English; he didn't speak any French. He didn't have a favourite painter and he didn't know Beethoven from Bach. And he didn't have an answer to 'Dear God, boy, what has your mother been teaching you?' So he had said nothing while his grandfather sighed and shook his head and made Leo feel even smaller. If he had known that the next comment would be even more unkind, he would have run for the train home there and then.

'This is what happens when bloodlines get corrupted. Maybe you'll do better once your father's been rinsed out.'

Who said such a thing?

A Nazi perhaps?

This time the voice in his head was his mother's and it was just as right as his father's had been. Nazi or not – and Leo was really starting to struggle with not – the damage had been done. He had left Herr Foss's over-heated office with *disappointment* hanging over his head and all his new classmates had smelled it. And nothing had changed in the last miserable month.

Leo drew his legs up to his chest, wishing that they weren't so bony. That they were the kind of legs that won races or would make him a star on the football field.

Fleet as greyhounds, tough as leather, hard as steel.

That motto was in every classroom; it was the measure of every boy who studied under it. And it wasn't the only one decorating the walls: the whole school lived by mottoes.

Men make history but we make the men.

If we lead, the world will follow.

Whatever his grandfather thought, Leo wasn't stupid. He had read enough magazines and books about the Third Reich to know where those slogans had their roots. When he'd read them out loud and played at being SS officers leading the charge into battle with his friends, the words had sounded inspiring. But here, where the boys chanted them at the start of every assembly like robots and the teachers used them as punctuation in their lessons, the slogans had begun to sound sinister instead.

He had also quickly learned that it wasn't just the mottoes which were going to pose him a problem: the standards they and the teachers set were impossible to meet. Leo had been a bright student at his school in Berlin, but the history he had been taught there was apparently the wrong kind and the authors he had read were degenerates. He had also been a good athlete but at Schloss Braunsberg he was permanently at the back of the pack. And the military-style drilling everyone was obsessed with – which was supposed to encourage discipline and loyalty, although he wasn't sure what to – was gruelling and endless and had cured Leo of any dreams of a soldiering career that he had once harboured.

He had still tried his best; he wasn't a quitter. He wanted to do well; he wanted to make his grandfather proud and prove to his mother that he knew what he was doing – even if he was increasingly sure that he didn't.

He avoided the boys like him, who were struggling and pretended they weren't. He worked hard at making friends with the golden-haired ones who ran every show and walked through the world as if they owned it. Unfortunately they took their lead from his unimpressed grandfather and didn't want him, or not until he'd proved his worth anyway. And the things they talked about... they terrified him. They didn't just insist that the murder of millions of Jews hadn't happened in the way that his friends in Berlin had said. They revelled in the fact that it had. Some of them had photographs of dead bodies that were far more detailed than anything in his magazines and so disgusting they made him feel sick. Leo had been scared to look at them, not only because they were horrible but because he assumed that he would get into trouble. Nobody did. The teachers didn't confiscate the images and dish out punishments; they smiled and looked through them with as much interest as the other boys. They pointed out locations as if they had been at the huge open pits where the shots had been taken. His grandfather had picked up one of the worst and said, 'Ah yes, I remember that.'

In their last row, Hanni had told him that Reiner was a

monster – that a change of name and a fancy suit didn't alter who he was underneath. Then Leo had refused to listen, but now? He couldn't shake the creeping suspicion that she was right. He didn't want to believe it, but surely only someone who was really cruel could smile at those photos. Or curl their lip at him with such contempt when he missed another target at the firing range and tell him to buck up and become a man and earn his place in the elite the same as everybody else. Or say 'useless' in that cold sneering way. Or tell him that Jews were a problem, that they weren't the right kind of people; that the world would be a far better place without them. Leo hadn't known what to do when his grandfather had said that.

That's not true, Leo. I brought you up far better than that.

His mother again.

Leo dropped his head onto his knees as the shame washed through him. He knew exactly what he should have done. He should have argued back. He should have repeated what he knew to be true, not whatever nonsense he had pretended to believe in to make himself sound big. That there wasn't any such thing as the right or wrong kind of people and that the ones who hated and hurt Jews, or anybody else for that matter, were the bad ones. And he should have stood up for his father, who was the best kind of man.

And for myself, because I'm part of him.

He hadn't. He had behaved as badly as when he'd said that the Holocaust wasn't real just to provoke a reaction from Hanni. He'd said nothing. He'd bitten his lip and looked at the ground and nodded because he was too scared not to when Reiner followed his nastiness up with: 'And you do want to be the right kind of person, don't you, Leo? You want to overcome the unfortunate side of your parentage and be at the top not the bottom of the heap?'

A sudden crunch of car wheels against gravel pulled his head up. He pressed his face against the window, not caring if his tormentors saw him, hoping with every breath in his body that it was his parents come to take him home. It wasn't. It wouldn't be – not since Herr Foss had sat him down in his private office and made him write that horrible note to his mother. He had been mean about her too.

'She's proving to be a problem again and I can't have that kind of distraction. So I'm going to deal with her properly this time and you are going to help me with that. So no more sulking, no more hanging round the offices in case there's an untended telephone you can cry into. You came here of your own free will, and you're staying, so why not make the best of it? Why not push yourself a bit harder and make me proud? I'm sure you can, you know, if you try. And wouldn't making me happy make you happier too?'

Leo had nodded at that. The way his grandfather could switch from nasty to nice in a heartbeat always mixed him up. But *I'm going to deal with her properly this time* had stuck in his head. He didn't know what that meant or what *you're going to help me* meant, but he didn't like either.

Why didn't I listen to her? Why did I think I knew best?

Whatever the answer, it was too late to go back.

He slumped into the recess again. He had made a terrible mistake and now he was stuck with it. Nobody was coming and he didn't dare run. And although he hadn't used the word directly and Leo didn't understand why him staying mattered, it was clear that his grandfather regarded him as some kind of a prisoner.

A bell rang on the floor below him, indicating that lessons were about to start. Leo knew he would get into serious trouble if he missed class but he didn't move. He didn't need another morning of being called stupid. He waited until all the doors had slammed shut and there wasn't a sound outside except birdsong and, once he guessed it was safe again, he knelt back up at the window.

The sun was high in the sky, sparkling off the snow which topped the highest of the mountains ringing the school. The lake was silky smooth and there was a stork perched on the top of one of the trees next to it as if it was practising to be an angel at Christmas. The view was beautiful – it should have been comforting and calming. It wasn't. Leo no longer found anything about the school or the landscape around it beautiful. He didn't want storks or pine trees or snowflakes; he wanted Berlin's busy sidewalks and bright shops. And Renny's bad temper, and his parents' strange marriage. And his mother, who he loved even if she no longer believed that.

He was alone and he was frightened. And all that he wanted was home.

CHAPTER 11

5 APRIL 1963, WEST BERLIN

Freddy rubbed his eyes as he stared at the photographs and the letters spread across his desk. He was exhausted from yet another night chasing sleep with a head that was too full of his fears over Leo. And now he had another set of images to add to the ones of his son marching with his arm raised and in step with Reiner. Images that this time were real, that he couldn't unsee.

'We need to find Emmi Schrade. I think she could be the key to finding out what was wrong with Luise.'

Hanni had arrived in Freddy's office late in the afternoon, smudged with dust and sticky with cobwebs and so wrapped up in the trail she was following, she hadn't noticed the dishevelled state she was in. The contrast between her messed-up hair and filthy clothes and her dark blonde beauty had turned heads across the station. It had winded Freddy. *It's my Hanni* had cemented him to his desk. Wipe away the years and there she was again: the girl he had met in the ruins of a bombed-out building, covered in brick dust and photographing a murdered body whose curious positioning she had described as *deliberate* a second before he was about to use the same word.

The day we became a team.

It had taken him a moment to catch his breath in Wilhelm-straβe. It had taken him more than that when she arrived in the station clutching her findings from the Lietzenseeufer attics. And she hadn't realised the impact she made on him any more this time than she had in the ruins.

'Emmi was my mother's maid in the 1930s but she was more than that – she was a friend and a confidante. And she was there the night things started to get bad with Luise – she was the one who chased me away from the nursery when I went to see why my mother was in so much distress. I'd forgotten that bit. The only person I could see at first when I tried to recon-figure the events was my father but then, in the attic, the whole of the picture came back.'

The force of her was white-hot. She ran through the memo-ries that had resurfaced as she rummaged through her family's belongings at breakneck speed, crashing into the news that someone else had been there too before Freddy could absorb half of what she was telling him. That revelation rang with alarm bells but she skated straight over his 'Slow down, Hanni, tell me that part again.'

'It's nothing to worry about. Greta didn't let him in, but from the way she described his appearance and his manner, it had to be one of Reiner's boys. Which is when I realised that getting into the house really did matter. If Reiner had his sights on checking it as well, there had to be something there to find.'

He didn't know if she was oblivious to the danger or simply didn't care, but he didn't like how easily she dismissed it.

'Okay but, with respect, that's not *nothing to worry about*. If it's true, it means that Reiner could be aware that you're looking for information on him and might go there, that he's on your trail. That he may know about the Gessner article or that we went digging for him in the GDR; that he could be physically following or at the very least keeping tabs on you. I know you say that you're not scared of him anymore, but you can't pretend he's not dangerous. Especially not now he's got Leo.'

Leo. That had slowed her down. It had made her acknowledge the need to move carefully. But it hadn't dented her determination to make something useful out of a pile of photographs and letters that refused to tell Freddy anything of substance at all.

'I'm not pretending he's no danger to Leo or to us, I promise. Quite the opposite. If he's on to us, we need to act faster and that's why I want to find Emmi. She left very soon after that night; she might have left at once, I'm not sure. But these letters prove that she stayed in touch with my mother, or she wrote to her anyway. I don't know if Talie answered them – they're so brief and so bland I can't tell. That might have been deliberate; perhaps she was scared in case my father read them. It also means that they might not be much use. But if you read between the lines, they suggest Emmi knew things about my sister's condition that I don't, so tracking down Emmi has got to be our next job.'

Freddy hadn't been able to argue with any of Hanni's assessment. The letters didn't have a return address on them and they asked that any replies be left care of a local café. And although they wanted reassurances that Talie was well and that *nothing had worsened,* Emmi never explained what *nothing* meant. If he had to guess, he would have said that not only was Emmi worried that her letters might be read; she was also worried about being found. Which didn't make him any more comfortable about Hanni racing off on the woman's trail. Or talking straight over him as he tried to say 'Yes, I understand what you're saying, but—'

'She was important. She was part of the family and Mother trusted her. Look, she's in almost every group picture that was taken at the house and also at some of the parties we went to. If my mother confided in anyone about what was happening with Luise, she would have confided in Emmi. So we need to find her, Freddy. I know it's a long shot given that she's been out of contact for almost thirty years but we have to try. I'm starting to think that...'

She had stopped then. It had taken a moment to get past *that*. Normally Freddy would have offered her some help to get through the sentence, but he was too busy trying to concentrate on the photographs she was waving at him, trying to focus his attention only on the small, neatly dressed woman on the edge of each shot. When Hanni started talking again, she'd sounded a lot less certain.

'I think Reiner was trying to hide the truth of Luise's illness, and I think that he might have gone to Hadamar for help with it. I don't know what any of that means but Emmi might, and it might be the missing bit of the puzzle we need to convince Leo that his grandfather is dangerous. So I know that you're already tying up resources to look into the hospital's background, but could you start another search too? Could you see if we can trace Emmi? We don't have anything else to try, Freddy. We're no closer to getting our boy back.'

Her voice had started to shake. Her face had lost its high colour. She had wanted more from him than a promise to divert manpower. Freddy understood why. The fear that gripped her was starting to run wider than Reiner's threat to Leo. The further they dug into Luise's last days, the more unsettling they became. Hanni needed him to find a quick and palatable answer to what had happened, and to do that with a ready heart. The first was difficult enough. As for the second...

Freddy had agreed to a second investigation at once – even though he was already sailing close to the wind by using his staff to pursue a personal matter. He had also promised to start straight away. Not because he was as convinced by the plan as

Hanni immediately presumed, but because he was desperate for her to leave. The photographs she had presented him with were too raw to look at while Hanni sat there all mussed-up and over-eager, the twin of the girl he had fallen in love with. It had been hard enough listening to her describing trips to Nuremberg and watching Hitler get honoured from the Adlon Hotel as normally as if she was describing an excursion to the seaside or a family picnic, but seeing the physical evidence of that life? That was another matter entirely. Freddy understood that Hanni's life had been lived among Nazis, but he had never been confronted with the reality of it before. Now that he had, it made him feel sick. And snared. Which was why he was still sitting at his desk hours after she had gone, trapped by images of Hanni shifting from a carefree little girl to a self-conscious teenager, her beauty deepening with each passing year, and utterly unable to tear himself away.

In any other context, watching that progression would have been a wonderful thing. Their lives had never been allowed the anchor that shared memories and shared families brought. Hanni's history had been hidden; his had been lost. There had never been family albums to pore over with smiles and locked hands. There had never been the moments of embarrassment caused by unflattering snaps and the shrieks of 'Oh God, is that really me?' he imagined other couples laughing over. And they had never had the luxury of tracing a family resemblance through the generations and trying to guess whose bright eyes or pointy chin had blessed or cursed their son. Freddy had felt that gap even more keenly since Leo's birth. And now Hanni had presented him with a timeline of her history which filled all her gaps in and all he wanted to do was recoil.

They wouldn't have let me be a part of them; they wouldn't have let me live.

The men in the pictures were in uniform, the sharp black and dark grey a chilling contrast to the pale dresses worn by their adoring women. And too many of the faces, never mind Reiner's, were known to him. Heinrich Himmler, the SS Reichsführer, was featured in one shot making a toast; the Führer's private secretary Martin Bormann was holding court in another. And one photograph, the one Freddy couldn't get out of his head, featured a laughing Hanni at its centre with Goebbels standing behind her, his hand resting on her shoulder, his smile reeking of ownership. Goebbels the Goat who groomed young actresses to be his mistresses on his film-set casting couch. Freddy couldn't think *did she?* – he wouldn't – but it was hard to shake off *she was in his sights.*

Stop it. She didn't choose to be put in his path; she didn't invite his attention.

He stood up, his blood suddenly too hot, and swept the photographs into his desk drawer, praying that out of sight would be out of mind. Telling himself that these pictures were as staged as the film from Theresienstadt which Reiner had forced him to watch. It didn't work. He couldn't get away from Hanni's *I took the photography scholarship Goebbels arranged because I wanted it.* Or the fact that the images she had treated as clues with no thought of their impact weren't directed scenes – they were everyday moments in a privileged life. Or that the truth of them, once seen, was a bitter pill to keep swallowing.

Hanni had attended glittering parties with the Nazi inner circle, with the same men who had written the laws which had reduced his family to nothing. She had accepted the patronage of a man who believed, and frequently said, that it was necessary to exterminate Jews like rats. If Freddy looked through all the albums she had discovered, he assumed that there would be a photograph of her shaking hands with Hitler. He couldn't see that and fall into a discussion about how to track down an old servant, or refer to Leo as *our son* and smile. So *you were a child, the responsibility wasn't on you* wouldn't stick anymore, although he had said it and meant it then.

He grabbed his coat and headed out of the office, barely acknowledging his team. He had to breathe fresh air before the walls crushed him.

Or before she does.

She was under his skin again. She had climbed there when Leo ran away, she had burrowed deeper at Buchenwald. He had almost succumbed to the feelings that she had dug up. He had sat in the hotel room next to hers on the night they had spent in Weimar, forcing himself not to go to her when every instinct kept propelling him towards her bed.

I have loved you my whole adult life.

He had imagined knocking on her bedroom door, saying those words, stepping over the threshold and into her arms. He hadn't done it. He had sat next to her in the car on the way back to Berlin wondering why. And then she had dropped the photographs onto his desk and his heart had remembered. The past wouldn't lie down. Whenever they moved forward, it kept creeping back and he couldn't let it. Never mind what Renny would do if he opened his life back up to Hanni, he couldn't survive his skin tearing open a second time.

The traffic noise had disappeared while he was walking. Freddy looked up and realised that he had wandered without noticing into Viktoriapark. That his feet were automatically leading him along the familiar path towards the bench opposite the waterfall.

Not today.

He stopped so abruptly he had to apologise to the young couple he almost knocked over. There it was, exactly as he had feared: the past rearing up again. Viktoriapark was the place where Hanni had first held his hand, where she had finally told him that she loved him. Where their broken hearts had reconnected through baby Leo. And where he had turned his back and walked away from her even though the pain of doing that had burned through every step. His head was spinning; his chest was too tight. He couldn't be in Viktoriapark and he couldn't escape her – she was everywhere. And everywhere he turned, so was Reiner.

Who takes away everyone that I love.

Freddy had told Hanni not to go running to the school to rescue Leo. He still believed that had been the right advice; he still hated himself for following it.

Freddy hadn't wanted to make plans and wait and hope that revealing Reiner's true nature would win back their son. What Freddy had wanted to do – what he still wanted to do in the early hours of the morning when sleep wouldn't come – was to collect his police gun, leap into his car, drive to Goslar and shoot Reiner dead. He had been forced to lock his gun away in the days after Leo's disappearance to stop himself doing just that. The strength of Reiner's influence – the cruelty of it – took his breath away every day. Freddy had lost his parents and his brother to the Nazis. He had lost part of himself in the hell that was Buchenwald. He had almost lost his sister. He had lost the miracle that was Hanni. And just when he thought he was finally emerging from the worst of the war's shadows, the Nazi who had destroyed his marriage had snatched his son. There were moments, sometimes hours, when the anger for all that he had lost and all that was threatened consumed him. When it unleashed a renewed hatred for Reiner that was visceral. Today, as he'd stared at the photographs, that anger had spilled out and some of it had landed on Hanni.

That wasn't logical. It wasn't fair. He couldn't help it. And no matter how much he wanted to, he couldn't escape the fact that the love he carried for her held Reiner's darkness at its core.

So I have to protect myself, and my child, or drown.

He pushed open the park gate, catching sight of his wedding finger as he did so. It was bare. It had been bare since he had finally removed his ring after one too many of the women he half-heartedly dated had complained that its presence made them feel uncomfortable. And now the pale band and the indentation that had remained behind for the longest time was gone too, the skin smoothed out and caught up with the rest of his finger. Freddy wasn't a man who believed in signs and omens but today he needed one. The visible mark which had said husband to the world had disappeared; perhaps it was time to disentangle himself from the rest too. To file the papers. To admit that the love of his life – because she would always be the love of his life – was gone.

His eyes filled; he couldn't see. He let the tears briefly fall only because there was nobody nearby to witness them. Then he dragged himself back to the station because there was nowhere else he had to be and if he didn't stay busy he would break. But Reiner was waiting for him there too.

'That report you wanted on the Hadamar facility is in, boss. It doesn't make for pleasant reading: whatever it pretends to be now, it was hell on earth there in the war.'

Freddy took the folder and waved to his deputy to shut the door. When he closed the file twenty minutes later, all thoughts of protecting himself and cutting his emotional ties with Hanni were gone.

I think Reiner was trying to hide the truth of Luise's illness. I think that he may have gone to Hadamar for help.

He opened the drawer where he had put the photographs and dropped the folder on top of them, trying not to dwell on what *help* might mean in such a God-forsaken place. He had to be wrong. Being right was unthinkable. Being right would destroy Hanni's world. And being right put Leo into the hands of a man who truly didn't have a heart.

Maybe I won't tell her; maybe I'll pretend there was nothing to find raced through his head. He dismissed it: secrets and lies wouldn't help Hanni any more now than hers had helped him. Besides, just because Reiner had gone to Hadamar when his child was sick, when his child had died, didn't mean there was a link.

But if there was – and if that link was even a fraction of the kind of horror story currently playing out in his head – then he couldn't be done with Hanni, because Hanni would need him like never before.

CHAPTER 12

10 APRIL 1963, WEST BERLIN

'So it's good news. Emmi survived the war. And because we had the photographs and also because the owner of the café where she collected her mail also survived and could give us a starting point, we've tracked her down. Thankfully, she stayed in the West, so that made the process easier.'

It was good news but Freddy didn't look particularly happy to be delivering it. He had reverted to his policeman persona, the businesslike and distant side of his personality which Hanni had hoped, especially after Buchenwald, wouldn't now stand as the currency between them.

Except I ruined everything again.

The photographs had scalded him, she knew that. They had brought him face to face again with the wrong Hanni. Wishing she had warned him what they contained before she had hit him with them wouldn't change that. She had been so obsessed with finding Emmi, she hadn't considered the impact of the pictures on Freddy until he was looking at the reality of her childhood and refusing to look at her.

Which was when I should have apologised and given him time to adjust.

She hadn't done that either. She had kept on talking instead, hoping against hope that he would view the images as clues and nothing more. Forcing herself not to snatch the whole bundle back when he flinched and turned white at the shot of her standing so close to Goebbels. That photograph was the worst: the way it had been taken, it looked like she was leaning excitedly into him. Hanni had felt sick at it too. She had wanted to say, *I might have seemed happy but I wasn't. I hated the way that he looked at me; I hated being near him. I hated being near all of them.* She had longed for Freddy to push the horrible images aside and say, *Don't worry, I know this girl isn't you.* But he had stayed silent, so she had too. Now the photographs lay like a scar between them and there was nothing she could do to repair it.

'There are a few missing years we can't account for. She seems to have married not long after she left your family's employment, but there is no record of a husband after 1945 and no indication that she had children.'

Hanni forced herself to concentrate as Freddy continued to read through the information typed on the sheet in front of him.

'Luckily for us, after the war she largely stayed in one place. She took a position as a housekeeper in one of the villas in Frohnau which stayed in private hands rather than being requisitioned by the army.'

Freddy suddenly stopped and his professional mask slipped. He was watching her with the same pinched expression he had worn when he looked at the photographs. Hanni wanted to shrivel.

'Which could mean that she already knew the owners. Perhaps they were contacts she made through your family. A lot of the properties around that area belonged to Nazis like your father who made themselves indispensable to the Allies after forty-five. Was Emmi a Nazi too? Did she have the same sympathies as him?'

It wasn't a question Hanni had considered before. It wasn't a question that would have been asked of Emmi or any other servant.

'I don't know. There was an assumption on my father's part that everyone in the house subscribed to his views but I've no idea if that was true. It's not as if anyone would have dared to stand up to him. Actually no, that's not right.'

She blinked, suddenly remembering the lost look on her grandmother's face as she stared at her son's black uniform and listened to him lecturing about bad blood.

'My grandmother hated everything Reiner believed in. She told him once that he had lost the right to be her son. He bullied her after that. He turned her into a shadow of the vibrant woman I loved. If any servant had said anything even half as blatant as she did, well I'd be surprised if they survived to be honest.'

It was an honest answer and the honesty broke through some of his barriers.

'I'm sorry. I'm struggling with a lot of this but that wasn't a fair thing to ask you.'

Hanni hadn't expected his switch from cool to warm and her eyes filled. Freddy dropped his gaze back to his notes as if he hadn't expected it either.

'Anyway, Emmi's retired now and apparently isn't in the best of health. But whatever the reason she joined the household, she seems to have become more to them than an employee. She has her own apartment adjacent to the main house and all her other needs are cared for.'

He slid the notes back into a file. 'And that's the full extent of our enquiry so far. I didn't want to make contact with her directly – it didn't seem appropriate to do that through police channels. But she is there, she seems to live a quiet life and she doesn't go out a great deal. If you want to visit her, which I imagine you do, I can make time to go with you today.'

The offer was a surprise. From his manner, Hanni had been expecting him to hand the notes over and tell her to come back with a report. And she didn't know if she wanted his company, not if that meant pulling him further into a past life that clearly revolted him.

'You don't have to do that; I can go on my own.'

Freddy shrugged as if he didn't care one way or another which option she chose, but there was a tightness to his jaw that suggested he cared very much.

'I know you can. But this isn't only about Luise; it's about Leo so I should be there. And I'm convinced that Reiner is on our trail. What I don't know is if he's behind or in front of us. He may have come to the same conclusion as you about Emmi holding important information about his past that he doesn't want anyone getting near. He may already have found her. I can't have you walking into that alone. So if you want to talk to her, can you indulge me and let us go there together?'

Hanni doubted that Reiner had given Emmi a single thought since she had left the Lietzenseeufer house, or before for that matter. He wasn't the kind of man who noticed servants unless they were in the wrong place and he had never bothered to learn their names. But Hanni really needed *us* and *together* so she nodded. It was obvious that Freddy was pulling away again, that – whatever the looks and the tentative touches of the last few weeks might imply – the thread that made them anything other than Leo's parents was barely holding. And she desperately didn't want him to voice the word she had sensed hovering around him since he had seen the picture of Goebbels' hand on her shoulder. There hadn't been a moment since Leo's birth when she had been ready to hear him say *divorce* and she wasn't ready for it now. He might have removed his wedding ring, which neither of them had acknowledged. They might not be married in anything but name but they were somehow still married. That mattered far more than she could tell him.

'Hanni.'

She shook herself back from the spiral she had been about to fall into. Freddy was holding out another folder.

'There's something else.'

When she reached out to take it, he wouldn't let go.

'What is it?'

He didn't seem to be able to find the right answer. Hanni looked properly at him and her fingers instinctively edged away from the cardboard. His mouth was twisted, deep lines scored his forehead. He wasn't being distant because he was angry with her or revolted by her. He was worried.

'You're spooking me, Freddy. Tell me what's in there or let me see it.'

He let the folder drop onto the desk and pushed it towards her, although he was clearly still reluctant to let it go.

'It's the report on Hadamar – it came in last night. Don't open it, or not yet. Give me a minute to tell you what it says.'

It was too late. His hesitation had made her nervous. Hanni pulled the loosely tied folder open, intending to read it through quickly. She didn't get any further than the opening line.

'I don't understand. You said Hadamar was a psychiatric facility during the war, the same as it is now, but this says it was a euthanasia centre. What on earth would Reiner be doing visiting a place like that?'

And then a memory crashed in and her stomach lurched.

'T4.'

'Hanni, will you wait just a second...'

She waved her hand at Freddy to be quiet so that she could pull together the terrible night in Prague and the horror stories Luca had spat at Reiner through a mouthful of blood.

'Luca said something about euthanasia and T4. He said Reiner had been involved in a set up or a roll out, I'm not sure which. The name didn't mean anything to me then and I'd forgotten about it until now.'

Freddy grimaced. 'I think a lot of people have tried to do that.' He shook his head as Hanni flinched. 'That wasn't an accusation – I didn't mean you, but there's levels of secrecy about the activities that came under the T4 banner that still aren't easy to cut through. And what my poor detective did find...' He shifted in his chair. 'Whatever Reiner's involvement, the report's a hard read. I know you have to read it for yourself. But don't take it away – do it here.'

His eyes filled with so much compassion, Hanni didn't want to read it at all.

'Is there something in here that's worse than I already know about him? Is that possible?'

'I don't know yet; his name's not directly mentioned, but even a vague link is a worry.'

Freddy's response didn't make it any easier for Hanni to start reading. Especially when *he's got Leo* instantly became the report's soundtrack in her head.

Hanni skimmed through the first paragraph. That explained that the programme had taken its name from the central co-ordinating office at number four Tiergartenstraße and gave the definition of euthanasia as a 'healing act to prevent pain and offer a kind release from suffering' which she knew the rest was about to subvert. It was the second paragraph which forced her to slow down.

Under the Third Reich, the concept of euthanasia no longer centred on assisting a terminally ill patient to die with dignity and without pain. Instead euthanasia became a tool to deliberately end the lives of those who were deemed to have no value to society. Those whose physical or mental incapacities branded them, in Nazi terminology, as 'useless eaters'.

Hanni couldn't get past the last two words; she couldn't breathe.

'Drink this.'

She grabbed the glass of water out of Freddy's hand and swallowed its contents in one gulp.

'*Useless eaters,* what kind of an expression is that? How could they label people so cruelly?'

She suddenly remembered who she was talking to and how he had been labelled, and she blushed.

'I didn't know this was Nazi party policy, Freddy, or something my father was involved with. I swear to God I didn't.'

His nod calmed her pulse a little.

'I didn't think for one moment that you did. Like I said, the programme was highly secretive, more so than the camps. I don't think many people outside the centres knew the full extent of what was going on. At the start, when the programme first became public knowledge, there were protests in some of the towns whose hospitals were used. The regime got very good at hiding the killings after that, but they didn't stop. And, well you'll see it for yourself when you read on, but plenty of people now think there's a link between the killing methods used in the T4 facilities – especially when they started experimenting with gas – and the industrial-scale murders carried out at Auschwitz and Treblinka and the rest. The work to prove that is only just beginning, but the progression from one disposable group to another is there.'

He fell silent as Hanni steeled herself and began to read more slowly through the rest of the page. She managed that without stopping until she got to the numbers. Over seventy thousand victims – people who couldn't advocate for themselves, whose families trusted that they were receiving specialist care – had been murdered in the first phase alone. Thirty centres had been established specifically to deal with sick children, or those who Nazi ideology designated as sick. The hatred that soaked through the figures was overwhelming.

'When did it start?'

She didn't want to know, or she wanted an answer that was far later than the one she dreaded was coming, but asking the question seemed somehow less daunting than turning the next page.

Freddy's fingers knotted. 'None of the information my team could access was definitive about that. The start date that is usually given is 1939, but the legal framework was in place by 1936 so I think we can hazard a guess that there were killings taking place any time after that. The Nazis were nothing if not meticulous about testing their programmes before they were fully rolled out.'

He wasn't looking at her; he couldn't look at her.

Hanni didn't want to be in the room. She didn't want to know about centres and killings and who was deemed to have enough value to live. Talie was in her head, throwing dates and warnings at her like jigsaw-puzzle pieces. Reiner was in her head, demanding perfection. Leo's white face was hovering. As for Luise… Hanni closed the folder and pushed it away. If she explained slowly and clearly what had happened to her sister, explaining it would make it true.

'Luise was frail. She died of scarlet fever during the 1938 epidemic. My father told me that. He showed me her death certificate – that's how I know the date. I wasn't there when it happened, or when she was buried, which everybody told me was a good thing. I could have died too, that was what Reiner said, and my mother would never have survived the loss of us both. It was scarlet fever that took her – there was nothing anybody could do.'

She didn't recognise her own voice – it had too high a pitch. And she didn't recognise Freddy's when he finally spoke.

'The problem is, Hanni, that there wasn't a scarlet fever epidemic in Berlin that year. I checked. According to the medical records I've seen – which I accept may not be complete given all that's happened to the city since – the last serious problem with that particular illness was in 1934, and even then it was treatable. So whatever killed Luise, I don't think it was scarlet fever.'

'I want to see Emmi. I want to go now.'

Hanni pushed the folder into her bag without reading the rest of it. What Freddy was saying didn't make sense. What he was implying wasn't a path she could follow. She didn't want to talk about it – or think about it. Except, for the whole of the silent car journey to the north of Berlin where the garden suburb of Frohnau was located, she was stuck in 1938 not 1963 and she couldn't think of anything else...

'Have a wonderful Christmas!'

'Don't forget to tell your father that we met Hitler at the resort and he shook your hand; he'll be so proud of you.'

Hannelore stood on the platform waving goodbye to the friends she had spent two weeks skiing with in Garmisch-Partenkirchen and resolved to do nothing of the sort. The skiing had been fun – it was a sport she excelled at – but the town itself had been too rich with swastikas for her liking, and meeting Hitler had not been the same highlight for her that it had been for her friends. He had been holding forth to the faithful in the hotel lobby when they wandered in from the slopes, discussing a speech he was writing and asking whether 'parasite' or 'leech' was the most fitting name for the Jews, or if anyone else had a word they preferred. The sadism in the answers had delighted him and sickened her. When the Führer turned and saw the girls watching and immediately insisted on personally greeting *such wonderful examples of our race*, her skin had crawled. So no, she wasn't going to mention that meeting at all. Not that there was anyone to tell it or any of the rest of the trip to.

Her mother wasn't waiting on the platform to meet her, as

she had promised she would be. Which meant that Luise wasn't there, hopping from one foot to the other with excitement at being reunited with her big sister. Instead, there was a uniformed chauffeur waiting to lead her away from the lively goodbyes and into a silent car. And when she arrived back at home, there was nobody waiting there either.

Hannelore marched into the house feeling very hard done by. Two weeks away should have ended in open arms and a warm welcome and something special and delicious on the table for tea. Not dimmed lights in the hallway and her father's rather forbidding secretary.

'You are to go straight to the study, Fräulein Foss. The Obergruppenführer is waiting for you there.'

Her father's study was the last place Hannelore wanted to be, but a summons there was not a summons she dared ignore. She checked her reflection in the mirror and straightened her hair while the secretary tapped her foot and both of them pretended that the chill shrouding the house wasn't worth remarking on. Reiner finished the memo he was writing before he asked her to sit. Then he put down his pen and informed Hannelore – in a tone that came back to her twenty-five years later as cool and detached as it had been then – that he had *unpleasant* news.

'Your sister has died.'

Four words, no warning and Hannelore's world cracked.

She managed 'No' and 'When?' and 'How?', the words appearing automatically from her mouth while her brain whirled and screamed.

'Last week, on the tenth. During the scarlet fever epidemic.'

None of that made any more sense than *died*. When she asked, 'But where is she now?' her father sighed.

'She is buried, Hannelore, I told you: it's been over a week. There was little purpose in bringing you all the way back so the matter was done without you.'

'I don't believe you. It's not possible.'

She twisted round in her chair, waiting for Luise to pop up and laugh and tell her it was a joke.

'Don't be ridiculous. And don't get hysterical – I've had quite enough of that. Here.' He was waving a piece of paper at her. 'I don't know why you would need proof; you're as bad as your mother, but here it is in black and white.'

Hannelore could see her sister's name and the date Reiner had given and the word *deceased* in thick black letters. She didn't want to. She shut her eyes to block the words out. It still wasn't possible, whatever the certificate said. How could Luise have died? And how could she have been allowed to die without Hannelore there to make sure the little girl suffered no fear in her last moments? And that was when the world began to spin and her stomach reached up through her throat. How could there be last moments for a six-year-old? How could there be anything but thousands of moments to come?

'I don't want to be here; I want my mother.'

Hannelore lurched to her feet. She was caught in a nightmare and Talie was the only person who could cure nightmares. She needed her mother's cool hand on her forehead, plucking the bad dream away, making everything safe again.

'Sit down, Hannelore. Calm yourself. You will leave when I say.'

She did as she was told but she couldn't feel the chair. Reiner reached for the bell pull by his desk and rang it.

'Your mother is not to be disturbed. She is sedated. It would be better for everybody if she stays that way. The housekeeper will take you to your room. I presume there will be food if you want it.'

Hannelore went where she was led because she didn't know what else to do. The silence was as thick as if the house had died with her sister. She didn't want food; she wanted warm arms and somebody to explain how this nightmare had happened. She sat on her bed, waiting for her father to realise how broken she was and to come and help mend her. She lost count of time. She couldn't cry. She didn't move until she heard him saying goodnight to the butler and the front door slam and a car pull away over the gravel. Then she went in search of her mother.

There was no light under Talie's bedroom door. Hannelore knocked, expecting Emmi to be standing guard. There was no answer. When she crept inside, the curtains were open to the moon and Talie was lying motionless in the crumpled bed. The normally immaculate room smelled stale. Lipstick and powder compacts were scattered confetti-like across the cream carpet. The wardrobe door hung open, revealing dresses half-toppled from their hangers.

'Where is Emmi, Mama? Why are you here on your own?'

Talie didn't answer. She continued to stare out of the window to where the snow was falling in white drifts across the sky. Whatever she was seeing, it wasn't the tumbling flakes.

Hannelore's heart burst open again.

'Can I get you anything, Mama? Can I do anything?'

She approached the bed, her hands out to straighten it, to settle her mother more comfortably against the pillows. Talie didn't turn, but she began to speak in a voice that was stripped of all its usual melodies.

'She's not there.'

Hannelore froze. Had her mother gone searching in the nursery? Had she been pumped so full of sedatives she had forgotten Luise was dead?

'I know, Mama. Father told me what happened. I know.'

But Talie couldn't hear her and she couldn't stop. She was still repeating the same words over and over when Hannelore finally abandoned the sickroom and fled.

. . .

'She's not there.'

'What?'

Freddy stopped staring out of the window at the palatial villas edging Frohnau Straße and turned round. Hanni had still been half caught in the night she had learned of Luise's death but she pulled herself together and said it again.

'My mother kept saying those words over and over the night I came home and Reiner told me Luise was dead. I thought she was so grief-stricken, or so drugged, she'd forgotten what had happened, but...'

Hanni stopped, rubbed at her face and regrouped. 'When Reiner sent us back from Theresienstadt to Berlin in 1945, my mother – who barely left the villa or her room when we were in Bohemia – wouldn't stay inside the house. I kept telling her how dangerous the streets were but she wouldn't stay away from them. She walked them every day for hours, sometimes until her feet bled. I thought it was grief again – that the shock of coming back to Lietzenseeufer had made her lose her mind. That she had forgotten Luise was dead all over again and was looking for her. But now I don't think that's true, or not in the way I thought then.'

She couldn't continue. What she wanted to say was absurd; it was the fault of the file about Hadamar putting crazy ideas into her head. She started to say *no, it doesn't matter, it's nothing,* but Freddy knew her too well.

'Tell me what you're thinking, no matter how far-fetched it sounds. I know you, Hanni: when you have a hunch, you're rarely wrong.'

'That's what I'm afraid of.'

She took a deep breath and kept her eyes locked on Freddy's.

'In 1938, when Mother said *she's not there* and when she went searching in 1945, what if she was telling the truth? My father told me there was a burial but my mother wasn't well enough to attend it. And he said that there was a grave with Luise's name on it in the Kaiser Wilhelm Cemetery, but Mother never visited it – she flew into a rage the only time I mentioned going. And I...' She shook her head. 'I couldn't bear to think of Luise lying alone in the dark, so after Mother got so upset, I never went to visit it either.'

'It's all right – that's understandable. And it's not too late. There'll be records of the burial; we can go and look for it whenever you want.'

He was still holding her hand, trying to make things right, but he hadn't understood what she meant. And if she didn't say it out loud, neither would she.

'But that's the thing, Freddy. I don't think finding the grave is what matters. What if my mother went wandering because my sister really was lost? What if by *she* Talie meant Luise? What if there is a plot and a plaque, but the grave is empty?'

She paused because the last question was too painful. But painful or not, it had to be asked.

'What if my sister was never there?'

CHAPTER 13

10 APRIL 1963, WEST BERLIN

The house in Frohnau was an elegant sweep of white walls and red roofs and was set far enough away from the road to be deaf to the traffic. Hanni led Freddy up the drive already on edge, bracing herself for another complicated explanation. Fortunately her opening 'I knew Emmi Schrade as a child and was really hoping to see her' immediately unlocked a warmer welcome than she had met with at Lietzenseeufer. Better than that, the housekeeper's smile and her 'She never has visitors – this will be such a treat' allayed any fears that Reiner's spies had beaten them there.

Freddy had been right about how well Emmi was regarded. The cottage they were led to was bordered by neatly clipped hedges and sported a fresh coat of paint.

'I'll leave you here rather than crowd your reunion. Give her a few minutes to answer though – she's not as spry on her feet as she was.'

It was good advice. The cry of 'I'm coming' reached them well before Emmi did and, although Hanni did her best to hide it, the woman's appearance was a shock. Twenty-five years had taken the plumpness from Emmi's cheeks and speckled her hair with grey, a change Hanni had expected, but whatever illness she was in the grip of had slowed her body more than the years alone should have done. And before Hanni had the chance to worry at that, she was lost inside a swooping and tear-dampened embrace.

'Hannelore Foss, I can't believe it. I thought I would never see you again. Oh thank God you made it through all those awful years. I've always wondered what happened to you. I even went back to the old house once to try and find out, but it was swarming with uniforms and there was no one to ask where the family had gone.'

It took a while to progress from introductions between Emmi and Freddy – which Hanni made using 'friend' rather than husband while neither of them looked at the other – through the hallway and into a cosily furnished sitting room. It wasn't until they sat down that Emmi's smile dropped.

'I've missed your mother so much. Did she make it through as well? Please tell me that she did – I would so love to see her again.'

Pain flooded her eyes when Hanni shook her head.

'No, she didn't, I'm sorry. She was killed in an air raid in 1945.'

Hanni paused. Pretending that Talie's last years had been happy ones would be a kindness to Emmi but it wouldn't help unpick what had led to her death.

'And she was lost to us long before that, which is the real reason why I'm here.'

Hanni told the story of Talie's frail state by the end of the war as simply as she could. Emmi stayed composed until the end and then her face crumpled.

'I should never have left her alone with him; I should have stayed and looked after her but I ran away instead. That's the most cowardly thing I've ever done, and there's barely been a day since when I haven't regretted it.'

Emmi had clearly held the tears she burst into then inside her for a very long time. Hanni slipped an arm around her shoulders until the flood eased and then she coaxed her, as gently as she could, back to her mother's story. It wasn't easy to do: the woman's pain was real and the sight of it reignited Hanni's.

'I'm so sorry that you've been carrying all this and I don't want to make anything worse, but I need to ask you, Emmi: by him, do you mean my father? Do you mean Reiner?'

Emmi nodded. 'I was afraid of him. All the servants were. You understand that, don't you?' She breathed a little easier when Hanni nodded. 'And I told myself that leaving would be all right as long as I stayed in touch and wrote to her and let her know that I was there, that there was always someone she could turn to and somewhere she could go. She never replied, which may have been his doing. So then I told myself that it was better for you that she stayed and that she would recover with time, even though I knew she never would. That she couldn't because he'd broken her.'

He'd broken her.

Emmi didn't appear to have made a mistake: she was upset but she was being deliberate. Hanni still had to be sure.

'Don't you mean Luise's death had broken her?'

Emmi didn't seem to know what to do with her hands – they fluttered between her lap and her face as if she wanted to disappear behind them.

'No, it was him. Or maybe it's the same thing in the end. Your poor mother's life was ruined either way. She tried so hard to keep her baby safe, to make sure the truth wouldn't get out, but it was hopeless. It was always going to be hopeless. What Reiner wanted always won, and he didn't want Luise.'

The temperature hadn't changed. The sitting room was as warm and snug as when they had first stepped into it. The sky outside hadn't turned black; there was sunlight streaming fresh and bright at the window. Knowing those things didn't matter. Hanni's body was so cold she wasn't sure it was still there. There were so many shadows pressing around her, she could no longer see Emmi or Freddy.

'Hanni, it's okay. Breathe and come back to us.'

Freddy – who had stayed quiet and let Hanni take the lead – was at her side, not pushing her faster than she needed to be pushed but there. She leaned into his shoulder. When he didn't move away, the world steadied. And when she took the deep breath he was asking her to take, her voice came back with it.

'My father told me that Luise died in a scarlet fever epidemic.'

Emmi looked away. Hanni swallowed hard.

'That was a lie, wasn't it? There was no epidemic and my sister was ill long before 1938. It started in 1936 or it got bad in 1936, on the night of the Peacock Island party. And you knew what was wrong, and no one was supposed to know, which was why you were afraid of him.'

Emmi nodded but she couldn't look up when she answered.

'I thought he never took any notice of the staff, unless we crossed him, but he'd taken notice of me. He told me that night, after he chased you away from the nursery, that he would kill me if I said a single word about what had happened to Luise. He would have done it too, except I was the only one who could keep Talie calm. But when it was over, that's when I was really in danger. He wasn't the kind of man who left evidence. So I ran. I abandoned her.'

Emmi was slipping into a loop of guilt and regret that was understandable but would overwhelm her and the story. As Hanni leaned forward to take Emmi's hand and try to help her hold on to the present, Freddy began talking. To her relief, his calm voice lifted the crying woman's head back up.

'Emmi, look at me, come on. That's it, that's better. There's no blame here. Reiner was a dreadful man and you were in danger – we know that. You had to protect yourself – there's nothing you did wrong. But we need to find out what was really the matter with Luise. Can you help us? Can you explain?'

There was such kindness in his voice, especially on *there's no blame*. Hanni knew that he meant it, that it wasn't a tactic intended to simply keep Emmi talking. The compassion lifted her own soul a little. It worked on Emmi too. There was a pause while she searched his face. Once she found what she was looking for there, she sniffed and nodded and sat up a little straighter.

'Thank you for that, for not judging me. I'll try – I'll do my best.'

She drew a breath and then the words came so fast it was clear that she was glad to be rid of them.

'The thing that the Obergruppenführer didn't want anyone to know, that he couldn't live with, is that Luise had fits and, as she grew older, they became increasingly bad ones.'

'Oh God, no. He would never have had any patience with something like that.'

Hanni couldn't help herself. *He didn't want Luise* had suddenly started to make the worst kind of sense. Emmi instantly stalled and wouldn't resume talking until Hanni promised her she could bear whatever was coming. When Emmi eventually resumed the telling, it was far more hesitant, and Hanni was forced to swallow so many tears she thought she would choke.

'You were right about the night of the party being the start: that was when she had the first one. It was such a shock and it frightened your mother, and me, half out of our wits. As for your father... He turned his back on Luise that night and he never looked her way again except as a problem. And after that night it got worse. Sometimes she could go for days and be fine, sometimes she couldn't get through a morning without four or five seizures. I've never felt so helpless in my life. Her poor little body would be twisting and turning and there was nothing your mother or I could do to soothe her.'

Hanni heard the words but her brain slid straight over them.

'Four or five fits in one morning? For two years? How didn't I know?'

Emmi's fluttering hands were struggling to escape. 'Because Talie and I got very clever at hiding them. We had to be: your father was riding high in the regime and nothing was allowed to get in the way of his ambition. He had no compassion – none of them did. You said he wouldn't have had any patience, but it was worse than that. He was afraid that if anyone found out that his daughter was ill and in a way that – for the likes of him – was such a taboo, he would be judged for it. He thought people would whisper about bad breeding or blood or some such nonsense and his career would suffer. Once he knew the first fit wasn't the only one, he refused to let her mix with anyone outside the house, even though Talie kept trying to give the poor mite some kind of a life. Luise was hidden and you were kept well out of the way.'

'What was wrong with her? Was there ever an official diagnosis?'

It was Freddy who asked. Hanni was struck dumb by how desperately her mother and her sister had suffered, and how blind she had been. By the new depths of her father's cruelty. *Is it worse than I already know about him? Is that possible?* She knew instinctively that it was. Something was chiming at her in the use of *bad breeding or blood*, a warning bell she couldn't yet quite make sense of.

'I don't think so; I don't think your father would take that risk. A doctor came the first time it happened but Talie wasn't allowed to speak to him and he never came back, although I think I overheard the Obergruppenführer talking to him on the phone once or twice.'

Emmi sounded exhausted. The ordeal of reliving those days

was clearly too much for her, but it was equally clear that there was more to tell. They had no choice but to encourage her to carry on.

'Talie and I had to become the experts. We read everything that we could and eventually we came to the conclusion that Luise had leukaemia, which is the true definition of bad blood I suppose. All the symptoms were there – they had been for a long time. Bruising, fatigue, constant infections, and the fitting. And everything we read told the same story: that there was no cure and that the treatment available was limited and likely to be worse than the illness.'

Bad blood.

There it was again. Hanni could hear Reiner's disgust ringing through her head the whole time Emmi was talking.

If only I'd known, I would have... She couldn't get further than that. What could she have done that Emmi and her mother hadn't tried? Her face must have betrayed her; this time it was Emmi who took Hanni's hand.

'Your mother was amazing; I want you to know that. We talk about her now as someone who was fragile and broken but then, when your sister needed her? You wouldn't believe how strong she could be. Maybe we could have carried on managing, I don't know, but the seizures got so bad and took such a toll on the poor child's body that Talie was terrified Luise would die in the middle of one. That was when she weakened and gave in to Reiner's demands that she send Luise away for treatment, which he'd been trying to force her to do for months. He over-whelmed her with kindness and Talie was so unused to that and so exhausted, she listened. When he persuaded her to let him take Luise to a hospital outside Berlin where no one would know him, she agreed.'

Emmi shook her head as though she was hearing warnings now that she hadn't heard then.

'He made it sound so reasonable. The plan was that Talie

would follow and stay once Luise was settled but that never happened. Reiner took Luise away but apparently the journey was too much and she died within hours of their arrival. He didn't even bring the body back, although there was a funeral with an empty coffin for appearance's sake, and he put out the story about scarlet fever to stop anyone asking questions. I'll never forgive him for that. For not giving Talie a last sight of her daughter, for making her collude in a burial that was a mockery. The things she shouted at him that night... she wouldn't stop until he had her sedated. And then he came looking for me and I ran.'

Emmi ground to a halt, her breath coming in jagged sobs. Hanni was aware of Freddy getting up, finding a pillow and a blanket, fetching water. All the things she should have done, but she was frozen.

She's not there.

Talie had known the truth all along and it had crushed her.

Emmi was crying again. 'Defective, that was the word Reiner used to use about Luise. And useless, a waste of life. Horrible, horrible words he should burn in hell for.'

Useless.

It was the T4 word.

Hanni's brain recoiled. She was half off the chair before she realised she was moving, desperate to run from revelations which hinted at a darkness she couldn't face when Emmi's hand latched on to her arm, with a far stronger grip than her thin frame suggested she had in her.

'He paid for his crimes, didn't he? Tell me he suffered the way he made them suffer.'

For a moment Hanni wanted to lie. She wanted to give Emmi the comfort of believing that Reiner had been punished for all the misery he had inflicted. She couldn't do it. And she couldn't hold anything back.

'I wish that was true, but he thrived – he's still thriving. And he's still dangerous. I'm a mother now too, Emmi. I have the most beautiful boy. And Reiner has him and I'm scared he's going to hurt him the way he always hurts… Oh God…'

Hanni suddenly realised the true extent of what she had done. She turned to Freddy, wondering how to say 'I've put her back in Reiner's sights again' without frightening Emmi. She didn't need to: Freddy had got there at the same time.

'Do you have any relatives or friends outside Berlin you might be able to go and stay with, Emmi?'

His tone was casual but confusion still clouded the woman's face.

'I'm not sure. There's not many of us left. My husband was killed in the war before I got a chance to know his family and most of mine are gone. There's a cousin in Munich who I was close to as a girl, but I haven't seen her in years. I suppose I could contact her and ask if she'll have me, if you really think it's necessary. If you think there's a need.'

Her wide eyes were begging him to say that no of course there wasn't, but Freddy couldn't indulge her with false hope any more than Hanni had.

'I think it's best not to take chances, that's all, until we can bring Reiner into custody, which I promise is the plan. And I can arrange everything if you'll let me, including a very comfortable limousine to take you there, and bring you back home again very soon.'

Emmi stopped hesitating the moment Hanni added, 'It would make me feel better if you'd do it,' and agreed to contact her cousin. Freddy made a note of the address while Hanni hugged Emmi and promised that she would stay in touch this time, and introduce her to Leo as soon as she could. It was only as they were leaving that Hanni realised there was still one unasked question.

'The hospital Reiner took Luise to – can you remember the name of it?'

Emmi closed her eyes. Hanni waited while the older woman's eyelids flickered. When she opened them again she was frowning.

'I can't get the name – it's been too long. He chose the place, I'm sure of that. He said there was a little town nearby where Talie could stay, a pretty one with the baroque architecture she loved. I remember that because I thought it was an odd thing to say, as if he was trying to make the place real and pleasant for her so that she wouldn't put up objections.'

Emmi stopped and nodded to herself. 'It was odd and it still feels odd now that I say it. Your father wasn't a man who cared about anyone's comfort, but he kept doing that, wrapping the trip up for her like a parcel. I know the town was near the city of Wiesbaden – he said she would like it there because it was more cosmopolitan than the countryside. I think he would have said anything to make her go along with what he wanted.'

A small town an hour's drive from Wiesbaden, noted for its glassware and the splendid altars in its churches.

Hanni could recall the description in the folder Freddy had given her because the location of the hospital was at such odds with its cruelty. She needed Emmi to confirm it all the same.

'Was the town or the hospital called Hadamar?'

Emmi's face brightened with the relief of finally being able to help. 'Yes, that's it. It's coming back to me now. He said it was a charming place, and particularly suitable for children.'

CHAPTER 14

13 APRIL 1963, UNIVERSITY OF WEST BERLIN

'The beauty of the devices we used was how simple they were to make. That really matters when you have no guaranteed access to supplies and no time to waste. And, even better, they turned every train into a potential weapon. Once the pipe packed with gunpowder was fixed into place, it looked like part of the track. Then all we had to do was run a fuse from it along to a detonator and whoosh! A plume of dirt, a rocket of flame and up goes the train with its cargo of Nazis, off the bridge, into the ravine, wherever we chose to send it. It was the best firework display I've ever seen, and we did it to dozens of them.'

All we had to do.

He made it sound so much simpler than Renny guessed sabotage under such dangerous conditions must actually have been. When one of the audience pointed out that their speaker for the night had also had to be fearless and driven and determined to purge evil out of the world, with no thought of injury or death, he'd shaken his head in embarrassment. And left Renny utterly spellbound.

Gregor – which everyone knew wasn't his name and only added to the thrill of being in his presence – wasn't like the usual speakers who addressed their group: the academics and aspiring politicians. Gregor had been an actual partisan during the war. He had spent his days hiding in woods and stalking Nazis, destroying trains and ammunition depots. And he hadn't been just any partisan: Gregor had been a Jewish one. Everything about his story left Renny – and her friends from the group who were as open-mouthed as she was – giddy.

Gregor had escaped the destruction of the Vilna Ghetto in 1943 which was an incredible feat on its own. Then he had gathered together a band of other escaped heroes like him and headed for the forests, hell bent on taking revenge. The cost of that had been terrible. Renny's eyes had filled up with tears when Gregor explained how most of his comrades had been caught and executed, and how most of their families – because, as he explained, the Nazis had used reprisals as a method of holding a whole population in fear – had suffered the same fate. Their sacrifice had been selfless and magnificent. Renny had clutched the hands of the girls on either side of her when Gregor said that, and hoped with all her heart that she would have been equally as brave.

'Every time one of us got away, a dozen lives were taken in exchange. Those attacks, on our loved ones and the people who sheltered us, were meant to stop us, to bring us to heel. It fed us. Their blood became our blood. Their sacrifice became our fuel. We bowed our heads and we mourned but we fought on.'

And I would have stood next to you, whatever the cost.

Renny had almost shouted that out loud; her whole body had thrilled with it.

Gregor was a poet, a consummate storyteller. He had brought the resistance inside the walls of their bland meeting room. The earthy dampness of the dirt-covered dugouts. The metallic sulphurous tang of the gunpowder they packed into their bombs. The crunch of leaves and bark and the sweep of the searchlights as the patrols came hunting. And as for the name of the group he had been part of, it was as perfect as he was. *The Avengers*. Renny could see them as easily as she could see Gregor: appearing out of the dark, ready to kill and destroy and to die like a troop of dark angels.

By the end of the talk, her imagination was running at full speed. She was there in the midst of the action. She could feel the branches whipping round her face as she positioned her rifle and took aim. She could hear the hum of the tracks as she fixed her pipe bomb in place and spooled out the wire. She could taste the danger, and it was sweet and addictive and she craved it.

By the time she met Gregor himself at the end of the talk, Renny could barely speak. He was even more electric in close quarters than he was at the lectern, and he was so impressed when she told him that she planned one day to become a fighter for their faith in Israel. When he suggested that the two of them move on to a quieter bar, for a drink, for a more intimate conversation, she would have fallen straight into his arms despite his age, which was closer to Freddy's than hers. If the organiser of the talk hadn't loudly mentioned Gregor's wife as she got up from her chair, she would have gone wherever he suggested. He left then but it didn't matter. His call to action had roared through the room.

'What happened here in Germany during the war wasn't some kind of evil aberration that could never be repeated. The hatred of Jews runs deep, so believe me when I tell you that it could happen again. We have to be vigilant. We have to carry our six million dead beating inside our hearts like a pulse. And when the enemy rears their heads again as they will, we have to be ready to pick up the fight.'

Renny was ready. She was fired up. She sat on the bus to Anhalter Bahnhof barely able to keep still and sprinted down Stresemannstraße towards home on feet made fast by tales of heroism, determined to persuade Freddy that Israel was where she needed to be and that the fight was in her blood.

And then she ran straight into a swastika.

'What in the name of God possessed you? The desk sergeant said you went at the man like a lunatic. Didn't you think for even a second about the danger? He could have had a knife; he could have had accomplices. And as for attacking him, I still can't believe you did that. It's a good job the paint pot you swung at him only caused a concussion and he didn't want his name in the papers or you'd be facing serious charges. What's next, Renny? Where does this end? With you in hospital? Or in a prison cell? I swear that's where you're heading. I love you, I do, but I can't keep cashing in my good name to save yours.'

Freddy had raged on long after Renny had stopped listening. She wished she'd hurt the Nazi far worse than a concussion. He deserved it. He'd carried on daubing the swastika on the wall after she'd shouted at him to stop. He'd laughed at her and called her a communist whore. So she'd picked up his paint tin and launched it at him and down he'd gone with a bellow louder than a stunned bull. If it hadn't been for that, the crowd that his yelling immediately attracted, and the fact that she was still dripping in paint when the police arrived, Renny was certain that she would have got away. And of course the thug hadn't wanted to press charges – he probably had a respectable job and a family. So Freddy had no right to keep ranting and telling her what an idiot she'd been. He should have been proud of her; he should have acknowledged her bravery. If he'd done that, the evening wouldn't have ended in yet another fight.

This one had been terrible. A no-holds-barred shouting match that Renny had woken up feeling ashamed from.

'You're a coward. You didn't have the courage to fight back in Buchenwald and you don't have the courage now. There's

Nazis on the streets, but you don't stop them. There's Nazis in the government, but you don't protest against them either. Instead you shout at me for doing the right thing and you don't even have the balls to rescue your son.'

She hated herself for everything she'd said but especially for that. She knew that standing back while Reiner got his claws into Leo was killing Freddy. She had caught him pacing the flat. She had heard him crying, and cursing, when he thought she was asleep. She knew that waiting for Leo to see sense on his own, or whatever strategy he and Hanni had decided to follow rather than running straight after the boy, was too much for him. She had still used his cowardice, as she kept on calling it, as a weapon.

Which is fine, because he hurt me too.

Except that wasn't true. Renny couldn't even convince herself that his barbs had been on the same level as hers. Freddy had told her that she was naïve, that the tales told by Gregor and his kind to whip up foolish young girls into believing they could take on the world were dangerous. That whatever good the partisans had done had to be weighed up against the horrific reprisals their actions had inflicted on their families and communities and that what Gregor was asking for now, including attacks on right-wing political parties, were crimes not heroic acts. Renny had taken issue with all his opinions but he had said nothing unkind about her in his arguments and his words had glanced off her. Whereas hers...

Renny climbed out of bed, wishing that her mouth didn't always run away with her. Wishing that she had been able to explain how inspiring Gregor was and what it meant to her to have found a group as committed to each other and to the hope of building a better world as she and her friends were. Wishing that he understood how much seeing a swastika on a wall so close to her own street had frightened her.

Which he would have understood if I hadn't started yelling.

Freddy was a good man – Renny knew that. She also knew that the only thing he wanted for her was to be happy. And he had rescued her twice from charges that could have had her sent to prison or kicked out of the university. At the very least she owed him a thank you.

Maybe we could start today better than we ended last night. Maybe we could find a way to talk properly to each other.

It would be a welcome change and it wouldn't take a lot to make it happen. Freddy was, as he frequently pointed out, her only brother and she did love him, even if she forgot to show that most of the time. Which was something she could easily change.

It was still early enough for him to be at home, so Renny wandered into the kitchen and began pulling open cupboards, assembling the ingredients for an apology pancake breakfast. It was only when she started to lay the table that she saw the note.

I'm going to be out of town for a few days working on some leads which will hopefully resolve matters with Reiner. I don't think some time apart will hurt us, Renny – if I'm honest, I think spending more time together at the moment is what's going to do that. You went too far last night. You said some terrible things that I hope you didn't mean and you gave me a hell of a fright. I need you to be safe, Renny. Leo is in danger and, whatever you might think, that's tearing me apart. I can't deal with having you in the same state as well. So, please, for me, could you give those so-called friends of yours a rest for a while? And could you try not to do anything else stupid while I'm gone?

There was love in the note but Renny chose not to see it. What she saw was an overbearing big brother who wasn't going to apologise, who wasn't going to see anything from her point of view. Who couldn't even be bothered to sign his message or tell her where he was going – he'd just delivered his lecture and gone. And left her feeling more alone and misunderstood than she would ever admit.

She was still standing by the table, the note crumpled up in her hand, not knowing whether to throw the coffee pot or cry, when the telephone rang.

'Renny, is that you? Oh thank God, we were certain they'd hold you in jail for this one. Everyone's talking about what you did last night. You're a hero. Will we see you at the meeting room tonight? You have to be there – you have to be part of this.'

It was astonishing how much better she felt within a minute of hearing Joel's voice – it was a testimony to who really mattered. Her friends didn't think she was stupid or naïve. They were proud of her.

'You inspired us. We've been up since dawn working out what to do next.' What higher praise was there than that? And they hadn't called her attack on the thug idiotic like Freddy had; they were calling it *step one*.

'It's what Gregor warned us about, the enemy rearing its head, and we have to listen to him and act. You know that office close to Hallesches Tor, the one everyone says is where the DRP work out of? Where their pamphlets are produced and they co-ordinate their graffiti sprees? Well, we've decided enough is enough. We're going to flush them out of it tonight and silence their poison. We're going to teach them a lesson they won't forget in a hurry.'

Renny went back to the kitchen once she had agreed that she wouldn't miss that opportunity for the world and worked her way through the mound of pancakes she had left warming in the oven.

'We can be the new wave of Avengers. We can ensure their name lives on.'

Her friends had a plan to clean up the streets and she was central to it, no: she was their muse and their beacon. There might not be trains to derail or soldiers to assassinate, but there were still enemies. Men who used paintbrushes and obscenities and twisted vulnerable minds like Leo's with their cheap words.

So-called friends.

Renny finished the last of the coffee and went to her bedroom to dress in the dark clothes Joel had told her to wear. Freddy didn't have a clue. They weren't her friends; they were her family. And unlike the family she was supposed to be part of, they didn't dismiss her. They understood her. They listened to her. They were loyal and they respected her fears and her views. And they didn't disappear on some mystery mission as if her struggles didn't matter. They didn't leave her alone.

CHAPTER 15

13 APRIL 1963, FRANKFURT, WEST GERMANY

Hanni sat in Freddy's office, gripping the edges of her seat, trying to breathe through a chest that was so tight it felt as if it was crushing her. First Leo and now this. The fear and the guilt were suffocating.

This is all my doing. This is because I agreed to wait and let Leo come to his senses when I should have gone straight after him and dragged him out of Reiner's clutches whether he hated me for it or not.

Freddy was talking. She forced herself to listen. It didn't help.

'I am so sorry, Hanni. She was a gentle soul; she didn't deserve this. And before you start blaming yourself, it's not your fault. I should have had her out of the city by now, but her cousin in Munich is away for another few days and Emmi didn't want to go to a hotel until she came back or let me ring the woman and explain. She wouldn't let me "cause a fuss" as she put it. I shouldn't have listened – I should have made her go anyway.'

A gentle soul.

Freddy had described Emmi in the same way on the day

they had visited her at the cottage. That was why he had said 'No, I don't' when Hanni had carefully pointed out that he didn't seem to blame the woman for not doing more to stand up to Reiner, without exactly saying 'the way you can't help but do with me'. And why, or so Hanni had assumed, he had followed that with 'I don't always understand the terrible hold he had on your family, but I'm going to try harder to', which had forced Hanni to stare out of the car window so that he wouldn't see the hope for the two of them in her eyes. And now gentle little Emmi was dead.

She had been found lying at the bottom of the staircase in her cottage with a gashed head and a broken neck and her hands flung out exactly as if she had fallen. The staging could not have been better. It was exactly what they had both feared might happen. Hanni still wasn't about to let Freddy take the blame.

'Don't do that. Don't try to make me feel better. Actions have consequences – Reiner drummed that into me from the day I could understand what the word responsible meant. And my actions have killed her. It was my idea to gather evidence. It was my decision to track her down. What else could that do except lead Reiner to her? The responsibility for what happened to her next – which wasn't a fall or a coincidence – is nobody's but mine. She wasn't safe from the moment we found her.'

Wherever the fault did or didn't lie, they both knew that much was true, even if there was no proof of foul play. The driver Freddy had sent to take Emmi to Munich that morning had become suspicious when she didn't answer his knock. He had roused the housekeeper and, when her voice didn't produce a result, he had broken the door down.

'And destroyed any evidence of an earlier forced entry in the process.' The young deputy stepped back as Freddy glowered. 'Not that I think we need to go looking for signs of that to be honest, sir – it looks like a straightforward accident. There was a loose nail at the top of the stair carpet and the side of the runner had come adrift. She could easily have caught her foot and fallen. And the housekeeper said she wasn't in good health, that she could be unsteady. Obviously we can run an investigation if you want us to, but nobody heard or saw anything strange.'

He tailed off and Freddy dismissed him with a curt, 'Let me think about it.'

'There's no point, is there? There won't be anything to find. You and I know that it's murder and that it's Reiner's doing, but we'll never be able to tie him to it.'

Hanni closed her eyes, overwhelmed by sorrow for a woman who had never been anything other than kind. Emmi had lived a secure, quiet life for twenty-five years and Hanni had destroyed that in three days. Despite everything Reiner had put her through to make her understand that other people got hurt when she defied him, she still hadn't learned her lesson. And now he had Leo and the stakes were impossible.

'I was careless with her too. I should have taken her home with me, or insisted we sent her to Munich straight away. I shouldn't have given Reiner a window to act. This isn't new. This is what he's always done: he strikes round, not directly at me. He shot a guard who sneaked me into Theresienstadt to take pictures so that I wouldn't dare ask another one for help. He put the man who showed me how the town worked on a death train. He kills the people I involve in our fight or the people I care about; he always has – it's his way of inflicting the most pain. And now he's had poor Emmi murdered and it's part of the same pattern. It's a warning for me to get back in my place, to stop chasing him. Or face the next consequence if I don't.'

'And are you telling me that consequence is Leo?'

Freddy's face was calm – any of the officers watching them

through his office window, which most of them were, wouldn't have any idea he was close to breaking point – but his fingers were a knotted mess.

Hanni had to turn away from the glass – her veneer of control was as thin as his and she wasn't used to being the object of scrutiny. Her stomach lurched as she answered.

'Yes, it's Leo. If Reiner wants to hurt me again, he's got the perfect hostage.'

Her voice cracked. Freddy was on his feet, his hands curled into fists, his face so red all the watchers on the other side of the glass instinctively flinched.

'Then what are we doing? To hell with waiting and building a case. We need to go straight to the school now, not to Hadamar. We'll drag Leo out whether he wants to come or not and then I'll wring Reiner's neck.'

It was exactly what Hanni wanted to hear; it was exactly what she wanted to do. She jumped to her feet as well, fired up for a fight that had been coming for years.

I hate you.

The voice was so loud she thought for a moment Freddy had spoken.

I hate you. Take me away from here and I'll run straight back. You'll never see me again.

Leo was in her head, twisted up with anger. Reiner was standing behind him and laughing. The fight was what she wanted but, if she lost that, if she lost her boy...

Hanni sank back into the chair, her whole body shaking.

'Which I want more than anything in the world, but what's changed? We're afraid for Leo, we're both sick with it even when we pretend not to be. We'll be afraid until we get our boy home. But he could still be under Reiner's spell, or furious with me, or...' she stumbled as she brought her real fear out into the light. 'Or what if he isn't physically in danger at the moment, but he will be the moment we go rushing in? I hate this; I hate every second he's away from us. But we still need to be careful. We still need evidence – we still need a charge against Reiner that will stick.'

She waited while Freddy sat down and gave him a moment to breathe.

'I'm right, aren't I? I wish I wasn't but you have to be able to go there with a warrant that holds tight enough to arrest him. We have to make his crimes public to make Leo truly ours again.'

He nodded, but he was still a furious and frightened father.

'What if it's too late, Hanni? What if Reiner has already hurt him?'

She hated the terrified catch in his voice. More than anything she hated how she had failed her son. But she knew her father, and that had to count for something.

'As scared as I am, I don't think he'll have done that. That's what I'm holding on to. He'll be trying to influence him; he'll be trying to turn Leo into one of his boys. Making him his heir would be such a great prize. But physically harming him?' She paused, wishing that she could give Freddy – and herself – the security of *he never would*. She couldn't go that far. 'He hasn't – I'm as sure as I can be of that. But he could. If we blaze in there with no cause except as angry parents and he feels threatened, or he wants to truly hurt me – and he always wants to hurt me – then he might.'

Freddy had to turn away from the window as his face collapsed. Hanni wished that she could go to him and hold him and take back every frightening thing she had just said. But it wasn't the place and it wouldn't be the truth, so all she could do was repeat her inadequate apology.

'I'm so sorry. I'm so very sorry for bringing all this into your life.'

He didn't reply. And he shook his head and left the office when she tried to say it again.

. . .

There was nothing to be done except to set out on the first leg of their journey towards Hadamar. Although, in the light of what had happened to Emmi, they couldn't do that until Freddy had sent a car to the Lietzenseeufer house to check on Greta and her family.

'They're out of the city, in Cochem on holiday according to the neighbours. I've put in a call to the local station to get a man out to their hotel and explain that they could be in danger in Berlin because of an ongoing investigation. Hopefully with that, and with what you told her when she let you into the attic, they'll decide to extend their trip. I'll make sure they're watched either way.'

That didn't put the family entirely out of harm's way but it was a relief and it got Hanni into the car.

The drive from Berlin through East Germany to the border crossing point at Helmstadt was long and tense and filled with rules whose pettiness set their already strained nerves further on edge. They had to surrender the newspaper Freddy had forgotten to remove from his bag as they exited West Berlin in case they dropped it somewhere en route and corrupted an innocent GDR citizen. They had to explain the nature of their trip so many times they began to believe that their story of a visit to relatives in the south of the country was true. The transit route they were ushered onto had only one rest stop with nothing to buy, and the speed limit was fixed at a level which might suit a Trabant but reduced Freddy's new Opel Kapitän to a crawl. By the time they made it through Helmstadt's multiple checks and reached the outskirts of Frankfurt – which they were planning to use as a base for the visit to Hadamar and after if needed – he was complaining his hands would be permanently stuck to the wheel.

None of that was pleasant. What was worse was the

awkwardness sitting between them. There wasn't a safe subject they could touch on. Emmi's death was too raw. What to expect at Hadamar was too fraught. Neither of them could talk about Leo without bringing up Reiner and how helpless they both felt in the face of his hatreds. Hanni didn't want to bring her creeping suspicions about what might have happened to Luise out into the open and when Freddy began a rant about Renny's latest outrage, she immediately closed him down with, 'I'm sorry, I know it's unfair and not the way I should behave, but I can't worry about your sister when my head's all messed up with my own.' She knew it was beneath her but she was too worn out to help herself. And when they found themselves locked into a conversation about how the GDR's collective approach to farming had transformed the landscape, they mutually agreed that perhaps silence might be for the best.

It wasn't. It was a weight. Hanni longed to break it but they were about to check in to another hotel and she couldn't face a repeat of the night they had spent in Weimar, separated by a wall, wondering if she could pluck up the courage to go to him. Wondering if he might come to her. Not when she knew for certain that, this time, neither of them would. How could they when the bond they had started to rebuild at Buchenwald had now stretched to snapping point? When Reiner was with them in every unspoken conversation and turned-away head?

The distance between them grew wider as they drove into Frankfurt and she hadn't the heart to reach over it. When they spoke across each other at the reception desk in a tangle of hastily whipped-up excuses, neither of them tried to hide their relief.

'I'll eat in my room tonight, I think. It's been a long drive. We can work out how we approach Monday's visit tomorrow.'

'We can make a plan for Hadamar tomorrow morning at breakfast. I'm far too tired to think of one now.'

Hanni fussed with her bag and let Freddy go upstairs first.

She went to her room only when she was sure that he would be safely inside his, pretending to herself that it was on a separate floor, that he was nowhere close. That he would fall immediately into a deep sleep and that imagining him lying awake and thinking about her was pointless. She told herself that she would be able to do the same. She got into bed determined to wipe out the day and start fresh. And within ten minutes she was up at the desk and poring over the Hadamar file.

Thank God I didn't do what I was tempted to do at the station and insist on coming here alone.

Hanni grew more grateful for that decision with every page that she turned.

> *Preparations for the killing of patients began in the 1930s with a review of Germany's psychiatric hospitals... Hitler entrusted the implementation of the programme to his personal physician, Karl Brandt, appointing him head of Aktion T4... Patients, including children and newborns, were selected if their future was deemed as 'unfavourable' and they were classified as unsuitable to have children of their own because of the risk of passing on physical or mental conditions that would impact on the Reich's future racial hygiene... both starvation and poisoning methods were used to terminate life before gassing was deemed the more effective method to effectively despatch the large numbers required...*

The report Freddy had commissioned, the one Hanni had been unable to finish in his office, ran to fifteen pages. Its factual tone spared her nothing – it was a horror show. It covered the whole span of the euthanasia programme, from its conception in the far too gentle surroundings of the Tiergarten, to the introduction of the vans used to gas small numbers of patients in the early days and finally to the six industrial-scale gassing centres, including Hadamar, which were established at its peak.

It detailed the comprehensive administration procedures that underpinned the programme, from the registration forms which the parents of children with marked medical conditions had to complete or face prosecution, to the letters of condolence that were sent out to those parents when their loved one succumbed to tuberculosis or pneumonia or one of the dozens of other fabricated natural causes the doctors decided to use. It detailed the conditions and deformities which fell under the T4 remit and meant certain death, including schizophrenia, epilepsy, missing limbs, paralysis and 'imbecility'. It described a process which was widespread, efficient and embedded. Which involved numbers of people both in its implementation and in maintaining its secrecy which went far beyond the handful eventually prosecuted. And a level of precision and order stamped through at each stage of the murders which was chilling.

The efficiency was the only thing in the folder which didn't shock Hanni although every page of it made her feel sick. She had seen how precisely the deportations had been organised in Theresienstadt. She had read the reports from the gas chambers at Auschwitz and knew how rigorously they had been managed. That the Nazis could run a streamlined killing programme didn't surprise her at all. What chilled her to the bone was the way a medical system which should have had care welded immovably to its core had become so horribly twisted.

Doctors and nurses had turned into murderers. No, they had been turned into gods, who, with a cursory examination and a tick or a cross, decided which of their patients should live or die. And most of them, like her father, had continued safely on in the world when the end of the war ended their reign of terror.

Hanni had followed the fates of the men who had drunk

champagne and thrown compliments at her at wartime recep-
tions in Berlin. She knew that Karl Brandt had been executed in
1948 after he had been condemned to death at the Doctors'
Trial and that six others had gone to the gallows with him. She
also knew that most of the staff involved in the experiments and
murders the Nazis had embedded throughout their medical
system had either escaped or walked away without charge. That
had certainly been the case at Hadamar, where more than
fifteen thousand victims had died. According to the report, only
twenty-five of the huge team working there had been brought to
trial. Those charged, including the chief physician and the head
nurse – who was still injecting patients with the lethal doses of
morphine she'd saved up as the Allies arrived at the door – had
been convicted but, as far as Hanni could see, no one could
claim justice had been done. Most of those imprisoned had
been released less than ten years into their sentences.

Hanni finally put the folder down when she came to the
section headed 'Healthy Jewish Children Killed at the Facility'.
She couldn't read it. She couldn't bear the thought of Freddy
reading it, although she knew that he would have done.

*And he would have imagined Renny dying among them, the
way he imagined her death so many times in the years before we
found her. He would have pictured her lying in one of the beds,
waiting for the needle that would end her life, and the darkness
that's supposed to be fading would have caught him back in its
grip.*

Hanni climbed back under the covers but she could see the
beds too, although she was desperately trying not to see Luise
tucked into one of them. Of all the grim roads Reiner had led
her down in the past, this one was personal. And this one was
lined with victims whose suffering – like the old and the abandoned in Theresienstadt – she couldn't shake. The Reich had
stripped so many people of their normal lives and rendered
them helpless and then they had reached down further again,

their fingers stretching to scoop up the most vulnerable and the damaged. The children and adults who deserved everyone's love and care, who had a value to their families if not to the Reich. Who mattered.

Who died because they weren't perfect.

The evidence was lining up; the clues were too strong to ignore. She didn't want to follow them.

Nothing was allowed to get in the way of his ambition.

That was true in so many ways, but surely even Reiner had a point beyond which he wouldn't go? Hanni needed to believe that. She needed all the suspicions crowding her head to be wrong. What she wanted was a scarlet fever epidemic that had swept through Berlin and the sad but explainable death of a sickly little girl. For her mother to have been maddened by grief and for Emmi's memory to be muddled or clouded by hatred for a man who had been cruel and uncaring and frightening.

But not a man who would arrange his own child's death, not a father capable of that.

It was the first time Hanni had let that thought move out of the dark edges of her brain. A deliberate end to Luise's short life was where the clues she was so unnerved by were pointing and Hanni knew better than most how to put clues together, how to spot the fine details. And yet...

Reiner had been an affectionate father to the little girl. He had held Luise in his arms, he had carried her on his shoulders. There were pictures in the photograph albums she had recovered in the attic of him smiling at his daughter as she crawled across the lawn towards him. There were others of Luise as a toddler sitting grinning on his knee. Hanni could remember her mother boasting to her friends about how good Reiner was with the baby. Surely she hadn't imagined that?

The sky was shifting from navy to indigo by the time her eyelids finally closed, and when she woke, fuzzy from lack of sleep and the fevered dreams that had swamped the few hours' rest she had managed, her first waking thought was the same as her last.

Thank God I don't have to face whatever is coming alone. Thank God Freddy will be there with me.

Hadamar was the answer; Luise's death was Reiner's Achilles' heel. Hanni had sensed that from the moment she'd found the hospital's name scrawled in Freddy's notes and matched the T4 programme with Luca's sickening allegations. Emmi's recollections and the lies surrounding Luise's burial had deepened her fears. Hadamar held the answer to what had happened to her sister; Hadamar held the trap that would catch Reiner. Hadamar was waiting.

And it's the last place I want to go.

CHAPTER 16

Renny couldn't help but be disappointed. Only three of them had turned up to the special meeting in the end: herself, Joel and David, who was new to the group and had an intensity about him that was attractive to Renny but unnerving apparently to most of the others. The turnout was disappointing but Renny was determined not to let the low numbers dampen her enthusiasm.

'One brave man who says no is worth far more than a dozen who hang their heads and obey.'

Gregor had said that during his speech and it had sounded to Renny – like everything Gregor said, whatever Freddy thought – like poetry. And it worked on the boys tonight: when she reminded David and Joel that they were following in Gregor's footsteps, they both stood a few inches taller.

Does it really sound like a poem? Or is that the voice of a man who likes to pass judgement?

Renny pulled her coat tighter across her body so that the others would think it was the cold wind whipping across the canal that was making her shiver rather than the doubts currently whispering their way into her head. Freddy hadn't been half as impressed as Joel and David by Gregor's words. When she'd retold her hero's stories to Freddy, he had immediately pulled them apart.

Well done to him for escaping and fighting back. I don't doubt he was brave, but resisting like that wasn't an option in Buchenwald, Renny, whatever he might like you to think. Resistance of any kind there was impossible. One disobeyed order or one wrong step meant a bullet; most things there meant a bullet. And if we were hanging our heads it's not because we were cowards, it was because we didn't want to be noticed, because we were trying to stay alive and sane in conditions you and your friends can't possibly imagine. Which took a bravery all of its own, whatever your sainted Gregor might think.

Freddy had shouted a lot during the fight that had consumed them both the night before but he hadn't shouted that bit. Renny would have preferred it if he had. The quiet way he had spoken and the sad slump of his shoulders had given his words a far stronger force than a raised voice would have done. And the heartfelt 'Don't believe him too easily about violence being the only choice: sometimes the bravest person is the one who puts down the gun or the bomb to protect the lives of the people he loves' which had followed. That in particular had played on her mind all day as she waited for the evening and Joel's promised direct action, even though she'd tried to tune Freddy's warnings out.

She wasn't feeling as confident as she had been about *direct action* either now that she was in place under the railway arch. That phrase had lost its sparkle when she realised that there were only the two boys waiting in the meeting room, rather than the lively crowd she had expected. She wished she'd taken the chance then to ask a few more questions about what exactly *flush them out* meant and where everyone else was, rather than delighting in the idea of being some kind of resistance goddess. She hadn't. And she hadn't been able to conceal her shock when Joel removed the cloth in the corner that he kept grinning at and shared the actual plan. Whatever she thought *direct action* meant, it hadn't included a stock of liquid-filled bottles with rags stuffed in their necks. Her horrified 'What on earth are they for?' had not gone down well. Joel had spoken to her as if she was an idiot.

'For the fight, what do you think? We can hardly win without weapons. Luckily David was able to source some weed-killer from his grandfather's shed and he's made these for us, which deserves a thank you, not your schoolmarm's pinched face. They're the simplest thing in the world to use. All you need to do is light a match and take aim and, to borrow another line from Gregor, *whoosh* and up the whole place will go.'

He had waited then, nodding at David as if she was supposed to clap or cheer him. Renny had managed to loosen her expression and smile but she couldn't speak. She had packed her share of the bottles into the bag he produced because she didn't know what else to do – the boys had stared at her as if she was about to fail an important test and she didn't want to disappoint them – or herself. And then she had followed the two of them onto the bus, copying the distance they kept from each other, sitting rigid as a statue with the bag full of weapons on her lap until it pulled up at Hallesches Tor and Joel nodded to her to get off. He had flicked his hand to a spot underneath the elevated trainline which dominated the area; she had trotted off like a good girl. Now she couldn't get *we don't know what we're doing* out of her head.

The boys were behaving as if they were in a spy film, and nothing about the proposed attack on the DRP office felt right. Renny curled into the metal arch under the track, hoping that there would be a sudden rush of people and the plan would unravel. She was out of luck. Twenty minutes had passed without anyone coming down the stairs from the station and the area had started to take on the deserted air Joel had said was essential before they could make a move.

Renny dug her hands deeper into her pockets and wished she had the nerve to run up the steps and away before the last train left. Never mind what was coming – this wasn't an area of Berlin that she liked. Too many of the buildings were empty or half-demolished, and stretches of it seemed to have been turned into a parking lot for trailers and trucks. It dawned on her that, if they could hide in it so easily, so could the kind of men who still wanted to march behind swastikas. It was one thing stumbling over a vandal and acting on instinct, but deliberately setting out to attack their premises in a section of the city they possibly controlled? Renny suddenly felt very small.

'Come on. There's no one around – this is it. It's time to get into position.'

Joel had appeared at her side without her noticing him coming. David was a few paces to the left. Both of them were dressed completely in black, the same as Renny. Joel's knitted hat was pulled down so low over his face she was surprised he could see. Perhaps he had sensed she was wavering because he put his hand on her arm and smiled.

'I'm proud of you, Renny; we both are. You're the only girl I know who'd have the courage to do this. Wait till Gregor hears what you helped us to carry out – he'll spread tales of your courage all the way to Jerusalem.'

Jerusalem.

The word worked on her like magic. Freddy disappeared from her head. Doubt disappeared from her head. They did know what they were doing and it did matter. The DRP were polluting the streets; they were creating a new climate of fear. Their offices and their leaflets and their nasty propaganda machinery deserved to go up in flames.

Renny grinned back at Joel. She picked up the bag of fire-bombs as easily as if they were feathers and ran across the street behind the boys, zig-zagging to avoid the street lights in the same way that they did. This wasn't pretend or playing at being in the movies. This was far more daring than yelling at politicians or swinging a paint can. This was the kind of action Mossad agents would take.

'It's that one. As far as we know they use the ground and the first floors.'

The building was thin and rickety looking, sandwiched between a taller one covered in scaffolding and one sealed up ready for demolition. It looked exactly like the kind of place where vermin would flourish.

'We need to spread ourselves around so that we can target the main windows on both sides.'

Joel was already moving to the left; David had slipped to the right but Renny's heart was suddenly in her mouth and her feet wouldn't follow them.

'Wait.'

Her voice bounced round the empty street, stopping both the boys who immediately waved their hands at her to signal for quiet. Renny dropped her voice as low as she dared, but it was vital that they heard her.

'Look up there. There's a light on in the middle office on the first floor.'

Joel frowned and shrugged. 'So what?'

Renny thought she had misheard him. She stared from him to the bottle he was already holding at the ready. David hadn't come back when she called, although she was certain he'd heard her concern. He was crouched at the far side of the building, swinging his arm as if he was testing his weapon's weight. She tried again, speaking more slowly in case they hadn't understood what she meant.

'If there's a light on, then surely there could be people inside. People who will get hurt if we throw burning bottles. You said it would be empty.'

Joel shook his head. 'I didn't. That might be what you heard, but it's definitely not what I said.'

Renny's throat went dry; her hands started to sweat. He had said that, surely? But then her brain switched back on and she realised that he hadn't said empty at all. He had talked about pamphlets and typewriters and destroying the work that went on in the office. He hadn't talked about the DRP members engaged in that work and Renny hadn't asked about them. She had assumed they would be gone by the time their gang arrived, that they weren't the target. And now he was staring at her as if she was the one in the wrong.

'Joel, please, you can't be serious. You can't throw firebombs into a building when you know it's occupied, when you could hurt or even kill somebody inside it.'

Joel had looked at her intently many times before. There had been an occasion or two, after meetings or parties when those looks had acted on them both like magnets and sent them into dark corners where nobody cared how passionate their kisses were. She was used to seeing admiration in his eyes. Now his face was full of contempt.

'Really, is that what you are? Another coward who can talk about winning the fight but not step up and act when it counts? That's disappointing, Renny; that's really disappointing.'

He stepped back. He glanced over at David and he nodded.

'You can't do it.'

But the boys lit their matches and they raised their arms and the bottles swooped up in a perfect arc of flame, and Renny realised far too late that they could.

The smoke was at ceiling height, rolling round the top of the walls and down the narrow staircase in a grey wave, thickening the darkness in the hallway.

'Is there anybody up there?'

There wasn't an answer at first, or not one Renny could hear above the crackling and popping sounds jumping out from the walls and the wood panelling lining the hallway. The first two firebombs had shattered the side windows on the upper floor of the building, sending a shower of glass and sparks onto the pavement below. Seconds later a scream had rung out which should have stopped Joel and David reaching back into their bags for another bottle. It hadn't.

'Stop it, do you hear me? Stop it!'

Renny had grabbed for Joel's arm as he swung again, knocking him off balance and his missile off course. The bottle fell with a crash into a patch of dry wasteland and the lighted rag fizzled out.

'What are you doing? Are you mad?'

He had pushed her away. He had another bomb in his hand and the matches out ready before she could grab the bag. He wasn't listening to the shouts pouring from the window above; he wasn't going to listen to her. He wasn't going to stop no matter how much she yelled. So Renny had done the only thing she could think of to do: she had run towards the burning building and crashed in through the front door, praying that Joel and David wouldn't throw any more bombs if she was inside. In the barely a minute that blind run had taken, there hadn't been another shower of glass, but it was clear from the smoke and the smell that the fire had taken hold without any boost from the boys.

'Is there anybody up there?'

The first answering 'Yes' was faint, the second was stronger and the 'Hurry, for God's sake, I need help' which followed was higher-pitched and terrified.

The smoke had begun climbing down the walls, stretching out towards the hall.

Renny instinctively dropped into a crouch, pulled off her jacket and wrapped it round her nose and mouth. Her body was immediately bathed in sweat. She inched forward, peering through the gloom, trying to see where the fire was coming from. And then she put her hand on the banister and jumped back with the shock – it was hot to the touch and the wood shivered and hissed, as if a river of flame ran through it. That was the moment when Renny stopped thinking. She leapt up the stairs two at a time and plunged into a corridor whose walls danced in the smoke as if they were swelling, hurtling towards the sound of the voice.

'He fell rushing to the window and I can't move him on my own – he's too heavy.'

The girl was kneeling beside the body of a much bigger man. His eyes were closed and his skin was grey, but his chest was moving, and as the smoke swirled closer, he let out a rattling breath.

'You take his legs and I'll take his arms and we'll drag him.'

There were no flames in the room yet, but the crack of timber from left and right and the taste of soot in Renny's mouth said it was eating its way towards them. There was no time to waste checking if the man had injuries which would worsen if they moved him: not moving him could only have one outcome. Luckily his companion hadn't succumbed to panic and didn't need to be told what to do twice.

'On three.'

Renny had never counted so fast. They got him through the door with muscles powered by adrenaline; they got him to the top of the stairs. The only light in the corridor now was an orange glow Renny didn't dare look at and the staircase was a wavering drop. Her shoulders tore, her eyes streamed. She stepped onto the first stair and almost toppled backwards as the man's weight tipped forward and threw her off balance.

'Drop his legs; come round here. We'll have to brace ourselves against the wall and the banister and try and pull him down that way.'

It worked for a moment or two, until the heat pushed Renny off the wood and the girl stumbled on the loose carpet and they both lost hold. The crunch as their cargo hit the floor below them was sickening.

'Run!'

They tumbled down after the man's body as the flames broke through the door nearest the staircase in a roar. Renny had no idea how they got him outside, or if he had survived the fall or their rough handling. She rolled onto the pavement, sucking the air into her screaming lungs, coughing so hard she thought her ribs would break. The girl folded into a ball beside her was doing the same.

'Thank God you saw what was happening. Who would do such a terrible thing? Didn't they hear us yell?'

Renny clambered onto her knees. There was no sign of Joel or David but the bag containing the firebombs which she had dropped when she ran into the house was still lying there. *I can't be here* pounded through her head as fast as her pulse. She tried to take a breath deep enough for her to get up and run but her body refused to co-operate. When she attempted to stand, she was back on her knees within seconds.

'Someone must have seen the flames – listen: help's coming.'

The sirens were screaming so loudly they could only be a block away. The girl had crawled over to the man who was groaning. Renny tried to get up again, but her head was spinning and the pain where she had wrenched her right shoulder and blistered her hands was too big to get past.

'I have to go – I can't be here when they come.'

The words came out of her mouth muddled with smoke and soot and making no sense. Her eyes smarted as though someone had rubbed grit in them. She was so tired. Her eyes began closing at the same moment somebody shouted, 'Don't go to sleep – stay with me!' It was easier not to.

The blue lights which had screamed to a halt a few feet

away faded. The street and the flames whose flare had turned the sky scarlet faded too. It was a struggle to breathe and Renny didn't want to make the effort when every attempt made her chest scream.

When all she wanted to do was let go.

CHAPTER 17

14–15 APRIL 1963, HADAMAR, WEST GERMANY

When Freddy appeared in the breakfast room on Sunday morning, his face was as white as the starched and stretched tablecloth and he looked as if he had slept, or not slept, in his suit.

Hanni pushed away the Hadamar file she had been planning to discuss with him. She stared at the sticky *Franzbrötchen* she had ordered because it was Leo's favourite and now couldn't eat and pushed that away too. She reached for the coffee pot instead.

'Are you all right? Has something happened?' She almost dropped the pot as her heart constricted. 'It's not Leo is it?'

'No, it's not Leo.'

He lit a cigarette and gulped down the coffee as fast as Hanni could pour it.

'It's Renny – she's been up to trouble again and this time she's in hospital. I got a call from the station to tell me in the early hours. There was a firebomb attack on a DRP office in Berlin last night and I can't work out if she was the ringleader of it or the hero who saved a man's life. Or – from the way she was dressed and the fact she knew what was in the bottles the police found at the scene – maybe both. But she's got smoke inhalation and burns to her hands, and from the sound of the way the building went up, she's lucky she wasn't killed.'

Hanni put her own cup down before the contents spilled over. Then, without second-guessing what she was doing or fretting over what it might imply, she wrapped her hands tightly around his. She was suddenly horribly aware of how selfish she had been in the car when he had tried to confide in her about Renny's increasingly erratic behaviour. She was determined to do better than that now.

'Then you have to go back straight away, Freddy – that's not up for discussion. Renny's well-being is far more important than whatever lead we're chasing here.'

His breathing settled for the first time since he had sat down, although his shoulders stayed hunched.

'I know I do, and I knew you'd understand so I've made the arrangements to go out on the first plane. But I still feel terrible for leaving you. And I don't know what to do with her anymore, Hanni, I really don't. It's one thing to have a cause and be passionate about it, but she seems to have lost all sense of perspective. She sees one swastika daubed on a wall and she thinks we're five minutes away from a second Holocaust.'

'What do you mean, a swastika? What have I missed?'

His face drooped. 'It was what I was trying to tell you before. This crowd she runs with used to be good kids but now they're getting more... militant for want of a better word. It's gone beyond meetings and hurling abuse at politicians they don't like, which is how she's filled most weekends. The other night she attacked a man physically and the only thing she was sorry for was that she hadn't inflicted more damage on him.'

He ran through the story of the paint pot and Renny's arrest, leaving Hanni mortified at how cavalier she had been when she had dismissed Renny's problems as being less important than her fears about Luise. And at how easily she had taken her eyes off Freddy's complicated relationship with his sister.

Freddy downed another coffee he didn't need and sighed so deeply the guests at the next table jumped. 'And now I'm worn out and I've run out of ideas about how to tackle her, so if you've got any thoughts on that, this would be the time to pitch in.'

'I'm so sorry.' Hanni said it again as he shook his head. 'I mean it, Freddy. I didn't realise how dangerously she was behaving or how worried you were and I should have done. Renny and I might not be close but I do care what happens to her.'

Might not be close was an understatement – most of the time they prowled round each other as Hanni waited for Renny to strike and Renny bristled with the longing to do it. But *care* was true. Care was what Hanni had thought would define their relationship when she first met the unnervingly self-contained little girl who turned out to be Freddy's long-lost sister. They had bonded over Renny's talent for photography. Hanni had imagined a life in which she would be, if not a stand-in for the child's mother, at least a loving older sister. Until Reiner ruined everything and turned Hanni into a monster. Since then, she had watched from a distance as the girl had grown more and more troubled. Then, after Renny had broken Leo's faith in his family, she had stopped watching at all.

And I left Freddy with too big a burden to carry. So I can't keep pretending I've nothing to do with what happens between them anymore.

Unfortunately, the thoughts she had wouldn't be the ones Freddy wanted to hear. He, however, was waiting and desperate, so there was nothing to be done but tell him anyway.

'Does Renny still want to go and live in Israel?'

Freddy nodded. 'It's all she wants; it's all she talks about. Or it is when she's not having a go at me for being a failed Jew and a failed brother.'

Hanni took a deep breath, conscious not only of how hurt and worried he was but that she was about to step onto shaky ground.

'Okay. Don't get upset and don't dismiss what I'm going to say, but do you think that maybe it's time to let her?'

She held his hands tighter as he frowned and spoke too quickly for him to interrupt.

'I'm not saying this lightly, or because I'm still angry with her and want her gone, although I wouldn't blame you for thinking that. But she's so unhappy and she has been for such a long time, and I don't see how that will change unless you really listen to what she's asking you for, instead of being afraid of it. And if you think about it, your situation with her is not so different from where we are with Leo. You said we couldn't keep telling him how terrible Reiner is, that he has to learn the truth in his own way, and you were right. Renny thinks Germany is the wrong place for her and that Israel is paradise. She won't stop thinking that or fighting you when you tell her that she's wrong, so maybe it's time to let her find out if it's true.'

The catch in his voice when he replied, and the fact that he didn't argue, told Hanni that he had already been up and down that path a dozen times since the station called.

'I can't lose her. I didn't go searching for her just to lose her all over again.'

The pain ran so deep in him, all Hanni wanted to do was soothe it away. But Renny's pain ran deep too.

'You won't. If you let her go and you let her see that you support her and that you trust her not to disappear from your life, then you won't.'

Whether it was because of the concern that rang through her voice, or because Freddy had already come to the same conclusion and simply needed reassurance that it was the right one, her words struck home. And unleashed a depth of emotion in him that she hadn't seen in years.

Before she could pull back or ask what he was doing, Freddy suddenly twisted his hands around so that they were gripping hers. He looked up and stared at her as if she was the safe harbour he'd been searching for. The longing in his eyes made her gasp.

'You always have the right answer and you know me better than anyone ever could. Oh God, Hanni, why can't we sort this out? Why do we keep getting knocked back when there's things I should have—'

Freddy didn't get any further. Wherever *should have* was going was cut short by the hotel manager appearing in a flurry at their table.

'A car is waiting to take you to the airport, Inspector, and a plane ticket is arranged. But you will need to leave at once if you are going to make the Berlin flight.'

Freddy dropped her hands. Hanni shook away his confused apologies with an 'It's fine – it will wait.' She really hoped that was true.

'I've left you the Opel. The keys are with reception.'

He hesitated. She had a feeling that he would have been able to express himself more easily if their hands had still been entwined.

'I'm not trying to tell you what to do, and I know there's no point in asking you not to go to Hadamar tomorrow as we planned. But will you promise that if you do discover something there, you won't act on it straight away? You won't go to the school and confront Reiner without me? I'll do my best to get back here in a few days; I'll be on the end of a telephone. I'll leave a lot more happily if I know you'll look after yourself when I'm gone.'

The manager coughed and looked at his watch, forcing Freddy to his feet.

'Hanni, did you hear what I said?'

She had heard him but she couldn't make promises she

wasn't certain she could keep. And she couldn't lie to him either. So she simply nodded, and she let him take what he needed from that.

The House of the Shutters.

That was the name which, according to Freddy's report, the locals had bestowed on the hospital during the war. Hanni drove along the road which led the short distance from the sleepy town of Hadamar and up the gentle incline of the Mönchsberg hill. She was exhausted from a sleepless night and spinning all kinds of horrors around Hadamar's name and the stories she had read about the facility. She emerged from the treeline expecting to find impenetrable granite walls and grey mists gathering around brooding towers. She was greeted instead by a square, solid and utterly unremarkable building sporting a raft of windows whose panes, rather than being screened off from the world, shimmered in the sunlight. It looked not unlike the older parts of the Charité Hospital which Hanni had regularly passed by without a second glance in Berlin. And there wasn't a scrap of comfort to be found in that.

The locals knew what was happening here. The shutters weren't visible things; they were the secrets everyone colluded in.

She was outside a euthanasia centre which had killed thousands of its patients and hadn't been torn down. That still functioned as a working psychiatric hospital.

Hanni parked the car a little way from the gates and turned off the engine. She wasn't ready to go inside and be greeted by a place that had apparently so easily washed off its history. She had come to confront what it had been, in the hope that old staff had returned, old staff she needed to speak to. She had to be prepared for whoever and whatever she met.

She closed her eyes and shut out the blossom-decked trees and the manicured lawns. She forced herself to see the hospital as it had been in the middle years of the war when its killing machinery was working at maximum capacity. When the grey buses drove twice a day along the road where she was sitting, bringing their victims from the smaller hospitals and nursing homes that fed into Hadamar. When the orderlies led their charges out of their seats and down the narrow fenced-in path not to the security of warm wards and comfy beds but to the basement and into a fake shower room where the gas was already plumbed into the pipes and lying in wait. When the chimney poured out its smoke and its acrid smells down onto the village and the residents there were the ones who shuttered their windows. It was a hateful thing to imagine – the images made her skin crawl and her eyes smart, but she couldn't not see them; too many people had done that. Hadamar had torn down its Keep Away signs and gone on with its life. Its wartime inmates hadn't had that luxury.

Hanni let the images spool. She gave herself the time she needed to consider the place, and the time she needed to steady her jagged nerves once that was done. Then she pressed the admissions button and drove through the gates. She had deliberately not called ahead – she hadn't wanted to risk a refusal, or alert anyone to her movements after what had happened to Emmi. She didn't know whether the relatives of those who had suffered inside the hospital's walls received a sympathetic hearing, or if any still came at all. And she hadn't concocted a cover story to explain her arrival because that would only get in the way. When the receptionist sitting behind her protective barrier asked Hanni what her business was and told her in the same breath that there was no patient visiting unless she had completed the correct forms, Hanni simply told her the truth.

'I believe that my little sister was brought here in December 1938 by my father, who was a high-ranking officer in the SS, and that she died here. I would like to talk to somebody about that please.'

The receptionist stopped being disinterested; a phone call was instantly placed. A few moments later Hanni was ushered into the office of Professor Katzmann, the hospital's director, and seated in a chair opposite his overly grand desk by a secretary who kept offering her coffee Hanni didn't want. The woman, who was markedly older than her boss, withdrew after Hanni's second refusal, but she left the door between her office and his slightly open. That set Hanni immediately on edge. She had stayed in her hotel room for the whole of Sunday once Freddy had left because she couldn't shake the idea that Reiner might have sent his boys after them into Frankfurt. She had no intention of trusting anyone at the hospital more than she had to.

'Can we close that? I'd rather she wasn't able to listen to what I have to say.'

The professor smiled and shrugged as if the matter was out of his hands. 'It's protocol, nothing more. Sometimes the visitors and the patients who I interview in here can be, well, a little upset is probably the best way to put it and not always in control of what they are saying or hearing. The door is kept open so that we both feel secure, and Frau Pelzer is the soul of discretion.'

He was managing her. He reminded her of Captain Walker, the American officer who had run public relations for the air force in the days of the Berlin Strangler – not easy to work around and well-versed in how to protect his organisation.

With no other choice, Hanni stopped looking to see if the secretary was placing the phone call that would betray her and launched into her story, running through the events leading up to her visit to Hadamar as concisely as she could.

The director sat perfectly still. He didn't react while she spoke, or when she paused to gather herself up before she explained her reason for coming, in the shocked – or sympathetic – way Hanni had expected. Her senses were immediately back on alert. *What if he's Reiner's man?* flashed through her head. It was a possibility. It wasn't the first time she had feared it might be the case. All she could hope was that, if Reiner really was on her tail the way that she suspected, she was still a few paces ahead. She took a deep breath and ploughed on.

'This is the difficult bit. It's not easy to say but there is very little point in me trying to sugar-coat or hide it given that I need your help. We know that the story of a scarlet fever epidemic in Berlin at that time is untrue. We also know my father was here on the tenth of December 1938 which is, as I said, the day Luise died. The seizures my sister suffered from were getting substantially worse by that point and...' She hesitated and decided not to use the word *evil* even though it was on the tip of her tongue. 'He was an ambitious man who wouldn't allow anything to threaten his Party standing. He's still an ambitious man now. But something happened here, Professor Katzmann, which caused my sister's death – I'm certain of it. I know Hadamar's history; I know what became common practice in this place during the war. I think Luise was one of its earliest victims, and I'm here to find out if that suspicion is true.'

It was the first time she had voiced that allegation out loud and it shook her, but not him. From the just-concerned-enough expression on his face and his soothing tone, she suspected it wasn't the first time Katzmann had heard a charge like it.

'That must have been a difficult episode in your life to relate, Frau Schlüssel. It clearly remains a source of great sorrow, as unexplained deaths so often do. But can I ask you why you have decided to make this journey and open this line of enquiry now? After so many years, when so much information has been lost and so many answers will simply never be found. Isn't it better to let the past rest?'

'For you perhaps.'

He flinched at that, but Hanni hadn't come to Hadamar to make its director feel comfortable.

'You are too young to have worked here in the thirties and forties, I can see that. Nothing that went on before your time here is your fault and I assume that part of your remit is building this hospital a better reputation. I don't have an issue with that, providing better doesn't mean that everything that it was is now hidden. I understand that there is little chance of finding anything in the records – even if there were complete ones, they're never the places where my father appears. But I was hoping that there might be other staff members, nurses perhaps or orderlies, who worked here when Hadamar was a very different sort of hospital. Who might remember that night and be willing to share their memories with me, if you could arrange for me to talk to them.'

His face shifted then. The smile disappeared. His tone became brisk.

'My staff are not here to be quizzed about events that occurred under a regime that demanded impossible things of the people caught under it. Even I don't question their backgrounds. If some of them did serve here in the war and have found employment in the wards once again, that is their business. I very much doubt anyone walked away from those days without scars. And I am sorry, but I don't think you have your facts as straight as you think you do. It is true that Hadamar became a euthanasia facility. Young or not, I'm well aware of that. But its T4 work began in 1939 after the war started and it dealt with adults, not children. Whoever your father was then or is now, and why he came here in 1938, is not something I can help you with. It's also unlikely to have had anything to do with that unfortunate programme. I am sorry. As difficult as this is, I'm afraid I don't have any more time to give you today.'

He put out his hand. She saw that he was fully expecting her to shake it and go. But Hanni wasn't ready to leave and, unlike Katzmann, she wasn't in the mood to be businesslike and efficient. She was furious. He was using the language of avoidance, as if *caught up* removed responsibility. He wanted to put the past to rest while it was still shifting. To settle certainties around it when there were no such certainties to be had. Once she started to point that out to him, she couldn't stop.

'Perhaps you need to investigate your place of work in a little more depth. This wasn't a solely adult facility, not that that would make its crimes any better. There were thousands of children poisoned and starved to death here under the remit of that *unfortunate programme*. For no reason except that the regime considered them to be what they termed *useless eaters*. And there were Jewish children murdered in this hospital who had nothing wrong with them except for their so-called "bad blood". And maybe you don't know, but I do, that in its worst days, when it was known as a "wild" centre because of the scale of the killings, Hadamar's patients didn't even get the most basic medical examination before the morphine went in. And throwing a date at me makes no difference. The Nazis never rolled out a programme before it was well-tested, so an official start in 1939, or 1940 or whenever you choose to pitch it, means nothing. And before you ask me how I know all this, it's because, unlike you, I've done my research and made it my business to. As for who my father is, well, you might know his name. It's Emil Foss. Have you heard of him?'

Katzmann's eyebrows shot up so fast the answer was obvious.

Hanni nodded. 'I thought you might have. He's another one with a good eye for public relations. The bit you're missing, however, is that in 1938 he wasn't Emil, he was SS Obergrup-penführer Reiner Foss and he was a close associate of Karl Brandt.' She nodded again as that name also registered. 'So you have done some investigating. My father ruined countless lives, Professor, and if the graduates of his despicable schools win the power he wants for them, he'll ruin countless more. I've had nearly twenty years to stop that and I've failed. And now he has my son under his control and that terrifies me. I have come to you because the only way I can destroy him is by finding a crime I can directly tie him to. I think that crime is here, at Hadamar. So, with or without your help, I'm going to keep digging until I can bring that into the light.'

She stopped, her chest heaving, convinced that her passion had won him over. Katzmann's face was now the ashen shade it should have been when she had described Luise's illness and its possible consequences; when she had used the hateful phrase 'useless eaters'. She could see him flipping through what he knew about the hospital, wondering what he had too carelessly overlooked, hopefully examining his conscience. She sat forward, waiting for him to recant and make a telephone call. Waiting for him to present her with a list of names of the staff members who could help her sift suspicion from truth. She really believed it would happen. Until Katzmann straightened his tie and slipped his professional mask back on.

'I am sorry for your loss, Frau Schlüssel – it clearly has affected you very deeply. But as I have already said, these events you are describing occurred a long time ago, in the middle of a war which, in my opinion, would be better left in the past where it belongs. My duty is to what Hadamar is now, not to what it was then. I hope you find your answers, I do, but they will be found without and not with my help.'

He stood up. He didn't put out his hand again for Hanni to shake it; instead he waved her to the door and left her no option but to get up and go through it. And then he closed it behind her with a sharp snap.

'Drink this.'

Hanni grabbed the glass that appeared in front of her and swallowed a mouthful of its contents, immediately bursting into a coughing fit as the water she had expected to drink turned into brandy. The secretary glanced across at the closed door, took Hanni's elbow and steered her into the corridor.

'You have to go. He'll come and check in a moment that you've left and I don't need another lecture from him about how our focus has to be on the future. Or to lose this job given how few there are in the area. He's not a bad man but he hates to be lectured, which you were definitely doing. And he's paid to do a job he's also determined to hang on to, which means that the past tends to be a carefully controlled country round here. You can't just go blundering through it – you have to pick your way with more care.'

Hanni stopped at the top of the stairs as the meaning of Frau Pelzer's words hit her. 'You know something, don't you? You heard what I said in there and you know something.'

'Perhaps. I'm not sure.'

She gestured to Hanni to go quickly down the stairs as the door opened behind them and the professor began calling her name.

'It was the date that stuck with me – December the tenth. It's the same night my brother left his employment here. When a part of him broke that's never been fixed.'

The admission – and the way it was phrased – was the last thing Hanni had expected but she didn't have a chance to ask questions. Katzmann appeared in the doorway and Frau Pelzer's voice turned instantly as brisk as his.

'If you really feel that you can't make the drive back to Frankfurt, madam, there is a hotel in the village – The Swan – which may have a room. I suggest that you try there.'

As she turned away and nodded politely at the director, she suddenly squeezed Hanni's arm. The gesture was over and done in a second but it left Hanni calm enough to do as she was asked and walk away. And with a sense that, despite Katzmann's refusal to help, the lifeline she was looking for might actually be coming.

.   .   .

'I don't know if he will talk to you and I haven't asked him in case he refused.'

Frau Pelzer sat down on a chair in the hotel's deserted restaurant and picked up the conversation where they had left it, as seamlessly as if Hanni hadn't been shredding her finger-nails for the last two hours.

'My brother isn't a well man, Frau Schlüssel – it's important that you know that. The war and the years since have not been kind to him. What I said about the way he left Hadamar with a part of him broken must have sounded a little dramatic, but it's the only way I can describe it. Tobias never went back there after that night. His life completely changed. He began drinking and, when he was badly injured on the Eastern Front, he began drinking more. He's a quiet drunk, not a belligerent one, but he's not at ease with the world and I can't predict how he will react when he meets you. But I think, for both your sakes, meeting with him is worth a try.'

The picture she was painting wasn't a hopeful one but Hanni did her best to ignore that.

'Has he told you anything about what happened to upset him the way you've described?'

The older woman shook her head. 'Barely a thing. He was in a very bad state, in the same kind of shock he was in when he came home from the fighting. He wouldn't go back to work. He told me to send a message to the hospital to say he was leaving the area. After the war he turned himself into a recluse and, with everything else that happened to him, I never had the heart to bring up the subject. I also didn't know if he would dare talk about it. Perhaps you don't know this, but the staff who worked at Hadamar then were forced to sign an oath of silence, and they were told that if they broke it, they would be sent to a concentration camp. That alone would have kept him quiet, but there was also a man there that night who terrified him. Who Tobias said – before he panicked and refused to say anything else – was evil. I've never forgotten the way he said that. And it resonated with the way you described your father today.'

She got to her feet, moving far more slowly than she had when she sat down.

'I've never been able to help my brother, Frau Schlüssel, although I've longed to. Maybe if you can get him to talk, it will take some of the burden he carries from him. All I ask is that you are patient and gentle and don't push him if he lets you down.'

The single-storey house she led Hanni to was on the edge of the village and it was a sad and tumbled-down thing. The roof was wreathed in bald patches where the slates had come unstuck; the plaster was flaking; one of the windows was cracked and badly patched up with cardboard. It reminded Hanni of the wrecked homes she had seen in Berlin at the end of the war where families had lived in cellars while they tried to rebuild their old lives out of rubble and ruins. Frau Pelzer, who had been about to knock on the door, caught sight of Hanni's frown and stepped back.

'I don't want this for him but he won't take my help, and he won't live with me.'

Hanni rarely blushed but now she was scarlet. 'I'm sorry. I didn't mean to judge.'

The woman's face softened a little. 'No, I don't suppose you did but everybody does. He's the town drunk now and that's all he is. No one but me can remember the lovely boy he once was. I should warn you too that the inside is likely to be worse and he will be upset at you seeing that, but I couldn't risk warning him you were coming and having him disappear. So, as I said, please be gentle.'

She knocked on the door and pushed it open, calling out Tobias's name. Hanni followed her into the dark and stale room which led straight from the front door feeling thoroughly chastened and determined to honour Frau Pelzer's request, no matter how frustrating the meeting might become.

'I've brought someone to meet you, Tobias. Why don't we get the place a bit more comfortable?'

Frau Pelzer was already tidying as she talked, sweeping books and papers off the chairs, clearing a place to sit, throwing logs on the smouldering fire and opening the heavy curtains. It was quickly done and covered over with enquiries about her brother's health and his day, and it left Hanni with a few moments to observe Tobias. He was thin, painfully so, and his skin had a yellowish pallor, but the smile he greeted his sister with was warm and she could trace what must once have been a handsome man in the sweep of his cheekbones. He was also wary of her, especially once Frau Pelzer had stopped fussing and moved on from swapping names to the reason for Hanni's visit.

'So, here's the thing. Hanni came to Hadamar today looking for answers about one of her family members. The director was no use, but I wonder if you might be the one who could help her find them.'

She took her time. She let each sentence settle on him before she moved to the next.

'It's about what happened in the winter of 1938 on the night you left the hospital, Tobias. It's about what you saw then. And I think it's about the man who was there – do you remember telling me about him? Hanni thinks that man may have been her father and she needs your help to understand what he did, and how that might be connected to her little sister's death. I know what I'm asking isn't easy, that casting yourself back to that day is frightening, but what do you think? Could you see your way to helping her?'

His breathing turned ragged; his leg started to shake. His first instinct was to say no – that was clear from the way his eyes widened and his mouth twisted. His second was to leave. Hanni was certain he would have done that at once if Frau Pelzer hadn't taken his hand and stroked it and kept him in the chair. She couldn't dive in with her questions; she had to follow Frau Pelzer's careful lead, but she couldn't think how to win his trust. Until she looked at the joined hands and the deep bond it represented and found the answer there.

'I can see how much your sister means to you, Tobias. So can I tell you about mine? Can I talk to you about my Luise?'

It worked. He was still perched ready to flee but he nodded. Hanni had come to the house hoping that Tobias would tell her a story and that its telling would not only help her, it would offer him some comfort and relief. She hadn't expected to be the one unburdening her soul, but once she conjured up a newborn Luise wrapped in her pink knitted shawl or the toddler dancing like a butterfly in the Lietzenseeufer rose garden, she couldn't stop spilling her memories. She didn't start with Hadamar; she didn't mention the hospital at all. Instead she talked about the birth of a long-wanted baby and a little girl she had carried around like a doll and she brought Luise in all her bright colours into the room.

'I've been so bound up with finding out how she died, I'd forgotten what a joyous little thing she was. I'd forgotten how much light she brought into our home.'

Hanni's eyes were wet but, for the first time in weeks, she wasn't sad and her sister wasn't just another lost victim. She was a real little girl again, and she was loved.

'I remember her smile. Even when she was...' Tobias shook his head. 'She had the loveliest smile.'

Hanni heard the words but she couldn't catch hold of them. Her brain was stumbling over *When?* and *Where?* and *How do you know that?* but she couldn't catch hold of those either. As she started to try, Frau Pelzer, who was watching her brother intently, shook her head. Tobias's eyes were wet too but his leg had stopped shaking.

'So many people chose not to see, didn't they?'

His voice wavered as if it wasn't used to making its presence felt.

'They looked away. From the cattle cars and the barbed wire. From the flames shooting out of the chimneys. From the burial sites. They looked down and turned their backs and made their worlds into very small places. They said "I didn't know" because they decided that they didn't. I envy them. All I can do is see.'

He looked up then and looked directly at Hanni. His eyes were so hollow, she was the one who suddenly wanted to leave. She didn't want to make a broken man relive what had broken him. But Tobias was talking again and his soft voice was hypnotic.

'When it started, I thought what we were doing was a kindness. There weren't many who came to us at first but the ones who did, it would break your heart. Kiddies who couldn't see or hear, whose limbs were all wrong, who cried out constantly from the pain they were in. Old people who'd lost their minds and been abandoned, who cried all the time too. They had no one, but we held them at the end and talked to them right up to the last second. I thought we were offering them mercy. I didn't know, I swear, that we were being trained up for worse.'

He stopped, took a shuddering breath, rubbed his eyes as if he was trying to scrub the images out of them. It wasn't easy to tell whether he was standing in the past or in the present. Hanni wondered if that was always the case.

'I believe you.' She did, and it suddenly mattered that he heard it. 'The regime was clever. It twisted people and ideals; it knew how to suck the unwary in.'

He nodded as if her answer helped him but his hands were trembling. 'I wasn't a monster. I learned that night what the plans for the hospital were and I wouldn't have stayed there for anything. But I can't prove that to you, can I? I ran away because I was afraid for my own life and I didn't tell what had happened or what was coming. And I didn't speak out against him or against anyone.'

Him.

Reiner was finally in the room and his presence there was a threatening thing. Tobias was already shrinking.

'You don't have to tell me, Tobias. I can see what it's done to you. I can piece what I know together in a different way.'

Hanni meant that too. There had to be someone else less wounded she could turn to, no matter how much longer the search took. And she could see from the frightened look on Frau Pelzer's face that she wanted the same.

'No.'

It was one small word but when Tobias said it there was a strength in him he hadn't shown since they arrived.

'Tobias, please, think of your health.'

But he slipped his hands free from his sister's and waved her to be quiet. And he wasn't looking at her or Hanni anymore; he was staring at the bottle of brandy on the sideboard. When he said no a second time, Hanni wasn't sure who or what the refusal was aimed at. But saying it gave him enough courage to take a far steadier breath.

'My health? That's kind of you to say, but it makes me sound like an invalid, not someone who's brought all this misery on himself. I haven't done very much with my life, have I? I've run away from most of it or drowned it in drink. I've been a coward.' He shook his head as his sister started to argue again. 'It's true, Nora. Plenty of men saw terrible things; plenty of men were injured, but they haven't all turned to the bottle and given up. I know what I am. But I'd like to be better. And if this is my chance, I'm not going to waste it.'

He turned back to Hanni and this time the man he could have been was there in his face.

'Is your father still alive? Did he commit more crimes during the war?'

She nodded and she gave him another way out. 'Yes, he is and he did. He helped set up concentration camps, he had a hand in running Theresienstadt, he supervised the start of the euthanasia programme. Somebody once said to him, "You volunteered for every obscene job that was available," and that was true. So many people suffered, directly and indirectly, at his hands then. He's still evil, he's still a danger now, including to me and my family. I'm trying to bring him to justice, for everything that he's done, before it's too late, and I think whatever happened at Hadamar could be my last chance. But I can't guarantee that he won't try to find you if he discovers that I was here or that you helped me. So I won't blame you at all if you want to stop.'

Tobias thanked her but he shook his head. 'You really want to know – you're sure of that? You can't let the past be, no matter what's been done and no matter what I have to tell you?'

It wasn't the first time Hanni had been asked that question but it was the first time she had longed to say yes. *No matter what I have to tell you* told her that she was standing on the edge of a story far darker than she had ever imagined. And yet there was no other way to go but on.

'I wish I could but I can't. You called yourself a coward. Well, I've been one of those too. And I can't be that tonight – the stakes are too high. So, whatever it is, I want you to tell me.'

Tobias held her gaze for a moment, then he nodded. 'Then I'll do my best. But I'm more sorry than I can say that you have to hear it.'

He closed his eyes and leaned back in his chair. And when he started to speak, he took them back to a night twenty-five years earlier that he could still all too vividly see.

CHAPTER 18

10 DECEMBER 1938, HADAMAR HOSPITAL

'I need you in the lower ground theatre tonight at six o'clock sharp. There's a special patient on the way in. We're keeping the team small and discretion is key so no names and no details. Leave the room when we're done. Is that understood?'

Tobias stood a little straighter as Dr Brath addressed him. He always stood a little straighter when the doctors were around – he was ambitious, he wanted to impress; one day he wanted to wear a white coat too. On the morning Herr Klein, the hospital's chief administrator, had singled him out – after Tobias had held on to a little boy's hand without once letting go and murmured kind words as the child slipped free of his suffering – and said, 'You have a good touch – you could do very well here,' Tobias had added inches to his frame. And now here he was being singled out again. His dream of becoming a doctor, which nobody knew about yet except his sister Nora, was coming close enough to touch.

'The patient is a child, which is why I need you on hand, Tobias, although it's very important that you don't enter the main theatre until I give you the nod. You're to wait in the anteroom until then, where you can see but not be seen.'

Tobias knew where Brath meant. The small room at the side of the operating theatre had a discreet one-way mirror built into its dividing wall because it was sometimes used for teaching purposes. He wasn't, however, used to not being a visible part of the team and – emboldened by *I need you* – he said so.

'It's better this way, believe me. The father has demanded complete secrecy for his visit, with only myself and a nurse present, and he's not a man we want to cross. In fact it's imperative that we keep him happy. He is a close confidante of SS Gruppenführer Brandt, Hitler's personal doctor, and could be instrumental in Hadamar taking a central role in the next phase of' – Brath stopped and changed whatever he was about to say – 'our growth. If he sees you, he'll start making trouble so stay out of the way. By the time I need you to step in, I assume he'll have gone.'

Tobias noted that but he noted *growth* more. He had guessed there were important changes coming for the hospital. The country-style doctors, who spent time getting to know their patients as if they were friends, had been replaced by uniformed men like Brath whose watchword was efficiency. More beds had been arriving than the current wards could hold. Construction work had begun in the basement, apparently for a new shower block although Tobias could think of half a dozen locations in the facility which would be more practical for that. And the drug cabinets were overflowing – they had enough stocks of scopolamine, luminal and morphine to poison or sedate an army. All of which suggested that Tobias was employed by a hospital whose work was under the Third Reich's spotlight and that could only be good. So 'growth' was fine but he was wrong-footed by 'father'.

Fewer and fewer of the patients who were being recommended to Hadamar had family, or family who visited them anyway. The hospital was increasingly the last stop for those, both young and old, with lives which were lived in a state whose struggles and agonies tore at Tobias's heart. That was why he saw his work tending to their last hours or minutes as a service, even if Nora was shocked by the number of deaths he had been present at. He didn't like talking to her about the hospital – she could be very judgemental. It had been something of a relief when all the hospital staff had been required to sign an oath of silence about their work: if he couldn't share what he did, she couldn't raise objections which were based on a false picture of the lives they were ending. But for a father to come? Tobias wasn't at all sure that was appropriate but he said nothing this time. He assumed that Brath was right: that the man would slip away when the last process began and that would be his time to take over.

Tobias was in place at five thirty. He assumed that the child in question would be blind and deaf and completely unaware of their surroundings but that didn't matter – the place they spent their last moments in should still be a kind one. He checked the instrument tray, even though that was the nurse's job – it was essential that everything went smoothly and there were no delays looking for syringes or needles or the correct dosage which could unsettle even the most absent of patients. Once that was done, he wheeled the heavy lights that wouldn't be needed into the corridor and spread a blanket across the bed which would hide the bare metal frame and soften its contours. There had to be dignity and there had to be kindness, whatever the demands of efficiency.

'Do you know who's coming in?'

The question was as surprising as the choice of nurse who appeared in the doorway. Amelie was new. She was also young and skittish and, in Tobias's opinion, not suited to this kind of work. Which she proved yet again as she started fussing with the tray he had already organised.

'How bad are they, do you know? Is it going to be quickly done? I can't bear it if there's screaming.'

Her hand was shaking, which wouldn't do. Tobias wasn't impressed that she would be assisting – he assumed that she'd been chosen for her stunning looks, not her ability. The SS offi-cers were obsessed with ordering pretty nurses around. But this was an important night for them all and he needed her calm before Brath came in and decided that neither of them was fit for the job.

'We're not given that information – you know that. And the screaming is sometimes nothing to do with us at all; it's a symptom of the condition that's brought them to us. But no, I don't imagine it will take long and we will have done whoever is brought here a kindness, Amelie. Maybe it's best to focus on that.'

That settled her. She smiled at him and complimented him on how well the tray had been set up. By the time Brath arrived, the theatre was quiet and organised and the praise Tobias loved hearing flowed.

'Right, he's here. Amelie, stand ready to greet him by the door. Tobias, get yourself into the ante-room and keep an eye on me. I'll give you the signal when I need you.'

The car rolled into position in the courtyard at the back of the building which bordered the smaller operating theatres and immediately turned off its headlights. Amelie smoothed her hair and ran her tongue over her lightly lipsticked mouth. Tobias slipped into the side room and closed the door with a soft click behind him. Once his eyes adjusted to the darkness, his view through the window was a clear one. He pulled a stool forward and angled it so that he could see the door and the bed. Every opportunity was one to learn from, and he wanted to see how Brath managed the father and the orderlies who would wheel or carry the patient in.

It took Tobias a moment or two once the door into the

theatre opened to adjust his understanding of what should happen to what was actually playing out in front of him. He had expected an SS officer. He had expected Brath to snap to attention and for Amelie's pretty face to purse into a pout. That all went as expected. But there was no stretcher; there was no wheelchair. What there was instead was a pretty little girl of about six years old, smiling up at her father as he nodded to the doctor and the nurse and walking perfectly capably into the room.

Nothing about this is right.

The words tore through his brain but he had no idea what to do with them. The child should have been twisted up, oblivious, locked into her own dark world. Not staring round the operating theatre and pointing at the tray.

'What are those for?'

Her voice was sweet and clear. Her frown at her father's 'Nothing for you to worry about' was the reaction Tobias would have expected from any curious child. Her grin at Amelie was the same. Tobias glanced at Brath, who was firmly not looking at the child, and wondered if he had been warned that she wouldn't have a visible mark on her. He looked over at Amelie who knew nothing and was as white as the sheets laid out on the bed.

Where does it end?

They were Nora's words and he didn't want them in his head.

If they can so easily act like gods with the patients you describe as damaged, where does damaged stop?

That had infuriated him. 'They're doctors.' That's what he'd told her. 'They act in the best interests of the people in their care – they took an oath.' But then Nora had started on a tirade about the SS and the kind of oaths taken by men who set up the concentration camps some of her less politically sensible friends had been sent to, or who thought it was acceptable to harass elderly Jews, and Tobias had walked out. The Party wasn't perfect, he knew that, but it rewarded people who worked hard and didn't make waves, and Tobias could get along very well with that way of doing things. Or he had until now.

He pulled himself back from Nora's doomsaying and tried to take a better stock of the situation. Maybe this wasn't the patient; maybe there was another child still to come in. That didn't make sense but neither did anything he was watching, so Tobias decided to wait for the stretcher he was certain would arrive. And then the little girl fell.

She went down hard, her limbs dancing as if they were being pulled in a dozen different directions. Amelie was instantly on her knees, turning the child onto her side, rolling a pillow under her head to protect it from the hard floor. Brath moved quickly too, rolling the bed back a few inches so her flailing arms wouldn't crash into the metal. And the father... Tobias couldn't take his eyes off him. He didn't bend down. He didn't call out the girl's name or offer her any words of comfort. He stepped back as her leg shot out, and he stared at her with utter disgust.

'Now you see what I am dealing with. This is what keeps happening. It's why I've been forced to keep her locked away.'

The child was calming now, her body finally growing still. The father continued to talk over Amelie's soothing.

'It happens without warning every day now and she gets weaker with every attack. There is no cure; there is no possibility of a useful life. It's a stain on my family's line and it's not a state of affairs that can continue.'

He was discussing his daughter as if she was a specimen. Tobias had never heard such coldness. And he didn't move any closer as the child started to stir. Tobias could see that the girl was awake now, or close to it, although her eyes didn't appear able to focus. Amelie gathered her up and put her onto the bed, tucking the blanket round her floppy limbs.

'What's wrong with her?'

Tobias flinched as the nurse asked. He jumped off his stool, ready to take her place when Brath marched her out of the room. Instead the officer suddenly became the heartbroken father he hadn't bothered to be when his child was fitting. He bestowed a smile on Amelie which turned her cheeks pink.

'Leukaemia – a disease of the blood as I'm sure you know. It's terrible, isn't it? Especially when she looks as perfect as she looks now.'

He nodded to the bed where the child was lying in a tumble of blonde curls, her dark eyelashes fluttering, her skin the colour of thick cream.

'She's as pretty as a doll, isn't she? But don't be fooled: that pallor is because she is dying. It's a cruel illness, and I don't want her put through any more of its miseries, so here I am, asking for your kindness and your help.'

Tobias didn't believe his sudden show of concern. It was a blatant pitch to win Amelie onto his side that made Tobias's skin crawl. He'd heard of leukaemia but that was all; he knew nothing about its treatment or prognosis. He waited for Brath to fill the gaps in, to challenge the officer and plead alternatives, but all the doctor said was, 'Are you sure this is what you want?' and even that was more than he should have done.

The man rounded on him, his eyes blazing. 'Are you questioning me? Are you suddenly a champion of useless lives? Has Hadamar lost interest in the programme?'

Tobias recoiled at *useless lives*. No one in the hospital, or at least in his hearing, had ever spoken so callously about their patients. He waited for Brath to point that out but the doctor was suddenly all head down and contrite, calling Amelie back to the bed to fit the restraints and prepare the injection. Tobias could see the nurse's hands shaking as she fastened the buckles around the girl's thin ankles and wrists; he could see the sweat gathering on her forehead and top lip. *You can't let this happen* raced through his head but he didn't know who *you* was. It surely wasn't him?

Tobias wanted it to be him. He wanted to push through the door and shout, 'Stop, this isn't what we do here. We're the last resort when all other avenues are done, when there is more suffering than life. We don't deal with patients who talk and smile.' Except he wasn't brave enough and he wasn't sure that them being the last resort was true anymore. Not while the officer was talking about some promise he'd been given that the procedures at Hadamar had been thoroughly tested and were speedy, and reputations going to the back of the line if they weren't. Or when Brath made his stupid boast.

'No one here is going to fail; we are more than ready to lead the programme. My doctors and my nurses are the best in the business. Show him, Amelie. You take the syringe and you do it.'

Tobias could see the chaos that was about to unfold the second the young nurse tapped the top of the needle and her fingernail scraped against it. Amelie was too young; the child was too beautiful. What Tobias couldn't see was exactly what happened next; the nurse's body blocked that part of his view. He couldn't tell whether Amelie's hand shook or the girl's arm jerked but the outcome was the same. The needle didn't go cleanly in. Amelie panicked and pulled back and the tip snapped. The child's eyes flew open and she screamed.

'Do something! Get another dose into her!'

Brath yelled at Amelie as the child's screaming tore through the theatre, but Amelie was crouched on the floor with her hands over her mouth and she wouldn't get up.

'We can't do it, Reiner, we can't. We have to wait. We have to get the child calm first.'

Brath was pleading but this Reiner he shouldn't have named wasn't listening.

'It gets done. You promised me it would be dealt with. So it gets done or you take the consequences.'

Everything switched into slow motion as each scene imprinted itself on Tobias's brain. Brath froze. Equipment clattered as Reiner swore and pushed Brath out of the way, as he grabbed the second needle from the tray. Tobias saw what came next this time perfectly clearly although he wished that he hadn't. Reiner tapped the needle and plunged. It went in as roughly as the first, but Reiner was stronger and it worked. The scream cut off and became a gasp which turned into a choking, and finally, although Tobias thought it would never come, into a silence that was just as terrible to hear. Tobias was flat against the glass, his tears streaking it, unable to close his eyes, unable not to see. And then the screaming began again and this time it was Amelie.

'You monster. You absolute monster. You've killed your own child. How can anybody kill their own child?'

She was on her feet, her face scarlet, her hands bunched as if she was about to hit him, hatred oozing from every pore. Reiner put down the needle and he told her to stop. She didn't. She carried on yelling 'monster' at him as if it was the only word that she knew. And a second later she was back on the floor, blood pouring from the perfect circle shot into her forehead.

'Clean this up and burn them both. And then prepare a death certificate for my daughter which gives the cause as scarlet fever.'

Reiner's gun was back in its holster; his face was a series of menacing angles. Brath was barely breathing.

'And be very aware that you're only alive because you're a fellow SS man. Don't make me regret that. This stays between us – that shouldn't need saying. If it does, I'll put a word in with Brandt and ensure Hadamar will advance like you all want it to. If there is even the breath of a leak, you and every one of your fellow doctors will find yourselves in Dachau. Do you under-stand me?'

He turned on his heel with a curt, 'I'll wait in your office,' before Brath got further than, 'Yes.' He didn't look back at his daughter.

It took a while before Tobias could move. It took a while before he could haul himself up off the tiles and make his legs work. It never occurred to him to run: Reiner might not have seen him but Brath knew he was there. He walked out of the ante-room expecting to be shot like Amelie, to be removed along with the rest of the evidence. Some part of his brain had accepted that, had decided that end would be fitting. But Brath barely looked at him when he finally emerged. He was too busy wrapping up Amelie's body in a blanket.

'You'll have to take them to the ovens while I get the paper-work done and get him out of here. The rest we can leave for the orderlies. Nobody will remark on bloodstains in an oper-ating theatre.'

'I don't want to.'

Brath passed him a blanket and waved at the child's body, so Tobias said it again.

'I don't care what you want and I don't need the added complication of getting rid of you too. So you'll do this and then you'll keep your mouth shut. What you do after that is up to you. Stay and get on with the job, which, trust me, won't get any prettier than this when the big numbers roll in but the rewards will be excellent. Or leave and work on a farm. I don't care. But you'll forget what you saw here tonight, exactly as I plan to. Or I'll give him your name and hand him the problem and you won't live long enough after that to make any choices.'

Tobias covered both the bodies as gently as he could. He carried them one by one down through the corridors which weaved under the hospital, whispering nursery rhymes to the little girl when it was her turn and telling her not to be afraid of the dark. He laid them side by side in the furnace and said the few words he could remember from the one burial he had been to.

And when it was all done, Tobias went home and he started to drink and he tried and he tried to empty his mind, but he never could erase the pictures.

CHAPTER 19

15–16 APRIL 1963, FRANKFURT, WEST GERMANY

There was a bowl on her knee, gentle hands holding back her hair.

'You poor girl. You thought he'd arranged it, didn't you? You never imagined he'd carried out the killing himself.'

Hanni couldn't speak; she could barely nod. She was hollow. Her heart was in a basement, beside a furnace, watching a broken man feed her sister and a nurse who had also deserved far more from life into the hungry flames. Her mind was spinning. Every time she thought she had discovered the depths of Reiner's depravity, he pulled her further down.

She wiped her eyes and her mouth, pushed the sour-smelling bowl away. Nora was right: she hadn't imagined this. She had expected brutality. An order to take Luise and to sedate her so heavily or feed her so poorly she would slip quietly away. She had expected to find the grounds for a manslaughter charge. What she had found was murder. Luise dying in agony as Reiner jammed a needle into her tiny arm. Pretty young Amelie paying for her humanity with her life.

I wanted a crime but I never wanted this. And now the same monster has my son.

With that thought, her mind plunged into freefall.

It's a stain on my family's line.

Bad blood.

The refrain which had been pounding through her head for days suddenly found its true shape.

Leo.

Leo who was Freddy's child. Who carried Freddy's blood in him. Who in Reiner's eyes was surely as much of a stain on his family as Luise had been.

What if Leo has disappointed or angered him? What if the other boys have discovered his father is Jewish? What would a man who could murder his own daughter do if that truth came out?

'Hanni, sit down, calm yourself. Breathe.'

She didn't know that she had stood up. She didn't know breathing was an act her body was still capable of. There was nothing in her head now but Leo and a burning instinct to run to Goslar and to drag him out of Reiner's murdering hands.

'Hanni, please. I know you're in pain and I will help you through that, I promise. But Tobias needs me too.'

Tobias jolted her back. He was slumped, his head lolling and his eyes still closed – he hadn't opened them the whole time he was talking. He had recited the story as if he was watching a film playing across his eyelids. Now he was grey and limp and he looked as if he was dead.

And his death will be on Reiner too.

Hanni subsided into the chair, unable to look at the stricken man's ravaged face, while Nora kissed Tobias's hand and demanded that he come back to her. It took an eternity. He didn't seem to want or to be able to surface, but in the end he stirred. When he did, his eyes immediately went searching for Hanni's. And that was the moment – when he looked at her with all the pity that she felt for him – when Hanni finally burst into tears.

The crying blew a storm through her body. It washed away the last traces of the hope she had been carrying that Luise's death had been a painless one. And it also washed away any doubt about what she had to do next. Two murders, both directly committed by Reiner, and both of them witnessed. The cost of telling, and hearing, what had happened at Hadamar had stripped them all down to the bone, but the crimes were there and the crimes could be used. If Tobias could stay strong a little longer.

Hanni eased herself out of the embrace Nora had wrapped her in the moment her tears began falling. All she had received from the woman was kindness and now she was about to ask for something whose price could be far too dear. She hoped Nora would forgive her; she wouldn't blame her one bit if she didn't.

'I'm sorry, Tobias, more sorry than I've got the words to express. I'm sorry for what you went through and what you're still going through. I'm sorry that you were dragged into my father's nightmare way of running the world. And I'm deeply grateful that you told me the whole story – I know that wasn't easily done.' She glanced at Nora who was frowning as if she already knew what was coming. 'But I've another favour to ask if you can bear it. I've been trying to bring Reiner to justice since the war ended and he's evaded me every time. He was too clever to be caught; he kept his name well away from the evidence. But now there is a chance. To destroy him and to get justice for Luise and Amelie and all the rest of his victims. And to save my son, who I think could be in worse danger than I realised. What you have told me about that night is the crime I need to destroy him with, Tobias, so—'

'You want me to swear to the truth of it and tell it again in court.'

Hanni's 'Yes' was shouted down, as she had expected it would be, by Nora's immediate 'No.' She turned to the woman to explain, and then she realised that explaining wasn't her place. Tobias had taken his sister's hand and was holding it tight, and although his face was still haggard and grey, his eyes were clear and focused.

'I have to do it, Nora. I've no choice if I ever want to climb out of this darkness I live in. I've let my life run through my fingers; I've let his life carry on. Who knows, perhaps if I'd intervened that night, perhaps if I'd stopped him or spoken the truth in the days afterwards, his life might have taken a very different path.'

He answered Nora's 'That's ridiculous – he would have killed you, he still might' by bringing her hand to his lips, and then he turned his attention fully on Hanni.

'If you can get him to a courtroom, I will be there too.'

Relief surged through her, blunting – for a little while at least – the sharpest edges of her grief.

'Thank you. You've no idea what a difference this could make. I'll tell Freddy, my... the detective who's helping with the case that you'll stand as a witness. In the meantime we can get your testimony written down and the facts organised and get an arrest warrant issued.'

She was desperate to make plans, to get all the details of Tobias's story captured but Nora's curt, 'We'll deal with that tomorrow,' reminded her of the toll the night had already taken.

'Nora's right – that can wait. You've helped me enough for now.'

Hanni sat quietly while Nora led Tobias into his bedroom. When Nora came back, her eyes were still blazing.

'You'll keep his name hidden from Reiner until the last moment.'

It was an order, not a question, but Hanni nodded anyway.

'Then I'll respect his decision and I'll say no more. But now he's exhausted and he needs his rest. You will come to my house with me and you will sleep, and in the morning I'll take you to a place that might help.'

Nora led the way to the pretty cottage she shared with her husband at a pace that didn't encourage conversation. Her head was clearly full of her concern for Tobias and, although she nodded at Hanni's 'I can never thank him enough for his bravery tonight', Hanni stuck to her word and didn't pursue the topic.

Hanni climbed into the bed she was shown to, wondering what kind of a place could help. She was desperate for sleep; she had been pushing a body that had been running increasingly empty since Leo had left and the story of Luise's death – and all the thickened fear for her son that brought with it – had drained the last of her reserves. The mattress was soft; the pillows were deep. Hanni crawled under the covers but sleep wouldn't come. Nothing would come except Luise's fear-filled eyes and Reiner's plunging arm. And Leo.

The place Nora led her to the following morning turned out to be an uneven and bleak-looking stretch of land out of sight at the side of the hospital. Hanni stumbled after her and didn't know what to make of it.

'Bear with me – let me explain. I once swore that I would never work here, but circumstances dictated otherwise and I don't know the true extent of Hadamar's history as well as I should. What I do know is that that stretch over there is a graveyard.' Her arm snaked round Hanni, who had started to sway. 'She isn't here – I wouldn't have done that to you without warning. As for who is... I'm not sure how many bodies there are. Locals say it's a few thousand but nobody has the exact figure or their names or knows what happened to the ashes of the many more victims who were cremated. None of the investigations into the killings here could ever get a clear answer to that. And that's the point of bringing you here. Whatever it seemed like yesterday, the past hasn't been entirely swept away from this place; there will be some remembering. Next year all this bare land will be transformed into a memorial garden and a cemetery. There will be plaques and statues and flowers. It will be a place where people can come and mourn and say goodbye.'

She hugged Hanni tighter. 'I told you that Katzmann wasn't a bad man. He will make sure that this is carefully managed and the worst of the story kept out of the public eye, but he will also see that it's done right. And I thought Luise should be a part of it.'

'What do you mean?'

Nora let go of Hanni's waist and reached into the bag at her feet. 'I thought you might like to plant this – it's a rose bush with pink flowers that would do very nicely for a pretty little girl. I'll make sure it stays safe when the works begin and Tobias will tend it when the garden is done. I was angry with you last night for talking about the trial, I won't pretend that I wasn't, and I was scared for him but then, this morning, he was stronger than I've seen him in years. Maybe his burden has lightened a little. Maybe coming here, and helping to look after the garden like he once did with the patients, will give him a sense of purpose again.'

She stepped away then and left Hanni to choose the perfect spot for the rose, at the highest point of what would become the cemetery, where its petals would always feel the warmth of the sun.

Once that was done, they walked back down the hill to the village in a silence which allowed Hanni to say goodbye to her sister. Rose bush or not, she would never come back. Hadamar could never hold anything but horror for her, and Luise deserved to be remembered in far kinder places.

'What will you do now?'

Nora had been right about Tobias: the hug he gave her as Hanni said goodbye to him was a far more solid thing than the broken man she had met at the start of the previous night could

ever have managed. He had promised to write everything out in
as much detail as he could and send it to her hotel in Frankfurt;
he had, apparently, already started. Hanni hoped that he would
manage to stay steady, that the bottle wouldn't reach out and
defeat him again once he had to relive the story or face Reiner
across a courtroom. She didn't insult him by saying that.

'I'm going to go back to Frankfurt to wait for Freddy to join
me there from Berlin. I'll make a start on preparing the case so
that he can get an arrest warrant ready for Reiner. Once we get
your testimony, we'll go after him and end this. And your name
won't appear anywhere until the trial starts, I promise.'

It sounded simple; it sounded achievable. As if twenty years
and more of hating her father finally had a finish line. She had
to make it sound like that, to stop herself hurtling straight to
Goslar.

Hanni got into the Opel and began the drive back to the
city. She refused to dwell on Luise – the car would have slipped
out of her control if she let herself do that. She refused to dwell
on Leo – she had to trust that her initial instincts were right and
that Reiner wouldn't harm her son unless she was there to
witness it. She kept herself calm by imagining the trial instead.
She let it play out in her head: Tobias on the stand talking about
dignity, the jury in tears at his testimony and Reiner caught by
his crimes as surely as Eichmann had been. *Life*. She heard the
life sentence pronounced, because surely life was what it had to
be. She watched Reiner crumple as he was convicted of two
murders, including his own daughter's. There wasn't a lawyer
in Germany, however far Reiner's web of contacts extended,
who could wriggle him out of those charges.

That certainty sustained her all the way to Frankfurt and
was further bolstered by the telegram waiting for her from
Freddy at the hotel reception.

RENNY MUCH IMPROVED AND VERY SORRY STOP DIDN'T
ACTIVELY PARTICIPATE AND DID SAVE MAN'S LIFE SO NO
CHARGES STOP AM STAYING UNTIL SHE'S OUT OF HOSPITAL
AND MOBILE THEN TO FRANKFURT STOP HAD DISCUSSION
RE ISRAEL YOU SUGGESTED AND RELATIONS DRASTICALLY
IMPROVED STOP

Hanni dithered for a moment. Her immediate impulse was to telephone him. To tell him everything that she had discovered and ask him to start the warrant process moving, but then she dismissed the idea. Telling Freddy what Reiner had done to Luise would be hard enough in person never mind over a crackling connection and, besides, she wasn't ready to talk. If she let herself linger on the images Tobias had planted so graphically in her brain or tried to give voice to them, her body would instantly stop working. She sent a simple *that's wonderful news* message because it was and headed towards her room, praying that this time she might be able to sleep.

'Frau Schlüssel, do you have a moment?'

Hanni turned with a smile which faded as soon as she saw the nervous expression on the normally unflappable hotel manager's face.

Leo.

Freddy was well, Renny was well. It had to be Leo.

I've called it wrong. I've failed him. Reiner hasn't waited at all.

'What's happened to my son?'

The question was instant and panic-filled because surely all her chances were used up? So many times the bad news hadn't been Leo when she had been convinced that it would be, and that kind of luck couldn't hold. And yet it did.

The manager frowned. 'Your son? No, madam, this has nothing as far as I know to do with your son. But I do need to speak to you and I would rather that it was in my office.'

Hanni followed him to the far plainer area beyond the elegant marble foyer, her mind whirring through what else could have gone wrong. Leo was still at the school and unharmed. Renny was getting better and wasn't going to jail. Freddy would be back in Frankfurt shortly and they had the basics of the case that they needed. She couldn't work out what else could be the matter, and then the manager told her and she couldn't work out why she hadn't seen the threat coming.

'Before he was called away, your husband indicated that the job you were both here to complete was a potentially dangerous one. That there may be' – he stumbled over what was clearly a very unfamiliar concept – 'people on your trail who could... cause a problem and that myself and my staff were not to divulge that you were here if anyone asked for you.'

'And someone has come looking?'

It was hard to stay composed when the manager nodded, but Hanni folded her hands and crossed her ankles and nothing started to shake.

'A young man arrived in the foyer after you left yesterday morning, asking an awful lot of questions. I have to say he wasn't very subtle. He didn't introduce himself. He was one of those types who thinks that charm will get him whatever he wants and doesn't like being told no.'

The description fitted Reiner's boys so perfectly, it saved Hanni the moment or two she would have wasted trying to convince herself it was a coincidence. She had presumed his people were on her trail; she had presumed he would show his hand sooner or later. It was almost a relief not to be waiting anymore. All that mattered now was that the trail hadn't led them to Tobias.

'He asked if you were staying here and what your movements were and whether you were alone. None of which we would have divulged about any of our guests, irrespective of your husband's warning. Anyway, it became clear very quickly that denying your existence wouldn't get rid of him, so I took a decision that I hope was the right one.'

The manager looked so worried that Hanni thought for one sickening moment he had overheard her and Freddy talking about Hadamar and had accidentally let that information slip. If he had, she was already running out of time to send a warning.

'What did you say?'

'I told him that your plans had changed and that you had headed back to Berlin with your husband and that you weren't planning to return. Did I do the right thing?'

He had done exactly the right thing. He had bought her time and he had removed Tobias from the firing line. The look on the manager's face when she burst out laughing and hugged him was priceless.

She shouldn't have laughed or relaxed her guard. She shouldn't have gone out.

Even as she was fastening her coat and hunting for her scarf, Hanni could hear Freddy's voice in her head telling her to stay inside the hotel and stay safe. If the manager hadn't sent Reiner's little spy away perhaps she would have done. But the sky outside her window was the prettiest shade of blue and her room was stuffy and closing in. And every time she stopped moving, her head filled with all the details of Luise's killing and kept switching her sister's face in the operating theatre for Leo's. Sleep was an impossibility. Staying alone was an impossibility. The only thing she could do to stay sane was to go out and find people to blend into, and walk too fast to think.

Hanni didn't know Frankfurt at all. Freddy had chosen the city as a base because it was close to Hadamar and also within relatively easy distance of the Harz Mountains. The only things she did know was that Frankfurt was famous for its pork sausages, which she had no appetite to try, and that, like so many German cities, its Gothic Old Town had been pounded to bits by the Allies in 1944 and what was left was in the process of being rebuilt. That sounded like something that might occupy her so she left the hotel in the direction of the cathedral without the proffered guidebook, preferring to wander and stop as the mood took her. Except the mood didn't take her at all.

As desperate as she was for distraction, she couldn't connect to the determinedly modern swathes of concrete and glass which dominated the city, or the wide roads which had turned the car into Frankfurt's king. In the end, the traffic fumes which sat like a fog across every street she turned into sent her in search of the water and green space. She couldn't connect to that either.

Unlike Berlin's network of waterways and canals, Frankfurt's river edged the city. It wasn't its beating heart. The water was sluggish and dark, and Hanni couldn't find a bench to sit on even if she had wanted to stop and stare at it. The path she had followed quickly turned rubbish-strewn and neglected; the grass verge running alongside one edge of it was thoroughly overgrown. And, apart from the occasional fisherman she could see huddled below her on the river bank, there weren't any people around. That also felt wrong. Berlin's towpaths and riverwalks were bustling places where a walker had to dodge children and dogs and courting couples oblivious to the world. Hanni would easily have found the crowd she needed there. Instead she was as alone as she would have been in her room and unable to hide from her fears.

After half an hour of following an increasingly bleak walkway which seemed determined to go nowhere of interest, Hanni was ready to give up and return to the hotel. She was also ready to act on her earlier impulse and call Freddy. Luise's story was too heavy to bear alone. Her increased worries over Leo were too much to bear alone. A poor connection or not, she needed Freddy's certainty that they would get Leo back and get justice; she needed his warmth to push away the shivers she was struggling to hold back. She didn't get a chance to ask for either.

The sudden sound was a footfall.

She heard it in the second before she turned round. A footfall that hadn't been there in the moment before. It was evenly paced, matching hers. It wasn't particularly heavy. There was no obvious reason to be concerned by it: if she had been in Berlin, she wouldn't have paid a set of footsteps behind her a second thought. Except she wasn't in Berlin and their speed was far too precisely mirroring hers.

And I've known all along this was coming.

Hanni kept moving. She didn't speed up or slow down. She didn't tighten her shoulders, although they wanted to tighten, or grab any harder onto her bag. She didn't look around. She was too busy weighing up her options, which were limited. The river was below her on one side; there was a high wall bordering the grass verge on the other. There was no one walking towards her who she could stop and speak to while whoever was so intent on shadowing her was forced to walk past. Which left running as her only other option and, given she had no idea where the path was heading, Hanni wasn't about to do that. So she turned round instead.

The man behind her could have been Valentin Gessner. He was tall and blonde and carried himself with the same unbreakable confidence. One glance told her he wasn't the type who went wandering about on scruffy river banks. And he didn't lift his hat or nod and walk on. He stopped at the exact moment she turned and confronted him.

'What do you want?'

Hanni didn't have time to play games and pretend that this was anything but what it was: a man deliberately following her with no good purpose in mind. She sized him up quickly, the way she had once had to size up a murderer when she had been the one doing the following. His hands were out of his pockets;

she couldn't see a weapon. But he was bigger than her and the width of his shoulders suggested that he was considerably stronger.

But maybe he's not as nimble or fast.

The wall bordering the grass verge ended a dozen yards or so behind him. Hanni could see a patch of wasteland which presumably led onto one of Frankfurt's never-ending roads; she assumed that was where he had sprung from. If she could get to that, she could make enough fuss to attract attention and help. All she had to do was find a way to get past him and then sprint along the path.

'I asked you what you wanted. Or have I made a mistake? Aren't you following me?'

She was determined not to show any weakness although her heart was pounding through her chest. It pounded even harder when he smiled.

'No, you are right: I am. And I'd been warned that you didn't frighten or back down easily. But I think I'll be the one asking the questions. Where have you been, Frau Schlüssel? Obviously not back to Berlin. The manager of your hotel needs to learn not to sweat so much when he lies. So where have you been and who have you been to see?'

The menace pouring from his stance and his face was completely at odds with his casual tone. Hanni – who had been assessing the ways to get away from him rather than focusing on what he might do if she couldn't – suddenly realised how much danger she was in. It took a huge effort not to jump back when he took a step closer.

'I asked you a question – two in fact. I would very much appreciate an answer.'

He couldn't know the full extent of what she had discovered, and neither could Reiner. Reiner hadn't seen Tobias in the hospital; he hadn't known Tobias was there. Even if her father had pieced enough together to guess that Hadamar not Frankfurt was Hanni's main destination, he couldn't fit Tobias into that picture unless Hanni put him there. And whatever happened next, Hanni was not going to do that any more than she was going to run. So she stood her ground.

'Nowhere that concerns you and nobody you know.'

He didn't get angry, which she was ready for. He laughed instead and that threw her off guard. Which she realised a second too late was his intention. He was behind her before Hanni saw him move. His arm was round her neck before she could duck out of the way. The weight of it clamped across her body was a shock. Her instinct was to struggle but that would only have made him grip harder so she refused to follow her instincts and she went limp instead.

'Don't think you're going to get out of this. Whether you tell me or not, whether you struggle or not makes no difference.'

The pleasure in his voice as he lifted her onto her toes was as terrifying as the hold he had on her.

'Your father is sick of you chasing after him, but he doesn't care anymore who you're talking to or roping in to your schemes. He's decided to cut the problem off where it really needs cutting: at its roots.'

Hanni felt his other hand travel over her back and slide down and away from her body. She had been a fool to think that there wasn't a weapon just because it hadn't immediately appeared. He was reaching into his pocket for a gun or a knife.

Hanni stopped thinking before *I'm going to die* overwhelmed her and became a reality. She forced herself to listen instead to the voice in her head telling her that she'd been in a situation like this before and she'd survived. She forced herself to feel her assailant's movements. One hand was in his pocket – there was nothing she could do about that. But the act of reaching had loosened the pressure round her neck and her shoulders – not by much, but by enough.

Hanni moved faster than she had ever moved. She jerked

her head forward and bit down hard on the hand closest to her face. His scream tore through her ear so she bit down again and this time his arm fell away.

Hanni pitched herself forward and out of his reach, hurling herself along the path. She was quick, but she wasn't quick enough. He didn't reach for a weapon this time; he used his fists and his feet. The blow caught her on the side of the head and sent her dizzy. The kick that accompanied it sent her off balance. And the push that he aimed squarely at the middle of her back toppled her over the side of the river bank and down.

There were no branches to grab. The concrete she fell against snatched her breath and spun her faster. There wasn't a moment to kick off her shoes or scramble out of her coat. There was nothing but pain as she fell and then there was nothing but freezing cold water.

CHAPTER 20

16–19 APRIL 1963, FRANKFURT, WEST GERMANY

'You are lucky to be alive, Frau Schlüssel. Very lucky indeed.'

Hanni was barely awake. Sounds were muffled; the room was blurred. The dividing line between the river and the hospital bed was still an unsteady one.

She blinked slowly – even the smallest movement demanded an effort which exhausted her – until the man perched on a chair beside her bed came more clearly into view. He wasn't one of the white-coated shapes she had briefly encountered as she swept in and out of consciousness. His voice was far louder than everybody else's hushed tones. He carried himself with the confident air of a police officer and Hanni wasn't ready for that.

She tried to sit up but her limbs were leaden and wouldn't obey, and the blanket which someone had tucked tightly around her gripped her body as fiercely as the icy black water had seized hold of her coat. It was hard not to panic and kick.

'Here, let me help you. You've got a lot of bruising so take it very slow.'

A softer voice, kind hands supporting her shoulders, a nest of pillows at her back.

Hanni let her eyes close briefly again while the nurse propped her up and warned her visitor – who had introduced himself as Inspector Wechsler and was, as Hanni had correctly guessed, a detective with the Frankfurt police force – that he would need to be quick.

'How do you know my name?'

Her mouth tasted brackish as if the river was still running through her.

Wechsler nodded to the handbag on the cabinet beside her bed. 'You must have held on to that when you fell, or for part of the way at least. It was found at the bottom of the bank. Your identity card and purse were still in it, so I'm assuming that whatever happened to you wasn't a robbery that went wrong?'

Hanni didn't have a better explanation than that to offer him so she ignored the question. 'How did I get out of the water?'

The detective frowned but the nurse was still hovering, clearly ready to chase him away if he caused Hanni any distress. He smiled instead of pressing her to explain what had happened, but the smile stayed well away from his eyes.

'You were hauled out by a fisherman who was standing underneath the point where you toppled in. Now that he's got over the fright, he's rather enjoying being a hero. He's hoping to make the front pages tomorrow.'

Which means Reiner will soon know I'm not dead. So the next target he goes for could be Leo.

Wechsler was too well trained to miss the flicker which passed across Hanni's face at that realisation. This time he pushed.

'Never mind how you got out; how did you come to fall in, Frau Schlüssel? Were you alone when it happened? Did someone attack you? I'm sorry to have to ask such difficult questions, but there are some oddities here. I found a hotel receipt in your bag and, when I called the manager there, he wasn't as

surprised as he should have been that you had met with an accident, although he wouldn't be drawn on why. Can you unpick
any of that for me?'

Hanni could but she didn't plan to. Whichever thread of
the story she chose to follow would lead to a tangle of revelations that could bury her for days. She didn't have days. And
she didn't trust the detective; she didn't trust anyone in Frankfurt. Whichever strand she offered him could find its way back
to Reiner.

*And then he'll send another man after me to do the job right,
or he'll hurt my child. Neither of which can happen.*

Reiner wasn't going to get the time to harm her or Leo.
Reiner wasn't going to get the time to do anything. Hanni's
head might be muddled about what to say to get rid of Wechsler
but that was all she was confused about. She was perfectly clear
on what had to be done with her father. She had decided that
the first time she had recovered consciousness.

'I don't know why he wouldn't be surprised and no, there
was nobody with me. I fell. I tripped on something and I fell
and I couldn't catch myself.'

It was exhausting to talk, to try and find the right words to
hide behind. It also didn't work.

The detective leaned forward with a sigh. 'Frau Schlüssel, I
hope that you believe me when I say that I have come here to
help you but that story simply doesn't ring true. I've been a
policeman in Frankfurt for a very long time and we have had
our share of tragedies in the river, but no one has *fallen* from
that broad section of the towpath before.' He paused and shook
his head as Hanni stayed silent. 'I think there is more to this
than you are saying. I think that perhaps you were pushed, or
possibly you jumped. Whichever it is, I need you to tell me the
truth.'

'I've already told you that. I fell – there's nothing more to
say.'

Her voice rose; the room started spinning. The nurse was at her bedside in seconds, her bossy manner instantly relegating the detective to the status of a naughty child.

'I warned you, didn't I, not to distress her? My patient is still very shocked and your questions aren't helping her recover. Come on now, leave her be. Let the poor woman get some rest. There'll be time for all this later.'

It was clearly a scenario that had been played out before. The detective was reluctant to go but the nurse was more than a match for him. He got up from the bedside and pulled out a business card which he placed on the bedside cabinet.

'If you wish to persist with this story then I can't force you to change it. But I would appreciate it if you would give yourself some time to think and then come in to the station once you've been discharged and continue our conversation. Will you do that?'

Hanni managed a nod, which partly placated him.

'Fine, well at least that much is agreed. I'm not accusing you of lying, Frau Schlüssel, but perhaps your memory is muddled and events may come back a little clearer when you are more rested. If this is more than an accident, if there is someone out there who could be a danger to the public, I want to know. In the meantime I'll continue looking for witnesses, and I'll give your husband a call and let him know what has happened.'

'No. Don't do that.'

The fog instantly lifted from Hanni's brain and she sat bolt upright, ignoring the nurse who was trying to get her to lie back down.

Wechsler stared at her. 'What? You don't want me to phone him? Why not? The hotel gave us his details – surely it's only appropriate to let him know that you've suffered an injury? Besides, he's a police officer, isn't he? I'm not comfortable keeping something like this from one of our own.'

Why not?

It was a reasonable question to ask. Hanni couldn't give him an honest answer to it.

Because Freddy will work out that this was deliberate the second you tell him. He'll work out that Reiner was behind it. And then he'll race here before I'm well enough to get out of hospital. I can't have that. If he finds out what I'm planning, he'll stop me even though he's longed to do it himself often enough.

That was too much truth to offer a policeman, so she gave him a different version of the truth instead.

'He's a policeman, yes, but he's my husband in name only. We're estranged. That's why he went back to Berlin: we tried a reconciliation and it didn't work. So I don't want him to know about this, not until I'm ready to tell him myself anyway. I don't know what he'll think or how he'll react.'

Hanni had planted a doubt and now it was Wechsler's expression that flickered. She could see the story piecing itself together in his head: the last-ditch attempt to save a marriage which had ended in a row, the despair that had followed. The desperate decision taken on a lonely towpath. She waited until pity crept into his eyes.

'But I will come in to the station as you asked, in case there are more questions you need me to answer. And I'll be fine now, I'm sure of it. As you said, I'm very lucky.'

That and the increasingly angry nurse was enough to send him away. Hanni slid back against the pillows, her body aching, her stomach sick.

I wasn't supposed to survive. I was supposed to be as dead as my sister.

There was no balance of power to fight over anymore; there was no pendulum swinging back and forth between her and Reiner. Murder was second nature to him and kinship didn't matter. He had sent someone to kill her. Once he knew that the attempt hadn't worked, he would send someone else and there wouldn't be any dodging his reach this time. There wouldn't be a hand to pull her back from a tumble onto a train line or to scoop her out of a river, or the news of a pregnancy to ward off his blow.

He's decided to cut the problem off where it really needs cutting: at its roots.

Reiner didn't make empty threats. Reiner had wanted her out of his way for a very long time and he had plenty of people apparently willing to do his bidding. And Reiner had Leo.

And none of that makes my father safe.

Reiner was ruthless but he had forgotten one vital thing: Hanni wasn't afraid of him anymore. More important than that, his perception of what fatherhood meant was a dark and twisted thing. He had never learned the lengths a loving parent would go to in order to protect their child.

The end was coming, the root was finally going to be yanked out, Hanni was at one with her father about that.

But she wasn't going to be the one who died. He was.

'Oh, thank goodness you're back and all in one piece. Is there anything at all I can get you?'

There was, but Hanni couldn't imagine how the fluttering hotel manager would react if she told him.

Yes, please. I'd like a gun. Something small enough to slip into my pocket. And a supply of bullets to go with it.

She settled for a telephone directory and a pot of tea instead. For all her aches and bruises, and the likelihood that she was still in danger, it was a relief to be out of the hospital and back in some kind of control of her life.

'Two nights' bed rest isn't enough, Frau Schlüssel. You have suffered a concussion that requires monitoring. There may still be problems with your lungs. I cannot agree to your leaving hospital so soon.'

But the doctor, for all his huffing and puffing, couldn't stop her.

Hanni had left the ward with a list of symptoms to look out for and an instruction to rest that she had no intention of following. She had lost two days; she couldn't lose any more: speed was what was needed. But as much as she wanted to, she couldn't leave Frankfurt right away either. Tracking down a weapon would need a day. Her aching head and shaky hands would need one more night in the hotel. There would have to be a quick visit to the police station so that Wechsler wouldn't take it into his head to go looking for her. So two more days. It felt too long, too exposed. Anybody could be watching. She'd had to plan for that too.

Hanni had gone straight from the hospital to a clothes shop where she purchased a far more drab hat and coat than she usually wore. She had scurried into the hotel lobby wrapped in those and gone straight to her room, summoning the manager to her there rather than risking attracting attention by standing at the busy desk. And when she went out again, clutching the meagre list of gun shops she had gleaned from the phone directory, she did it under the presumption that Reiner knew she was alive and was back on her trail. She kept to busy streets and she kept her head down. She was careful and quick but, whatever her furtive movements might have suggested to the contrary, she wasn't afraid. Hanni was set on a path that had been waiting for her for years; all she wanted to do now was run down it.

She didn't make it past the first bend.

I need a gun. I need a gun.

That thought set the rhythm her feet followed through Frankfurt's bustling streets. But what Hanni hadn't realised was how difficult it was for a civilian to get hold of a firearm. Reiner had never been without his Luger while she was growing up. Freddy had carried a police-issue Walther PPK handgun for as long as she had known him and she had used the same make on the training course he had insisted she completed when she first joined the murder squad. She had spent so much time around detectives who slipped on their holsters as easily as they slipped on their jackets, she had stopped noticing the weapons. So she assumed that weapons were easy to get and – beyond finding the names and addresses of the stores in Frankfurt licensed to sell them – Hanni hadn't done any research into the mechanics of acquiring a gun. Which meant that all she raised in her search was suspicion.

'You can't buy one without a permit and you should have applied for that weeks ago. You're not from round here, are you? That's not a local accent. What do you need a gun for anyway? Maybe you'd better tell me that, and where you're staying, and your name.'

She got the same reaction in the three shops she visited and in the antique stores she tried next where the guns available were mostly hunting rifles which were far too big for her purpose. After the fourth grubby shop, where the only thing on offer was a Wehrmacht pistol solid with rust and the same list of questions, Hanni started to imagine the telephones ringing from store to store and a bank of chattering switchboard girls who were all in Reiner's pay. She gave up and retraced her steps even faster to the hotel, arriving there with a throbbing head which made her too slow to dodge the manager.

'I have some good news for you, madam. Your husband will be back with you on the twentieth. You have just missed his telephone call.'

'You didn't tell him about my accident, did you?'

The terse question wasn't the response he expected and it wiped the smile off his face. Hanni didn't have time to soften that or her reply to his confused, 'But surely he already knows?'

'He doesn't and, if he calls again, I would prefer if you kept it that way.'

Hanni hurried from the lobby while he was still groping for words. She knew that she was being horribly unfair, that the poor man simply wanted to make her feel better, but there was nothing good about his news. As odd as it felt, for once Freddy's arrival was the last thing she needed.

Unless I make it work for me by stealing his gun.

It was a ridiculous idea; she dismissed it the moment it jumped into her head. Freddy might not be carrying his firearm and, if he was, he was always meticulous about its whereabouts.

And the second he hears what happened to me on the towpath, he'll have me under lock and key until Reiner's been caught.

She didn't bother to waste any time over *so I won't tell him.* That would require levels of pretence Hanni was determined never to resort to around Freddy again. She wouldn't be able to keep the attack a secret from him and she didn't want to. What she wanted to do was throw herself into his arms and sob out all the fear for her life and for Leo's that she had buried deep inside her since she woke up in the hospital. And give air to the grief and the fury over Luise's death which was nestled beside it. Once Freddy saw the depths of that, or if he got the slightest inclination of what she intended to do, neither she nor his gun would be allowed out of his sight. So it couldn't be Freddy's gun but it had to be someone's. It took Hanni a while to solve that. Her thoughts were still a jumble; her head wasn't entirely her own. But in the middle of the night when the darkness carried too many memories of the black water closing over her head, the solution finally came to her.

Come in to the station once you've been discharged and continue our conversation.

A shop hadn't delivered what she needed, but a shop wasn't the only place where she could pick up a gun.

. . .

'I am very glad to see you, Frau Schlüssel. I would have called into your hotel today if you hadn't come. A few things have come to light since we last spoke that I'm anxious to go through with you.'

Hanni wasn't finding it easy to concentrate. She was too busy trying to drink in as many details of the office and its location as she could. Whether there were usually so few people working on the floor; how many exits and entrances there were; how she might be able to distract one of the few officers bent over their desks for long enough to steal their firearm. She was also trying to block the voice in her head telling her that her plan was madness, that all it would lead to was her arrest. None of that left much room for Wechsler.

'Did you hear me, madam? I said that I have some ongoing concerns around the incident on the towpath that I would like us to discuss. Are you able to do that? Are you recovered enough?'

Hanni pulled herself together and nodded and did her best to give him her full attention, but it was hard to focus on whatever was worrying him when her brain was trying to solve far more important problems.

'All right then.' He glanced down at the papers piled on his desk and pushed one of the sheets towards her. 'I know that you said you were alone at the time of your... fall, but we now have a witness who seems to contradict that. According to his statement, he saw a man hurrying from the riverside within the timeframe that you went into the water. That might not mean anything in itself of course, but the gentleman in question was clutching his hand to his chest and the witness noticed blood on it. Does that, or this description, mean anything to you?'

Hanni scanned the paper he was pointing to which was a

very accurate depiction of her attacker. She shook her head and pushed the testimony back across the desk.

'I'm sorry, but it's like I told you at the hospital: I didn't see anyone else there. If there was a man like that, he must have come later.'

Wechsler sighed and pulled up another sheet of notes. 'I did hope that you would have a better answer for me than that. I don't like coincidences and this is too big a one. So I think that the two of you are connected and that our mysterious injured man had you in his sights that day. Your husband isn't just any policeman, is he? From what I gather, he is very well thought of in Berlin and he's handled a number of high-profile murder cases. So my question is, has some kind of danger followed you here? Has some case spilled over from his city to mine? Is that what is really happening, Frau Schlüssel? Have you brought an assassin onto my streets? Or are you still going to tell me that you tripped and you fell?'

He wasn't pretending to be compassionate anymore; he was watching her as if she was suddenly the threat. Hanni registered that but what she registered more was that Wechsler wasn't wearing a jacket or a gun holster. And that what she needed was to give him something he could spin a story out of in the same way she had done in the hospital. She blinked and began to buy herself time.

'That's what I'm supposed to tell you, yes.'

His body quivered like a hunting dog's, exactly as Hanni had hoped that it would.

'What do you mean, supposed to?'

Once again, just as she had done before, Hanni kept him on a hook and didn't answer.

'Could you let me see the description again? My memory is still horribly clouded, but you've been so kind to look out for my welfare and I do want to help you, whether I'm meant to or not.'

He glanced back down. The sheet she had asked for was

caught under the rest of his notes and it took him a few seconds
to pull it back out. That was all the time Hanni's detail-focused
eyes needed to scope out the office and find his jacket hanging
on a stand by the door. If the jacket was there, the holster could
be with it. This man wasn't Freddy; he was careless, easier to
distract. He was worth taking a gamble on.

Hanni rubbed a hand across her forehead as he handed her
the notes and winced as she scanned them. All it needed then
was to add a shake to her voice that it wasn't hard to maintain.

'My husband and I are estranged – I was telling you the
truth about that. And, yes, his job is a very dangerous one –
that's one of the reasons our marriage didn't work – and I think
the case he's working may have put me in the firing line, and
maybe other people in Frankfurt too. But what happened with
this man was all so quick and there's so much I'm not permitted
to say. I don't know why I came here to the station, except that
you were nice to me and I'm not very used to nice. But I've
already said too much. I just want to leave here and go back to
Berlin. I've booked my ticket for this afternoon so please can I
go now?'

She stopped and gulped and left Wechsler trying to catch
up and thinking that she was close to tears. It had been the right
way to play him. Now that he had the sniff of a case to cling on
to, he was immediately all concern.

'Frau Schlüssel, please don't upset yourself. We have plenty
of time to get to the bottom of this. If needs be we can arrange a
later train – or a car if you would prefer that.'

She managed a smile and a request for a cup of tea that
made him jump to his feet. He looked through the open door,
but whether he was expecting a secretary or a junior officer to
come to his aid, there was nobody around.

'Give me a moment. It's a busy day. I'm sure I can find what
you need.'

And then he was gone, bustling out of the room, clearly

completely unfamiliar with the mechanics of how refreshments normally reached him.

The instant he was out of sight, Hanni leapt to her feet and ran to the coat stand. It was as she thought: Wechsler was no Freddy. The holster was there under his jacket, the gun hanging from it. The weapon was inside her pocket in seconds.

Hanni had never moved so fast. She hurtled through the outer office and down the stairs and past a desk sergeant who was far too occupied with an angry-faced man to notice her.

Her luck held. There was a taxi idling outside the police station. When she jumped out of that at the hotel, the reception was empty. She ran straight to her room, changed out of the drab clothes she had worn to the police station and into a far more elegant outfit. She didn't pack anything beyond a few essentials which she stowed into her handbag – if Freddy arrived back before she did, missing clothes and a missing case would serve as a clue and if she didn't make it back at all... That was an outcome Hanni couldn't think about.

The next hurdle was getting the Opel out of the basement without anyone seeing her. She managed that challenge too. Her confidence soared. As she pulled out of the garage, each step that had to follow became instantly achievable.

If this had been a film, if Hanni had been watching herself, that confidence would have faded in seconds. She would have started screaming *stop* at the moment she walked into Wechsler's office. But Hanni wasn't considering her actions or thinking forward at all. She hadn't questioned her decision to steal the gun. She didn't stop now to think about what Wechsler would do when he realised it was missing. She didn't stop to think about the reality of what taking it meant or what she was intending to do. Or how she could shoot Reiner and protect Leo from the reality of that. Or return from Goslar and greet Freddy as if the world hadn't suddenly imploded. She had blanked out every negative thought in her head as determinedly as she ignored the shake in her hands and the ache in her temple.

From the moment she seized the gun until she turned over the car engine and drove out of Frankfurt, Hanni operated on instinct and had only one focus.

The tree was diseased but the tree was still growing.

The time had come to tear the tree down.

CHAPTER 21

'I understand your concern, Inspector Wechsler, I really do. That's not a discovery any station wants to make, but I can assure you that the loss must be a coincidence. Hanni telephoned me not long before you did to say that she was safely on her way back to Berlin and, whatever may or may not have happened to her in Frankfurt, she is not the kind of woman who would resort to a firearm. Or steal anything. I'll ask her to call you when she arrives, but I doubt she'll be able to help.'

Freddy replaced the receiver in its cradle but he was still hypnotised by it. When he finally managed to snap himself free and turn round, Renny was standing in her bedroom doorway with an all too familiar frown on her face.

'Hanni hasn't called. You've been pacing the floor waiting for her to contact you since you left the message that you were coming. So why did you lie to him and say that she had?'

'I didn't, I...'

He stopped as he realised that the look wasn't the judgement he was conditioned to expect but concern. He hadn't yet adjusted to this new, gentler version of his sister.

'Because I'm worried about her and what she's planning to do, and I didn't want a policeman I don't know to suspect that.'

He followed Renny into the kitchen but he couldn't sit down. The story of Hanni's accident and then her disappearance at the same time as Wechsler's gun had gone missing was far too disturbing to let him relax and it didn't improve with the retelling.

'You don't think it was a fall, do you?'

He shook his head and drained the cup of coffee Renny passed him far more quickly than his jangling nerves wanted him to do.

'No, I don't. That kind of premeditated and anonymous attack has got Reiner written all over it and it's not the first time he's tried it against her. She's discovered something at Hadamar – I can feel it, the same as I could sense that she was avoiding me. I should have kept calling the hotel and forced her to talk but—'

'You were too busy worrying about me.' Renny moved the coffee pot out of his reach and replaced it with a plate of sweet rolls he ignored. 'And now you think that she's stolen a gun and gone after him.'

That was exactly what Freddy thought, but the words said out loud created an impossible scenario. Hanni wasn't a killer. She might hate Reiner but she couldn't point a weapon at him in cold blood and fire, Freddy would stake his life on it. Or put Leo in danger by doing such a desperate thing.

'She could.'

He didn't know Renny was able to read him so well; he was going to need to relearn her.

'Think about everything he's done, Freddy. Never mind all the crimes and the horrors he's inflicted on the wider world, he's ruined her life in so many ways. If Hanni's found out something worse than you already suspected about the way Luise died, that maybe makes Reiner an even worse threat to Leo.

Would it be such a surprise if she snapped?' She frowned again as he stared at her. 'What? Why are you looking at me like that?'

'Because you sound like you care and I'm not used to it.'

A month ago Renny would have bitten his head off for suggesting such a thing. A month ago she had been all jagged edges. Since the firebomb attack, she wasn't that girl anymore. She didn't lose her temper or call him a fool, and she met his stare without flinching.

'That's because I do. I care very much about you, and about Leo, which means that I need to stop holding you back by hating Hanni. I think I stopped doing that a long time ago if I'm honest, but I've been seeing the world in black and white for an awfully long time. That's over with now, but whatever is going on between you and her isn't. Whatever you pretend to yourself or to me, you love her. So if you think she's in trouble, you have to go now and help her get out of it.'

Freddy knew that – he had known that from the moment he put down the telephone receiver. The urge to get straight on the road was the other reason why he couldn't sit down.

'You thought I'd fight you, didn't you? You've been waiting for me to tell you not to bother with her anymore.'

Renny waved away his stammering attempt to deny what they both knew was true and left the kitchen, reappearing with a map which she spread out across the table.

'If the school is near Goslar, then your nearest airport is Hannover. You can hire a car from there and drive the rest of the way. It's too late to leave now but let me call Tempelhof and see how early they can get a police inspector and his assistant onto a flight in the morning.'

It took a moment for *assistant* to register. By the time it did, Renny was already on the telephone and booking two tickets.

'You can't come with me – it's far too dangerous.'

She was the one who couldn't sit down now. She ran round

the flat, pulling a suitcase out of the hall closet, sweeping in and out of the bedrooms and rattling through drawers.

'Which is why I'm not letting you travel alone. If what you suspect is right – that Hanni is on her way to try and kill Reiner – and if she manages to do it, you're going to need me there to look after Leo.'

She didn't have to say 'and you too', but the promise was there in her actions.

'And you can't go after her without more support than just me. You've said yourself that Reiner has eyes – and presumably bodies to do his bidding – everywhere. What if he knows she's on her way? What if he's planning to strike first? I'm not going to volunteer to go to the school with you; I'd only get in the way, but you need to make contact with the local force in Hannover and put them on standby.'

The suitcase was on the table on top of the map; his over-coat was already in it. Freddy sat back as Renny whirled through the packing. The empathetic and practical woman who was determined to organise and support him was such a contrast to the weeping girl he had found bandaged and in shock in a hospital bed – and to the angry and battling girl he had spent so many years living with – it was hard not to feel overwhelmed by the change in her.

'I don't want to feel like this anymore. I want to be happy; I want to belong.'

That had been so hard and yet so hopeful to hear. When she had looked up from her hospital bed and seen him standing in the middle of the ward, her distress had wiped away all the arguments that had ruined the past. Freddy had sat on the bed with his arms around her until Renny stopped sobbing, murmuring 'I know' into her hair. And when she was finally quiet, he hadn't taken her to task for the danger she had put herself and the occupants of the bombed building into. He hadn't attacked her with questions or got angry. He had swallowed all his fears and his misgivings the way Hanni had asked him to do and he had put Renny first.

'I think it's time we talked about Israel. About you making a home there.'

He'd had to repeat it. He'd had to add, 'If that's where you want your future to be, then I'll do all I can to make it happen,' and smile so she knew that he meant it. Then Renny's arms had gone around him and her eyes had come back to life.

And now here we are: making plans together and healing. And no matter where she goes or how long she's away from me, I won't ever lose her again.

'Thank you. For having my back. For being the sister I need.'

His words stopped Renny in her tracks. The smile she gave him made his heart steadier.

'It'll be all right. It has to be. You'll get there on time. He won't hurt Leo or break you two apart again.'

She was so young, so full of hope. Freddy couldn't remember a time when he'd been either of those things, but he nodded because she needed him to and he tried his very best to believe her.

CHAPTER 22

19–20 APRIL 1963, GOSLAR, WEST GERMANY

Hanni drove with her hands locked onto the wheel, watching the miles disappear, only stopping when she needed to consult the road map Freddy had stored in the glove compartment. For the first hour of the journey she kept her eyes fixed on the road ahead and avoided looking in the rear-view mirror, convinced that there would be a parade of blue lights stretching behind her if she did. Nothing appeared.

Away from East German roads and allowed to cruise closer to its top speed, the Opel covered the distance between Frankfurt and the small town of Goslar in a little over four hours. That was quicker than Hanni had hoped for but it was still close to sunset by the time she arrived. She didn't want to break her journey: the school was only another half an hour away. Every instinct told her to push on.

Except Hanni was no longer acting on instinct. She'd had a long drive to reflect on where that course of action could have landed her, and she was certain that stealing a gun from a police station had used up all her day's luck. Reiner's flagship school had lived in her head for years, but she had no reference for its layout other than a handful of grainy photographs she had seen thirteen years earlier in Prague. Everything about the place was an unknown and she had no desire to blunder around its grounds in the dark. She had no desire to take any more risks at all, not with the prize so close. And not if a too-hasty act could put Leo at risk. Whatever else happened in the next twenty-four hours, she had to keep Leo safe, and Hanni was under no illusions about how difficult that would be. If Reiner realised that she was on her way to reckon with him, he would use her son as a human shield.

Reiner on his own territory in front of her, Wechsler full of suspicion behind and her window to do what had to be done closing. It was hard to weigh up which option carried more danger: driving on or staying put.

Except no one knows I've come this way, so maybe there's no one on my trail yet. If Wechsler is looking for me, he'll be looking towards Berlin.

It had been a flimsy story about leaving, conjured up in the heat of the moment. A phone call to the train station would reveal it as a lie. All Hanni could hope was that the detective wouldn't pursue it. That he would assume she had lost her nerve and bolted and taken whatever danger she represented with her out of his city. And that he wouldn't immediately discover the loss of his gun or connect the two events any time soon.

Or telephone Freddy.

That was the biggest flaw in her very flawed plan. Freddy knew that Reiner had played a key role in Luise's death and he hadn't wanted her to go to Hadamar alone in case the truth was worse than they suspected. He would piece together the story of a missing gun and a missing injured wife in a heartbeat and he would guess where Hanni was heading, even if he refused to believe what she was intending to do when she got there. And he would do everything in his power to stop her. But he was hours behind her and that was all *perhaps* and *maybe* and *will he make it?*, whereas her need to face and defeat Reiner was certain. Which meant that a delay might not be ideal, especially when she was so close, but it would have to be borne. There would, after all, be no second chances.

So close.

The words settled around Hanni like ice as she drove into the small town. This was Reiner's kingdom. His school must have brought wealth and jobs to the area; if his influence was spread thick anywhere it was here, no matter how hard it was to see his shadow. Goslar was a charming place, a setting for a fairy tale filled with medieval towers and half-timbered houses with shingled red rooftops. It was currently packed with families meandering happily through the cobbled streets and lingering in front of its brightly lit shop windows. On any other day it would be the perfect place to stop and be distracted, to rest her tired bones and breathe, but stopping and exploring was another risk Hanni couldn't take. Even pretty places had fast-running rivers and dark corners and people who chose not to see. Even fairy-tale settings could be rotten beneath.

It's one night, no more, a matter of hours. By this time tomorrow, Reiner will be dead.

Hanni parked the car outside a small hotel which was a little more faded and a little less busy than the flower-covered ones which crowded the main square. She signed the register with a made-up name and paid her bill with small notes that wouldn't attract comment. And then she went to her room and hid herself away until dawn.

Her confidence began to plummet the next morning, half a dozen miles outside Goslar, when exhaustion finally broke down the walls she had built around her since the towpath attack and the voice shouting *stop* roared back in.

She hadn't slept. She had barely eaten since she left the

hospital. She had spent so much of her energy refusing to focus on anything but getting a gun and getting to Reiner, she had nothing left over, and her tired brain felt as if it had developed a dozen little cracks. If she let her concentration drift even for a moment, *don't do this or you turn into him* filled up her head. The gun in her pocket began to feel like a weight that could bury her, not a comfort.

It didn't help that the school was located in such a secluded spot, so well protected from prying eyes. There was nobody close enough to be called a neighbour. It was set back from the road behind ornamental gates patterned with sharp-tipped ivy leaves and topped with a pair of stone lions who looked menacingly real. It was also on a far grander scale than it had appeared in the photographs. From where Hanni was standing, tucked into a copse of trees opposite the main entrance, the driveway looked wide enough to host one of Goebbels' most elaborate parades. Even if she could somehow manage to talk her way past the intercom system fixed to the side of the gate, driving along its expanse alone would be a far too vulnerable thing to do. She would stand out, even though she had done her best to blend in. Hanni had come dressed in a dark blue shift dress with a matching swing coat and low-heeled buckled court shoes, intending to look the part of a prosperous parent. Now she wished she had worn ski pants and heavy boots, something more suited to climbing walls and hiding in shrubbery.

She checked her watch. It was eight thirty, too early perhaps for the stream of parents she had hoped would arrive on a Saturday morning, to take their sons out for the day or shout themselves hoarse at sporting fixtures. Too early yet to give up.

So close.

But now it wasn't the proximity to Reiner which prickled her skin; it was the fact that Leo was somewhere on the other side of the gates. To be so near and yet so separate from him was agony. To have no idea how deeply Reiner had got his claws into her boy was terrifying.

And what if I make things worse? What if I fail and he runs to his grandfather and rejects me again? Or what if I succeed and he hates me forever?

She was drowning again, the icy water pulling her under, unable to tell which way was up and which way was down. Unable to push *whatever I do, I'll lose him* and *he'll never understand* out of her head. She turned back to the car; she turned back to the gate. She had to hold on to a branch to stop herself spinning.

Another half hour passed in a haze of indecision. The day began to warm. Hanni stayed rooted to the spot, her hand in her pocket, her head split in two as, for the first time, she properly considered the reality of what she had come here to do. Trying to imagine the action of killing and unable to see herself squeezing the trigger. Reconciling herself to going back, to pursuing the case through the court, to doing the right thing. To accepting the impossibility of her plan and walking away. And then a long black Mercedes purred past her and the gates opened but didn't close. A few moments later another limousine appeared and then an Opel not unlike the one she was driving added itself to the line sweeping down the drive. Within another twenty minutes, the cars had formed a steady line, some disappearing, some driving out again almost immediately with a boy or two in the back. Throughout all the activity, the two halves of the gate stayed firmly apart.

Hanni hadn't gambled wrongly, or not on the school's timetable at least: Saturday was a busy day full of families coming and going, an easy one to mingle in with. And the newspapers hadn't over-exaggerated the kind of parents Reiner's schools attracted. Every one of the cars that sped past her was a luxury model. The men in the driving seats were solid and shiny; the women sitting next to them were heavy with boredom and furs. The boys loaded into the back of the cars driving out could have been cut from the same high-cheekboned and blonde-haired mould. Reiner was cultivating an elite, a whole regiment of Valentin Gessners to go out and do his bidding, exactly as he'd promised her he would do when he had unveiled his plans in Prague.

He is the rotten thing here. Everything he touches turns the world bad.

Hanni held the gun tighter. What she was about to do was as right as it was wrong. Leo would have to understand. Freddy would have to make him understand. She had spent too many years of her life stepping back, letting Reiner flourish, not taking aim. That was done.

Hanni smoothed her dress, checked that the gun wasn't spoiling the lines of her coat and got back into the Opel. The cars were still coming, slowing almost to a crawl. With a final pat of her pocket, Hanni pulled out into the traffic and joined them.

The cars streamed steadily along the curving drive, peeling off at regular intervals towards what Hanni assumed were dormitories or sports fields. The school was so dazzling close up, it was hard to concentrate and monitor exactly where the other visitors were going.

Palatial was the best word she could think of to describe the expanse of buildings which greeted her as she reached the widest point of the drive. The main entrance was flanked by a pair of sturdy columns which wouldn't have looked out of place at the Parthenon and accessed by a double flight of stone steps which demanded trailing skirts and a fleet of horse-drawn carriages to do them justice. The main building was square; the rest was a swoop of white wings glistening with diamond-paned windows which radiated out on both sides. As Hanni drove past the second of those, a cloister appeared linking the right-hand wing to a dome-topped octagonal building with the baroque air of a church. Every inch of the complex breathed privilege and wealth. It was also a photographer's dream. She slowed the car to a crawl as the sun bounced in an arc off the walls and the windows and draped dappled shadows across the cloister's carved arches, picturing the detail in the shots she could take.

Leo must have been overwhelmed by the scale of it when he first came; he must have thought he'd stepped into a storybook.

The image of her son scurrying through the school to his classes and the thought of what he might have been taught there snapped Hanni out of her trance. Nothing here deserved her camera; nothing deserved to be made grander. The line of cars had thinned out a little as some of them turned off the main thoroughfare, but the church appeared to be the destination for the majority.

Hanni followed them, making her way to a large car park where she slid the Opel between two low-slung black Daimlers which would have looked perfectly at home at an SS rally. That the men who climbed out and stepped round to open the passenger doors for their waiting wives were dressed in business suits and not the uniforms Hanni's brain had instantly conjured up came as a welcome relief. She still had to force herself to smile as she stepped out to join them, to focus on the couples in front of her and not the ones marching through her imagination.

'Are you here for the debate?'

One of the women had noticed her husband noticing Hanni and stepped immediately between them. Hanni nodded and whispered a silent thanks that she wouldn't have to build a story entirely from scratch.

'I am, yes. It's also my first one so I'm feeling a little out of place. My husband usually attends this kind of thing but he's away on business.' She smiled as the woman, whose face had relaxed a little at *husband,* rolled her eyes. 'Well I don't need to explain all the burdens of that to you now, do I? But I do have to confess that I'm rather nervous and not quite sure what to do or to expect.'

'Don't worry about that. We can look after you, and as to what to expect – well, the best way to describe it is that you're in for a treat.'

The unspoken appeal to *I'm a neglected wife and isn't it a bore* had worked. A gloved hand attached itself to Hanni's elbow and swept her into the group.

'Dear Herr Foss calls these sessions his training ground for government and he's utterly right. You'll see for yourself what he means when they get started: the boys are so eloquent and so witty. I swear one day they'll be running the world.'

Hanni joined in the laughter but slipped away from the self-congratulatory couples who had surrounded her the instant the ushers who were there to guide the audience into the building began shepherding them inside. *Dear Herr Foss* was bad enough; *running the world* was frighteningly accurate. It took all Hanni's self-control not to lose her grip on the grounds she was standing in. It would have been the easiest thing in the world to fall back in time to the palace gardens in Prague where she had listened in horror to Reiner laying out his plans.

My army will fight its wars quietly. My boys will be perfectly suited to every role that they take.

Take was the key word. Reiner's pupils weren't the kind who stood back and waited, and neither was Reiner. He would use his influence to make sure that every position his pupils got their hands on, whether that success was in industry or finance or in the media or politics, would be the only positions that mattered.

He's rooted their ideals in his fascist view of the world and now they will go out and seed them everywhere that they go. How could any parent be proud of that?

Maybe they wouldn't be; maybe they didn't know. Maybe if

they did, they would be horrified and pull their boys out of Reiner's clutches.

Hanni whirled round, convinced she was surrounded by hoodwinked families who would be stunned if they knew the truth. Ready to launch into a lecture that would derail Reiner's life without her having to physically end it. And then she caught sight of a father clasping hands with his son and she stopped. What if she was wrong? What if everyone knew exactly the type of man Reiner was, and they didn't care? Or they actively supported him? And who would listen anyway if she tried to explain that the education system which she could hear more than one parent describing as wonderful was actually poison? That it was something Hitler himself would have applauded? Or if she began listing Reiner's war crimes? She would be dismissed as a crank, or a danger; she would be hounded out of the school.

And then he would be the one coming after me.

'Madam, if you would like to attend the debate, now would be a good time to take your seat. We can't let anybody in once the speeches have started and it would be a shame to miss today's event. We've some of our brightest speakers lined up.'

Even if Hanni could have commanded an audience it had gone, following a group of young men who were greeting their guests with the same blend of politeness and charm as the one who was smiling at her. A group, now that she looked at them properly, who were all dressed as oddly as him. His suit could have been worn by Kaiser Wilhelm at the turn of the century – it was only lacking a chest full of medals. His black coat was cut short and tightly fitted at the waist before flaring out into tails. The collar above his white bow tie was so stiffly starched, he could barely lower his chin. His outfit was so far removed from what the fathers around him were wearing, he could have been a time-traveller.

He saw Hanni staring and smiled. 'You must be one of our

newer parents. It's rather formal isn't it, this rig-out? But tradition matters here. Wait until your son is old enough to wear this part of the uniform – you'll be as proud of him in it as he is.'

The thought of Leo dressed and behaving in the same mannered way, as if all eyes were on his performance, was chilling. Hanni muttered something noncommittal and followed her guide into the chamber in silence, blinking as the light instantly dimmed. The boys arranged in two opposing sides on the stage were dressed in the same outdated fashion as the ushers, although the speakers' bow ties were red. But it wasn't the lines of speakers who demanded Hanni's attention, or not once she had scanned their faces and determined that Leo was too young to be one of them. What had caused her heart to skip and then to speed up was the debating hall itself.

Why can't they see it? was her first thought, followed by the sickening crash of *what if they can?*

The colours of the room – from the curtains framing the stage to the school crest picked out on the banners edging the walls, from the tail suits and stiff shirts worn by the boys to the pamphlets outlining the day's topic which awaited each guest – were uniformly red, white and black. Oak leaves and edelweiss sprigs had been carved into the benches where the parents were sitting and shuffling. The light was provided by candles and torches and a drum roll called the audience to silence. The signs and allusions were all very subtly done, but they were unmistakeably there. It was as if Goebbels had waved a wand over the chamber and sprinkled echoes of the Third Reich through its entire fabric.

Hanni stared around the packed benches, watching each face as closely as she dared. No one seemed uncomfortable. No one flinched as they glanced at the motto picked out in thick black gothic lettering above the stage. *Be More Than You Seem.* They should have done: it was a close adaptation of the one the Napola schools had used while they educated the future leaders of the Thousand-Year Reich. Nobody flinched either when silence fell and the solemn boy standing to attention at the lectern read out what was announced as the event's opening prayer:

'We often heard the sound of your voice
And listened silently, with folded hands,
As each word sank into our souls.
The pure faith that you have given us
Pulses through, guides our young lives.
You alone are the way, the goal.'

However Reiner had packaged it to his pupils, whether as an ode to God or a reflection of the comradeship and loyalty Hanni assumed ran like an artery through the school, what the boy was reciting wasn't a prayer. It was part of a song once sung by the Hitler Youth. Its title had once been 'In Praise of the Führer'. Plenty of the fathers in the room must have been in that organisation in their younger years and sung it at the tops of their voices, but nobody else seem disturbed to hear it again now. Nobody else looked as if they were about to be sick.

Hanni pushed her hands under her knees and gripped the bench as the debate began. It was unbearable to listen to, some fabricated premise about a belief in tradition being the hallmark of a true German. A premise whose roots, like everything else in the chamber, were deformed things. The speakers tossing the subject about were exactly as eloquent as Reiner's fan club had promised. Their poise and wit were remarkable. Everyone except Hanni seemed to be utterly entranced by their performance, swept along by a wave of arguments that relied far more on confidence and a flair for entertaining the audience than any interest in substance. The watching crowd was so enthusiastic, it was a while before Hanni realised that hers wasn't the only head which kept sinking. There was one boy among the crowd of cheering younger pupils whose face was pointed determinedly down, who was sat at the end of a bench with a noticeable space around him. Who looked as lost as she felt.

Leo. It was Leo. Sitting apart, not joining in.

It was all Hanni could do to stay on her seat.

Look up, look up. Find me.

She wanted to shout, she wanted to leap from her place and run to him. Instead she focused her attention on the downcast head, willing him to sense her, to feel her presence through the air. Her eyes were aching by the time he finally looked up.

'Leo. My boy. My love.'

She had said it aloud, not that anybody heard her above the thundering applause. But Leo could see her – he was staring straight at her, so she said it again, slowly so that he could read the words on her lips. He didn't move; his face remained frozen.

Hanni waited for his reaction, her nails digging into her palms. She waited for contempt, for fury. For him to alert the teachers enthusiastically joining in the applause to the enemy in their midst. In that moment whatever he did or said didn't matter: it was enough simply to see him. But Leo didn't do anything except stare. Until he blinked. And his mouth opened and he answered her in a silent plea that said *Mum* and then *help.*

'I hate it here and I hate him. I was so wrong about everything. I'm so sorry.'

He was shaking as he fell into her arms and his words were garbled and muffled by tears.

He hasn't fallen under Reiner's spell. He hasn't been broken.

The fear that had set Leo trembling was heartbreaking but the knowledge that Reiner hadn't destroyed him ran through Hanni with all the warmth of a well-tended and safe hearth. Hanni held her son close, breathing him in, painfully aware that even a few weeks away had physically changed him, that he had grown lankier and taller; that she had to stretch a little further to kiss him.

But he is still my boy and all the best parts of him are here.

And he was still in danger; they both were.

'We need to get out of sight.'

She pulled him into the shadow of the debating house's high wall. Leo had been careful when she had nodded to the door and he had slipped out of the hall – he had waited until the main speaker had taken the stage and begun whipping up the applause. That didn't mean nobody would come looking. Hanni needed to get him off the school premises and to safety, but Leo needed to talk.

'I wanted to come home almost from the same day that I got here, but he wouldn't let me leave. I don't understand him. One minute he's telling me I can be anything I want if I try and the next he acts as if he can't stand me and he thinks I'm useless at everything. He only seems to like me when we're in public. And he made me write that letter telling you I was happy when I wasn't. It's about you, isn't it? He's keeping me here to upset you, which wasn't what I meant to happen. He's horrible; he's not a hero. He's not what I thought he was at all.'

He was crying again and trying hard not to. Hanni dried his tears with her fingertips and took tight hold of his hands, her heart lifting as she realised that everything she and Freddy had hoped would happen when they made Reiner's crimes public was already done. Leo loathed his grandfather; he hadn't fallen under his spell. Her task had suddenly grown easier.

'I know you didn't want any of this. But yes, sweetheart, this is about me. I've been fighting your grandfather for years but that was never supposed to involve you. And it's not your fault, Leo. Nothing that's happened or will happen is your fault.'

His frown was a mirror of Freddy's. 'What do you mean *will happen?*'

Hanni shook her head, conscious that, even if Leo hadn't

been missed, one of the parents who had tried to befriend her might have noticed her slipping out. That somebody might already be asking questions.

'It doesn't matter now. What matters is getting you out of here.'

A look flashed across his face that a month ago she would have taken for sullenness. She now realised it was fear and an inability to find the words to express that.

'I messed up too, pet. I didn't answer your questions the way that you needed. I didn't trust you to understand. And when you left...' She shook her head. 'I wanted to come after you straight away, I really did. You have to know that. I didn't abandon you, I promise, and neither did your father. We've been working on a way to get you back since you left, but we were so afraid that—'

'I'd have fallen for his charm and his lies and wouldn't come with you if you'd turned up here and tried. Well he didn't stay charming for long, and I'm more than ready to be done with him.'

Leo hadn't just grown taller; he'd grown up. Hanni nodded.

'I wanted him to be a hero though. I really did.'

His voice cracked. Hanni squeezed his hand and he managed to steady himself.

'I wanted you to be wrong and I wanted to be one of his boys, which is what they call themselves here. I don't now. Everyone who worships him is a robot – that's what all the rules here make you into. You're not meant to care about anything except your classmates and the school. Nobody talks about family, or not in the way that you do – the outside kind doesn't count here. Everything's about loyalty and honour and forging future networks which are going to change the world. The teachers say that all the time but I've no idea what it means. And when he's not pretending that he's delighted I'm here, I'm not good enough for him to be proud of me. I'm *average*, I'm *weak*. And I'm part Jewish which he says is the worst sin in the world. He's obsessed with that. He's obsessed with elites. And he's obsessed with stamping out *bad blood* and I sometimes think that includes me.'

Leo stopped and rubbed his face. Hanni somehow managed not to panic and pull him away with her as the truth she'd been fearing burst out but let him find the words he was struggling with instead.

'I must sound so stupid. My grandfather the Nazi is obsessed with everything the Nazis were obsessed with. He did it all, didn't he? All the things that Renny said about him were true. He's heartless and hateful. He caused the deaths of thousands of people and he doesn't care.'

Leo's face suddenly hardened and aged. 'I hate him. I hate what I said before about the murders in the war being lies and what I nearly turned into. I hate what I've put you and my dad through. I never want anything to do with Reiner or Emil or whatever he calls himself or anyone like him again. I hope he comes to the worst kind of end. I hope someone makes him suffer.'

Leo was an angry and betrayed child lashing out. His words weren't permission. Hanni knew that he would be frightened and horrified if she told him that she intended to inflict exactly that kind of suffering on his grandfather. But it was what Hanni needed to hear – about her son's state of mind and about what Reiner deserved – and the relief pushed a new wave of strength through her.

'The debate's coming close to an end.'

Leo turned as voices rose inside the chamber. Hanni could hear applause and laughter, the sound of more willing participants seduced by the promise of power and greatness trickling down onto their sons. Of more boys and their parents caught up in the dazzle of Reiner's glittering futures, seeing the false gold that littered the surface and not the black underneath.

'We have to go.'

Leo was pulling at her sleeve.

'He'll be in his office now but he likes to sweep in once the speakers have finished and hold court for the parents. There's a reception in the cloisters afterwards and they all line up to clap him when he appears.'

And this was it, the moment she had been dreading. She had found her beloved boy and now, rather than holding on to him, she had to send him away with no way of knowing when she would see him again.

Maybe this is what our future will be, a handful of snatched meetings.

That could have stopped her, that could have bundled her back into the car clutching him tight. But Reiner was about to be feted and fawned over, and next week he would be fawned over again. If he could deliver the successes these parents and the ones on his waiting list were paying for, he would be fawned over for years. The legacy that adulation would spawn was far worse than losing years of freedom with her son. So it couldn't be *we have to go* no matter how much she wanted it to be; it had to be *you have to.*

Hanni reached into the pocket of her coat which didn't contain the gun and pulled out an envelope. 'How long do I have before that happens?'

'Half an hour, maybe forty minutes at the most.'

It was enough time to do what she needed. She held out the envelope.

'Leo, sweetheart, you have to do what I tell you now and without asking questions. You have to leave here at once and get yourself to Goslar. Do you know the way?'

He nodded. 'I think so.'

'Good. It shouldn't take more than an hour if you walk at a fast pace. When you arrive, go straight to the train station. There's money in here, more than you'll need to get you home

to Berlin. Take the first train that you can and then head straight
to your father's apartment. Can you do that?'

He nodded again.

'Okay, that's settled then. But you mustn't talk to anyone at
all, not on the way to Goslar or on the train, and you mustn't
give anybody your name. That's really important, Leo. Do you
promise?'

He nodded again but she could see he was bursting with the
questions she'd told him not to ask.

'I can't come with you. I have to speak to your grandfather
and I have to do that alone. And I have to know that you are
safely away from here while I do that so that I can concentrate
on him.'

'And what about you?'

It wasn't a question Hanni had expected so she didn't
understand what he meant.

'Will you be safe? If you go and challenge him, will you be
safe too?'

She wanted to say *of course* and *there's nothing to worry
about* but Leo had moved out of childhood and past the safety
net of false promises.

'I don't know. But if I deal with him the way I should have
dealt with him years ago, then you will be and your father will
be, and that's all I care about.'

There was a pause while he scanned her face and then Leo
reached out his hand and touched Hanni's cheek in a gesture
that was both so old and so young she had to bite down on her
lip to stop herself breaking.

'His office is on the first floor of the main building, up the
stairs to the right. His secretary is never there on a Saturday.'

'Thank you.'

Hanni had already dropped his hands; she was about to
turn away, afraid that if she let the goodbye linger she wouldn't
be able to let him go. His sudden grab for her and the ferocity of

his hug took her by surprise and she swung into his embrace, forgetting to shield the heavier side of her coat. Leo stepped back as the weight of the pocket bumped into him.

'What's that? What have you got? What are you going to do?'

His voice cracked and turned him back into a little boy. And Hanni couldn't say or do anything to make him feel better.

'You have to go, Leo. You have to walk away and not ask me.'

He didn't want to. She almost had to push him to get him onto the path. When he finally gave in and did as she asked, it took all Hanni's self-control not to throw away the gun and run after him.

I might never hold him again.

The clock was ticking, her window was closing but Hanni was slumped against the wall, her bones turned to liquid. She couldn't move. Not until Leo disappeared round the bend in the drive and was gone and she had drunk in every last drop of him.

CHAPTER 23

Unlike the busy debating chamber and the crowded playing fields Hanni spotted in the distance as she drove back along the drive, there were no cars parked outside the main building and the reception hall was deserted.

Hanni stood in the doorway, counting the number of doors that ran off it, alert for the slightest movement or noise. Now that Leo was out of harm's way, now that she was only feet away from her father and there were no barriers left between them, Hanni had wiped away all the doubts and surrendered herself to the act that was coming.

She moved slowly, taking care. She didn't run straight across the foyer towards the wide central staircase. She was too conscious of the sound her heels would make clicking across the marble floor. She kept to the edges instead, following the thin strip of red carpet which formed a border to the black-and-white tiles. She kept to the edge of the stairs too as she went up them and held on to the banister, partly to give the impression to anyone who came in behind her that she wasn't in a hurry, partly to steady her hand.

The first-floor corridor was as empty as the entrance hall

below. Hanni quickened her pace as adrenaline started
pumping through her body. And somewhere between the top of
the stairs and the turn to the right Leo had told her to follow, the
years started to blend one into the other. Halfway along the
corridor and she was no longer thinking about Leo, or Freddy, or
herself. She was no longer walking down a school hallway. In
Hanni's head the hall now had a powder-blue carpet and silk-
covered walls hung with paintings of long-dead relatives. And
the room she was heading towards, her head still ringing with
the terrible scream which had just spun out of it, was guarded
by a man with no heart.

OFFICE OF THE SCHOOL DIRECTOR: EMIL FOSS

The brass plaque on the door brought Hanni back to the
present with a jolt. The name was out of place: for a moment it
meant nothing to her. And then it meant everything. That easy
slip he had made out of one identity and into another with no
questions asked was shorthand for everything that had gone
wrong since the war.

No justice, no one responsible. Everybody moving on as if the
horrors of the past were someone else's doing and not to be poked
at. Everything riddled with secrets and lies.

Hanni stopped with her hand on the doorknob. She closed
her eyes and let it come. The fury she had been holding at bay
since Tobias had laid bare the truth of Luise's death. The hatred
for Reiner that had consumed her as he described the first
needle breaking, the second needle slamming in. She let the fire
that image had lit deep within her burn through her body. She
let its horror take her father's shape. And then she opened her
eyes and she nodded and the next breath she took was a
clear one.

. . .

Leo had been right: there was nobody waiting to act as gatekeeper in the outer office. Reiner was unprotected, alone.

Hanni moved silently through the immaculate room towards the inner door. That was ajar. She could hear a one-sided conversation spilling through it, punctuated by an all-too-familiar laugh which scratched nettle-sharp across her skin. She waited for the conversation to end, for the sound of the receiver clicking back into place. For Reiner to be without help. She didn't waste time working out what her first words would be or at what moment she would reach for the gun. She assumed that whatever came next would find its own pattern.

More laughter. A promise to meet at some future date which Reiner would never honour. A click.

Hanni pushed the door open and went in. This office was twice the size of the outer one, with a window facing the lawn which stretched almost from floor to ceiling. It was also decorated, as Reiner's offices always were, to impress. Wood panelling and crimson wallpaper covered the walls, and a gallery of photographs of the school's many balls and galas, which all featured Reiner at their centre, hung on display. Her father's preferred surroundings hadn't changed since the days when he'd been employed by the British in their offices at Fehrbelliner Platz, setting up schools for the city's bombed-out children.

When he laid down the groundwork for this.

His surroundings hadn't changed and neither had he. *The dashing Herr Emil.* That was how the young secretaries had described him in 1947; Hanni imagined it was how a good proportion of the mothers described him now. He was standing behind his desk, slipping his arms into a beautifully tailored suit jacket, smoothing his tie; becoming the charming school director his audience expected. The sight of him made her sick.

Not that he acknowledged her. He didn't greet her; he didn't look her way. Maybe because the carpet was thick and the door was silent and he hadn't heard her. Maybe because he was used to staff and servants who knew better than to speak until they were spoken to. Whichever it was didn't matter to Hanni; he would see her soon enough.

She waited, watching him get into his role. And then he looked up and the mask slipped. Shock flashed across his face, followed seconds later by a hatred Hanni was happy to see there. It was his true face. It was the last face Luise would have seen. Its presence told her she was right.

'Hannelore, I wondered when you might appear. If only you'd given me warning, I would have arranged a welcome party and a tour.'

It was the quick recovery she expected from him. It was also a bid for control. Hanni let him carry on. It wouldn't be long before he realised his mistake.

'It's a remarkable building, don't you think? Did you know that it once belonged to Göring? I think he'd approve of what I've done with his legacy. Some of the artwork you'll see displayed on the walls came from his collections. He was quite the magpie in his day, but I'm sure you remember that. You did use to enjoy talking about art with him.'

It was a clever move, reminding her of the circles he had once moved in and the privileged life she had lived as a result. Reminding her of the power he still wielded. Playing games. Hanni let him have that too. She slipped her hand into her pocket and wondered briefly if he thought she was cowed by his posturing. She wasn't; she doubted she would ever be cowed by him again. It was time she made him aware of that.

'I'm sure that he was. I doubt that there was a gallery or a confiscated home in Berlin that he didn't rummage his fingers through. But that's not the crime I'm here to discuss.'

Reiner adjusted the line of his jacket and dusted an invisible speck of dust from his sleeve. 'Crime, really? Are we going down that road again? And what's the charge this time: kidnapping?'

His sigh was deliberately theatrical. Hanni equally deliberately didn't react.

'In case you've forgotten, daughter dear, Leo came here of his own accord. Can you blame him given the ramshackle way you've raised him? The boy wants structure; he wants to make something he can be proud of out of his life. He's got ambition and he understands what it takes to get on in the world. Or is that a crime in your eyes too?'

He had stepped back closer to his desk as he was talking. Hanni assumed that he didn't trust her, that he had a weapon of some sort too. But his was inside a drawer not a pocket and would need a grab to get it he wouldn't have time to make.

She shrugged. 'Not at all. I want Leo to be ambitious; I want him to find his place in the world. I'm happy that he does too. And I'm even happier that he understands he won't find the way to the life he deserves at your school.'

Reiner stopped reaching for his desk drawer and stared at her. Hanni allowed herself a small smile as he frowned.

'He's not here anymore. He's gone and he's safe, so whatever you were planning to do with him to break me is done.'

She shook her head as he glanced at the telephone. 'Don't bother. You won't find him; he won't come back. You got it wrong with him, that's the best part of this. He came here looking for a hero and you showed him a monster instead. He saw you for what you are and he hates you. He hates everything that you did and everything that you stand for. Do you know how happy that makes me? You opened his eyes and now I'll never have to tell him again how rotten you are. You wanted to warp him and you taught him to look below the surface instead. Maybe I should thank you for that. You failed, Reiner. He was yours for the taking, but you don't have the love and the humanity in you that a good boy like Leo needs and he saw it. You failed.'

There was no more pretence of boredom. There was no more baiting. There was no father in the room, no daughter.

'What do you want, Hannelore? If your sad little son is gone, why are you still here? Don't tell me that this is another futile attempt to make me pay. Didn't you learn anything about how pointless that is in Prague? Or on the towpath in Frankfurt?'

There was menace in the line of his shoulders and the curl of his fists and Hanni knew better than to ignore that. But there was also a flicker in his eyes as he glanced at the desk drawer which felt like unease.

And the longer I stand here without buckling, the deeper that unease will run.

He was still talking, his tone growing increasingly strident.

'What is the matter with you? I warned you more than once to stop this ridiculous contest between us but you still can't let the past die. Even though nobody else cares about it but you. You're a fool, Hannelore. The world has marched on and you've got no place in it. So nobody will miss you when you're gone.'

It was a joy to realise how easily his threat bounced off her. She was too in control now to even be angry.

'If there's a fool here it's you. Don't you follow the news? Do you really not know that, since Eichmann, the world has moved back in step with me? People do care. They're going to start looking back and asking why and who and how do we stop it happening again. If anything is over, it's your sad little dream that you can bring the Reich back with your brainwashed boys. Nobody wants that anymore, except for a handful of fanatics and fools who will soon disappear back into oblivion. Along with you.'

He wasn't listening. He was so used to winning he only

heard what he chose. He thought he was back on familiar territory – that was obvious from his smile.

'This is about closing the schools, isn't it? You're wasting
your time but be my guest, have a go. What do you think will
work best? Telling all the parents who are waiting to applaud
me that the education they pay a fortune for, which is already
delivering graduates into the best universities and highly
successful careers, is part of a fascist conspiracy? Good luck
with that. Your son was too fragile to cope with our methods;
you're a single mother and unstable. How difficult do you think
that story will be to spin? If it's my schools that are the great
crime you've come here to accuse me of, I think that we're
done.'

'It's not.'

Her hand gripped the barrel; her finger found the trigger.
This was her moment to make Reiner understand exactly why
she hated him so much and what price he was about to pay and
she had no intention of hurrying it. She took her time explaining. She let him run the possibilities through his head.

'But there is a crime that needs punishment. I'm surprised
you don't know what it is, given how closely you've been
following me. Maybe you really haven't put the pieces together;
maybe you're too used to getting away with it all. And you were
clever, weren't you? You hid all your sins in plain sight. All the
camps and the killings you had your hands in and yet you never
once signed anything; you never once took a visible lead. You
literally buried the evidence and swapped your whole identity,
never mind your name. But no one is that clever, Reiner. No
one can do the things you did and leave no trace. For every old
lady who ends up at the foot of her stairs, there's always a corner
you didn't look into, a door you didn't look behind.'

She had his attention now. Every inch of him was focused
on her.

'I followed your trail, step by step, crumb by crumb. I

started with a scream from my mother's bedroom that you blamed on a nightmare and I unpicked my whole life to find out the truth.'

She nodded as his face blanched. 'You're with me now, aren't you? You're standing beside me in Luise's bedroom, watching her become the kind of child you didn't want. You're next to me at Hadamar, leading a little girl into an operating theatre by the hand. An innocent little girl whose only *crime* was that she was sick. Who trusted her father, who didn't realise that he was hollow, that there was a void where his heart should have been. Who trusted him to do what he was meant to do and care for her.'

It was the first time she had ever seen him unable to speak.

Her words wouldn't stop flowing. 'Well you did that, didn't you? You certainly took care of her. I've called you a monster before, but I didn't know the real depths of it; I didn't have a clue. But somebody did; somebody saw. There weren't three of you there that night – there was a fourth. There was a witness who watched the needle break, who watched the nurse fall. Who watched you step in and murder my sister.'

There was a moment when the world stopped. When her words swelled and filled the room and tore the arrogance and the certainty from Reiner's face. When a long-dead little girl was suddenly alive again and screaming in fear. And then Reiner lunged for the drawer.

'Stop. Step back.'

The gun was out, nestled in her hand, aimed directly at the point where his heart should have been. He stepped back but he didn't raise his hands. She almost admired him when he opted for contempt not surrender.

'Put the gun down, Hannelore. You're making a fool of yourself.'

She brought her left hand up to cup her right and braced

her feet. Reiner's fear, because it had finally flooded his face as she took up a shooting position, steadied her.

'You can't do this, Hannelore. Never mind the prison sentence you'll get – Leo will never forgive you.'

'I will.'

The voice came from the doorway. Leo was behind her. He had come into the room as silently as Hanni had. Reiner faltered but Hanni didn't turn, she didn't flinch, even though Leo began talking directly to her. Even though there were other noises now too. A door slamming below them, feet clattering on the stairs. Hanni kept her eyes on Reiner and her finger on the trigger.

'I will forgive you, Mum, if you shoot him. He deserves it. He deserves to die as afraid as all the people whose deaths he arranged. And he is afraid, look at him. You did that; you broke him and I'm glad. So I'll understand and I won't blame you, but I don't want you to do it. I don't want to spend the rest of my life visiting you in prison. I don't want you to become a killer like him.'

'Listen to him, Hanni.'

For a second she thought the voice was Reiner's. She thought he was flinging himself like a coward onto Leo's plea. It wasn't till it continued that she realised the man speaking to her was Freddy.

'I know you. This isn't the kind of justice you want, that you've been waiting for all these years. This isn't making Reiner answer for Luise or Talie or all his other victims. This is a quick death. This could be a martyrdom. Don't give him that.'

One pull on the trigger and it's done. One pull and he's gone.

Reiner was doing his best to look unconcerned, but he was sweating. Hanni could see the sheen of it on his brow. And his hands, which he had finally raised, were shaking. He believed she could do it. He believed that she was no longer afraid. Her body responded; her finger began squeezing the trigger.

'Please, Hanni, don't. Put the gun down. Let Leo keep his mother; let me do my job. There's a whole team behind me – he can't get away. And I've got the witness statement from Hadamar – Wechsler sent it to Hannover this morning. We have a case, there will be a trial, but only if you lower the gun. If you shoot, there's nothing I can do. You'll both be lost. I can't bear that and neither can your son.'

She was so tired. From all the years living under Reiner's shadow, from all the years battling him. From all the wrong decisions she had made. And Freddy's voice was so warm, so filled with love.

I don't want to do this. I want to live my life, whatever that will be. I want a future with my boy. I don't want him to see me with blood on my hands; I don't want that to be the shadow that destroys him.

Her arm fell and the room rushed past her. Freddy raced towards Reiner, barking at him to kneel down, to stretch his arms out behind him. Someone eased the gun out of her hand. There was shouting and orders and people everywhere. There was Leo, with his arms wrapped round her, holding on to her as if he was terrified she might fly away. And there was Reiner, handcuffed and a prisoner but still alive.

'Get your eyes down.'

Why is he smiling at me?

The officer who had hold of Reiner's arm was on the wrong side of him. Leo stepped back as the prisoner was bundled towards the door but Hanni wasn't quick enough to avoid the brush of Reiner's shoulder or escape his mouth as it grazed past her ear.

'Get him away from her.'

Freddy's shout was too late. The words were said.

Hanni's hand flew instinctively to her pocket, but the mistake was made and the gun was gone and nobody would listen when she screamed, 'Give it back!'

CHAPTER 24

20–21 APRIL 1963, HANNOVER, WEST GERMANY

Reiner's boys were not about to let their leader go lightly.

By the time Freddy shepherded Hanni and Leo back into the foyer, the prison van had left but a crowd had assembled in front of the steps.

'Ignore them. They don't know what happened in here. They don't know who you are.'

Hanni found that hard to believe. The glass-panelled doors had blurred faces and sounds but she could sense the hostility brewing. And outside wasn't the only place where she was in trouble.

'I appreciate that she's your wife, Chief Inspector, but she stole a weapon from a police station and that's not something we can easily sweep away. And as for what we witnessed upstairs, how am I supposed to describe her behaviour if not as intent to kill? She'd barely surrendered the gun before she was shouting at us to give it back.'

Freddy had tried to shield Hanni from the heated discussion which broke out around her once Reiner was gone, but her actions had compromised any authority his rank might otherwise have granted him. The argument went round and round in a loop – his opposite number from the Hannover force threatening charges, Freddy pleading extenuating circumstances and promising co-operation if they would let her go. He kept glancing at Hanni while he was talking, as if he hoped she would step up and explain herself. She couldn't help him. Her head was too full of Reiner's parting words to think up any of her own.

'What did he say to you when they took him out? Why did you start yelling?'

Leo had asked her that in the office and he asked it again as they came down the stairs, despite Freddy telling him to give her some time to recover. Hanni hadn't replied. She couldn't say Reiner's words out loud: that would make them true and then she would fall completely apart. Neither Freddy nor Leo needed the added burden of that. All she could do was keep walking and not thinking and pray to any god that would listen that he was wrong.

'Is there another way out?'

Leo had also spotted the gathering boys and, although he was trying to be as brave as he had been when he'd walked into Reiner's office, the hand he slipped into Hanni's was trembling. Freddy glanced around but it was a reflex: he had already checked and come up with nothing.

'No, I'm afraid not, but I'm with you now – we can do this together. It's only a short walk to the car and then we'll be gone from here. I've told the officers searching your grandfather's office to make sure no one else leaves, and we're heading to Hannover not Goslar so that should throw anybody with stupid ideas off our trail. It will be all right, I promise.'

Hanni didn't believe that either – she knew when Freddy was pretending confidence and when it was real – but she followed him out of the building, keeping her eyes down as he'd asked them both to do, even though that made her feel like the criminal. They barely made it to the bottom of the steps before the first body pushed in between them and the waiting police car.

'Whatever you've charged him with, you'll regret it. He's done nothing wrong. He'll ruin you.'

Freddy kept moving, his body acting as a shield around Hanni's. He didn't reply to that threat or the next.

'You won't get away with this. You don't take one of ours and walk.'

Hanni glanced up. The shout could have come from any one of the boys circling around and moving in closer. Or from one of the grim-faced parents who flanked them. It was the call to unity the rest of them had been waiting for: *one of ours* spread through their ranks in a menace-filled rumble.

'Hurry up.'

Leo had her hand in a vice; Freddy was pulling her. The only sensible thing to do was to sprint the last few steps.

Except I'm not the one in the wrong here. I'm not the one who should be publicly shamed.

It was the right thought but the wrong time to be having it. As Hanni's head came up so did a hand on the edge of the crowd. The stone sailed through the air, coming too fast for a warning, too fast to duck. It caught her on the side of the temple and it stung.

'Get in the car, now, before this gets worse. Come on.'

Freddy yanked at her arm, throwing her towards the open door; Leo was screaming at her to move. But the blow had snapped Hanni out of the shock which had gripped her since Reiner bent down and taunted her, and she wasn't about to be bundled away.

'How dare you. You call him your leader and you shout about loyalty, but you don't know the first thing about him. You don't have a clue what he's capable of.'

Her shout was so unexpected, it silenced the mob.

'There's nothing innocent about him. He's a killer and I'm going to prove it.'

'Get in the car, Hanni. Before they tear you apart or you ruin the case. I'm not going to tell you again.'

Freddy was holding the door; Leo was already inside. Hanni hesitated, her mouth thick with accusations, but there was a new sound coming towards her, a hiss that surged with a hatred she knew would destroy her if she didn't back down. And Leo – who knew better than anybody what his classmates were capable of – was crying and begging her to stop. His terrified face got her into the back seat, and just in time. As the driver started the engine and tried to pull away, the crowd surged. Fists banged against the car roof, faces pressed ugly and shouting against the windows. The driver took his foot off the accelerator but Hanni was ready for that.

'Drive. They'll scatter or they won't. I don't care which.'

It wasn't her place to give orders but Freddy added his 'Do what she says' and the driver rediscovered his nerve. There were shouts and jeers and bodies hurling after them, but the car forced a path through the yelling and away.

The police cordon Freddy had been promised finally appeared. No one followed. Leo's sobs turned to cheers; he thought it was a victory.

Hanni knew it was anything but.

'Are you going to tell me what he said? I didn't want to push you when the others were around, but you need to tell me now.'

Saturday had disappeared in a flurried arrival at the hotel where Renny was waiting. Hanni had crawled off to her room as soon as Renny's apologies and Leo's hugs had let her go and fallen into a dreamless sleep she hadn't woken from until Sunday morning had almost slipped away too. The rest of the day had belonged to Leo and Renny. The four of them had wandered around Hannover's royal gardens and marketplace admiring the sites, arms tucked around each other. Pretending that Reiner wasn't locked in a cell less than a mile away.

Hanni had survived the day by refusing to discuss or to think about what had happened with her father and letting Renny hold court about Israel when they regrouped for dinner. It was after nine by the time Leo reluctantly gave in to exhaustion and went to bed. Hanni, whose nerves were worn tissue-thin, would have followed him but Renny's 'You two need to talk' was too direct and too quick for her. Before she could argue, Renny had gone, leaving her and Freddy alone in the hotel lounge and Hanni with nowhere to hide.

'Please, Hanni. What on earth did he say to make you shout for the gun?'

She put down the glass of wine she hadn't tasted and shivered as Reiner's voice crept back.

'You should have shot me while you had the chance, but you didn't, so you've lost.'

She blinked as Freddy groaned.

'He sounded so certain, I believed him. That's why I shouted. Because I felt as if I'd made the biggest mistake of my life by not killing him. I still do.'

She waited for Freddy to say something. To tell her not to worry, that it was the last threat of a desperate man. Her heart sank when he didn't. When he carried on staring at his hands as if his knotted fingers might hold the answer, she couldn't keep the panic from her voice.

'Oh God. You think he's right, don't you? You don't think anything's changed. You don't think that we've got a strong enough case to get him to court. You don't think we can win. He's going to worm his way out of this like he worms his way out of everything.'

Freddy was out of his seat and by her side on the sofa in an instant. That was reassuring. The way he took her hands in his and cradled them and finally looked straight at her was reassuring too. But his words weren't, and his words were what mattered.

'I don't know, Hanni. That's the honest truth. You had a gun pointed at him – he could make a strong case out of that and go after you. And as for what we've got against him... It's not great. There's only one witness who can place him in the operating theatre at Hadamar. A witness who – if Reiner is true to form and with the connections he's got – could be tracked down and intimidated or worse, no matter how much we try to protect him. Or could simply lose his nerve. Reiner's reputation will take a hammering, but as for the rest... I want to tell you that we've got him, that he's going to prison for years. I can't. I'm so sorry.'

Nothing he said was a surprise. Hanni had been living with the knowledge that Reiner had almost certainly slipped through her fingers since the moment he had whispered his amusement into her ear. To hear it articulated so bleakly was still a shock.

'I should have shot him, he's right. I was an idiot not to. I was a coward like I've always been a coward and now look what I've done. With all the support he can rustle up, he'll come back from this stronger, more dangerous – I know it.'

Freddy's grip on her was so tight it should have been painful. But all she could feel was the fear in his eyes.

'No. No you weren't – don't say that. Shooting him in that moment would have been easy. You were brave enough to stop, to think about Leo, to not damage our son. Oh God, Hanni, when I think of what might have happened, of where you could have ended up if you'd fired...'

His voice suddenly disappeared, lost under a sob that tore through his body. A second later Hanni was locked inside his arms, her head on his chest, kisses raining down on her hair.

'I nearly lost my mind when I saw you holding the gun. All I could think was she'll never survive this; she'll shoot him and it will kill her as well as him. You're not that person; you've never been that person. And the thought of you locked away in a cell for the rest of our lives, of never being able to hold you, of never being able to tell you all the things I should have said years ago. I think I would have died too.'

His words came in a torrent Hanni could barely keep up with, but the love burning through *our lives* and the rest was unmistakeable. And when she finally managed to disentangle herself from his embrace and look up, the love was there just as strong in his face.

'I thought you would never want me again. I thought that part of us was dead.'

She had carried that pain for so many years with no hope of curing it. When he shook his head, when he bent down and he kissed her, her heart found a new beat.

'Not dead, never that. Buried maybe for far longer than it should have been, but not dead.'

It was everything she had wanted to hear, but she slipped her fingers against his lips as he bent down to her again. She had to know if this was shock talking or if it was real.

'I'm still me, Freddy. I'm still his daughter; I still lied for years about that. Remember the way you felt when you looked at my family photographs. Can you live with that? Can you live with who I am?'

He kissed her fingers and moved them from his mouth. 'Who you were, not who you are. You didn't choose him, Hanni. You didn't choose the life he put you in.'

The words were the right words but the ground was still unbearably fragile.

'Freddy, listen to me. Don't do this if you're going to change your mind. Don't give me this if you're going to take it away again when we're out of here and back in the world. I can live without having you; I've learned to do that. I can't live with losing you all over again.'

He moved back. For a moment Hanni thought he was moving away. But his hold on her hands didn't falter.

'I'm not going to do that, I promise. This isn't some spur-of-the-moment thing. Yes, I thought I was going to lose you and that fear stripped everything else that's gone between us away. But these feelings are real, not a reaction I'm going to regret – I've been hiding from them for years and I don't want to do that anymore. Or live with the past anymore; I'm worn out fighting its ghosts. It's nearly cost me Renny – and Leo. It cost me you for long enough. I want to find a way forward. I want to find that with you.'

It's everything I wanted to hear.

There was still one question left.

'And you want that no matter what happens with my father? Even if he goes free and the whole mess starts over again?'

'Yes.'

One heartfelt word – it was all that was needed.

This time she didn't raise her fingers to block his lips. This time she smiled and leaned into him and she let the kiss come. She let it be what it was: everything.

The phone call woke Hanni with a jolt. She stumbled out of the tangled sheets to answer it before she remembered whose room she was in.

'You're blushing like a schoolgirl; stop looking so embarrassed. As far as the Hannover station are concerned, we're an old married couple.'

Freddy grinned at her as he took the receiver but his amusement didn't last long. The boyish look he'd been wearing even in his sleep disappeared a moment into the conversation.

Hanni took one look at his frown and began to get dressed.

'It's started, hasn't it? He's set the wheels in motion to get away?'

Freddy replaced the handset and nodded. 'He's hired a lawyer, one of Berlin's best and most expensive, and he's demanding that not only are the charges against him dropped, a whole set are pressed against you.'

He glanced at his watch. 'We don't have a lot of time. Once his legal team get here and start demanding a hearing and bail, especially since they will have the money to back up their demands, the chances of holding on to him beyond another night are slim. We might not even manage that.'

He grabbed for his shirt and moved past her to collect the rest of his clothes. 'It isn't the start to the day I'd been hoping for.'

It wasn't what Hanni wanted either. It was far too abrupt a pull out of his arms. But it was what she had known would happen as soon as Monday morning dawned.

Freddy was watching her as he scrabbled for his shoes. 'I thought you would be more upset. Am I so easy to walk away from?'

The comment was offered as a joke but Hanni knew better than to take it that way. Their coming together was new enough for him to be as terrified that it might crack open again as she was.

She went to his side, slipped her arms round his waist and gave him the kiss that he needed.

'You know that you're not. I'm not surprised, that's all. I knew he wouldn't let the grass grow. But I'm ready for him this time. I know what we need to do.'

What Freddy hadn't realised was that Hanni hadn't fallen asleep as quickly and as deeply as he had once their re-learning of each other was done. She had stayed awake instead, hugging her new-found happiness close, picturing the new life with her son and her husband that beckoned. And determined not to let the *whole mess* start over and ruin it.

Hanni had no more doubts: Freddy meant every promise he had made her that nothing would come between them again. But Hanni also knew Reiner. He would never forgive her for humiliating him, for casting doubts on his reputation because, no matter how cleverly he wriggled away from his crimes, mud would stick the way that it always stuck. He would come after her, and Leo and Freddy if she let him, with a fury like she had never seen. Hanni couldn't allow that. So somewhere in the hours between Freddy's last lingering kiss and her eyes finally closing as dawn filtered through, Hanni had come up with a plan.

CHAPTER 25

22–25 APRIL 1963, WEST BERLIN

Fifteen years. It seemed unimaginable that the last time she had stood on the corner of Clayallee facing the headquarters of the American forces in Berlin had been fifteen years ago.

Berlin had been a very different place then, cut off from the world by a Soviet blockade of its roads and rail lines and rivers and dependent on a burgeoning black market and Allied airdrops for its food and fuel supplies. And stalked by a killer who had held the city in fear for months and left a trail of dead bodies behind him which was far longer than even Hanni and Freddy had guessed.

'I won't miss it. I know you all tried hard to make me happy here, but Berlin has never felt like home. I've never liked it; I've never felt part of it. I can't wait to be somewhere new.'

Hanni had understood why Renny had said that when they were at dinner in Hannover and the girl's head was bursting with Israel, but she couldn't share the sentiment behind it. Hanni's whole life had been spent entwined with the city and its fortunes, for good and for bad. Every borough carried an echo somewhere in its streets or in its parks of love or loss. Berlin was part of her history, part of her blood. Hanni couldn't picture herself living anywhere else. Or she hadn't been able to. Now she watched the laughing servicemen and women streaming around a compound whose cinema and brightly lit shopping mall were so unmistakeably American and she wondered if history was enough.

Or if I should break free from it all and not just from Reiner.

Not that breaking free from him was by any means certain.

'It's a long shot – you know that, don't you? Even if we can get anyone to listen, we'll need to get the co-operation of the British authorities in Hannover and the Americans in Berlin and the East Germans to pull it off and that's a major hurdle in itself.'

Freddy had heard her plan out and helped her persuade a sleepy Leo and an equally sleepy Renny to get up and forgo breakfast and get into the car. He'd driven back to Berlin with all the speed Hanni had demanded, but he hadn't been convinced.

'I'm not saying it isn't a brilliant idea. If it works, it will bury him. But it's a lot of links that need to hold steady and it's not even a military matter.'

But that was an argument Hanni expected that he and everybody else involved would resort to and she was ready for it.

'It could be – that's the point. My sister's murder was carried out as part of the T4 programme – surely that makes it a war crime? And it proves Reiner was a Nazi so it has to make him a suitable candidate for one of the prisoner swaps we're all meant to pretend don't happen.'

Freddy might have been able to question whether anyone would do what Hanni wanted but he couldn't question her logic. And that was all Hanni needed: to have him on her side again, to be part of a team. That and the kiss he had given her that morning for luck.

. . .

It needs to be the highest person you can get me in the chain of command, and preferably someone who remembers the Strangler.

Freddy had delivered exactly the contact that Hanni had asked for. Lieutenant General Harry Carrell, the police point of contact at Clayallee, not only remembered the Berlin Strangler's murder spree, he had flown with the killer during the 1948 Airlift. He was also a far stiffer prospect than the last American officer Hanni had dealt with. Colonel Walker had been a public-relations professional who knew how to deflect potential problems with a smile. Carrell was too conscious of the medal ribbons coating his chest and his position to be as human as that.

'What you are asking, Frau Schlüssel, is unconventional at best. Whatever the more scurrilous newspaper reports might suggest, exchanging prisoners between East and West is not a significant feature of American, or German, diplomatic policy. And the man involved here – your father – whoever he may have been once or whatever he may have done, has no military record. I'm no protector of war criminals, but I fail to see how I can help you.'

Hanni chose not to respond to that – it was too obviously a precursor to him wishing her goodbye. She focused instead on what he hadn't denied.

'The exchanges might not be central to policy, but they happen. The newspapers didn't make up the story about the American pilot who was swapped for a Russian colonel last year and – or so my journalist contacts tell me – there've been others done more quietly since and they've involved all sorts of different people. I've got the details on file.'

That wasn't true. She didn't have contacts or a file; she was as reliant on rumour about what happened at crossing points in the early hours of the morning as everybody else in Berlin. She had gambled on the fact that Carrell would be too protective of military movements to challenge her, and she had gambled correctly. Her manner, which was clearly more confident than he was used to seeing on the other side of his desk, had also rattled his composure.

'That's as maybe, but this is still not our issue to resolve. And don't start suggesting that we owe you for all the unsolved crimes we were able to pin on Tony Miller in forty-eight, which I assume will be your next move. The supplies we lifted into your city to stop it from starving was ample payment for that.'

That had indeed been the next argument Hanni had been planning to try, but it wasn't her last or her strongest one. She had already noted the silver-framed photograph on his desk; now she was ready to use it.

'I know you are a busy man and I know how strange this request is. But it is a military matter, I promise you, and it's more than that. It comes down to what it means to be human. My father should have been tried at Nuremberg but he was too clever to leave his fingerprints on any of the lives he destroyed. And I have been trying to bring him to justice since 1945 without success. His crimes are endless. He flayed men alive at Theresienstadt; he pushed women and children onto the trains there. He was involved in the set-up of the concentration camps and the T4 programme. He was an ardent Party member and his life was dedicated to making the Third Reich's machinery run more smoothly. And I know you will say that there were thousands of men like him and I imagine that you will be sorry that only a fraction were ever prosecuted. All my father's crimes were terrible things; all of them should have been answered for. But now there's one he committed that I can prove he did, and that's why I'm here.'

She nodded at the picture of the smiling woman in the frame and the giggling little boy and girl she was cuddling. 'How old is your daughter?'

Carrell frowned at the personal question. 'She's eight. But I don't see what that has to do with anything.'

Hanni folded her hands onto her lap where he couldn't see them trembling. 'You will. You see when my little sister was six and as pretty and as full of laughter as your daughter, my father took her to Hadamar Hospital and watched as she was strapped onto a bed. And then, when the nurse who was supposed to inject a cocktail of drugs into her that would stop her heart panicked and couldn't do it, he picked up the syringe himself. He murdered Luise, his daughter, because she had leukaemia and fits and she didn't match his requirements for the perfect Aryan child. And then he murdered the nurse who called him a monster for doing it.'

All the colour had drained from Carrell's face. Hanni gave him a moment to digest what she had said and then she continued.

'I'm not saying that was his worst crime. Other children, and adults, died because he hated their blood and they have all been forgotten. But we have names for these victims and a witness to the killing and Reiner is under arrest and in prison. The problem is that my father has money and connections and he will, I have no doubt, find a way out of this. Then he will kill me and probably my husband and my son. Or you could help stop that. There is a young American journalist in Hohen-schönhausen prison in East Berlin who you haven't been able to extract. We have a guarantee from the Stasi that they will swap him in return for Reiner, who they've been after for years. My sister and all the others who suffered at his hands will finally get justice. Isn't this one of those moments where everybody wins?'

Hanni sat back. She had to trust that she had managed to make the numbers of the war's dead, who were faceless to him whether he meant them to be or not, into a more personal story. There was nothing else she could say. Whether Reiner disap-peared from the world or flourished in it was out of her hands. She had played her part; Freddy had gone back to the East and played his. Now all she could do was wait to see what kind of man Carrell was beneath his medals.

He didn't say anything. He picked up the photograph of his family and stared at it. Then he swallowed and he nodded, and Hanni – who had been holding herself together through sheer force of will since she came into his office – had to bite back a lifetime's worth of tears.

It was still dark when they arrived at the Glienicke Bridge which spanned the River Havel in Wannsee and formed part of the border between West Berlin and the East. The sky hadn't quite decided whether to be day or night and stars dotted its inky blue.

Hanni climbed out of the car and pulled her coat tight against the damp wind. She hadn't been to this section of the city or crossed the bridge they were standing on since she was a child. The East Germans had closed it as a crossing point to Westerners in 1952, and since the Wall went up, access to the road which ran over it had been restricted to the military. Now it was a place where nobody in Berlin went but everybody knew. Glienicke was the spy bridge, a place of secrets and subterfuge that had already spawned a wealth of stories. Nobody went there and nobody witnessed the exchanges that supposedly took place at its centre, but everyone could describe how those played out. Prisoners clasped hands with each other as they crossed from prison to freedom, or back to prison if the rumours about the way returnees were treated in the East was true. Some didn't walk but came back silently in coffins. Some of them were greeted on the far side with shots. Every swap grew more theatrical with its telling. All Hanni wanted was for the transfer to go smoothly, which it should. Everyone had delivered their side of the bargain, or this far at least.

By the time Reiner's lawyer arrived in Hannover, full of

indignation and demands, Reiner was gone – returned to Berlin due to a 'confusion' over where the legal meeting was due to take place. The lawyer raced back to the city but paperwork had been lost and orders hadn't been received and Reiner was on his way back to Hannover, or was in Frankfurt or was somewhere else that wasn't here. The lawyer shouted and he demanded explanations and he filed a series of complaints, but what could be done in the face of all the apologies Freddy made sure the furious man was smothered in? The lawyer was helpless. Reiner was left languishing in a cell in a prison on the outskirts of Berlin where none of his contacts mattered. And now, if the timetable Carrell had outlined was still working, he was on his way to what surely had to be the end of the line.

Hanni edged forward onto the bridge, being careful to go no further than the soldier guarding the car which had delivered her and Freddy to the swap site had told her was permitted. The figures in front of her were shadows and blurred shapes. There was no movement. There was no sense of urgency. There was no sound beyond the wind rippling across the black water below her. It didn't feel like a place where something momentous was due to happen.

'What if there's been a change in plan? What if the Stasi don't want him?'

Freddy slipped his arm round her shoulders. 'That won't happen. Apart from the fact that I'm Rühl's only contact over here so any changes would have to go through me, Reiner is too big a catch. Rühl will bleed him dry about his past contacts and his present ones and he'll make him pay for Luca. And then they'll make political capital out of his crimes and the West's failure to punish him, even though I promised Carrell that they wouldn't. They'll feed off this for months.'

Hanni knew all that was true. But none of it would hold weight until she saw Reiner walk across the bridge and into the East.

'He's coming.'

All of a sudden, things moved up a pace.

A car was approaching from behind. There was movement in front. The officer in charge of exchanges – who had briefed her on what to expect the previous day without divulging his name – began walking towards them, his waving hands pulling the rest of his unit into position. Now that the sun had decided to rise, Hanni could see a small hut at the centre of the bridge and a striped barrier and darker figures moving towards it from the Potsdam side.

'It's on.'

The officer was by her side, his gaze sweeping the access road, his body on alert. 'We've had word that our missing journalist has been delivered safely to Checkpoint Charlie so we can send Foss over.'

He shrugged as Hanni frowned at him. 'The East like to change the script and keep us on our toes. To be honest I prefer this way to an actual swap: there's one less chance of a detainee refusing to do as he's told.'

Hanni hadn't considered the possibility of that but she didn't have a chance to ask what would happen if Reiner argued or ran. The car they had heard approaching was turning onto the bridge, slowing down and waiting for a signal to proceed. The officer waved his hand and then he turned back to Hanni.

'He won't have been told where he's going, although he may be making sense of it now. And he won't know you're here unless you want him to see you. Do you?'

He had asked the question the wrong way round. Hanni didn't care if Reiner saw her but she had to see him. She needed to be sure that there was no way out. She nodded.

'Go over there then, to the side of the bridge. I'll make sure that he's driven at a crawl past you and that the window is open.'

The car inched forward. Hanni glanced back at the barrier.

The soldiers on the eastern side were visible now. They had their guns cocked at the ready.

'Hanni. He's here – it's now.'

Freddy had his hand out. She took it and held on tight as the car drew level and the window rolled down. Reiner was in the back, his wrist handcuffed to the man at his side. He was asking something, gesticulating with his free hand, pointing through the window at the struts flashing past him. And then he turned and he saw Hanni, and whatever had mattered so desperately to him a moment before disappeared.

There was so much for Hanni to say and there was nothing to say except 'Goodbye.'

He understood then. There was a horror in his eyes Hanni had never seen there before.

She stood back. She let the car move on. She watched as it drew to a halt at the barrier, as Reiner was bundled out and shoved forward onto the wrong side and into a circle of guns. She waited for the order to move that cracked through the still air.

And then she squeezed Freddy's hand and she walked off the bridge with her husband into a new day.

CHAPTER 26

23 JUNE 1963, EAST AND WEST BERLIN

'Are you ready? This hasn't been a simple thing to arrange and you'll make me look a fool if you change your mind. That's not going to happen, is it?'

Rühl sounded uncertain and unlike him. Hanni – who had paused only to stop her heart pounding so that she could focus on what was coming – didn't need to think twice before saying no.

It had taken her two months from leaving the bridge to crash back down to earth. For two months, she had been surrounded by enough love to stay floating.

First there was Renny, who had turned back into a whirl-wind who couldn't stand still, although this time she was a happy one.

She began planning to leave Berlin the day they got back from Hannover. By the time Hanni and Freddy returned from the bridge, she was already outside the offices of the Jewish Agency waiting impatiently for them to open. Once they did, she charmed or terrified them – neither Hanni nor Freddy wanted to speculate which – into working at her speed. She had everything organised in a fortnight. A train to Marseille and then a boat to carry her on from the French port to Haifa. A placement at a kibbutz for the summer, followed by a transfer to the University of Jerusalem. Her energy was tireless, her enthusiasm infectious. Hanni ran round behind her helping her buy the tickets and the clothes she needed for her new life; Freddy ran behind them both, bemoaning the state of his wallet and loving the delight which shone from his sister's face. Her leave-taking turned into a party because Renny refused to look at any sad faces. Even Freddy managed to hold on to his smile. And then she was gone, leaving behind a far quieter Leo.

He wasn't a whirlwind. He was slower to move away from the shock of seeing Reiner for who he really was and seeing Hanni almost pulling the trigger. He approached each day carefully and turned a little younger, a little quicker to go looking for his mother's arms. Neither Hanni nor Freddy wanted to push him out of that. They kept him away from school on the promise that they would find him a new start when the summer holidays ended. Hanni let him help her at photo-shoots, watching with delight when he picked up a camera and said 'show me' and discovered an eye. That was the day she told him, and Freddy, about Ezra Stein and felt their little unit starting to strengthen. So Leo was slow but he was healing. And then there was Freddy.

Freddy was a gale and a calm place and home. Freddy was both the man she had met almost twenty years earlier, full of surprise and delight in her, and the man he was now who had learned the value of love. They were old to each other and new; their bond was deep and it was fragile. It needed care. It needed to grow wide enough to contain the scars and the moments when they looked at each other and remembered the hurts. They both believed that would happen; they both believed in each other. They were learning new ways to be.

For two months Hanni floated, buoyed up by her son and her husband and the girl who had hugged her before she stepped onto a train and whispered, 'I'm happy you're back in his life.' She refused to look back; she refused to discuss anything about her father. And then she woke up on a bright sunny morning convinced that Reiner had talked his way out of the East and all the shadows poured back in.

'I have to see him. I have to know that it's real. That he hasn't managed another reinvention.'

It didn't matter that the East German authorities had done exactly what Freddy had said they would do and splashed the story of Reiner's exchange and the extent of his war crimes all over the pages of *Neues Deutschland*. Hanni convinced herself that was a propaganda piece with no substance. It didn't matter that his schools had already begun closing as the news of his arrest, and the charges, leaked. Hanni convinced herself that he would reappear exactly as he had done the last time, with a new name and a new plan to subvert anything good. The bridge stopped being real. Her last sight of him surrounded by East German soldiers stopped being real. It was unimaginable that a man who had got away with so much and so often could have been caught. So Freddy had put himself in the Stasi's pocket yet again and arranged for her to go to East Berlin and see the truth for herself.

'I'm not going to change my mind – there's no need for concern. I'm ready.'

The walk along the side street where the driver left her to where Major Rühl was waiting, at one of the hidden entrances to Hohenschönhausen prison, had been a longer one than the few minutes Hanni's watch said. She had been made to come alone. Freddy had been refused entry to the forbidden zone which housed the prison compound; he had been forced to wait for her at Stasi Headquarters. He hadn't even pretended a smile when Rühl had told him not to worry, that she would almost certainly come back. None of that had stopped her.

She followed the major through the empty courtyard and

up a short flight of steps, doing as he asked and only looking ahead. Not that there was anyone to see in the courtyard or the prison's corridors. Hanni knew that was deliberate. Rühl refused to tell her how many prisoners the building held; Hanni guessed from its size there were hundreds. She could sense them, standing to attention without a sound as the lights above the locked doors switched from green to red as they walked by. The silence was too full for the prison to be empty.

'In here. If you stand at the window, you'll have a perfect view.'

She was looking outside but it wasn't outside. The walls of the narrow yard were open to the sky but a sheet of mesh covered the place where the roof should have been and the prisoner stumbling round and round its cramped space was looking down not up.

'It's what we like to call a tiger cage. It's an interesting design: the outside world is there and yet it's not. The prisoner knows he's come outside the building; he can feel and smell the fresh air, but he's forbidden to look up and see the sky which is what he so desperately craves. If he raises his head, not only will he get a severe beating but he won't be allowed out again here for months. It's one of our more subtle ways of controlling them, but it's very effective.'

Rühl's amusement – because that's what it was – barely registered. All Hanni's attention was focused on the broken prisoner below her. He was small; he was nothing. Shorn of his hair and his expensive suits and surroundings, he was insignificant.

The guards took my name and my hair and everything I had been and turned me from a man into a plaything for their entertainment.

She wished Freddy could see Reiner now, fitting the words he had used to describe his own treatment in Buchenwald.

Freddy's anger – which he never referred to but Hanni knew still burned – needed the symmetry of that. As for her...

Reiner's limp and his twisted right arm suggested that the guards had had plenty of sport with him already. Because it was Reiner stumbling round the cage – Hanni no longer had any doubt about that. The square he was walking in was tiny, barely ten paces; every time he turned, she caught a glimpse of his face. It was a mottled mess of green and yellow faded bruises but there was no mistaking the line of his cheekbones or chin.

'I can send an order to make him look up. If you need to be sure.'

Hanni shook her head. She had wanted to be certain that he could never touch her or her family again – she hadn't come to gloat or turn his incarceration into a game. She wasn't him.

'I don't. I can see that it's my father. That's all I came for.'

'He's not going anywhere – I can promise you that.'

Rühl's voice had softened. When Hanni glanced round at him, his face was full of compassion.

'There's nothing the guards here hate more than Nazis. He'll finish his days inside this place and they won't be easy ones. You can let him go, Hanni. You can be done with the past. He's not your burden anymore; he's ours.'

'He said that to you – those exact words?'

Freddy had managed to stay professional when she and Rühl arrived safely at the Security Ministry but his composure cracked the second they were back across the checkpoint and in their own car. He had to pull over at once to hold her.

'If he did, there's more layers to him than his role over there would have you believe. Maybe I should try and get him to defect.'

Hanni laughed and wriggled out of his embrace. 'He said it kindly and he meant it. And he was right. Reiner's in a prison that doesn't officially exist; he doesn't have a name anymore, just a number. There's not a lawyer in the world who can spring him from that. Reiner Foss is nobody. He's gone for good.'

Hanni didn't have to add *unless I let him come back*. Watching her father walk away into the darkness on the other side of a bridge had left a gap in the ending. That gap was now firmly closed. And she didn't have to ask if Freddy could also let him go: that he loved her every day proved he had already done it.

They drove on in silence, Freddy weaving his way through the early evening traffic towards Rüdesheimer Straße, Hanni staring out of the window at streets which no longer carried a shadow. Although they carried something that was out of place.

'What's going on? Can we stop and see?'

Hanni peered out of the window at the mass of flags and bunting and rosettes which had turned Schöneberg into a field of red and blue stars and stripes. Freddy slowed down, much to the annoyance of the drivers behind him, and slotted the Opel into a vacant spot. He was staring at her as if he didn't know whether to laugh at her or scratch his head.

'You can't have forgotten surely? Kennedy's coming – the American president? He's making a speech here the day after tomorrow. I've been tied up in security details for weeks.'

Hanni had forgotten. Her head had been so full of Reiner she had been sleepwalking for days. Now she was wide awake and deeply regretting that, because they had been crossing to the East, she hadn't brought a camera.

'Gessner was meant to be on the reception committee but he's been dropped, I heard that this morning. It seems like he's been dropped from the race for the federal government as well. The mud is sticking a lot wider than Reiner. Some of his pupils will be lucky to get a job at all.'

The poison had stopped. Freddy had kept telling her that but now Hanni had seen the crushed state of the root and she believed it. She grinned as a woman walked past pushing a pram so festooned with rosettes there was barely room for the baby.

'It's quite a circus.'

Freddy shook his head. 'Wait till the day itself. We're expecting the whole city to flock here, which could be a security nightmare, but his people are all over everything. It's impressive. There's a lot we could learn.'

Hanni glanced at him as he watched the workmen putting up yet another string of banners. The integrity of his role mattered so much to him and yet here he was, two favours down to the Stasi. Freddy hadn't complained and he'd brushed off her questions when she'd asked what he'd be expected to do for Rühl or his masters in return. Hanni wasn't naïve enough to imagine that would be nothing. She slipped her hand into his.

'Could we start again do you think?'

'I thought we already had.'

Hanni hurried on as he frowned. 'I don't mean that; I don't mean us. I mean could we start a life somewhere new? Not because we're running from the past, but because we are finally finished with it and ready to write our own future.'

He followed her gaze towards the podium where the flags were fluttering. 'Do you mean in America?'

Hanni shrugged. 'Perhaps. Leo would love it. You've said before that you would love a chance to go and immerse yourself in their methods and I think there would be an audience receptive to my work. So perhaps America, yes.'

He didn't answer straight away but, when he leaned down to kiss her, Hanni could see a new light dancing in his eyes.

She wrapped her arm round his waist and nestled into his shoulder as they watched the streets getting ready for the biggest event the city had seen for years.

He would agree to a move – she could see that in his smile. But it didn't matter where they decided to build their home –

Berlin, New York, Renny's kibbutz in Israel; somewhere different entirely.

The only thing that mattered was that, wherever the world took them, they would be where they were supposed to have been since they'd met standing among the ashes of the war.

Side by side, holding hands.

Together.

A LETTER FROM CATHERINE

Dear reader,

I want to say a huge thank you for choosing to read *Her Last Promise*. If you did enjoy it, and want to keep up to date with all my latest releases, just sign up at the following link. Your email address will never be shared, and you can unsubscribe at any time.

www.bookouture.com/catherine-hokin

Language and how it is used is particularly important to a writer. That might sound very obvious but it is a truism I have come back to again and again while writing fiction based around World War Two, and it is particularly significant for this novel. I wrote about the language games used to cloak the reality of what was happening to Europe's Jewish population in *The Secretary*: the use of 'cargo' for example, to describe what was being moved during the deportations instead of the more truthful 'people'. Euphemisms were a commonplace feature in the reports written about the Final Solution and they were an equally common feature in dialogue around the T4 euthanasia programme.

As I am sure many of my readers know, the National Socialist Party was an expert user of propaganda and this is clearly in evidence in the 'softening up' of attitudes towards euthanasia. Two films were widely shown in Germany with this aim in mind: *Dasein ohne Leben* (*Existence without Life*) in 1939 and the unashamedly tear-jerking *Ich Klage an* (*I Accuse*) in 1941. Both were designed to encourage the belief that 'mercy killing' was a humane act, with the latter using terms such as 'right to die' and 'make the poor woman's suffering less painful' to describe the beautiful main character's plea for a dignified release from multiple sclerosis. In reality, the Third Reich was eliminating thousands of people in the most inhumane conditions and the language they were using among themselves was the phrase I have used in the novel, the chilling 'useless eaters'. It is perhaps a warning to all of us to never get complacent about the power of words.

I hope you enjoyed *Her Last Promise* and if you did I would be very grateful if you could write a review. I'd love to hear what you think, and it makes such a difference helping new readers to discover one of my books for the first time.

I also love hearing from my readers – you can get in touch on my author Facebook and Instagram pages, Goodreads or my website.

Thank you again and I look forward to bringing you more stories.

Warmest wishes

Catherine

www.catherinehokin.com

facebook.com/Cathokin

instagram.com/cathokinauthor

ACKNOWLEDGEMENTS

It has been a real delight to write a series and spend so much time with my characters. Four books obviously means that there are a lot of overlaps with sources, but, as always, there are some specifics I would like to acknowledge as being very important to this book.

For background to the education system and attitudes/experiences of children in Nazi Germany: *The Third Reich's Elite Schools* by Helen Roche, *A German Generation* by Thomas A. Kohut, *Boy Soldiers* by Helene Munson, *A Model Childhood* by Christa Wolf, *The Folly of Youth* by Lance Schmidt and *Hitler's Children* by Guido Knopp. For Jewish resistance stories, *The Avengers* by Rich Cohen. For concentration-camp information, *The Society of Terror* by Paul Martin Neurath and *It Is Impossible to Remain Silent* by Jorge Semprún and Elie Wiesel. For matters around euthanasia and T4, *The Origins of Nazi Genocide* by Henry Friedlander.

If you are, like me, a movie buff, can I also recommend the 1959 movie *The Bridge,* the German film *Before the Fall* and *The Eichmann Show.* The Storyville documentary *Final Account* is also excellent.

I am also grateful to Dr Randall Bytwerk of Calvin University for giving his permission to quote the Hitler Youth song lyrics. The *German Propaganda Archive* which he curates there is an excellent resource.

And now to the thanks which may sound familiar to anyone who has made it this far! They go as always to my agent Tina

Betts for her unfailing support across this series and all the books that have gone before. To Emily Vega Gowers, you will be missed. To the Bookouture marketing team, especially Sarah the magician. To Daniel and Claire and Robert, none of whom can remember which book we are now on but they keep cheering anyway. Much love to you all.

Made in United States
North Haven, CT
17 June 2023